The
Wedding
Season

The Wedding Season

SU DHARMAPALA

SIMON & SCHUSTER
AUSTRALIA
A CBS COMPANY

THE WEDDING SEASON

First published in Australia in 2012 by
Simon & Schuster (Australia) Pty Limited
Suite 19A, Level 1, 450 Miller Street, Cammeray, NSW 2062
This edition published in 2013

A CBS Company
Sydney New York London Toronto New Delhi
Visit our website at www.simonandschuster.com.au

National Library of Australia Cataloguing-in-Publication entry
Author: Dharmapala, Su
Title: The Wedding Season
Subjects: Sri Lankans—Fiction. Women—Fiction. Melbourne (Vic.)—Fiction.
Edition: 1st ed.
Dewey Number: A823.4

ISBN: 9780731815623 (pbk.)

Editor: Janet Hutchinson
Cover design: Christabella Designs
Internal design and typesetting: Midland Typesetters, Australia
Printed and bound in India by Replika Press Pvt. Ltd.

The paper used to produce this book is a natural, recyclable product made
from wood grown in sustainable plantation forests. The manufacturing
processes conform to the environmental regulations in the country of origin.

PRAISE FOR
THE WEDDING SEASON

'Lots of fun – *A Suitable Boy* meets *Bridget Jones's Diary*
with a bittersweet twist'

– Kylie Ladd, author of *Last Summer*
and *After the Fall*

'A fabulous debut: heart warming, with emotional depth.'

– Lisa Heidke, best-selling author of
Claudia's Big Break and *Stella Makes Good*

DEDICATION

For my mother, Lalitha Dharmapala,
who nagged and cajoled me to write.

For my cousin, Brigbala Dharmapala,
who badgered me to write.

And for my old boss at GE, Stuart Moran,
who asked me why I didn't write.

ACKNOWLEDGEMENTS

Writing, by its very nature, is a solitary business. You don't know if your writing makes sense or is simply a mass of words held together by the thin thread of insanity in your head. It takes patience and endurance to support a writer.

To this end I wish to acknowledge the support and wisdom shown to me by Shelagh Reynolds and Julie Hugenholtz. I am so sorry for giving you a million paper cuts.

For her gentle guidance I wish to thank my writing guru Liz Kemp.

Lawyers are very useful people by way of friends. Their eagle eyes rarely miss inconsistencies and their concisely worded boots in one's rear gets one off the procrastinating couch faster than the speed of light. So I thank my friends Monika Smith and Adeline Hiew for their invaluable assistance in pushing me along, reviewing drafts and contracts.

For my cultural reality check, I wish to thank Anusha Jayasinghe. It is so reassuring to know that it is not just me.

I also wish to acknowledge the luminescent Anjanette Morton from Rick Raftos. Thank you for believing in me.

PART ONE

Mangala Yoga

CHAPTER 1

An Email

Imagine this if you can: a single woman in her thirties who is happy. Nope, I didn't think so. I didn't think you'd be able to do it. But here I am, in my thirties, single and I am totally happy. I may be the only woman in the Western world in her thirties, single and happy; but I am honestly happy and unafraid to say it.

My mind was buzzing with these mutinous thoughts when the lights changed and I gunned my BMW past the tram in a flawless execution of the Melbourne Tango, swerving hard to avoid the parked cars along Albert Park Road and somehow dodging an exquisitely coiffed office worker in stilettos trying to get across with her life intact.

I glanced back guiltily; I hated giving tram drivers cardiac arrests on the job. Especially when I was on my way to work myself!

A few hundred metres later, I turned down the narrow laneway that led to the cavernous carpark under my office in South Melbourne. I slowed down as I reached the guardhouse, reducing the volume of the Bollywood Beat track blaring through the surround sound system, and pressed the button to lower my window.

'Good morning, Miss Shani,' Abdul, the ancient car park attendant, said with an elegant little bow. I never bothered to hide my predilection for Bollywood music from Abdul; he knew all about my favourite vice.

'Just call me Shani,' I protested. 'You know we don't do any of this "Miss" stuff in Australia.'

'That is fine, Miss Shani,' he replied, wiggling his head. Abdul was of the old school and I doubted he'd ever call me by my first name no matter where we lived. I tossed my hands up in frustration. This suddenly reminded me of something.

I reached to the passenger side floor, gingerly picked up a Harrods carry bag and carefully presented it to Abdul as if it were a nuclear bomb.

'For you Abdul – chicken buriyani from my mum.' Okay, so it was a tiny white lie. My mum had packed the fridge at my unit in Blackburn with rice and curry over the weekend, and I'd be completely curried out if it weren't for the fact that I could flog my lunch each day to Abdul.

'Thank you, Miss Shani,' he said, bowing rapidly over and over again like a dashboard dog.

My iPhone beeped at me as I entered the lift, telling me that I had somehow missed a call while I had been parking my car. I looked at my phone. Yup, it was Mum. I saw Max Ferguson, the other senior group accountant, do a quick jog to catch the lift, so I held the doors open for a moment.

'Very nice,' Max complimented me, a little breathlessly, on my wine-coloured, ruched Burberry knit dress.

'Thank you,' I smiled serenely – and coolly – back. Max was a bit of a flirt, and I wasn't into office romances.

'Good weekend?' he wheezed, wiping his pudgy sweaty brow with an oversized handkerchief.

Oh, how could I explain my weekend to Max?

I was supposed to have met my older brother for a quick coffee at TGI Friday's yesterday, during the tiny window of time he had spare during a trip down to Melbourne from Sydney. Except I was ambushed by a blind date my mum had sicced on me! I should have known that my yuppie brother would never be caught dead at TGI Friday's.

But I went anyway, and was sitting there, waiting for my dear elder sibling, when a complete stranger accosted me. 'Are you Shani Devapura?' the man wearing cream pants belted up to his chest and a stripy pink polo t-shirt had asked.

'Yes,' I replied warily.

'Oh good. Your *ammi* said you'd meet me here,' he replied with a gap-toothed grin. The evening went downhill from there.

I couldn't dump this debacle on poor Max, so I took refuge in a solid social lie and replied, 'Fine!' brightly and turned the tables on him. 'So how was your weekend?'

For my sins, I was treated to a ball-by-ball account of a cricket game Max had gone to at the Melbourne Cricket Ground.

The lift stopped with a soft ping at the fourteenth floor and I made a hasty escape into the luxurious confines of my wood-panelled office. Max had wanted my opinion on whether a certain player was a 'chucker'. Sorry, but as far as I'm concerned, chucking is something that happens in a toilet bowl after a big night out.

I fired up my computer, enjoying the plush neutral decor of my office overlooking Port Phillip Bay and deliberately ignoring a further three missed calls from my mum. I knew what she'd be up to, and I didn't want to play.

How could I make my mother understand that it was possible for a woman in her thirties to be single and happy? I had tried. Many times. But my mother seemed to think my unmarried status at the ripe old age of thirty-two was a cause for serious alarm – a code red alarm, complete with sirens, bells, whistles and defibrillator machine. I know it's difficult for many people to imagine. But here I am, in my thirties, single and happy.

For the record, I am not a lesbian either. Not that I haven't seriously considered it in the past, attempted it once or twice – you can never know unless you try more than once – but alas, no. I just do not feel that way about women.

It's not as if I'm an unemployed burden on my parents either. I am the Senior Group Accountant at George Elliot & Co, a chain of upmarket department stores based in South Melbourne (trust me when I say I *enjoy* my staff discount card that I truly do *enjoy* it). I report directly to their Chief Financial Operations Manager. I own my own home and I have no credit card debt (no mean feat considering the above mentioned staff discount card).

Unlike most other women who also seem to have it all, I am not a bitch either. I volunteer at a homeless shelter once every couple of weeks, I go to temple, and I donate blood regularly. What's not to love about me? Just ask my mother!

So why, if I am a totally happy, independent, heterosexual female of thirty-two years, do I still listen to my mum, and go out on the disastrous blind dates she sets up? Three words for you (four if you are being pedantic): I am Sri Lankan.

Okay, okay, okay ... I am an Australian citizen, with the certificate to prove it, but I am of Sri Lankan *descent*. Which means that we listen to our mothers. Not just because we love them, and certainly not because they cook and clean for us until *they* die – as they constantly remind us. No, it's the guilt factor. Sri Lankan mothers are guilt mongers to rival the very best in the field, including Jewish mothers and the entire Roman Catholic establishment.

Happy to be at work, far from Mother's interfering ways, I fired up my email and what was left of my post-weekend euphoria vanished like a packet of Tim Tams on a girls' night out.

An email from Mrs.Peiris@srilankans.com. Who the bloody hell uses their title in their email address?

On cue, my phone rang.

'Have you got the email?' Tehara demanded without preamble.

'Hot and smokin' in my inbox.'

'I bet you a tub of Nuts About Chocolate that old woman Peiris has finally managed to flog off one of her daughters. And I bet you a second tub that it is Jayani, not Gayani.'

Who bloody well names their daughters Jayani and Gayani? Oh, yeah, Sri Lankans do. My name is Shamini, the older brother I should have seen last night for coffee is Gamini and my younger brother, Gehani.

'You know what this means though?' I asked Tehara, thinking of the larger picture.

'Yup, the wedding season is off with a bang this year! We need to catch up and coordinate, *machang*. When is a good time for you?'

'We'll see each other tomorrow night, like we always do.'

'Look here, I'm not bloody doing wedding season again without preparation. You know the other two won't get any grief ...'

'Well, that's because Amani is married like a good little girl and Una doesn't count. Her skin's so pale Dulux uses her as a standard for their pure white range,' I replied distractedly, my eyes skimming over the week's sales figures.

'Well duh ...' Tehara's beeper cut her off. 'I'd better get this. I just sedated one of my patients.'

'Oh darling, the only people who *like* hanging out with you are comatose,' I teased lightly. Tehara was a psychiatrist who specialised in dealing with people with bipolar disorder, the really extreme cases who liked to swing from chandeliers.

'Yeah, yeah … Come to the hospital around 1 pm and we'll catch up. We need a good plan this year, *machang*.'

'Okay, chief,' I replied, hanging up.

I clicked the email open and my heart sank.

As I'd feared, it was a formal marriage announcement prior to the official hand-engraved invitation from the happy couple. Or the happy parents, more to the point. Old woman Peiris had finally managed to 'flog off' one of her daughters.

I kept reading and my heart sank further. It wasn't the younger, malleable, prettier sister who was about to get married; but rather the bane of my existence, the perfect example of a well-brought up Australian-Sri Lankan woman – Gayani.

I said I was happy, but I never said my life was perfect. And as I took a deep swig of my morning latte, I realised that the 'happy' status of my life was about to get seriously challenged.

CHAPTER 2

Breadfruit Curry Anyone?

That night, I reluctantly made my way to my parents' house. I normally tried to limit the number of visits to Devapura Mansion to no more than four times a week for the sake of my sanity. I especially avoid going on Mondays as my mother, in combination with Monday-itis, is an excellent recipe for a migraine. I really wanted to avoid going there tonight because I had a well-substantiated premonition that things were going to go worse than usual.

Am I psychic? Hell no. I *am* an accountant and we're paid to figure out trends.

My premonition was kick started almost as soon as the day began. I was focused on my month-end sales figures spreadsheet, when my mother rang for the fourth time. Like the first three calls, I ignored it and let it go to voicemail. Three minutes and forty-five seconds later she rang again.

Again, I let it go to voicemail. Excel wins over my mum any day of the week.

Two minutes later, and I mean exactly 120 seconds later, she rang my mobile phone. Shit. I glanced up at the wall clock and I realised that it was nearly 10 am.

The postie had been. *Shit.*

She rang me for the eighth time about ten minutes later. I now refused to answer her call purely on principle.

Thirty minutes and six more missed calls to my landline and mobile later, I returned her call. I hate to admit it, but I play this game with my mother often. It boils down to a matter of who controls my life, and she has far too much input into it already.

This time, our conversation started off relatively innocuously. We completely disregarded the horrible time I had had with my date last night thanks to her.

'*Ammi*, it's Shani. You've been trying to call me?'

'Yes, I've called you so many times. My phone bill is already so high! Why don't you answer my calls?'

'Well, I wanted to see if your need to speak to me was greater than your concern for your phone bill and twenty phone calls later I decided that it clearly must be,' I replied sarcastically. 'I'm busy. Did you want anything?'

'I just wanted to know if you're coming for dinner tonight.'

Strange, she is usually a lot more direct about what she wants than merely offering a polite invitation to dinner. I waited.

Then she chucked the doosra at me with Muralidaran-like skill. Cricket is part of Sri Lankan culture, absorbed with the breast milk. Even a sport-hating female like me knows about Muthiah Muralidaran and the doosra, even if I can't quite get my head around the concept of a 'square leg'. All cricketers seem to have perfectly normal legs. Actually, that Daniel

Vettori from New Zealand has particularly fine legs, if you ask me.

'I'm making breadfruit curry in coconut milk with prawn *sambol*.'

This was serious.

'I'll be there,' I replied briskly as I cut off the call and speed-dialled Tehara. I didn't expect to catch her 'cause I thought she would be on hospitals rounds, but I was in luck.

'Hon, I'm gonna have to go to Casa Devapura tonight. I have to cancel our date.'

'Oh come on! Can't you ditch your mum? Surely you've learnt how to ditch your *ammi* by now,' Tehara teased.

'*Machang*, she's making breadfruit curry in coconut milk with prawn *sambol*.'

There was a moment of complete silence. Then:

'She's on a mission,' Tehara whispered softly.

'Yup.'

'I'll let my answering service know to notify me if you call. I'm technically not on call tonight, but *machang*, ring me if you need me.'

I really love Tehara. She has a heart of gold.

'Over and out, *machang*.'

Now, let me take a moment to explain the whole breadfruit curry with prawn *sambol* trap. First the history and then the economics. Breadfruit, sometimes mistaken for jackfruit, is a large, green fibrous fruit originating from the South Pacific. The British, bless their anally retentive, stiff upper-lipped souls, brought it to Sri Lanka, along with venereal disease, tea and indentured slave labour in the form of Tamil tea plantation workers. We live with the fallout to this day.

Breadfruit and tea were nice little earners; Sri Lankan tea is now prized the world over and breadfruit is a staple in our diet. Venereal disease and the indentured slave labourers who went on to join the Tamil Tigers are slightly less prized by the general populace – at about the level of the cane toad in Australia.

Breadfruit has a second claim to fame in addition to its benefits to Sri Lankan society. It's the reason behind the mutiny on the *Bounty*. Yup, in 1787 mad King George III sent William Bligh and Fletcher Christian on the HMS *Bounty* to Tahiti to bring back cargo holds full of breadfruit. Christian fell in love with a Tahitian chick, fell out of sorts with Bligh, and now we have a really bad Mel Gibson movie.

Mad King George never got to taste breadfruit, because his son locked him in an asylum and threw away the key. We Curries could never put our parents in an asylum, no matter how much they deserve it. And that is because we believe in karma. Maybe the perfidious son, also King George, should have believed in karma, too, because he died of overeating and without an heir. My mother always used to say, 'You can't avoid karma's speeding fines.'

But the third claim to breadfruit's fame is that, cooked in coconut milk with prawn *sambol*, it is my favourite food of all time. It is the one narcotic I am unable to resist. If it were a Venus fly trap, I'd be a plump, delicious blowfly. If it were a fluorescent light bulb, I'd be a mindless moth. I think you get the picture. Breadfruit is my Achilles heel and my mother knows it.

My suspicion that my visit to my parents was not going to be pleasant was reinforced by the constant stream of phone calls I took from my mum over the course of the afternoon. For every five calls she made, I answered once.

Every time she'd call, it would be about something relatively innocuous. Could I bring a carton of milk? Could I get an extra loaf of bread? Have I considered colouring my hair the same shade of red as Julia Gillard? (WTF? Firstly, I don't have a boyfriend who is a hairdresser. And secondly, who can keep tabs on the myriad shades of red the woman goes through? She changes hair colour more often – and more rapidly – than I can text message the sale price of the Nine West platform sandals to Tehara.)

I knew it was serious once I had the request to change my hair colour. My mother is always serious when she hints I should alter my appearance. She hopes that something as fundamental as the 'wrong' hair colour may be the reason I am still single.

The fragrance of breadfruit curry hit me halfway down the street from my parents' house. We could never hide from the Ku Klux Klan if they ever became prevalent in Australia; all you'd need to do is drive around the suburbs of Melbourne with your nose out the window to smell the curry coming from our homes. Masters of disguise we are not.

My mother was upbeat, almost 'normal', right throughout the main course. This was standard *modus operandi* though and I knew not to let down my guard too much. Sri Lankan mums never like to spoil their children's appetites. I only wish the same courtesy would be extended to dessert.

And for the record, *Ammi's* dinner was delicious. Breadfruit in a light creamy coconut sauce with slivers of ginger, fresh green chillies and whole mustard. It was the perfect foil for the tart sambol with fresh, crisp prawns stir-fried with caramelised onions, curry leaves, tomatoes and served with a squeeze of lime.

And it was over an equally delicious dessert of yoghurt with honey that the campaign started in earnest. I was handed the invitation to the wedding along with my bowl of yoghurt. It was orange, made of garishly shiny cardboard, and made in Sri Lanka. I could feel the poor quality of the lotus cut-out through the envelope.

'Did you know that it was Gayani who is getting married?'

'Yes, I got an invitation via email. Why don't I organise your spice drawer for you, *Ammi*?' I asked desperately, trying to distract her. I hated sorting the spice drawer. You always needed two people to sort through the hundreds of variants of spices used in Sri Lankan cooking.

'She is younger than you, you realise!'

'Yes *Ammi*. Did I tell you what Tehara got Amani for her baby shower?'

But my mother was not to be sidetracked, continuing relentlessly:

'She is not as pretty as you. Have you seen her moustache? And her sideburns? You don't have any facial hair and you're still not married!'

'That's because I wax,' I interjected quickly, but closed my mouth in resignation when I saw the determined glint in my mother's eyes. I might as well get this over and done with.

'Don't you get smart with me!' her voice rose rapidly. 'Even your Aunty Sonali's daughter, who is five years younger than you, is married! Why, why, why have the *Devas* forsaken me? Why is my daughter the only one unmarried? Why can't I ever be the mother of the bride?'

I was tempted to remind her that Tehara was not married either. But best not to goad a rabid dog. I sat while she continued the onslaught.

'So, can you tell me why you don't want to get married?'

'Because I don't see the need for such a sacrifice.'

'What do you mean *sacrifice*?' my mother hissed, her normally large eyes squinting into ominous little slits. My mother was good looking for her age. Her hair was still glossy black and her light-brown skin was supple and unlined. But, like most Sri Lankan women, she'd started to spread a little around the middle in the last few years.

'*Ammi*, I am thirty-two years old with my own house, car and job. I travel the world when I want to …'

'Yes, with those *kara* friends Tehara and Una …' my mother interrupted. Bizarre how my friend Amani had lost the tag '*kara*' (meaning sluttish, sly, devious) as soon as she had got married. Taking a leaf out of my mother's book, I continued as if she hadn't spoken.

'So, why should I give up my perfect existence to cook a man *paripu* every night and wash his socks? Now, I just come over here when I want to eat curry and you do my laundry and housework by sneaking into my place twice a week.'

'If I didn't do it, you'd have no clothes to wear and your house would look like a pigsty.'

Damn. I hoped I had truly distracted her by referring to my bad housekeeping habits, but no, she could not to be swayed tonight. She rapidly changed tack, going for the ultimate argument.

'You must get married because you'll get lonely. Tehara will be married off soon ...'

'Not bloody likely,' I muttered under my breath.

'Una will find a nice Australian boy, and then you'll be left alone. What will you do when *Thathi* and I die? You'll be left alone. All *alone*. Your brothers will have their wives and families, and you will be *all* alone. Do you want that?'

'My fate could be worse than that you know. I could end up married to a man I hate.'

She paused to catch her breath and marshal her arguments once more.

'Why won't you meet Bhatiya Fernando, Aunty Sonali's nephew? She says your horoscope *ponrondang* match letter for letter!'

'Because he lives in the UK.'

'You could fly out there to meet him.'

'I am not flying twenty-four hours to meet a man who may turn out to be a complete twat.'

'But you go to Europe with Tehara and Una every year!'

'For the pubs and fashion! Duh!'

'What was wrong with the Kalupahana boy?'

'He smoked.'

'You could have got him to quit. And the Tilekaratne boy?'

'He had a lisp and he covered me with spit every time he spoke. How can I share the rest of my life with someone who can't even pronounce my name without spitting?'

My mother dismissed this with a wave of her hand. 'Ever heard of a hanky?'

'And Shamil Udabage? He would have been perfect. He is a doctor, drives a nice car and comes from a good family.'

And he is also gay, I thought grumpily. I wasn't about to out him to my mother though. My mother is of the firm belief that there are no Sri Lankan homosexuals. It's not as if we don't have a population crisis in Sri Lanka where 20 million people, the population of Australia, are crammed into a landmass the size of Tasmania. If you ask me, a few gay boys were exactly what the Paradise Isle needed.

'You know, your biggest mistake was letting Rohan Wick-ramasinghe go!' she continued.

I rolled my eyes. Not this again …

I had met Rohan during my first week at university. I thought he was gorgeous, but he already knew that and was completely full of himself. I didn't have the razor sharp tongue to cut him down to size and make him a half-decent human being. But my best friend Amani did and they have been happily married for the last five years.

'Why no answer, Miss Smart Mouth?'

Ammi then launched down another familiar path and my hackles instinctively rose.

'You know what the problem with you is? You have a big mouth,' she continued.

'My mouth and teeth are perfect. Dr Jayasinghe, the ortho-dontist, said so. Remember?' I replied, grinning widely to show her my teeth.

'See, you have a big mouth! You have an answer for

everything. Men don't like women who talk. They like quiet women who listen to what they have to say. If you were nicer, kinder and better, then someone would marry you. Try to be nicer.'

'I am nice.'

I was getting weary of this talk. We were two minutes away from my mother listing all my behavioural infractions since babyhood.

My mother's eyes narrowed again. The ideas were running out now, and I could literally hear the cogs in her head turning as she searched for the final hit that would clear the MCG grandstand of my resistance. I quickly shovelled the rest of the yoghurt into my mouth. This was not going to end well. It never did.

'It's because of that boy, *nay*?'

'Which boy?' I asked warily. But I knew exactly which boy, alright.

'That white boy.'

'You mean, Jacob Thuan?'

'Yes, him.'

My mother lowered her voice conspiratorially. 'You know, they can fix these things now?'

I looked at her, puzzled. This was new.

'Fix what? I don't want to get back together with Jake,' I said, confused and emphatic at the same time.

By now, I was pretty sure my father was intentionally ignoring our conversation as he raised the volume on the TV once again. I could hear Richie Benaud's dulcet tones calling the cricket.

'The precious treasure you threw away at Jacob Thuan's feet. Sonali told me that there is an operation they do in India to repair them. Nobody will know, and you can do it when you go to Sri Lanka on holiday this year. A ticket to India is only $100 more,' my mother said quickly and quietly as she clutched me firmly, her fingernails gripping my upper arms.

Comprehension slowly dawned. She wanted me to repair my hymen.

This, after all the phone calls and the guilt tripping finally broke my patience. I cracked. I was so incensed that fury robbed me of my usually stellar vocabulary. I stood there, gawping like a stunned mullet.

I was not sure what I was angrier about. Was it the fact that my mother felt she could discuss my sex life with me or the fact she'd discussed my lack of virginity with *bloody Aunty Sonali*? My left eye started twitching dangerously. My mother noticed this and wisely let go of my arm. I took a deep, shuddering breath and said calmly, 'I am going to leave now. Do not call me until I call you.'

'Shani, don't you want your life to be perfect? You have a good job, a nice house and a good family. All you need is a husband,' my mother pleaded.

I turned around and glared at her as I walked briskly out of the front door, marvelling that I had somehow managed not to slam it. I was so incoherent with rage that, as I barrelled down the driveway, I nearly ran over my younger brother, Gehani.

'Hey, what's up *Akki*?' he asked like a goofy, overgrown puppy.

'*Ammi*!'

He held his hands up in surrender. He knew what I was going through. I sometimes thought it was a miracle he was still living at home, but maybe that was more a tribute to my mother's superb cooking skills than anything else.

The only coherent thought that kept running through my head as I gunned the engine was that my hypocritical mother prayed twice a day. So how did she get round the fourth precept – the one that involved a promise not to lie? I was pretty sure that having a hymen repaired to snare a foolish man into marriage was about as big a deception as you could perpetrate. So much for Gautama Buddha's edicts of not practising deceit!

CHAPTER 3

My Peeps

I'd left a message on Tehara's answering service by the time I negotiated my way out of my parents' driveway. It contained exactly three words. COME. OVER. NOW.

Tehara called back by the time I reached the end of the street.

'How bad was it on a scale of one to ten?' my personality testing-addicted friend asked. Everything is about the MMPI for psychiatrists. The Minnesota Multiphasic Personality Inventory was Tehara's tool of trade. She'd made us all do it as a part of her training.

'100.'

'Reinforcements?'

'Yes.'

It took me less than ten minutes to drive home, but Una was already sitting impatiently on the doorstep of my unit like a flame-haired beacon, holding a box of Ferrero Rocher and a tub of Kentucky Fried Chicken.

'Amani is bringing the Nuts About Chocolate,' she called out, as I got out of my car. She winced as I slammed the door. 'You're going to ruin your car, you know.'

'Yeah, yeah,' was all I could mutter as I negotiated the lock to the front door and the alarm system my paranoid parents had insisted I install.

Una had walked in, switched on the lights and started to open a bottle of wine by the time I had finished punching in the security code. She poured me a large glass of red with a much smaller measure for herself and Tehara. She didn't speak to me until I had had a deep swig and collapsed onto my camel-coloured sofa, kicking off my stilettos. 'Change out of your work clothes first,' she commanded, as I closed my eyes. 'You know you'll feel better.'

She was right. I went to my room and changed. I looked at myself in the mirror as I brushed out my hair and I must admit my mother was right. I am prettier than Gayani. One of my exes once described my skin as milk coloured with saffron; my large, dark brown almond-shaped eyes turned up naturally at the corners. My mouth was small though, not in line with the current fashion for more generous lips. But my favourite feature was my nose, small and tilted up delicately at the end.

And I waxed. Regularly. Since the age of sixteen. So, unlike most South Asian women, facial hair was something I was not particularly plagued by either. I had been a distance runner at high school and university and I maintain a trim figure by running the Tan Track at least twice or three times a week. I was by no means a beauty queen, but I wasn't butt ugly either.

I heard more voices and a door close; the rest of the cavalry had arrived.

Amani was the first person I saw when I walked back into

the lounge room. Even after knowing her for nearly twenty-one years, her beauty still took my breath away. It was no wonder that Rohan had fallen in love with her at first sight, never mind the fact that he'd been flirting like mad with me for weeks before he'd met her.

I went over and hugged her, though it was rather difficult to get to her with a six-and-a-half-month pregnancy bump in the way. But with the extra pregnancy kilos, she had the nicest body to hug. All soft and yielding.

'Spill,' Una and Tehara commanded in unison.

I gave them a rundown of what had happened.

'Your mother wants to get your *hymen* fixed? You have got to be joking,' Una commented, chortling into her wine.

Tehara, Amani and I glared at her.

'Has hanging out with three Lankans for nearly twenty years taught you nothing? We never joke when it comes to cricket or hymens,' Amani said, in all seriousness. And she would know.

'Forget I asked. I should have remembered. Just ignore her,' advised Una.

'But what really pisses me off is that she discussed it with *Aunty Sonali*,' I continued.

'You know it's not Aunty Sonali's fault. The problem lies with Sri Lankan men. They all want to think they are Marco Polo. Going into uncharted territory,' Tehara added sarcastically.

'You stole that line from *Chasing Amy*,' Amani said.

Did I mention that my friend Amani is an actual practising lawyer, unlike myself? I studied law at uni, but was never admitted to the Supreme Court.

Amani has spent the last seven years working for the Department of Public Prosecutions. She did her rotations through the Criminal Courts, the Family Court and finally landed happily in the White Collar Crime area of the DPP, pursuing tax frauds and accounting cheats. She can also be very particular about intellectual property theft, and to this day is the only person I know who can speak a coherent sentence while still providing approved citations from the Law Council of Australia.

'So sue me,' Tehara retorted.

'So original, not!'

'Well girls, as always, I haven't received a wedding invitation yet,' Una said, interrupting the budding argument. 'But I got a text message from Gayani – asking me if I'd be a part of the opening dance.'

'Of course she knows you'll be dancing with us. When have the four of us ever danced without each other?' Tehara asked.

'Since now,' Amani said grimacing, and waving a hand over her bulge. 'I'll be ready to pop close to the wedding, so I can't see myself doing our Club Bollywood moves, can you?'

'Then we'll need to rearrange things a bit if it'll only be the three of us,' Una continued. 'How many weddings this season so far?'

'I've got four invitations so far – the Veeracone's, Peiris's of course, the Wijersuriya's and the Kohanagoda's,' Tehara said. 'I'm doing no more than six. I fly out to London for a conference the first week in June.'

'Four for me, and the same ones as you,' I said. 'I overheard Aunty Manel say to Aunty Vinita that her sister had heard from her friend, Aunty Chitra, that this year is not good for weddings. So, unless you *have* to get married, like Gayani, most people will hold off until next year.'

'I heard that too. My *ammi* told me that Aunty Jaya heard from Aunty Karuna, who heard from Aunty Kusuma who spoke to a professional astrologer that there are only a few *nekath* days this year,' Amani piped up, around a mouth full of chocolate ice-cream.

'Yeah, I heard my stepmother mumble something about poor *nekath* the other day. Apparently, that's put the kibosh on everything else. It's supposed to be a very bad year; loads of people will die and stuff like that,' Tehara mumbled.

Three for three. All saying the same thing. The bad *nekath* rumours must be correct. Good old *nekath* days. I glanced up to send a silent prayer of thanks to the *Devas*. Trust the bad *nekath* to cut back the ordeal of a very long wedding season.

Let me explain.

The Sri Lankan wedding season runs from mid-April to late June, with a tiny hiatus sometime in May. Which means in practical terms that the season starts after 15 April, or Singhalese New Year, and runs till the end of June with a break for Vesak, the birth of the Buddha, in May.

This is a win-win situation for almost all the parties involved. With the back-to-front seasons in the land down under, most Australian brides like to have spring/summer weddings from October to March. With dates of April and May, Sri Lankan weddings rarely clash with so-called 'Skippy' weddings. Wedding function centres win too, with almost a full year of wedding bookings thanks to the Lankans. And Sri Lankan parents love it as well, because they get 'off-season' discounts for their kids' weddings. As I said, everybody wins.

Except the Sri Lankan brides. They are obliged to freeze their tits off in scantily cut *saree* blouses in the middle of autumn and winter. I once went to a wedding where the bride was so cold, her nipples showed like pebbles against her *saree* blouse. She looked like a *Sports Illustrated* swimsuit model in a photo-shoot set in Iceland. I noticed. My friends noticed. The groomsmen, we were sure, noticed (as evidenced by their bulging crotches and sheepish grins). The groom grimaced every time he looked at his bride. Whether from arousal or embarrassment, I never knew.

All this discomfort because of *nekath*, or auspicious days.

Everything in Sri Lanka is governed by these auspicious times, calculated by a horde of mercenary, superstitious astrologers. People start new jobs on good *nekath* days. House foundations are laid on good *nekath* days. Women schedule their c-sections on good *nekath* days. Even the bloody elections are scheduled to be on a good *nekath* day, though ironically it'd only be good for one party – the party that rigs the most votes, and pays the astrologer the heftiest bribe.

Good *nekath* days for weddings apparently fall from April to June. It's really easy to book a wedding in Sri Lanka the rest of the year, but you need to book at least three years in advance to have your wedding between April and June.

Apparently, this coming year did not have good *nekath*. In Sri Lanka, business would virtually grind to a halt and people would just loll around waiting for good *nekath*, so that life could begin again. Meanwhile, we had things to discuss.

'Let's call it four weddings,' said Tehara, business-like as ever. 'Una, you can borrow my blue *gagra choli* and I can wear your bottle green *saree* from two years ago ...'

'The one with the vintage lace edging? And the lace blouse?'

'Yes.'

'I love you, Tehara!' Una replied, bouncing on her seat.

'Shani, you can have the new *choli* Rohan's mum got for me from India as well as the *saree* he bought me for our anniversary last year, ' said Amani.

'You're sure?'

'Yup, this Goodyear Blimp will be a yummy mummy-to-be in her new MaxMara maternity ensemble.'

'To all four weddings?'

'No one is going to notice.'

'Didn't you wear the *saree* to the New Year's Eve party? People will notice.'

'We'll add some sequins to it and make it up a little different.'

'Tehara, you can borrow the pink *saree* and the golden brown *saree*,' Una offered magnanimously.

'Okay, so we need to get two outfits each,' Tehara continued. 'I'll call Mrs Fernando and make an appointment.'

'We also need to choreograph the dances. Gayani wants us, obviously, to lead her dance. I think we'll probably be asked to lead the Kohanagoda dance, too, 'cause I've, like, known Sanjay forever. We'll get the couples to come over on a Sunday to choose the music and get themes for the dances,' I said.

The only reason, according to my smart-alecky little brother Gehani, that Una, Amani, Tehara and I were ever invited to weddings, was because we never said 'no' to leading the bridal couple in their first, Bollywood-inspired, group dance fest. I couldn't really argue with him. The simple matter of the fact was that we looked good on the dance floor, damned good.

'Fabulous,' came the chorus, as the girls gathered their things and made moves to leave.

We agreed not to meet for our standard Tuesday movies and mayhem. Tehara needed to catch up on some paperwork. And Amani just needed to sleep.

CHAPTER 4

Three Lankans and a Skip

In truth, Una, rather than Tehara or Amani, was my best friend. She was number one on my speed dial list. In fact, Una was number one on the speed dial list for Tehara and Amani as well. We weren't game to find out where the three of us ranked on each other's lists, but we were sure we were all in the top four.

The fact that Una was the collective best friend surprised no one who knows her. She is an Intensive Care nurse and the kindest person I know. We've all been friends since high school. But, like everything else in our lives, it's a bit more complicated than that.

I had immigrated to Australia from Sri Lanka with my family when I was eleven. We'd arrived in October, too late in the year to start in a new primary school, especially since I'd be going into high school in the new year. So, my dad and I lined up a nice local high school near our council flat in Springvale for me to go to and I liked it on sight.

There were stray dogs in the school yard, just like my old school in Sri Lanka. There were a couple of broken down cars in the playground instead of play equipment. Just like my old school in Sri Lanka. Broken windows. Again, just like my old school in Sri Lanka. And there were tons of other Lankan kids at the school and hardly any 'Skips', as I'd learned to call non-Asian Australians. Exactly like my old school in Sri Lanka.

However, within weeks of arriving in Australia, an enterprising uncle, a friend of a friend of a friend, took me to a scholarship exam. Only I didn't know it was a scholarship exam. Much to the delight of my parents, I passed with flying colours and was admitted to St Catherine's in Toorak, as a full-scholarship student.

I was almost fresh off the plane with an accent a mile wide. The grazier princesses had a new lamb to mulesing without anaesthetic.

Don't get me wrong, it's not like there weren't other 'ethnic' girls there. There was a bucket load of Chinese chicks, and a full complement of Indian and Sri Lankan princesses. Tehara fell into this group – she'd been there since kindergarten. I thought she was an arrogant bitch and I hated her immediately. Amani and I actually ran an 'I hate Tehara' club for about a month in Year 7.

Amani, like me, started at St Catherine's in Year 7; but unlike me, she'd been born here in Australia and her parents had worked their butts off to afford to send her to the school. She had no discernible accent and she 'fitted in' better. She worked each of the social groups like a pro – the Oriental Princesses, the Grazier Princesses, the Jewish-Australian Princesses, the Indo-Sri Lankan Princesses and the scholarship nerds. And by the end of the first week of school, she was flitting between all the groups like the adept social butterfly she was.

It also helped that, even at the age of twelve, Amani was beautiful enough to stop traffic. She always had the Scotch College boys offering her lifts in their BMWs, even when we were thirteen and the boys at least eighteen.

By the end of the first week of school, I had a sum total of zero friends (even the nerds rejected me because of my awful accent) and was working on an escape plan involving expulsion. I needed to get back to that school in Springvale.

But Amani's lunch box got in the way.

As with most kids, even rich, snooty ones, every one peeks in each other's lunch boxes. The grass is always greener on the other side, right?

This fine Friday, Amani's mum had packed her a lunch of sandwiches filled with spicy tuna. I have since had Amani's spicy tuna sandwiches and I can honestly say they are delicious. Alright, maybe I'm acclimatised just a little – being raised on spicy breast milk, you could light a blast furnace in my mouth and I wouldn't notice the difference. However, Melissa, the daughter of a prominent Melbourne QC, who'd been brought up on meat and three bland veg, didn't have a hope in hell of surviving a chilli bomb wedged between two slices of high fibre white bread. Amani still swears she did not twig to this before she handed the sandwich over to Melissa.

It took the Toorak princess all of ten seconds to start screaming once she'd bitten into a green chilli. It also didn't help that she went on to have an allergic reaction to the flavonoids and had to be rushed to the emergency room.

All the girls in our year thought the whole thing was hilarious. We also thought it would blow over by the following week. Especially if someone else had a more unfortunate misadventure, which Annalise Wright did. She caught the train home the following Monday afternoon with her skirt tucked into the back of her knickers.

Unfortunately for Amani, Melissa turned out to be the vindictive sort. She convinced anyone who would listen (anyone without a brain anyway, of which there was a surprisingly large number at our school) that Amani had shoved the sandwich down her throat in a crazy plot to kill her and rule the school. By the following Friday, Amani was labelled a curry-pushing murderous bitch. Her social collateral plummeted to the same level as mine. Her perfect life was in tatters.

That Friday afternoon, I was at the station, waiting to catch the train home when I saw Amani. She was gutted; misery and depression were etched in every line of her drooping body. Tears were streaming down her face when she looked furtively behind to see who was watching her. By the way she stood, poised, I thought she was about to jump in front of a train. Surely she wasn't that stupid, I thought desperately.

Unfortunately my first instincts had been right. I didn't stop to think further and, fired by adrenaline, I ran up and pulled her from the edge of the platform. She fought my grasp. I yanked her back and slapped her. We had a fist fight with our hair flying out of our ponytails and our school bags strewn on the platform. Right there at Toorak station, with the Scotch College boys egging us on. A real class act.

I landed a particularly lucky punch that made Amani's nose bleed, and the fighting stopped. She started crying and ran away, leaving me to catch the next train home and explain to my mother why I had blood on my uniform.

I looked forward to the following Monday. Expulsion had to be definitely on the cards. The Scotch College boys would have made sure the headmistress knew about our little altercation before she went to bed that day. St Catherine's made such a big deal of ladylike behaviour, especially in public, and delighted in expelling potential ladettes. And frankly, Amani and I had behaved more like mud wrestlers on speed than the gentlewomen our school desired us to become.

Expulsion also meant a one-way ticket back to the local high school. Goodbye ivy-covered sandstone, hello cement brick! Mission accomplished!

So on Monday, with a jaunty little skip to my step, I made my way back to school. I was so confident that I didn't even take my books with me. As predicted, the headmistress intercepted me at the gates and took me to her office. Amani was already there.

However, Amani surprised me. Before the headmistress started with the lecture to precede the inevitable (and longed-for) expulsion, Amani told her that she had started the fight with me and was really sorry. She made it a piece of high drama, complete with tears, snot and pleas for clemency, even tingeing her speech with a whiff of hysteria until the principal had to give her a little drink of water to calm her down. And she pledged to do detention every day until the end of the year *and* be the bathroom monitor (the most despised job in the school) until she finished Year 10, if she and I were spared expulsion.

I tried interrupting a couple of times, to say that she needn't include me in her pleas, but she ploughed on like a freight train. And much to my disgust, it worked. We weren't expelled. The headmistress gave Amani detention for two months and I got a verbal warning. In hindsight, I think Amani gave the poor woman a migraine and she just wanted us out of her office for some peace and quiet.

Outside the headmistress's office, Amani turned to me and asked, 'How did you know I was going to jump?'

'Your foot was already in front of the train, *modi*.'

'Pretty obvious, huh?'

'Jah.'

'Thank you. Stay with me,' she pleaded.

Saving someone's life by pulling them away from a speeding train isn't something you can easily forget. I felt I needed to make sure the effort wasn't wasted. We sat together in class from that day and we've been friends ever since.

One of the perks of becoming Amani's friend was that I suddenly got the entire insider's gossip on the other Sri Lankans. During the first lunch Amani and I shared at school, she gave me a rundown of all the Year 7 girls.

'You see that Manel?'

'Jah.'

'She is Dr Kularatana's daughter.'

I gave Amani a blank stare.

'Dr Kularatana! The one who owns a chain of bottle shops next to the medical centres! My *ammi* says it's bad karma to own a bottle shop, so all the good karma he makes as a doctor is wiped out.'

I nodded gravely, storing all these bits of information to later be repeated to my mother. I knew she'd want to know. Gossip isn't just a hobby with her, it's an obsession.

'That's Subarshini. Her father is a lawyer and her mother is an orthodontist. They paid megabucks for their house in South Yarra. My *ammi* got invited to their house warming *Dhanay* and she told me that they had fifteen monks attend.'

'Really? Where did they get all the monks from?'

'Well, they go to temple in Armadale – you know, the one with only the one monk. So they sponsored fourteen more to come over from Sri Lanka.'

'Oh, is there more than one temple?'

'Uh huh! I bet you go to the temple in Springvale, like us?'

I shrugged to say yes. That was when Amani explained the temple pecking order to me, or rather, the social strata of the Sri Lankan community in Melbourne.

'The doctors, lawyers, accountants and the Lankans who came here before 1985 go to the temple in Armadale,' she explained. 'We don't go there 'cause *Thathi* is only in IT. Your *thathi* works for Toyota, right? Well, he has an office job so we all belong at the temple in Springvale. The mechanics and their sort, they go to the temple in Dandenong.'

Somehow, I didn't have the guts to tell Amani my father had been a mechanic before he'd worked his way up to being a manager at the Toyota plant. She was my first friend in Melbourne and I wasn't going to let *anything* get in the way of our friendship.

'Now, you see that girl with the pudgy, oval face. Her name is Tehara, her father is Dr Jayasuriya.'

I nodded vigorously. Finally a name I knew. I'd met Dr Jayasuriya the week before to get my asthma assessed. He was a lovely GP with a practice near Springvale station.

'Not that Dr Jayasuriya! The other Dr Jayasuriya! He, like, came out here in the sixties, studied at Melbourne Uni and currently holds the chair of Psychiatry there as well,' Amani parroted, with an air of importance.

I didn't know what psychiatry was, much less what a Chair of Psychiatry might be. Did it have something to do with carpentry? Whatever, it sounded important and I was suitably impressed.

'His first wife committed suicide while they were on holiday in Sri Lanka. And here is the really interesting bit: he married Tehara's mum straight away in Sri Lanka and brought her back to Melbourne a year later. My *Ammi* says that when they visited, Tehara was already born and she didn't look like a newborn either. She was a big toddler,' Amani whispered, secretively.

Tehara, who was on the other side of the playground at that time, turned around right at that moment and caught us staring at her. I wondered if she could possibly have heard us from that distance. She gave us a dirty look and stalked off with her nose in the air.

Tehara seemed to have a perfect life though. Her mother picked her up every day after school in a Volvo, she had two pairs of Doc Martens and three hyper colour T-shirts. I never got a hyper colour T-shirt, however much I had begged. Tehara also spent her holidays flitting between Melbourne, Colombo and her father's holiday house in Tuscany.

However, the summer we all went into Year 8, Tehara's perfect life was ground to dust like the last crumbs in an extra large bag of Bhuja Mix. We found out all about it well before school started in January, via the trusty 'Curry Reuters' gossip network.

Tehara normally spent the summer holidays at her father's tea estate in Badulla. The family would fly out from Melbourne first class on Christmas Eve and have Christmas lunch on the estate bungalow veranda overlooking the majestic Knuckles Ranges. Her father would soon disappear to relax out in the wilderness, watching the mountain leopards and the like for the next week and a half; while Tehara and her mother would visit with relatives and gossip.

That year, however, two days into the annual Jayasuriya holiday Mrs Jayasuriya disappeared. Tehara's father didn't appear at the estate for another four days and the poor girl seemed to spend most of the intervening time alternating between bouts of crying and vomiting.

Enquiries were soon made into the whereabouts of the second Mrs Jayasuriya; fears were held that she had gone the same way as the first. Fortunately – or maybe unfortunately – not.

The second Mrs Jayasuriya had run off with the estate manager instead. When Mrs Jayasuriya was finally taken to task over her abandoned husband and child, she threatened to kill herself rather than return to Melbourne. Tehara's father promptly washed his hands of his second wife and returned with Tehara in time for the last day of the Test match between Australia and the West Indies at the MCG.

To add to the traumatic experience, Tehara's father called her into his study the day before the start of school and told her to pack up all her stuff. She was going to board at St Catherine's for the rest of the year while he went to London for his sabbatical. He returned in time for the Christmas trip that year with his third wife in tow.

Once her mother ran away, Tehara was ostracised by the girls from her Indian and Sri Lankan set. Their mothers didn't want Tehara hanging out with them; apparently loose morals were more contagious than the bubonic plague. So by the end of the first week of Year 8, Tehara had lost so much weight that she regularly passed out during class.

In the same way that I saved Amani, Una saved Tehara.

Una was a boarder too. She'd spent much of Year 7 not finding a group of friends. She hadn't fitted in with the other grazier princesses who'd swanned into school in their fathers' Range Rovers with their Country Road clothes. I doubt Una has ever set foot inside R.M. Williams!

And it was all because Una was the daughter of a pair of hippy organic farmers from Daylesford – at a time before it was cool to be into organic farming and after it was cool to be a hippy. When Una came to Melbourne for high school, the other graziers' daughters had somehow got wind about her parents' lifestyle and treated her as if she were a junkie. Girls at school kept going through her stuff, convinced they'd find hooch in her possession.

Una, to her credit, took it all in her stride, calmly. I have never seen Una rise to a taunt or a nasty comment. So, when Una had found Tehara distraught that first day of school in Year 8, she organised for a room transfer. Una didn't push Tehara, or talk to her much, but let Tehara know she was there if she needed someone. By Easter break, Tehara could finally hold down a meal and sleep most of the way through the night.

This was about the time the Tehara and Una show amalgamated with the Shani and Amani show. Thanks to that vindictive Melissa.

Every year, the Year 8 girls from St Catherine's put on an Easter concert for the old folk who lived at the Catholic retirement condominium in Kew. Alleviating the boredom of the elderly was character building, according to the moral arbiters at St Catherine's. What they didn't know, of course, that these old folks drove to Kew Junction in their Mercedes-Benz SLKs to get packets of cigarettes after the concert.

That year, Amani and I had decided to shake things up a little. We had decided to put on a little dance called Bollywood Bhangra.

Tehara and Una, on the other hand, were going to do magic tricks with a lot of smoke. (How lame was that? We've been giving them stick for it ever since.) They had this grand entrance planned, where they would use sparklers in a darkened auditorium to start their performance.

As it happened, Amani and I had done a rousing performance in our floaty sequined *gagra cholis* with bells on our ankles. We'd practised the transition with Una and Tehara; it ought to have gone smoothly.

'That was bloody fantastic,' I whispered to Amani as we danced off the stage to a standing ovation.

'What is she doing?' Amani asked urgently as she looked down the steep stairs to see Melissa.

'Una told me that Mel was going to do the sparklers.'

'But we're supposed to be off the effing stage before she does!'

When the sparkler near my feet caught fire Amani had the presence of mind to step back, but she froze in horror once she did. As the lights went out, my floaty, filmy synthetic skirt with sequins and bells went up with a whoosh!

It took the teachers just a few seconds to bring the lights back up, but my skirt was already in flames. Una, who was already on the stage, never lost her cool. She walked over and yanked off my flaming skirt.

Pandemonium raged for a few moments as everyone focused on dousing my ruined skirt. And as it calmed down, I realised I was standing in front of a crowd of 200 in my holey panties. I wanted the ground to open up and swallow me whole.

So there you go. I saved Amani, and Una saved both Tehara and me. We were bonded. Not just by the fact that we genuinely loved each other, but also by the fact that we owed each other our lives. Literally.

CHAPTER 5

Did they Build an Exit to Dandenong?

Saturday saw the four of us sitting in Tehara's brand new Merc driving towards Dandenong along Melbourne's newest addition to the freeway system, Eastlink. Amani was riding shotgun, owing to her increasing girth and the fact that almost anything could make her stomach heave. A couple of weeks back, I was driving past a fish and chip shop with her and she covered my new gym bag with the falafel she had had for lunch. Never again.

Una too, has been a victim of Amani's oesophageal pyro-technics; she was still trying to get her shagpile rug clean after Amani christened it while she'd been playing Wii tennis. Apparently, the motion of tennis coupled with the flickering lights from the TV had set her off. So we felt, quite reasonably, that it was Tehara's turn to get vomited on this time.

'I've spoken to Gayani,' Amani started without preamble,

popping a raisin in her mouth. 'I told her that if she cannot pick her music and the type of dance she wants by next Tuesday, her default wedding song and dance would be *Mahive*.'

'She's only the bride, it's not like she's got a choice or anything,' I drawled sarcastically.

'Has anyone met the intended yet?' Una asked.

'Nope,' Amani said, popping an almond into her mouth. The woman was certainly eating for two, if not three.

'Wonder what he's like?'

'Blind would be the obvious answer unless Gayani has had a serious run in with the Brazilian Butterfly,' Tehara said.

We all agreed that Gayani's upper lip did give Merv Hughes's handlebar moustache a run for its money.

'Which is the exit to Dandenong?' Tehara asked as the freeway loomed endlessly in front of us.

'Not sure. Just follow the signs,' Una said.

'I heard that he's a Sri Lankan qualified engineer,' I said, turning back to the topic of interest.

'Should I take the exit to Police Road?' Tehara asked, looking confused as she always did once she crossed over Burke Road. As far as Tehara was concerned, civilisation ended at Camberwell.

'Haven't you driven this road before?' Una asked.

'Of course not! I only ever drive up and down Punt Road!'

'Don't exit at Police Road, *modi*. You'll end up too far south and you'll have to drive all the way past the cemetery. Keep going,' Amani commanded. 'So, how is the *magul* business going?' she asked, turning to me.

'*Ammi* and I have agreed to not talk about potential grooms until Sinhala New Year. Apparently then, my Jupiter is going to intersect with my Venus, thus making me highly marriageable. An astrologer has told her to not even discuss marriage with me before then.'

Which meant that *ammi* and I were friends again ... I can rarely stay angry with her for long.

And, yes, my mother has an astrologer in Keysborough on retainer. She spends more money with him than on her telephone bill; and, let me tell you, the woman talks a great deal on the phone.

'Ahh, you are coming into *Mangala Yoga*,' Una intoned sagely. 'Did your mother tell you how long the *Yoga* was going to last for?'

Tehara and I caught each other's eye and smothered grimaces of incredulity. Una sometimes thought she was psychic; I'm more inclined to think she was psycho.

'Three months. Pretty much from the start of the wedding season until the end. *Ammi* said my *Mangala Yoga* has corresponded exactly with good *nekath* except for the last day. The astrologer said I should not meet men on the last day of the wedding season.'

So here's the deal on *Mangala Yoga*. According to Vedic astrology, a person can only get married if they meet the right person at the right time. And *Mangala Yoga* is the period in your life when you are most likely to meet a person you can marry. It doesn't come around every year either. It may come around once or twice in a person's lifetime. It's like a flower that blooms once every hundred years. Or the salmon mating season. Everything has to be in alignment for a woman to nab a man.

The con-artist astrologer my mother had on retainer had convinced her that I was coming into *Mangala Yoga* this *nekath* wedding season. And if I didn't get married this time, I wouldn't have another chance until the next *Mangala Yoga* period rolled around. Which could be, like, never. My mother had hit über panic stations.

'Oh, good!' Una piped up, excitedly. 'Aunty Sonali's nephew Bhatiya will be in Australia on holiday in the next few months. I practised matching your horoscopes together and they are perfect! You guys could be soul mates; that's how well you are matched.'

'Since when do you have a copy of my horoscope?'

'Since Aunty Sonali showed it to me!'

'Since when does *Aunty Sonali* have my horoscope?'

'Since your mother gave it to her to match it with her nephews!'

'Shani, your mother does have a point, though. You're the odd one out, *machang*,' Amani piped in.

'Don't you all gang up on me now. You know why I'm single.'

'Should I take the Corrigan Road exit?' Tehara asked, starting to sound worried.

'No, keep going,' Una called forward before turning back to me. 'So, why did you dump Matt?'

Matthew Jones, Business Development Manager, my last friend with benefits. We 'saw' each other for six months.

'He was getting a little like an octopus … all tentacles and clingy.'

'Have you considered the fact that you may have commitment issues? Men aren't the only people who have issues with relationships, you know,' Amani said smugly, chewing on a carrot stick.

'Oh, look who's talking. Didn't you, like, go out with ten guys before you settled with Rohan? And you lost your virginity before any of us!'

'That was because I was willing to give it a go. You used to be so petrified that you'd bleed to death that you hung onto your virginity like a life raft,' Amani returned. 'Besides, let's not forget you were lusting after my hubby for yonks.'

'I was not!' I retorted, hotly. I had got over my unfortunate crush on Rohan a very long time ago.

'Shaani, what Amani is trying to say is that we are worried about you and want you to be happy, love,' Una said soothingly while sending Amani a silencing look. 'Be nice! She is pregnant!' Una hissed at me angrily, poking me in the ribs.

'It must be the next exit,' Tehara muttered to no one in general.

'So why don't you want to get married?' Amani pressed.

'Because everyone I know who is married is miserable.'

'I'm not,' Amani returned with a smug little smile.

'You and Rohan are the exception. My parents, with their arranged marriage, ignore each other to the point of rudeness. Every day I have to listen to my mother complain about my father – the only time my father bothered to call my mum last year when she was away at my grand-dad's funeral for two weeks was confirm that she'd paid the Foxtel bill before she went and to make sure he needed to microwave his frozen curry dinners for five minutes instead of two! He spent two whole weeks in his underwear watching cricket and eating rice and curry straight out of takeaway boxes. He didn't use a single plate and he rinsed his tea cup every morning so he could re-make his tea in it!

'And your father, Amani, drove your mother to near obsession with Buddhism – the more he wanted to drink and party, the more your mother wanted to pray and meditate. Remember the time your father got sprung for running a poker game in the garage while your mother had the house packed to the rafters with monks for overnight Buddhist chanting? And Tehara's father ...' I kind of lost steam as I looked at Tehara.

'Go on, say it. My father is a self-centred, egotistical arsehole who covers his many faults by spreading his money far and wide. *Should I take the next exit?*'

'Exactly! Almost every person I know who gets married needs to compromise on something. They end up bitter and angry because they are not living the life they've always dreamed of. Why trade nice holidays, fancy clothes and unlimited self-indulgence for washing a man's socks and making him *paripu*?' I asked.

'And, don't forget, bearing his children,' Una said, significantly.

'Cause you'll be lonely, sexually frustrated and cold in bed,' Amani responded in a smartarse tone that made me want to slap her.

'I'll never get lonely cause I'm Lankan. Just look at all the family I've got. Besides, I can always get a "fuck buddy" if I need to. If I'm cold in bed, I'll get a hot water bottle … and do you honestly think a man provides you with unconditional love and support?' I asked Amani, pointedly.

Rohan and Amani had had an ongoing, often loud debate about when to start a family for the last five years. We'd all been pulled into the discussion at some stage and it'd come to the point that we had started avoiding social gatherings with the two of them. First Rohan had wanted a child and Amani hadn't. Then Amani had wanted a child and Rohan wanted to wait. It went on like a bad tennis match for years with neither side yielding a point.

Until last year's Melbourne Cup. Amani had too much champers at the Bird Cage and vomited up the pill she'd had that morning along with a large portion of smoked salmon, steamed wontons and camembert wrapped in prosciutto. Amani has a head as hard has the three-carat diamond on her ring finger and she looked hot in her new Carla Zampatti frock, so she and Rohan had made good use of the stretch limo they had hired to get them back home. Una and I reckon the child will be a bogan since it was conceived in the back seat of a car.

'I read somewhere that if you really want unconditional love and support …' Una was saying.

'… you ought to get a Jack Russell terrier,' I finished for her.

'You should *give* unconditional love and support, was what I was going to say,' Una completed with a glare.

'Girls! We've just passed Cheltenham Road. Does anyone know where we are going?' Tehara asked. Nobody was listening.

'We just want you to be happy,' Una said calmly.

'Maybe she *is* a lesbian,' Amani added.

'Maybe I am.'

'Hon, watching back-to-back episodes of *Nigella Bites* does not make you a lesbian.'

'Maybe if I got groped by another chick it would be?'

'Darling, if you are referring to the time you got groped at that lesbian bar, I am going to have to disagree. I've prosecuted Hell's Angels more in touch with their feminine side than those dykes,' Amani pointed out.

'Fuck girls, can I have some input here? We are halfway to bloody Frankston! Where the fucking hell is the exit?' Tehara yelled. That got our attention.

'How come you don't know how to get to Dandenong? We've only been going there most of our lives!' Amani pointed out.

'Shani usually drives. I never take notice of how we get there!'

'Shani? How do we get there?' Amani asked.

'Mate, I usually take the suburban roads to Dandenong. I never take the freeway.'

'Why not? Freeways are faster! Especially from where you live,' Una pointed out with maddening logic.

'For one thing, I never drive my car when I go to Dandenong. I always drive my dad's and my parents don't believe in paying to use a road when sitting in traffic suits them just fine.'

'And why don't you drive your car to Dandenong?'

'As if Miss Anally-Rentitive-Accountant here would risk her German steel in a suburb full of ethnic drivers,' Amani replied for me.

'I am NOT anally retentive!'

'Shani – I don't even need to peek down your size eight jeans to know you are wearing pink cotton hipster undies today. And why do I know? Because you colour-coordinate your underwear by the day of the week!'

'I bet you she's even wearing her T-shirt bra – she hates wearing structured bras on the weekend,' Una teased as she quickly leant over and pulled at my top quickly to have a peek.

'Hey, stop that!' I protested, smacking at her hands, but she was too quick.

'Yup!' she chortled with glee. 'You are so predictable.'

'I rest my case, Your Honour,' Amani finished.

'Can we stop fucking talking about fucking Shani's smalls and focus on the road?' Tehara swore again, her frustration boiling over now.

'Haven't you got sat nav?' Una asked in a small voice.

Amani was now trying to bend over her considerable girth to get to the sat nav system, but she couldn't reach it. Tehara could not get to it either, judging it wiser to keep her eyes on the road and her hands on the steering wheel. End result, we ended up in Frankston.

We finally pulled out into a side street and started using the sat nav.

'What's the address?' Tehara asked tersely.

'Foster Street, Dandenong.'

'*Diese Adresse existiert nicht.*'

'What was that?'

'The sat nav,' Tehara replied.

'Try it again,' I said, a little desperately. Frankston isn't the safest suburb for a car full of Sri Lankan chicks, even if we did have a token Aussie with us.

Again we heard; '*Diese Adresse existiert nicht.*'

'Haven't you used your sat nav before, Tehara?' Amani asked in exasperation.

'Of course not. As I said, I only ever drive up and down Punt Road. Guess I'll have to take it back to the dealership to have the language reset.'

'That's if we live long enough! Do you have a Melway?' I asked.

'Err. No. That's why God invented sat nav!'

'Okay, let's ask for directions,' I said.

A car full of women should surely be able to ask for – and get – directions, right? WRONG!

Everybody we pulled up alongside seemed to think we were the hounds of hell at their heels. An old man in a motorised wheelchair actually went into an automated carwash to get away from us. Surely that kind of reaction was only warranted if we had rocked up in a hotted up ute with a great big Eureka flag sticker on it? I'd have thought a brand new Merc, with four professional women inside and not a gun in sight, deserved a more measured response.

'How about we try a service station?' Amani asked, as we watched a ten-year-old boy pull a switch blade out of his trackie dacks.

Again, easier said than done.

We pulled into the first service station we came across and Tehara and Una went in to ask for directions.

'Hi,' Tehara had said ingratiatingly, to the Asian service attendant.

'You buy petrol?' the attendant had asked.

'No.'

'Then you buy chocolate?'

'No.'

'Then you buy milk. Sorry, no milk. Fridge broken.'

Tehara started to get a nervous tick in her left eye.

'No, we just need some directions. Do you know how to get to Dandenong?' Una asked.

'No. I no know. I just student.'

'Please?' Tehara begged, nearly in tears.

'No, get out! I call police!' the attendant started screaming.

'Okay, okay!' Tehara pleaded. 'Can I buy a Melway instead, then?"

'Why no sat nav?' the Asian attendant replied, looking dubiously at the Merc. 'No Melway here. Get out!'

Tehara was too traumatised to stop at another service station, so we decided to retrace our steps – all the way to Melbourne – carefully reading the signs this time.

So two hours after we were supposed to have got there, we finally arrived at Foster Street in Dandenong, or, as we called it, Little India.

'I need something to eat, right now,' Amani rasped and ran into a little Indian corner store before Tehara had even cut the engine. Clearly this was a crisis – Amani hadn't had anything to eat for forty-five minutes.

The rest of us slowly got out of the car, feeling a little car sick. Yes, you can get car sick, even in a Merc.

'Who designs a road without signage to a major suburb?'

'A stupid twat,' Una chimed in.

'A *bloody* stupid twat!' was all I could mutter as I steeled myself to look through metres of coloured silk. I knew we weren't going to buy anything here. We'd only come to Dandenong to make sure we weren't going to buy anything anyone else would be wearing. We were going to see Mrs Fernando in about an hour, where we would actually buy *sarees*, confident in the knowledge we'd be buying one-off designer numbers. Serious *saree* shoppers didn't buy on Foster Street; they bought from select *saree* boutiques which operated out of people's rumpus rooms or converted garages in the suburbs.

We were barely out of the car when Amani came out of the store, stuffing greasy samosas into her face like she'd been starving for months.

Una touched my arm lightly and nodded in the direction of a couple emerging from one of the *saree* shops in the distance.

'Is that … ?'

'No … it can't be …' I replied, squinting into the distance.

Amani whipped around to have a look and had to quickly smother a look of incredulity. 'It *is* Gayani … and that must be …'

'… her fiancé.'

'Maybe it's a long lost relative instead!' Tehara hissed, jealously.

Because the man Gayani was with was gorgeous.

Tall, which is unusual for a Sri Lankan man. Well-dressed in chinos and casual shirt. Even more unusual for a Lankan male. And when he smiled, he revealed really good teeth. He'd even had bloody orthodontic work done! Outrageous.

As the couple neared, we held our breath. Maybe we were mistaken. But no, it was Gayani. She still had enough facial hair to be confused for Merv Hughes. Surely her dowry couldn't be that big. Her parents weren't über rich. They went to the temple in Springvale, just like my parents.

'Hi girls,' Gayani said with a fake smile and upbeat voice. The cow normally didn't deign to speak to us.

We all managed weak smiles.

'This is Sarath, my fiancé. We just went to look for some *sarees* for the bridesmaids. I want them in yellow,' she gushed.

They were going to look awful. As a general rule, Lankan women cannot wear shades of yellow without looking like anaemic lemons.

'How are you going? Amani, don't you look … big,' Gayani said with a smirk.

And there we were, just the six of us, in a parking lot

on Foster Street in Dandenong making small talk. Gayani's fiancé soon revealed himself to be a completely sane, normal human being with no obvious intellectual impediment. At one point, he walked away to deposit their shopping into his Land Cruiser. Clearly, he was not visually impaired either. He was not parked in a disabled spot. He was parked right next to Tehara's Merc. The question on all our minds, as we listened to Gayani's prattle, was how the hell did she land him?

After about five minutes, we made signs to move. We really needed to get on with things. And Amani wasn't looking too good either.

'Tehara, could you unlock your car?' Amani said desperately. 'I think I need a drink of water.'

'We'd better head off, too,' said Gayani as Una and Amani rushed back to the car, almost out of earshot.

'So, what do you do?' Tehara asked as she unlocked the doors with a click of the remote.

'I am a civil engineer,' Sarath replied politely.

'She must have slipped him one,' Una muttered urgently to Amani, unstopping the bottle of water.

Amani was now sitting in the passenger seat drinking, looking clammy and green.

'Have you designed or built anything we know?' I asked.

'Nah, it must be the money,' Amani whispered to Una in a serious tone.

'He was the chief engineer on EastLink,' Gayani said loudly and proudly, making sure both Amani and Una heard even though they were several feet away, catching Una by surprise as she opened her mouth to say something to Amani.

On cue, Amani's stomach heaved. Una jumped back to get out of the way of digested samosa, nuts and raisins only to be trapped by Sarath's Land Cruiser. Her yelp of surprise gave extraordinary volume to what she had meant to only say in a whisper.

'It must be a *guliyak*,' Una yelled.

There was a deathly silence.

Gayani's look spoke daggers as she and Sarath made a quick getaway. Amani, strangely, had perked up now that the contents of her stomach liberally coated Una's shoes and Tehara's hub caps.

'He is not blind, so he must be stupid. Not only is he marrying Merv Hughes, he also built a fucking freeway with no signage,' Tehara said with biting sarcasm as she watched Gayani and Sarath drive away.

CHAPTER 6

Love at First Bite?

Okay, my nearest and dearest, including my family, think I am anally retentive. It is a claim I will fight in public till the bitter end, but in my heart of hearts, I must admit there *was* a teeny, tiny, grain of truth to the accusation.

While *they* liked to consider my meticulous nature to be a character flaw, I liked to think of it as positive attribute. I mean, I liked things to follow a certain order, and I did things a certain way only because they yielded the best results. I wore cotton undies on weekends *because* they were comfortable and likewise with the T-shirt bra. Amani had fluked when she'd predicted the colour. It didn't make me boring and predictable, it simply made me dependable. A worthy trait in an accountant!

And it was a trait I was putting to good use as I pored over the sales data of the past year to predict the following year's performance, humming quietly to myself, smiling. I was so engrossed in my numbers that I didn't realise that my boss, John, was standing right next to me.

'You really enjoy data analysis, don't you?'

'What's there not to love? Thanks to my love of data analysis I, unlike millions of women across the world, do not need to depend on Anna Wintour or Kim Kardashian for fashion advice. See, I have statistically valid data that tells me that Jimmy Choos are a darn sight more fashionable than Manolo Blahniks 'cause Mr Blahnik's sales have been in decline for the last six quarters in a row!'

'You crack me up, Shani, you really do!'

'I am not kidding … look …' I said, turning my computer screen around. 'Sales of Blahnik shoes have been more than woeful since the second quarter of the last financial year. And all this fashion knowledge comes with the added benefit of doing actual work of creating a purchase strategy for Patricia from Procurement!'

'I believe you! I believe you!' John defended himself, holding his hands up in the manner of a person surrending. 'Could you join Max and I for a few minutes please?' he invited, leading the way back to his massive corner office. I followed him with my unplugged laptop.

'So, I have been discussing the board report with Charles – Charles Worthington, the CEO – and he and I agree that this year we'll do it a bit differently,' John announced as soon as Max and I sat down in the comfy chairs across from his desk. 'Instead of running the board reporting team by myself, I will be looking to the two of you to run two separate teams whose results will be amalgamated into the final report.'

'Shani – I want you to run the Human Resources and IT report to enable you to get a better understanding of Max's side of the business. And Max, I want to you run the Infrastructure and Procurement report – Shani's side of the business,' he said, looking us both in the eye. 'It is a demonstration of the great confidence we have in both your abilities that we hand this responsibility onto you … Especially since we will be doing succession planning the month after the board meets.'

Max and I stole quick glances at each other. It was game on. John could not have made it any clearer that one or the other was being groomed to take over his role eventually. And I certainly relished the thought of being the CFO of one of Australia's premium retailers by the time I was thirty-five.

Both Max and I diligently took down our instructions and left John's office. As I turned towards my cubicle, Max turned to me with a smirk and muttered, 'May the best man win!'

He was not going to fight clean.

'Or the best woman!' I replied as I reached my desk, dismissing him coolly by picking up the ringing phone.

It was Una.

'She's slipped him a *guliyak*,' she started without preamble. Almost two weeks after we'd run into Gayani and Sarath in Dandenong she had yet to give up this line of conversation. I'd chatted to her about this about twenty times already.

'In all probability, yes, Una.'

'So, it really works then?' she persisted.

'Who knows? It may work in some instances and not in others,' I said sympathetically, my focus immediately shifting from my spreadsheets to my friend. Losing the love of your life was no easy matter, no matter how long ago it may have been.

'Do you think … ?'

'NO! We are not going back there,' I cut her off.

'Oh … okay,' she replied forlornly.

'I'll see you tomorrow at rehearsal,' I reminded her, hanging up gently.

It was only two weeks until Gayani's wedding and three until Sanjay's. We were having both couples over in an attempt to speed up the rehearsal process. Sarath had proved that not only was he myopic but he also was the proud owner of two left feet. If a miracle didn't occur between now and the wedding, the Peiris wedding dance was destined to tarnish all our reputations on YouTube.

My phone rang again. It was Una. Again.

'You don't think …?'

'No way, no how, not in a million years,' I replied firmly. 'But you'll find someone you love as much, one day,' I said in a much gentler voice.

'Okay,' she said sadly and hung up.

Poor Una. When Una was a little girl, she fell in love with Hugh, the son of a family friend in New South Wales. Hugh was everything Una had ever dreamt of in a man: tall, dark and handsome. He was also captain of his school and he could sing like an angel.

The crush that started when she was five had turned into full-blown infatuation by the time she reached high school. It then became a three-ring circus – complete with another woman – the summer before Una started university.

Every summer, she would go up to New South Wales to visit Hugh's family with her parents. There, she'd spend a few weeks hanging out, supposedly with his sisters, only she'd flirt like mad with Hugh. For his part Hugh was only kind to Una, letting her follow him an exuberant cocker spaniel.

Una finally lost her braces after four excruciating years, and she'd sprouted some C-cup boobs. That summer, she went up north, fully prepared to do anything to get Hugh's attention. She was also armed with the name, number and address of an astrologer and *tho-il karaya* in Sydney. A sad by-product of her lengthy association with Sri Lankans was that she truly *believed* in this stuff.

Things started off really well, at first. Hugh didn't call Una a 'squirt' or ruffle her hair. He actually remembered she didn't drink beer and offered her a glass of wine at dinner instead of cordial. As far as Una was concerned, they were just moments away from visiting the Australian Diamond Company for a glittering tribute to their love.

Una even started planning her wedding one Friday night after this brief discussion.

'So Una, what do you have planned for next week?' Hugh had asked.

'Nothing much. I was going to hang out with your sisters. Chris also said he had a little job for me,' Una said, glancing over at Chris, Hugh's father, who was an accountant.

Chris often brought people's tax files home to be sorted and was always trying to rope the kids into helping out. A 'little job' was code for a few hours of wading through people's expense receipts. Una didn't know what she'd be letting herself in for and Hugh knew this.

'Um, ah ... how about this? Why don't you come with me to my new job? It's at the Cessnock Correctional Centre.'

'But I thought you were going try your hand at acting,' Una said confusedly. Hugh had just returned from spending a year in Perth, where he'd studied acting.

'Yes silly, I've got a tiny part in an ABC series,' he said winking. 'Trust me, you don't want to help Pop with his "work".'

Una had the church, reception venue and style of dress picked out by the end of dessert. She just had to figure out whether to serve vanilla or chocolate cake at the reception.

On Monday, Una was on top of the world when she walked onto the set with Hugh. The first inkling things were not going to plan came when Hugh introduced Una to everyone on set as 'one of my little sisters'.

Things went from bad to worse when the lead actress turned up. Hugh was clearly smitten with her. She was older, wiser and definitely worldlier than Una. And worst of all, she was blonde. She treated Hugh like he treated Una, like a younger sibling. And, like Una had done to him, Hugh just hung around the actress, waiting hopefully for any crumbs of attention.

Around this time, I was on holiday in Sydney with my family. Did I ever tell you about how similar my family's holidays were to the *National Lampoon* movies? That year we went to Sydney, not because any of us had a particular yen to see the harbour city, but because Sri Lanka was playing Australia at the SCG.

On our first night in Sydney, I made my way down to the telephone box at the Lane Cove Caravan Park to call Una.

'He's in love with her,' Una wailed piteously through her sobs.

'You don't know that,' I replied, desperately trying to placate her.

'She is gorgeous. She is blonde and she is older than him. Men like older women, right?'

'I dunno …' What did I know about men? I was only eighteen and a virgin!

'You've got to help me! If he falls for her, it'll be the end of the world.'

'How can I help? I'm supposed to be going to the Sydney Opera House tomorrow!' I protested. The forecast of heavy rain had meant that the start of the test match was going to be postponed.

'The *tho-il karaya* Aunty Sonali told us about in Sydney. We've got to try him!'

'Look, I don't know where he lives, or even how to get there.'

'I've got his address and telephone number. I'll get an appointment tomorrow. You have got to come with me,' Una pleaded.

'You know this *tho-il* business is complete bullshit, right?'

'Nuh-uh, not according to Aunty Sonali. Her sister's daughter Malinthi is happily married with three children because of him, the one in Sydney!'

I'd always thought Una had spent an unhealthy amount of time with my mother's friend, Aunty Sonali. She was a purveyor of useless rumours and hopeless mystical stories where everything was resolved by the intervention of astrologers or *tho-il karayas* (Sri Lankan witch doctors – a profitable sideline for many astrologers, allowing them to peddle protective amulets alongside *guliyaks,* charmed oils and *nekaths.*)

Una had been hooked on Aunty Sonali ever since the first time they'd met over milky tea and lemon puffs at our flat in Springvale. In Una, Aunty Sonali found fertile ears and a willingness to believe, whereas Amani, Tehara and I just treated her with muted irritation.

'That could have been a one off.'

'But then there was ...' Una rattled off a dozen names, all of whom, according to Aunty Sonali, had found happiness through consulting this particular *tho-il karaya.*

'You've got to come with me,' Una pleaded. 'I don't speak Sinhalese.'

'Okay, okay ... get an appointment and I'll think of something,' I said as I hung up.

The next day, I begged off the visit to the Sydney Opera House by pretending to have period cramps. The trusty red excuse never fails to deliver. My mother gave me a suspicious look, trying to count back to when she thought I had my last period; my father and brothers just ignored me. I'm sure they didn't want to think about my 'female' problems.

The trip to the astrologer/*tho-il karaya* was a complete farce. He lived in a dingy bedsit in Redfern alongside a dozen or so other illegal immigrants. His darkened 'office' stank of dried urine, incense and the overflowing dumpster across the road. He had a couple of framed photos of Ganesh, Shiva and Durga, garlanded with wilted marigolds on a dusty altar along with a few peacock feathers and a rather serious-looking dagger.

The man took one look at Una and added an extra $50 to his standard fee. He listened to me translate for about fifteen minutes, wrote down Hugh's birthday and took a vial of water from where it was, hidden under his chair.

I interrupted at this point.

'*Mahataya*, I thought a *guliyak* was like a lump of raisins or a biscuit that has been charmed. I didn't think it'd be water,' I said, very concerned. Hey, I had grown up in the tropics; I have a healthy fear of waterborne diseases.

'*Nona*, it is the nineties. Today, we use charmed water, simple to give prospective groom,' he said with a dismissive shrug. 'Now I pray.'

He closed his eyes and started charming the water, holding the sealed vial close to his mouth. Every so often, he would fan the peacock feather over Una's head and over the vial, making both Una and I light-headed from the smell of stale sweat combined with Brut as he lifted his arms. Brut, the after-shave that accurately described the man who wore it.

After twenty minutes of this, he handed Una the vial with the following instructions:

'Now, you be listening to me *Nona*. You make good hot Sri Lankan tea, two cups only. You put half into groom's cup, another half into bride's cup. Two must drink at one time. You get married one year. Now give me $100.'

Una took the vial with a big smile. She'd just got a job on the set making tea for the actors. It was going to be all too easy.

The next day on set, Una laid her trap for Hugh with meticulous care. As filming wound down for the afternoon tea break, she made two cups of Sri Lankan Broken Orange Pekoe with loving care. As instructed, she divided the contents of the vial equally between the cups. She greeted Hugh with a big smile as he made his way to the little kitchenette and handed him his favourite mug, while clinging onto her own.

As Hugh lifted the cup of tea to his lips, the script director barged in, obviously in a snit. She was followed by the lead actress.

'Fucking stupid,' the script director railed.

'Yeah, bloody stupid,' the lead actress seconded. 'No prison psychologist would suggest inmates be vegetarian to reduce their violent tendencies. Who the fuck hired this tosser?' she asked as she started to make herself a cup of tea.

Hugh was desperate to get her attention, so he plucked the cup of tea out of Una's now nerveless fingers and gave it to her.

'You don't mind, do you,' he said to Una with a wink.

And Una watched with horrified fascination as Hugh and Deborra-Lee, the actress, drank their cups of tea together. By the second sip, the actress's eyes had glazed over.

CHAPTER 7

Check Mate

We were already running late for Gayani's wedding by the time Una, Tehara and I had left the *saree* dressers. What? Did you honestly think normal people could wind themselves into six-yards of *saree* without giving themselves a headache? Oh please.

Tehara was driving us in; but there was some nonsense about being 'on call' or something, so Una and I were making the most of the opportunity to get, in polite terms, maggotted.

'How's the big project going?' Tehara asked, negotiating the Saturday afternoon traffic around Windsor.

'Kind of alright. The bastard of the thing is that Max has managed the accounts for infrastructure for the past five years and I am really struggling to get the past twelve months of data from him,' I said, picking a microscopic speck of dust off my *gagra choli*.

I was dressed in a nude-coloured tight skirt and bustier with silver beading and matching *dupatta* I'd bought at Mrs Fernando's. It shimmied and slithered faithfully to my figure as I moved. The hairdresser had blow dried my hair straight, parting it exactly in the middle and pinning the simple beaded *tikka* that matched my earrings close to my hairline above my forehead. I had decided against wearing a necklace; I hated being overdone, festooned like a bogan Christmas tree.

'Is there another way you can get the information you need?'

'Short of doing a direct query from the main database, no. Anyway, a query like that would take at least four weeks and I would be really cutting it fine to complete my report in time.'

'And you really need to kick arse on this project,' Una piped up, chugging on a glass of Veuve Clicquot.

Una looked simply spectacular in Tehara's borrowed bottle green *saree*. She'd decided against wearing the lace blouse, and had the dresser drape the *saree* like a strapless dress. Her titian hair was done up in an elaborate set of curls that cascaded wantonly around her head with a string of pearls threaded through them for good measure. She wore a green *bindi* on her forehead that brought out the vibrancy of her emerald eyes.

'Didn't you say the CFO gets to go to the Milan and Paris fashion shows each year *in* the company jet? There's no "if's" or "buts" about it. You MUST get this job.'

'No pressure or anything there, Una,' I replied dryly. 'I never expected it to be easy to get the data from Max but I never thought he'd be this much of a bastard about it.'

'Have we met Max?'

'I am sure you've met him a few times at drinks. I don't socialise with him. He's not my cup of tea; he is a real snake when his wife's back is turned!'

'Is Max that pudgy bloke with glasses?'

'Yup – that's the one. He also has mop of curly hair and really bad acne!'

'At his age?'

'A few of the buyers from cosmetics have been tempted to drop some samples off at his desk. But we all kind of get a nasty kind of pleasure from seeing him scatch his face all the time,' I replied with more than a touch of sarcasm.

'He isn't popular then?'

'Hard to say. He has a team of twelve compared to my team of six and they are really close mouthed. We really know nothing about what goes on in his group.'

'I thought he was cute – teddy-bear like cute, you know. And harmless.'

'Appearances can be deceptive. I gave him a copy of my data on a USB key three days after our meeting with John. But Max only gave me the last three month's data yesterday.'

'What's his excuse?'

'He took his copy of the data home and he can't find it!'

'In terms of excuses that's up there with "my dog ate my homework".'

As we drove over Princess Bridge, a sharp gust of wind buffetted the car; a small draft of cold air slipped through the tiny crack in the window I had opened for ventilation.

Una shivered theatrically. 'I've just had that feeling … you know the feeling I get when I am about to have a premonition,' she said in a hushed voice.

Tehara rolled her eyes.

'It was a gust of wind, Una … just a gust of wind. A natural phenomenon.'

'I have got a bad feeling about him,' Una announced calmly and in a deep voice as if she were the embodiment of the Oracle of Delphi. 'No good will come of your association with him.'

'I can't not associate with him. I have to bloody create a board report with him!' I defended. 'Tehara, you've got to get her on some anti-psychotic drugs!'

'She's not psychotic, just delusional! You've been hanging out with Aunty Sonali again, haven't you?' Tehara asked, exasperatedly, taking a different tack.

Over the years, Una had become ever closer to Aunty Sonali. They spent countless hours sipping sweet milky tea, comparing the predictions they make by looking at Vedic horoscopes to those detailed in *New Idea*. Unfortunately, Una now thinks she can read Vedic horoscopes so none of us are now safe from her grasp.

'So what if I have?'

'Earth calling Una, come in, Una? If horoscopes were the be all and end all, then all Lankan marriages would be perfect,' I pointed out wryly, draining my second glass of champers.

'My grandmother whinged for years that my parents had an eighty per cent match on their *porondang,* and still their marriage failed,' Tehara piped up.

Una and I didn't have the heart to tell her that the reason her mother left her father was because he was a complete arsehole and nobody needed Vedic astrology to know that.

'Well, I've matched yours and Muthu's horoscopes to practise,' Una told Tehara, excitedly.

'Stop right there! I am *not* listening. We all know Muthu and I are never going anywhere.'

Two years ago, Tehara had a raging debate with a neurosurgeon, Muthu, at a medical conference, as to whether a patient's psychosis was neurologically based or psychologically based. After twenty minutes of slagging each other off, Muthu and Tehara had retired to the penthouse suite at the Sydney Sheraton to sort out their differences. I sincerely doubt they've been out of each other's pants much since.

'Is Muthu coming tonight?' I asked.

'Of course he is. He is Dr Shivalingam's son, after all. You don't offend the old guard,' Tehara replied.

Tehara and Muthu were both children of doctors who'd come to Australia as a part of the Colombo Plan. On the surface, they were the perfect couple. Both doctors. He studied at Scotch College, she at St Catherine's. A match made in heaven, right? Wrong.

Muthu is a Tamil.

'I don't understand how you socialise with each other but can still hate each other?' Una asked, confusedly.

'It's all about subtlety,' I explained airily.

'Sri Lankans, both Tamils and Sinhalese are very subtle people. We live side by side. Hell, we don't have much choice, Sri Lanka is only the size of a small cattle station in WA,' Tehara explained.

'We socialise with each other, go to each other's houses, celebrate Divali and Sinhala New Year together,' I continued.

'But you can still blow each other up at a drop of a hat?' Una asked.

'Don't confuse social niceties with deep racial hatred. We've only been trying to bump each other off for about 2000 years.'

'I just don't get you people,' Una said with a resigned sigh.

No, and I doubt you ever will. Australians are so dichromatic. Everything is either black or white, they cannot understand the subtle shades of grey or nuances of history that drive the inhabitants of our small island.

My phone rang. I was surprised to see that it was not my mother's but Max's number that flashed up at me.

'Hello Max,' I said, carefully modulating my slightly slurred, alcohol-affected voice.

'Guess what! I found the CD of the data!' he wheezed excitedly.

'That's great, Max, can I get it from you on Monday?'

'Actually, I am off to Sydney on Monday and won't be back till the end of the week.'

I rolled my eyes. I could not afford to lose another week of work.

Where do you live?' I asked between gritted teeth and took down his address.

'Can we swing by South Yarra, hon? I really need to pick up this CD of data. It's only about five minutes out of our way,' I begged Tehara. She rolled her eyes.

Max's sour wife answered the door even before I could knock.

'Oh, don't you look … hmm … so ethnic!' the South Yarra toff drawled, looking down her surgically altered nose.

'Hmm, quite. Where's Max?'

'In the study,' she said, pointing me down the narrow hallway of their double-fronted Victorian villa to a massive ante-room off the lounge. Max was sitting at his desk with his eyebrows furrowed, looking at the figures I'd given him the previous week.

'Thank you, Max,' I said, stretching out my hand to take the CD. But he whipped the plastic case back and turned around.

'Actually Shani, I don't understand your numbers. Could you run me through your thinking here?'

'It's a pretty standard P&L statement.'

'I just don't get these columns. Could you run me through them?

Was he kidding me? I was dressed to the nines to go to a wedding, and not to mention, slightly pissed and he wanted me to talk about a Profit and Loss statement any accounting undergraduate in nappies could decipher.

'Why don't we run through it when you get back from your trip?'

'Well, I will only be able to give you my data at the same time then,' he drawled evilly.

The afternoon sunshine streaming through the window behind him was making his glasses opaque. I knew then that Max was an adversary I could not underestimate. So I capitulated and started explaining some basic elements of the data.

Then my mother called.

'Shani, where are you?' she demanded in a shrill voice.

'Chillax, *Ammi*, the ceremony is not until 5 pm and it's still only 4.30.'

'But they are having drinks!'

'So? They always have drinks before the wedding,' I feigned ignorance. I knew what she was getting at. The early bird gets the freshest worm. I was supposed to be the worm to be picked up by an enterprising bird/boy. The whole thing tended to fall apart if either the bird or worm was absent.

'Shamini Devapura, where are you and how long before you get here?'

'Ma, ma … you're breaking up … we're going under a bridge … *shh … crr … shh*.'

'Are you still in Richmond then?'

'I can't hear you … you're breaking up,' I said and promptly cut off the phone.

About two minutes later, Tehara stomped into the room. 'Honey, your mother is on the war path,' she said, with a distinct quiver to her voice. 'I just got a call from her.'

'I figured that. This'll only take a second,' I replied and turned to Max. 'We run a standard ledger – no double accounting, but we do payment summaries for payroll each week.'

'Shani, you will need to run through your whole accounting standards. This makes no sense.'

I tried desperately to think of a way to get out it *and* rescue the CD of data that he was now using to scatch a massive zit on his chin!

Trapped.

'Oh okay, why don't we meet at the office after lunch tomorrow so I can explain it all to you,' I suggested with a resigned sigh. Maybe I'd still be able to sleep off the hangover I felt I deserved.

CHAPTER 8

Welcome to the Mardi Gras – Sri Lankan Style

As luck would have it, we made it to the reception just as the groom progressed onto the gaudily festooned balcony. Gayani had gone for an outdoor *poruwa* ceremony, so one of the balconies at Crown Casino that usually provided a spectacular view of Melbourne's cityscape had been transformed into a miniature replica of an Indian palace, complete with cheap Indian lanterns and garlands of marigold. The *poruwa* was in the shape of two kissing peacocks made of papier-mâché and dotted with sequins. It was completely over the top, tacky and, in my view, entirely Sri Lankan.

As we ducked and weaved through the throng of guests towards my parents, I could hear familiar whispers. The whisperers were Lankan, so they were actually quite loud.

'Is that Dr Jayasuriya's daughter?'

'No, I didn't think Dr Jayasuriya had a daughter.'

'No, not that Dr Jayasuriya, the other one.'

'Oh, the one whose first wife committed suicide.'

'*Anay,* yes, and his second wife ran away with the estate manager.'

'Poor Dr Jayasuriya.'

'You think they'd find something else to gossip about by now,' I said to Tehara who wore a mask of boredom to cover the hurt. 'How many years ago was it?'

'Why bother with new stuff when the old stuff is still juicy?'

My mother was practically spitting chips as we neared. 'Look,' she said, grasping my upper arm. 'That boy over there,' she pointed to a couple chatting away in the corner, 'is a lawyer. He was alone when he came. Now he is talking to the Anurudda girl. Shani, I am trying my best but you *need* to cooperate. Your *Mangala Yoga* only lasts for three months as of today, so if you don't get married now, you won't get married for another three years!'

'Focus, *Ammi,*' I said. 'The bride is about to enter.'

If only a bride walking down the aisle was a simple affair … But, no. Our wedding couples are not blessed with a gentle stroll in tune to Wagner's Bridal Chorus. That would be too simple for us. Instead, we are treated to a processional production akin to the Gay and Lesbian Mardi Gras. There are dancers, drummers, jugglers, street performers and every school kid in the Sri Lankan community who has ever been in a dance recital.

Una's composure cracked twenty minutes after the procession started. 'Just shoot me, okay?' she begged.

'Not on your life, you'll want to see Gayani.'

Finally, the bridesmaids turned up, all eight of them looking like anaemic lemons just as I had predicted. To add insult to injury, Gayani had made them all wear chandelier earrings with heavy necklaces, which must have weighed a ton.

Somewhere along the way, Una and I had started to nod off,

thanks to the bottle of champers we'd drunk and the heat in the stuffy room. 'Wake up, the bride is coming,' Tehara hissed, nudging us.

Finally, Gayani came in, clutching her uncle's arm.

'Well I'll be damned,' Una muttered.

'Someone's dropped her a card to the Brazilian Butterfly … and she's used it!'

Everybody sighed with relief. Not only because the ceremony was finally about to start, but also because … well … Gayani simply looked radiant. She'd obviously spent quality time with a pot of hot wax and her *saree* was faultless.

'She cleans up just fine,' I whispered back to Tehara and Una, astonished.

'That could have been you,' my mother hissed angrily.

As soon as the ceremony started, everybody started talking. The fact that Lankans talk right through a person's marriage ceremony may seem weird to most, rude almost, but that's because you just don't understand. And I mean you literally don't *understand* it. The marriage ceremony is entirely in ancient Sanskrit and nobody, not even the marriage celebrant, understands it. For all the bride and groom know, they could be buying cows instead of exchanging vows.

'Very good thing she nabbed him quickly,' one old biddy commented as the ceremony mercifully ended and the happy couple took their first steps off the marital podium to the deafening noise of drums and trumpets.

'Finally!' another added. 'I heard she only came into *Mangala Yoga* three months ago. Look, she is already married.'

My mother caught the tail end of this conversation as everybody rushed from the ceremony to the reception hall to grab their spot in the buffet queue. She knew how to stop them in their tracks, though. She grabbed hold of my arm, raised her voice and called out: 'My daughter, Shani, she comes into *Mangala Yoga* as of today!'

You could have heard a pin drop.

CHAPTER 9

Spearmint Rhino

I wanted the floor to open up and swallow me whole, but before I could turn around and rip strips off my mother for trying to sell me like a fattened pig at a hicksville market, the woman was swamped. One minute she was standing next to me, and the next she was surrounded by a sea of middle-aged Lankan women, all holding their mobile phones out at her.

WTF?

As I was pushed along in a tsunami of wedding guests, I was able to steal a glance at one of the extended mobile phones. OH. MY. GOD. The mothers have taken pictures of their children's horoscopes and stored them on their phones!

My mother was already turning some women away. As one walked off, she gave me a sour glance and muttered, '*Kuja* in the 7th house, good luck finding a partner for that girl.'

Another lady walked away, her phone beeping. She glanced

at it and then looked at me. 'Now I have your horoscope,' she said, jiggling her head. 'Not too malefic,' she said with a slight grimace. 'Things can be fixed with a *pooja* or two.'

God help me, my mother was texting my horoscope to complete strangers!

Tehara, Una and I beat a hasty retreat to the bar and were nursing a nice little G&T when my mother came bustling up, flanked by two or three ladies I vaguely recognised from temple. 'Shani, there are some lovely boys I want you to meet,' she said, flashing me a smile loaded with malice.

Just then, as if by divine intervention, the opening bars of the wedding dance started up and my mother didn't stand in the way as Una, Tehara and I made our way to the dance floor. Thanks to her grandiose and very public announcement, she knew the boys would be checking me out anyway. And what better way to exhibit the goods on sale than for the said goods to make an exhibition of themselves while scantily clad in a hipster *choli* and a *saree* blouse that made most bikini tops seem conservative?

Anyone who thinks those Bollywood production wedding dances are just for the flicks is dead wrong. People really do dance like that at Lankan weddings. Hey, we've got to do something romantic at them. It's not like the bride and groom can kiss each other at their own nuptials. *Cheekaya*, that kind of *kara* business only happens at Western weddings.

The whole point of the Lankan wedding dance, to put it crudely, is to dick tease. You have a phalanx of unmarried girls on one side of the dance floor, dressed to kill in skimpy *cholis* and *sarees*. They start up the dancing, gyrating their hips, stomping their feet and flicking their skirts to ensure the contingent of guys on the other side of the dance floor take notice. Subtle as Spearmint Rhino.

And it's not as if the guys can do anything about it. They can dance as close to us as they like, but there's strictly no touching. So they dance and prance around, indulging in acrobatic feats limited only by the amount of coordination they've lost by the volume of alcohol they've drunk before the wedding. The theory is that the more a guy can drink and still be able to dance, the better the catch he is. A real man. Indeed.

Gayani's wedding dance was no different to all the others we'd done. Una, Tehara and I lined up behind Gayani. It was her day to shine and tease her poor man's lust. It's a wonder a groom is at all coherent on his own wedding night, really. With all that blood running south all day, he should be too light-headed to perform.

The opening bars to *Mahive* went smoothly enough – so far, so good. We did this groovy move that involved shaking our hips while trying to hide behind our hands. As the tempo increased, we really got stuck into it, swaying our hips, stomping our feet and throwing our arms up in the air in choreography carefully stolen from the zillions of Bollywood flicks we'd watched over the years. Aish Rai, Preity Zinta and Shilpa Shetty had nothing on Una, Tehara and I. *We* were the queens of Bollywood as we shimmied, shook and strutted our way forwards and backwards on the dance floor.

The dance ended with the happy couple in the centre, grasping a length of *saree* silk while the other dancers formed a circle around them.

By that time, I was flanked on one side by a fine-looking young man I'd never met before. By the way, I wouldn't want you to think I'm against having a boyfriend at all. It just seems too mercenary to me to hook a guy solely in order to marry him.

'Hi, my name is Shani,' I said, flirting cheekily. 'And this is my friend Una.'

'Yeah, I know. My mum told me you've just come into *Mangala Yoga*,' the guy said with a little smirk, checking me out from head to toe. 'Not too bad, suppose I could do worse.'

What a tosser! I grabbed Una and stalked off the dance floor.

'What was wrong with him?'

'You need to ask?'

'Yes I do! The man just may want to marry you and you act like he has tried to cut out your ovaries. What exactly is your problem with marriage, Shani?' Una asked in exasperation.

'Like I've told you a million times …'

'Yeah, yeah, you don't want to wash a man's socks and cook his *paripu* but that is just convenient bullshit. You know it, I know it. So, spill!'

The crowded reception room at Crown Casino wasn't exactly the place for a deep and meaningful chat, so I grabbed her arm and walked out into the foyer. Tehara and Amani joined us as we walked out the door.

Amani had heartlessly left Rohan surrounded with a group of aunties, all of whom were teasing him about his impending fatherhood. He shot Amani a look of desperation which she ignored as she sailed out of the reception hall.

'I'm not going to save him. Damn fool forgot to pick up his suit from the dry cleaners yesterday, so I had to miss my pedicure to pick it up today. And then he ducked up to the shops get some polish for his shoes and got sidetracked at Bunnings for two whole hours looking at power tools!

'Anyway,' she continued, 'this sounds much more interesting. Why don't you want to get married?' Amani asked as soon as we sat down on some strategically placed couches outside the reception room.

'What if the man I marry turns out to be a complete arsehole? You never know until you're married what a man is like!'

'What do you mean?'

'What if I am miserable? What if he becomes a complete bastard? Men change!'

'You can't live your life afraid of what ifs,' Tehara said quietly.

'Whenever I have been with a guy, I can never really *be* with him because I'm always thinking of how I can get away. As quickly as possible. Maybe I am just one of those women who can't stay with a man,' I said in a rush.

'Don't be stupid,' Amani scoffed. 'You just haven't met the right man, that's all. And you're such a control freak as well.'

'Says she who has her underwear sorted by colour *and* the days of the week!'

'You just have to get into a relationship and try. You'll never know unless you do; and I mean, *really* try. You're so afraid of being trapped that you never give a guy a chance,' Amani returned.

'What is wrong if I *just don't want to*? Why must a woman's happiness be tied up in a man?' I asked, completely exasperated. 'Not everyone dreams of white *sarees* and *poruwas*. Most women I know who are married have compromised so much that they don't even remember why they got married in the first place.'

'Because being alone is not a natural human state!'

'Who says?'

'Everybody does. If we were meant to be alone, why do we have the biological urge to get together with someone?'

'Maybe I don't have the urge!'

'Sure you have the urge, you just don't know it,' Amani persisted, as if she were speaking to someone simple.

'Stop treating me like I'm an imbecile!'

'Well don't behave like one!'

'I just don't want to get married because everyone thinks it's the right thing for me to do. I want to get married if and when it is right for me.'

Una held up a hand, stopping Amani and me in our tracks.

'Shani, if that is how you really feel, we respect that,' Una said quietly, with Tehara nodding vigorously in agreement.

'But ...' Amani cut in but was silenced by Una's cool, steady stare. She gave a reluctant nod.

I knew the conversation was shelved, not over. They would not stop until I confessed everything.

'We'll even help you tackle your mum,' Tehara volunteered.

We all stood up, *Charlie's Angels* style. Together, we'd kick butt, whoever came our way.

We re-entered the reception venue in a totally 'nobody's gonna screw with us' mode. We glared at a group of guys lounging in the doorway; they scattered to the wind like the chickens they were. Only our Lankan *Charlie's Angels* act didn't last for long. Like a poorly packed bag of lentils, we were picked off one by one as we came back into the room.

First, Amani was ambushed by Rohan who had managed to escape the clutches of the evil aunties. 'Hey Shani, I hear your mother is auctioning you off tonight? What's the selling bid?' he asked cheekily.

'Oh, bite me, Rohan!' I snapped.

He turned to Amani. 'Jesus Christ, those aunties are nosey. They wanted to know whether our IVF doctor was Lankan!'

'Excuse me?'

'They assumed that bubsy here is an IVF child because it took us so long,' he said, looking surprisingly rattled. 'One went as far as asking whether it was me who had the problems. Doll, I need a drink,' he said as he made a beeline to the bar, dragging Amani with him.

My brother Gehani turned up with a couple of drinks. He is a physiotherapist and has been in love with Una since he was ten years old. He is normally quite goofy and funny, but Una renders him socially awkward.

'Ummm ... Una, you're looking pretty today,' he said, swallowing convulsively.

'Yeah, thanks Gehani. How's school?' Una asked absently, swaying to the music.

'I graduated from uni five years ago!'

'Oh. Excuse me,' Una said in a distracted tone and wandered off to join some other friends on the dance floor.

Gehani looked defeated. You'd think he would have given up by now.

As Tehara, Gehani and I made our way to our table, Tehara's phone rang. She looked at the number briefly, trying to decide whether to let it go to voicemail or not. When the number flashed again, she picked up the call and answered it. I knew it was serious the second her face took on a set expression.

'Okay, I'll be there in ten minutes,' she said to whomever on other end of the line.

'Ditch baby, ditch,' I begged. 'Please don't leave me here alone.'

She took hold of my hands and looked me in the eye. 'There's a jumper on the one of the city skycrapers.'

Tehara was one of five highly trained suicide negotiators in Victoria. And she had the highest track record of successful preventions. I knew when to back off.

'Good luck,' I said to her as I gently kissed her cheek.

As she neared the double doors of the reception venue, a man appeared from the shadows.

'Are they together?' Gehani asked, picking up something indefinable from their body language.

'Yes.'

'Tehara's *thathi* will hit the roof when he finds out.'

'Who cares about Dr Jayasuriya? The greater concern is Muthu's parents! They'll go ballistic. Their only son! Marrying a Sinhala chick. He'll get disowned.'

Tehara and Muthu moved off into the shadows. I thought I saw them gently kiss, before Tehara headed off.

'Hey Muthu, fancy seeing you here!' I called out.

'Yeah, I'm representing my parents,' he said, looking a little sad.

'Things okay?

'Yeah … I just …' he replied, looking morosely at the door.

'Hmmm,' I replied, gently touching him his arm. 'I know.'

'Hey, I heard about the auction!' he teased, only to glance up to see my mother bearing down on us. 'You know what, I think I'll get a drink,' he said, moving adroitly in the direction of the bar with my traitorous brother, following him like a conjoined Siamese twin.

CHAPTER 10

The Dare

So, I found myself quite alone when I was ambushed by my mother. 'Come with me,' she commanded in military fashion. 'Shoulders back, head up, you've got good breasts and a nice figure, even if you do drink too much.'

'*Ammi*, stop right now. I am not going to meet a line-up of "boys" just because you want me to!'

'Don't you give me any trouble about anything, there are at least ten boys here I want you to meet,' my mother said, grasping my arm. As she tried to drag me off she seemed to forget I was at least ten centimetres taller and five kilos heavier than her. And I used my height, boosted by my killer stilettos, to my advantage. I peered over her to try and intimidate her.

'Aren't you listening to me?' I hissed, trying to keep my

voice down. 'I am not going to meet even one of those boys, and certainly not ten or twenty!'

'Yes, you will meet them,' she whisper-shouted back, futilely pulling me along.

'What can I do to convince you to stop this?'

'Just meet the boys!'

'I won't,' I replied, stomping my foot like a three-year-old. My mother was the only person I knew who could reduce me to the emotional status of a toddler.

'And why not?'

'Because I don't want to. Besides, I don't think arranged marriages work in this day and age.'

'But your father and I are still together!'

'But that does not mean you're happy. Where is he by the way? *Thathi*?'

'In the Sports Bar watching the cricket,' my mother bristled uncomfortably.

'You've spent the last forty years married to a man who loves cricket more than you!'

'No marriage is perfect. Besides, what if you find a man who loves housework? Your unit might even be tidy for once,' she retorted. Then she sighed, sounding uncharacteristically defeated. 'What can I do to convince you to meet these boys?'

I wasn't fooled for a minute. 'Nothing,' I replied, throwing my hands up in frustration.

'After all I've done for you, the least you could do is to meet these boys.'

'But I don't want to meet anyone in such an artificial setting. It puts pressure on me, and them, and I always end up sounding like a bitch.'

'Then don't speak. You talk too much anyway.'

'How am I supposed to get to know them, then?'

'Why do you have such a need to *know* everything? Why not go … what's that saying … go with the flow?'

'Because that is just stupid and you know it. People get divorced all the time here, because they go with the flow and find out later what a bastard they've married,' I returned, completely stumped. Did she *want* me to live unhappily ever after?

'Only white people get divorced, not Lankans.'

'That's not true, I know many Lankans who are divorced.'

'Yes, that's because they are all *kara*. Besides they don't come from decent families,' she said, nodding her head wisely. She then tried another tack. 'Your father and I sacrificed everything for you and your brothers. We left our homes and our families so you could have a better life here in Australia. You owe it to us to be happily settled.'

'But, *Ammi*, I am happy. Don't you see, all this talk about marriage is what's making me *un*happy!' I cried.

'How can you be happy without everything? Your life is almost complete, all you need is a man to make it perfect,' she pleaded. 'What if I made you *hoppers* and *seeni sambol* every week?'

'I'll be the size of a house in a month and nobody will want me!'

'But Shani, you have to get married. Do you want to be an old spinster? All by yourself? With nobody?'

I must confess that this was the one argument that got me thinking. Spinsters have such a bad rap all over the world. The word conjures up unwelcome images of a greying older woman, stuck in a dingy flat with her cats, drinking tea. And doing embroidery. Or knitting.

But then I thought of all the people who'd got married, and things had ended badly. My own parents. Amani's parents' marriage, which we all knew was diabolical. Tehara's father and his many wives. Britney Spears and KFed. Madonna and Sean Penn. Madonna and Guy Ritchie. Elizabeth Taylor and her squillions of husbands. Princess Di and Prince Charles.

Was it really worthwhile to get married just for the sake of it?

Then I thought of all the single chicks who did it just fine without marriage. Julia Gillard. Germaine Greer (maybe I didn't want to be exactly like her, a bit too femi-nazi …). Elle Macpherson. Although they may have been in relationships, these women stood on the world stage by themselves and were confident women who didn't need men. Their lives were like the cake and the icing all rolled into a delicious Swiss roll of complexity and satisfaction.

How could I weasel out of this with my dignity intact? It came to me like a bolt of lightning. I would raise the stakes to an impossible level.

I drew myself to my full height and issued this edict to my mother: 'I won't meet one man then. I'll meet 101 men. When and only when you've found 101 men who: a) match my horoscope; b) are over five feet six inches tall; and c) don't live with their mothers; then I'll meet them. And you can't send them to me in dribs and drabs hoping to reach the target down the track, either. I want to see all the information on all 101 of them, before I meet the first one face to face!'

Surely that would settle the matter once and for all. Normally, my mother could not organise her way out of a wet paper bag; hell, I sorted her spice jars every week or she declared herself unable to cook. So how would she be able to organise such a large number of men to meet me? It was like a tale out of *The Arabian Nights*.

My mother looked horrified. 'Don't be stupid! How can I organise such a thing!' Then she looked cunningly at me. 'Maybe you can help me?'

'No way! You've got to be kidding. You have to do it all by yourself and no cheating. And don't think you can ask Una or Tehara for help, either. *And* there's a time limit, too,'

I added, folding my arms across my front. 'I have to meet all the men before the end of 90 days.'

'But the three months will be more than 90 days.'

'I will only meet men in the next 90 days, and not one day more,' I said piously. 'Take it or leave it.' I was sure I had the upper hand but, as usual, I'd underestimated my mother's legendary stubbornness.

'Fine,' she said. 'I'll take it! Shake on it.'

'Let's go one better,' I said. 'Let clasp our hands together in *namaste* like proper Sri Lankan ladies.'

CHAPTER 11

Temples and Tiaras

I woke up early the morning after Gayani's wedding, safe and warm in my own bed. I didn't even have a hangover because Tehara had done a bunk, Amani could not drink and Una had disappeared onto the dance floor. There is no fun to be had drinking alone, so I went home sober as a judge. This fine Sunday morning, I forced myself out of my cosy bed, and believe it or not, I went to temple.

Let's be honest. Given the chance, I drink like a fish. I lie relatively frequently, especially to my mother, and I like to party like a drag queen. Not the makings of a good Buddhist girl, I'll admit; but I believe Buddhism is a completely utilitarian philosophy and inclusive as long as you *try* to adhere to its tenets. Yeah, yeah, you say, but that's my story and I'm sticking to it.

So this Sunday morning, I found myself sitting cross-legged on the floor, meditating, in the lovely warm confines of late nineteenth-century Presbyterian church in Armadale (bought by the canny trustees of the temple to avoid inconvenient zoning issues.)

That morning, the resident monk gave a lovely sermon on living in the present moment and letting go of the past. I loved going to temple on a Sunday morning; it was so wholesome, it was so healthy and it was so invigorating. Plus it was only five minutes away from Amani and Rohan's house in Hawthorn. So we all usually landed there for Sunday brunch. Did I mention that Rohan, when he's not being a smug twat, is a whiz with the sandwich press?

Amani and Rohan lived in a gorgeous terrace house. They bought the place just as they'd finished university, when real estate prices in inner-city Melbourne were still affordable, and had lovingly renovated the old lady, restoring it to its Victorian splendour complete with iron fretwork and sandstone paving.

It also helped enormously that Rohan is an architect and has the soul of an artist. Last weekend Amani showed us the beautiful mural he had painted in the baby's room. It was a soulful depiction of their life together and their unspoken hopes for their child. Rohan can be very gentle and soft-hearted, especially when it comes to Amani. The man would have twisted himself into a pretzel for her, if she'd asked him.

'Hey Rohan,' I called out cheerily, as I walked through the house and straight out the back door into their garden overlooking the Yarra. The stint at temple had put me in a peaceful enough frame of mind to appreciate the birds twittering in the branches overhead.

Sitting in the corner on a sun lounge and looking a touch seedy was Una, nursing both a coffee and what looked suspiciously like Rohan's patented hangover cure: lime juice mixed with red cordial and a splash of vodka.

'Fine friend you are!' I said to Una. 'Do you have any idea what you left me to face yesterday when Tehara went to save the world and you did your *Dancing Queen* number?'

Rohan came out to the garden carrying a tray laden with croissants, Danishes, and piles of BLT sandwiches. Muthu followed him with the coffee plunger and mugs.

Una had the grace to mumble something that sounded vaguely like, 'I dunno … sorry …' She didn't look me in the eye, which naturally made me quite suspicious. Something was up, I was sure. Our group was completed when Amani and Tehara joined us in the garden. Judging by the smile on Tehara's face, she'd had a successful night.

'Guess what,' I said, more than a little miffed. 'Now I have to meet 101 prospective bridegrooms in the next three months to get my mum off my back.'

'Maybe you'll meet someone you like,' Amani said, with a delicate tilt of her head. The morning sun streaming through the leaves of the large magnolia tree in the back yard could not compete with Amani's luminescent beauty. Out of the corner of my eye, I saw Rohan look at his wife. My breath caught in my throat. Even after ten years, he still had same look of amazed devotion and love in his eyes as the first time he'd seen her through the busy library doors.

Rohan and I had had a study date – I was supposed to be 'helping' him with a commerce subject he had to pass to get his architectural degree. I had been waiting for him outside the doors of the university library that blustery autumn morning when Amani saw me, changed tack from heading to the chemist, and came up to me to ask for a tampon instead. I looked down momentarily as I fumbled around the bottom of my bag to find the item of sanitary protection, only to look up and find my date had fallen in love with one of my best friends! Strangely, he didn't have any problem with that subject after he met Amani.

I could understand why Rohan had immediately fallen in love with Amani. Her skin was light as almond meal and as flawless. She had a wide mouth with classically bow-shaped lips over perfectly even teeth. Her hazel eyes, a throwback to some Persian ancestry, were fringed with thick dark lashes that never needed mascara, and were flecked with gold, like diamonds on a streambed. When she smiled, you couldn't help but smile with her, as her eyes lit up and her cheeks dimpled cherubically.

'Isn't there a man drought?' Muthu asked. 'Aren't you girls in your thirties all about closing the deal? From what I see around the place, most chicks are handing it out like lollies to land a guy!'

Tehara, to her credit, smacked him across the shoulders.

'What?' Muthu asked with surprise. 'That's all you ever read. There is a man drought with fifty-two per cent of women in Australia still single. And you don't want to leave your biological clock ticking for too long, speaking as a physician of course. Shouldn't you be glad your folks are trying to find someone for you? Take the pressure off you, so to speak?'

'Muthu, I spent my twenties trying to land guys. I was handing it out just like anyone else so that some guy would go out with me. And you know what, when I eventually did land a guy, it didn't take long for me to find out that I didn't want to be with him,' I said. 'Remember Jacob Thuan? I worked on landing him for three months and then I only went out with him for one, before I cut my losses.'

'Yeah, he was a bit of a psycho,' Amani agreed.

'A bit? He was an absolute arsehole. He would not let me see my friends. I had to spend every waking moment with him. And he *always* had something to say about what I wore, what I did and what I ate!'

'But that doesn't mean all guys are psychos, you just have to find the right one. You may need to kiss a lot of frogs to find that prince.'

'Yeah, and I might get cold sores in the process, or even glandular fever!'

'Herpes simplex is considered an STD,' Muthu piped up, earning him a glare from Amani. 'But, getting back to the most important thing for you girls, don't you want the big white wedding and all the trappings like yesterday?'

'No,' I said abruptly. 'Besides, not everybody looks good in white!' As much as I liked Muthu, he had no right to stand on the moral high ground when he and Tehara were stuck in a no-win situation.

'But the Lankan process of horoscope matching should eliminate all the real psychos and idiots anyway, right?' Una said, speaking for the first time. She removed her glasses and we all gasped. She'd had a big night out, alright.

'Honey, if that were the case, all Lankan marriages would be made in heaven and the divorce rate would be pretty low,' I corrected. 'And we all know that is not the case. My parents, a prime example, have been married for nearly forty years and my father has spent the last thirty-nine of them glued to any device that will tell him the cricket scores. If cricket were a woman, my mother could sue for divorce on the grounds of adultery!'

'My parents hated each other too, as you probably know,' Amani confessed. 'And I mean they *hated* each other. They met twice before they got married, got hitched because their parents forced them to, and made each other miserable. My father wanted to have fun, while Mum ... all she ever thought about was suffering and praying. It was always going to be up to the toss of a coin to see who would die first to get away from the other.'

(The answer is her father, by the way. A diet of heavy curries, laced with coconut milk and fried rotis, will catch up with anybody eventually, especially if it is washed down daily with a good measure of Scotch and two packs of Lucky Strike.)

'And the divorce rate for immigrant families in Australia is no different to the divorce rate in the general population,' Muthu added.

'I agree with Shani,' Rohan finally spoke up. 'I don't think people should get married unless they already know each other and are committed to making a life together. When my sister got married, all she actually wanted was the wedding. It was an end in itself. She spent months designing the *poruwa*, the *saree* blouse, the bridesmaids' *sarees* and the flowers, and planning the reception down to the *nth* degree. But now that she is hitched to the guy, all she ever does is complain about him.'

'Hear, hear!'

'Besides, I really don't want to see Shani cutting some bloke down to ground meat every week with that cleaver she calls her tongue. I'd have to dob her in for cruelty to animals,' Rohan teased.

So much for support! I flicked him a birdie and continued. 'Everybody is obsessed about landing a guy and getting married. There is so much pressure to "close the deal", but what if the deal is with the devil?'

'What if you meet someone you actually *like* through the process?' Amani insisted. 'And heaven forbid, even fall in love!'

'Then I'll pursue it. But I sincerely doubt that a man my mum picks because he is tall, fair, handsome and of sober habits will automatically suit me. Especially not if he is of sober habits! And you know, a good marriage is not only about love. It's about whether two people can work together to build a life.'

'So, you don't believe in love?'

'Love is just an over-production of oxytocin,' Muthu interjected, 'speaking as a neurologist, of course.' Nobody paid him any attention.

'Of course I believe in love!' I said, indignantly. 'But I have seen plenty of people fall out of love when they can't pay the bills.'

'Then what are you looking for?'

'A man with whom I can build a life. And I'm not such a fool as to think there are very many of them out there.'

'What makes you so special?' Amani demanded.

'Nothing! I just think it's going to take a brave man to put up with my insane family and even crazier friends.'

'So, how many guys have you promised to toast ... oops ... meet? Maybe even have a chemical reaction with?' Rohan enquired.

'One hundred and one! But my mum can't organise herself to go to Woolies, much less organise for me to meet that many guys. It'll never happen,' I said confidently. 'Anyway, I had better go. I need to meet Max,' I said as I stood up, stuffing another Danish in my mouth.

'You know, I have a bad feeling about him,' Una called out as I walked away.

'Doesn't mean you're psychic,' Amani, Tehara and I called back in unison.

CHAPTER 12

What's with Push Presents? What will Women Want Next? An Ovulation Present?

It was two weeks since the wedding and my mother had yet to report back on the status of the 101 grooms. I relaxed back into my normal and comfortable life – well, as relaxed and comfortable as life could be, living close to the random attacks of Max Ferguson. The man had taken to putting more roadblocks in my way than Tullamarine Freeway at peak hour.

Once I had explained the basic premise of my accounting methods to Max, he'd insisted on me presenting it to his whole 'team'. I use the word 'team' loosely as I have never met a more disengaged group of people in my whole life. Nor had I ever met a group of people who'd mastered the fine art of synchronised eye rolling. Everytime Max said something stupid – which was often – they *all* rolled their eyes in unison.

However, Max continued to fail to give me the data I required. I was tempted to go to John but that might look like

I was incapable of managing Max, so I ended up befriending one of his team members who copied the data for me onto a CD.

I had taken a quick look at the data mid-morning and after lunch cleared out my entire calendar and the following few days, for good measure to clean up the mess. The reason why Max had been unable to understand my accounting system was because he had no system at all! As I hopped on a tram into the city for my lunch date, I could not stop wondering how he'd got away with it for such a long time.

No, don't get excited. It wasn't a real date. I was only catching up with Rohan to help him buy a present for Amani. Yes, even after ten years of being together Rohan *still* agonises over gifts for his wife. I would have found the whole thing completely barf-worthy had it not been for the fact that I loved the both of them very much.

I had organised to meet Rohan on the steps of the GPO on Bourke Street and spied him relaxing in the scorching autumn sun between the flower stall and a man holding up a placard proclaiming 'The End is Nigh'. It was an unusually warm day in May with the temperature hovering around thirty-eight degrees and Melburnians were making the most of the last blast of warmth before the cool of winter.

'Everybody reckons this bloke is pessimistic,' Rohan drawled as he stood up to peck me on the cheek, gently inclining his head towards the prophet of doom. 'But I think he's actually optimistic. I mean, he's been here for at least the last twenty years.'

'And he's still on message and on brand! Many of Australia's Fortune 500 companies struggle to be on message for more than six months!'

Rohan threw his head back and laughed. 'Lead the way, my credit card is at your disposal!'

'Have you decided what you want?' I asked as we went into the first jewellery store we'd made an appointment at.

'Hmmm … can't decide between earrings or a bracelet.'

'How about a ring?'

'I gave her an eternity ring for our last anniversary, remember, a little early, grant you, but I don't want to repeat myself,' he replied as a fussy sales assistant greeted us with a grandiose little bow.

'And how can we help you beautiful people? You make such a lovely couple. An engagement perhaps?' he sang.

'We're not a couple,' both Rohan and I rushed to hastily clarify.

'I am looking for a push present … oops … a present to celebrate the birth of our first child for my wife and Shani is here to help me choose. She is as close to my Amani as a sister,' Rohan explained as I gave the man a little wave.

Anyway, we spent the next forty-five minutes looking through hundreds and hundreds of rings, bracelets and earrings in all the jewellery stores along Elizabeth Street until we finally landed at Tiffany's on Collins Street. While Rohan and I had similar tastes in wanting sleek, polished designs, we both knew Amani favoured chunky jewellery – which oddly suited her delicate frame.

'How about this? I think she'll like it!' I said to Rohan, picking out a white gold bangle from the Atlas range. It was decorated with Roman numerals and diamonds.

'I am not sure …'

'Well, I am. Besides, it's Tiffany's. You can exchange it if you need to.'

'No … it'll never be exchanged. You know that!'

'What? Amani will tell you if she doesn't like it. Lord knows, but *she* will tell you,' I reassured him.

'No she won't. Haven't you heard her lectures on the politics of marriage? Don't let your partner get the upper hand on you?' Rohan indicated to the sales assistant that he'd like the bracelet and handed over his credit card.

'And how would telling a man you don't like a gift be classified as "getting the upper hand"?'

Rohan shrugged. 'Remember the shopping spree I bought for her when you girls graduated? I found out last year when we were at my brother's wedding that she thinks shopping sprees are a poor choice of gift. It demonstrates "lack of caring" apparently, or so she advised my brother when he was thinking of getting his fiancé a similar gift.'

'That was years ago! But I thought all that "politics of marriage" garbage was her blowing hot air. You sure she's not having you on?'

'No, it's real. Usually I don't mind that she keeps secrets. I think some secrets are good in any marriage. It keeps the mystery,' he replied, raising his eyebrows evilly. 'But as of late, things have got really bad. I just don't know what's going on with her.'

'She's just being self-protective. Can you blame her? Her parents are/were diabolical!'

'Yeah, I gathered that. It's worse since she's been pregnant. Something is going on and I just can't get through to her.'

'Maybe it's the hormones. She'll be fine once the baby comes,' I reassured Rohan as he collected his purchases and we walked out into the sun. As we turned to one of the many restaurants in the Block Arcade, Rohan's phone rang. There was trouble at one of his work sites out of the city.

'I will make this up to you, Shani,' he reassured me as he rushed off.

My stomach made some audible rumbling noises as I jumped on the tram back to South Melbourne and I knew I wasn't going to be able to get to dinnertime without stuffing my face full of chips from the vending machine. And I hate eating chips; I really do. They give me zits and I didn't have time to go for a facial before the Kohanagoda wedding. So I decided to do the next best thing. I decided to call in at Mama

Wong's dim sim van at the South Melbourne Market on my way back to work.

As I hopped off the old bone-rattler tram, my mouth started to water at the thought of hoeing down on a crisp dim sim smothered with soy sauce. And that was when I saw a familiar waddle making its way through the crowd.

What the hell was Amani doing here in the middle of the day? And in this heat? The northerly winds from the vast desert plains of central Australia were like a blast furnace. They literally desiccated everything in their path; fruit sellers weren't selling fresh fruit here, they were selling dried fruit!

I changed course and tracked her through the crowded market, dodging the Friday afternoon early markers who'd snuck in to pick up their weekend groceries. Not that Amani was difficult to find; her pregnant waddle not only gave her away, but it slowed her down as well.

'Hey, cheeky babe,' I called out as I neared her, deciding not to tell her that I knew what her push present was. Amani would not let twenty years of friendship stand in the way of prising out a little secret like that! So, it was only when she turned around to greet me did I see that her face was streaming with tears.

'What's wrong, honey?'

Enfolding her in a big hug, I towed her towards a coffee shop and had her seated before she knew what was happening.

'Is there something wrong with the baby?' I asked as soon as we sat down.

Amani shook her head wordlessly, biting hard on her knuckles to stifle another sob.

'That's a "no", correct?' I asked for confirmation. You always need to double check these things with Lankans. We're an odd race of people who nod our heads for 'no' and shake our heads for 'yes'. It takes me a couple of weeks every time I travel to and from Sri Lanka to recalibrate my brain as to what the acceptable gesture is in which country. I usually just vaguely circle my head while I acclimatise. It seems to work.

'Yes,' she said softly, and kept crying.

I decided I'd play twenty questions instead. It's not like I had anything better to do, even though I might just have to break into Amani's handbag to get to her stash of Mylanta. I could definitely taste my gastric juices now.

'Has Rohan done something?' The bastard! He was so sweet not a half hour ago.

'No.'

'Who's upset you then?'

'*Ammi*,' she said, sobbing in earnest.

'Okay.' I sighed with semi-relief. 'What has Aunty Chandra done now?'

'Rohan and I did all the shopping for the *Dhanay* yesterday and we even picked up gifts for the monks. *Ammi* rang this morning and asked if we'd picked up the gifts. I said yes, we were planning on giving each monk $50 plus a collection of toiletries.'

Amani stopped to catch her breath. The gifts sounded perfectly reasonable to me.

'Then she reminded me that the head monk was about to go off to Canada and had made it known he would like a pair of Ugg boots. I said I wouldn't have time to pick them up before the *Dhanay* and she started in on me,' Amani explained, between sobs.

'Apparently, I have a car and can go anywhere, anytime, unlike the poor pregnant women in Sri Lanka who have to catch buses everywhere. I told her that it was really warm out and that I was tired and she said that "tiredness" is something we create in our minds.'

'Honey, you know that your mother, like my mother, is a sandwich short of a picnic. We've been through this before; Lankan women lose their marbles along with their tight waistlines once they hit menopause. They just go completely nuts!'

'Then she said I was an awful daughter, because I had to stop ferrying her to temple at six in the morning when my morning sickness was bad. Apparently morning sickness is something I have created in my mind, too. Mind over matter, she keeps saying to me. If you can control your mind, then you can control anything, she tells me.' The stream of words was relentless. 'Then she started with the silent treatment, you know, not hanging up but only answering in monosyllables. This went on until I agreed to come here and buy the bloody Ugg boots!'

It was a bloody shame that Aunty Chandra couldn't control her mouth, much less her mind. My mother was a saint compared to Aunty Chandra!

'Have you told any of this to Rohan? What does he think?'

'Oh don't be silly, Shani! Of course I haven't told Rohan. You don't get the politics of marriage, do you? My mother cannot be worse than his mother, or else his family will have one up on me. And I just can't hide some of the things my mum does, so I don't need to add fuel to the fire.'

WTF? Maybe the pregnancy hormones *had* really got to Amani. I tried a different tack.

'Honey, you know you can't listen to her. Don't get upset. It's not good for the baby.' I knew as soon as the words were out that I had said the wrong thing.

'Don't you think I know that me being upset is bad for the baby?' she snapped. 'I feel like a bad mother enough, already. I mean, I should be able to sacrifice my own comfort for my child. So I am here, buying bloody Ugg boots on a sodding thirty-eight degree day!'

'Okay, bad mother, then how about this? You sit here and order us a couple of coffees and some toasted paninis and I'll go and hunt down the Ugg boots. Do you know the size?'

'No!' Amani said with a fresh wail. 'How can I think I could be a mother if I can't remember to ask for the size of footwear? Do you think we should put this baby up for adoption? Surely he or she can't want a mummy like me?'

'Hey, stop that!' I commanded. 'You are going to be a fabulous mum. I'll ring the temple and get the size. You just relax,' I said as I fished my iPhone out of my handbag.

On the down side, I now had to slog through the market in search of Ugg boots for a monk. On the up side, I felt completely justified in calling my boss and telling him I had a family emergency I needed to attend to. After all, Amani was the closest thing I had to a sister.

CHAPTER 13

Dhanay and Horoscopes

I honestly never intended to be a cultural tour guide, but just call me by name and tip me well when you finish your odyssey into the nutty world of the Sri Lankan diaspora. Because by now you must be wondering what this whole *Dhanay* gig is all about.

When Prince Siddhartha Gautama embarked on his journey of enlightenment (it was a lo-o-ong journey, it took seven years, and frankly, I would have given up the first night and gone back to my princely digs), he became a wandering mendicant ascetic. Since 'wandering' meant he no longer had access to the royal kitchens, the Bodhisattva had to carry a begging bowl for alms.

He would wander the highways and byways of India, stopping at people's homes begging for food and was grateful for whatever they could share with him. Once he became enlightened, the invitations to people's homes became formalised and he would give a sermon in appreciation of his hosts' kind generosity. This has become even more formalised into ritual that we know today as *Dhanay*. Which translates roughly as 'donation'.

Today, the Buddhist monks, decked out in their princely saffron robes, represent the Buddha and they come into our homes for their single daily meal. It is a beautiful ritual where we share food that has been lovingly cooked and, in return, they usually share a few words of wisdom and give a little blessing. The good karma that is accumulated through this charitable act is supposed to be very beneficial.

So, you have people giving *Dhanays* at the drop of a hat. *Dhanay* is offered when people move into new homes, before they get married for good luck, after they marry for longevity, before they start jobs, after someone has died, and when someone is about to have a baby. It's a beautiful ritual; everyone gets to feel good from being charitable, it involves delicious curries and everyone is happy. Right?

Wrong.

This is because, as usual, Sri Lankans have added a few embellishments to this once simple ritual. Where's the fun in keeping things simple?

Firstly, we wake up at an ungodly time of day to cook an insane amount of food. I once questioned Aunty Chandra as to why we couldn't be a little more restrained in the quantity and variety of food we offered and was told I was being stingy and not in keeping with the spirit of charity.

Secondly, we can't sample what we're cooking while we are cooking it. This is a big no-no. The food has to be consumed by the monks before anyone else touches it. I can never eat at 5 am and by the time I've been cooking non-stop for three hours, I am well over curry and desperate for a trip to Maccas.

Trust me when I say I could go on.

I spent the night before Amani and Rohan's *Dhanay* at their house. It was just easier to go there after spending the afternoon in South Melbourne with Amani. We'd had a lovely time sipping drinks in a beer garden watching a parade of buff gay boys strutting their stuff.

As a result, I had been roped into helping Aunty Chandra cook. Actually, I volunteered to save Amani the pain. No woman who is nearly full term should be cooking for fifty people. I don't care what anyone says about mind over matter.

So, it was an exceedingly seedy me who was woken up by the saintly Aunty Chandra at 4 am. Honestly, I was so disoriented it took her at least three attempts before she was able to successfully rouse me. After that, the pace was relentless.

'*Puthay,* now that you're up, can you please wash the rice, cut the fish, clean and wash the vegetables, sort out the plates and fry the pappadums. Tell me once you've done those things. I have a list a mile long to get done. You'll be blessed for helping me,' she said in a quiet but firm voice.

'Hmmm ...' was all I managed as I chugged blearily on a mug of hot, milky, sugary tea. Aunty Chandra, a true patriot, thinks coffee is the work of the devil sent to destroy the tea industry in Sri Lanka. She cannot and will not brew a pot of coffee even if someone's life depended on it.

'I'd better go and wake Amani up. All this nonsense about morning sickness and needing rest. When I was pregnant in Sri Lanka, I used to get up and cook breakfast and lunch for the family of six. You girls today are too soft,' she announced firmly, making her way to the master bedroom.

It took a few seconds for the intention behind the words to sink through my alcohol-addled, sleep-deprived brain. I launched myself off the kitchen stool and cut her off at the hallway, arms akimbo.

'Aunty, you know, I'm sure we can manage the cooking,' I improvised quickly, trying not to knock her out with my morning breath. Normally I could only handle a few minutes of it myself, before I made a mad dash to the bathroom for some Listerine.

'Nonsense,' she scoffed, ducking my arm.

Aunty Chandra is a little lady, standing barely four feet ten to my hulking five feet five. She is slender, bordering on skinny, which gives her a false appearance of fragility. Due to her 'extreme' adherence to Buddhism, she no longer dyes her hair or does any grooming beyond the absolute minimum of brushing her teeth and having a daily shower. This has dried her skin, giving her the appearance of a dandelion puff, with her large halo of grey hair and a body like a dried twig. But her age doesn't stop her moving fast when she wants to.

I scooted around her again, stopping her at Amani's bedroom door.

'Aunty Chandra, let's just let her sleep in till 6 am,' I pleaded. 'I am really fast and I am sure we can get everything done without Amani.'

'But this is her house and her *Dhanay*. She must do it!'

Mercifully, there was a quiet knock at the door.

'Aunty, why don't you go and get that,' I said wildly. There was no bloody way Amani was going to wake up at 4.10 am and I really didn't want to start a cold war so early in the morning. Some things are just better left till at least mid-morning.

I listened at the door for a few moments to make sure neither Rohan nor Amani had been woken by the altercation between Aunty Chandra and me. I was really happy to hear only the gentle snuffles of sleep and the odd snore from Amani.

And who the bloody hell comes knocking at this time of morning anyway?

I heard Una's perky voice and Tehara's measured tones down the hallway and gave a huge sigh of relief. Thank goodness the troops were here. There was no way I was going to be able to handle Aunty Chandra by myself. Not in my hung-over state.

'So, Aunty Chandra, what would you like us to do?' Una asked cheerily.

'I was going to wake Amani, it's her *Dhanay* and she should do most of the work!'

'You know Aunty Chandra, Tehara, Shani and I are all potential *punchi-ammas*, (well *loku-amma* in Tehara's case), and can do the work on behalf of the baby. We need the good merit as much as Amani, if we are to be good aunties,' Una fibbed. The logic was at best screwy, but Una's wide-eyed innocence, sincerity and whiteness won the day.

'What do you need us to do?' Tehara asked, determinedly donning an apron and a pair of onion goggles.

Aunty Chandra took to the invitation like an English general confronted with a whole battalion of over-eager Anzacs at Gallipoli. Which proved to be an apt analogy because we, too, were slaughtered at the break of dawn.

Aunty Chandra had us cut and clean the vegetables (twelve different varieties including bitter gourd which is a fiendishly tricky vegetable to clean properly), grind the spices, cook the curries, clean and prepare the fish and prawns, and fry an unending stack of samosas, cutlets and pappadums. Every time one of us suggested something like cutting the vegetables differently, or using different spices to flavour the curries, she'd threaten to wake Amani to do it properly. By a little after 7 am, she had the three of us well and truly cowed.

As dawn broke across the Melbourne sky, Una, Tehara and I were exhausted and smelly from the all cooking oil congealing in our hair. Not that it was uncommon for us to feel this way on a Saturday morning; only it usually comes with the consolation of having imbibed a considerable amount of alcohol and chain-smoked enough fags to smoke out a whole school of Tasmanian salmon.

'Aunty Chandra, I'll go to the bathroom first for my shower, and then Una and Shani can follow,' Tehara said as she dried the last pot and put it away.

It was amazing that Rohan and Amani had been able to sleep through all the banging of pots and chinking of china.

'What? You girls have no stamina! No, no, no, you have to wash the dishes for the *Dhanay*!'

'Oh, Amani's already done that. See, I helped her stack the dishwasher last night,' I pointed out, opening the dishwasher with an elegant bow.

'*Chee chee chee*, you can't ask people to eat from plates that have been washed in a dishwasher. You don't know if the chemicals have been cleaned off properly. Take them all out and hand wash and dry them again, please.'

'But, but ...' Tehara started, looking as if she could throttle Aunty Chandra. Even Tehara's psychiatrist patience was at an end.

I quietly stepped on her foot. It was only 7 am and the day was bound to be long. Amani needed as much rest as she could get.

'Fine,' Una sang with fake perkiness, twisting the tea towel into knots behind her back.

So, we re-washed and dried all the dishes and cutlery. Then Aunty Chandra had us sort out the napkins. Amani and Rohan finally made an appearance just as she was about to get us to re-arrange the lounge room. We could see from the smirks on their faces that they'd been up for a while, hiding in their bedroom.

Amani still looked tired and uncomfortable, though.

'You have finally decided to join us, huh?' Aunty Chandra asked her daughter. 'We've done all the work and all you need to do is relax. You are very lucky you have a mum like me who will do all the work. Soon, you'll be doing all the work, so you'd better get used to it.'

As the three of us took turns with the shower, Aunty Chandra kept ordering the remaining troops around doing a million other little tasks. Rohan was despatched to the supermarket to buy a list of things that was a mile long, including a whole stack of paper plates, paper napkins and plastic cutlery as back up.

'Amani, have you made the dessert like you promised to?' Aunty Chandra quizzed as Amani sat at the kitchen bench sipping her tea and munching on some toast liberally spread with butter and Vegemite.

'No, Aunty Sonali said she'd make it for me instead,' she replied absently, as she stretched over to pop another piece of bread into the toaster. She did another little stretch with her hand pressed against the small of her back.

'What?! *Chee chee chee*, surely you are making *something* for the *Dhanay* with your own hands? Think of the health of your baby. You must make something!' Aunty Chandra cried hysterically.

'Okay, okay, I'll make Mars Bar slice,' Amani improvised. Quick, easy and really didn't require much effort. Amani took a quick peek through her pantry and rang Rohan on his mobile to get the missing ingredients.

About ten minutes later, Aunty Chandra spoke up again. 'Amani, where is the desiccated coconut for the *pol sambol*?'

'I bought fresh coconut the other day and it's in the freezer. Remember? You said to buy fresh coconut because it tastes nicer,' Amani replied, sounding perplexed.

'*Aiiyo lamayo,* that's only when you are cooking for yourself. The monks can't eat fresh coconut because most of them are diabetic and have to watch what they eat. Ring Rohan and ask him to get some desiccated coconut,' Aunty Chandra commanded.

'But he'll almost be home now. Is it really that important?' Amani protested, still nibbling on her toast.

'Amani, I cannot believe you are asking me that question. What sort of daughter did I raise? Do you want to make the monks sick? *Do* you? Because you will be responsible, you know! Do you want bad Karma?'

'Of course not …'

'Do it for the health of your child! You and your husband don't know anything about sacrifice …'

'Okay, okay, okay … I'll ring him,' Amani said reaching for the phone, swearing under her breath. 'Okay, *Ammi*, we're getting the desiccated coconut,' she said a few minutes later as she reached for her last slice of toast.

'You eat too much! Eating like that, you are going to get diabetes and you'll have trouble delivering the baby,' Aunty Chandra scolded, whisking the piece of toast out of Amani's hand and tossing it in the bin under the sink.

I turned to see a telltale brightness in Amani's eyes.

'Actually, the causal link between over-eating during pregnancy and gestational diabetes has yet to be proven. Though you are more likely to get gestational diabetes if you are already obese when you fall pregnant, and since Amani wasn't, I wouldn't worry about it,' Tehara observed, sounding like she'd just swallowed a back issue of the *Lancet*.

'What would you know? You're only a psychiatrist. Not even a real doctor. Depression and mental illnesses are all results of bad karma. Pray, and it will go away,' Aunty Chandra snapped.

'Okay, Aunty Chandra,' I piped up. 'Why don't we go outside and rake the leaves on the pavement. The elm trees are shedding their leaves and it's red all over!' I pushed Aunty Chandra along the hallway while miming to Amani and Tehara to practise deep breathing, calming techniques.

'No, no, no Shani, can you please vacuum the carpets? I don't think Rohan did a good job last night.'

So I started vacuuming, hoping that the noise would drown out any conversation between Amani and her mother.

Thirty minutes later, everything seemed to have calmed down. Rohan had returned and been despatched to the supermarket yet again to buy some other forgotten trifle. And he was back for the third time. It was half past eight and everything was finally ready. Amani, Tehara, Una and I paraded in front of Aunty Chandra in our fresh clothes like primary school kids dressed for their first day of school.

'So, is everything ready?' Una asked.

'Yes,' Aunty Chandra said with a smug little smile. 'And it's only eight thirty. Why, at other *Dhanay* houses, people are still cooking when the monks arrive!'

'Why, is it extra good merit to have everything organised two hours in advance?' I asked, sarcastically.

Una jabbed me in the ribs, probably anxious to avoid a further war of words. Geez, the girl had pointy elbows.

'Rohan, I hope you are about to go and pick the monks up now!' Aunty Chandra commanded once she was content we looked suitably pious and well-dressed.

'I was planning on leaving at about nine. It only takes forty-five minutes for the round trip,' Rohan said.

'No, go now! You never know if you'll get stuck in traffic!'

'But I'll be going against traffic. And it's Saturday, anyway,' Rohan replied wearily.

Aunty Chandra strode over to Rohan who was chowing down on his bowl of Weetbix. She snatched it away and put it in the sink. 'Go, Rohan and don't be late!' she commanded and turned her back on him.

It was a testament to Rohan's laid-back character that he didn't frogmarch his mother-in-law out the front door. Lord knows, I was tempted to do it myself. He pulled me aside on his way out and whispered urgently, 'Don't let Amani's mum drive her insane. We saw the obstetrician last week and Amani's blood pressure is a little on the high side.'

'Is she alright though?'

'She should be okay ...' Rohan hesitated for a moment.

'I am sure she's fine,' I reassured him.

Once Rohan had left, Aunty Chandra then turned on us again. She had us re-arranging the furniture yet again while Amani made the Mars Bar slice.

'Amani, where's the bottle of mineral water I asked you to buy?' Aunty Chandra called from the lounge room into the kitchen.

'You didn't ask me to buy mineral water!' Amani called back. She really looked like she was in pain, now. I was starting to think her father must have died on purpose, just to get away from her mother.

'Yes I did.'

'No, you *didn't*.' I could hear an edge to Amani's voice that said she had just about had enough of her mother.

Fortunately we were distracted by a ring at the door. My mother walked in carrying, in addition to three superbly cooked curries, a smallish document box tied with a pink ribbon. On the ends of the pink ribbon hung little brass weights shaped like kissing peacocks. The symbol of marriage.

'*Aiyubowan, aiyubowan*!' my mother called out cheerfully, as she led a horde of loudly babbling Lankans into the house. The guests had also brought their contributions to the *Dhanay* in the form of more curries.

'We saw Rohan leave. It is a good thing he went early. You don't want to get caught in traffic,' my mother commented as she cornered me in the kitchen. 'Shani, look what I have for you!'

'What?' I asked absently, leaning back to hear the conversation between Amani and her mother over the din of the chattering guests.

'Aunty Sonali's daughter had blessed water at her *Dhanay* and she sipped it during her labour and it went perfectly!'

'I'll have blessed water too. Look, we can use an old wine carafe and I can have Rohan decant the water into a mineral water bottle later.'

'No, no, no. Aunty Sonali's daughter said that she used a mineral water bottle and it was sealed, and that is what made it perfect!'

'Surely the contents are more important than the container?'

'Why can't you do the right thing by the baby? This is not for me, this is for the baby! I really wonder what kind of mother you are going to make, Amani. Have I taught you nothing about sacrifice?'

Aunty Chandra then turned to my mother. '*Anay balandako* Jayanthi, these young girls don't do anything. I've cooked the *Dhanay*, cleaned the house and done everything and she can't even go to the shops to buy a bottle of water. What is happening to our girls? They have no sense of duty.'

'*Anay* yes, I've organised for Shani to meet some boys, but she gives me such a hard time. All we want is the best for our children, don't you know? We sacrificed so much for them and they can't do even the smallest thing for us,' my mother chimed in.

'Smallest thing' being marrying a man *she* picks for me?

Right now, the last thing Amani and I needed was to be in the middle of a 'my daughter is worse than your daughter' competition between our mothers.

Tehara walked past us to the back door muttering, 'Follow me for a quick getaway!'

Unfortunately, just as I made to follow her, my mother grabbed my arm. My heart sank as I saw Amani, Tehara and Una rush out the back door, calling back to Aunty Chandra that they were going to buy a bottle of mineral water. I couldn't bear it if they left me behind.

'Shani, look what I have for you!' my again mother said as she handed me the box tied with the pretty ribbon. *Uh, oh!*

'What's that for?' I asked, suspiciously.

'You said you wanted information on all 101 grooms before you'd meet any one of them. Well, here it is. Every single profile, typed up on a computer, horoscopes checked and everything!'

'Remember that I said they all had to be at least five feet six and not living with their mother.'

'They are all over five feet six and none of them live with their mothers!'

'That is just not possible, *Ammi*. All Sri Lankan boys live with their mothers. I'm sure if you looked up the dictionary for a definition of "mama's boy", there'd be a picture of a Lankan boy being spoilt by his mother.'

'Well, none of *these* boys lives with his mother. They all came here as international students and most of them live by themselves.'

'But why the rush? It usually takes your astrologer at least two weeks to match a single horoscope!' I was grasping at straws and my mother knew this.

'He offers an online service now. He matches horoscopes through an RSS feed and gets everything back to you in twenty-four hours!'

When did Vedic astrology become so high tech? More importantly, how the bloody hell did my mother get so organised? I smelt a rat.

'Did Una help you?'

'No, but Gehani did. And since you only wanted to meet boys in a "natural" setting, I have put your mobile number on this great service offered by, hang on, I can't remember its name ... hang on ...'

I tried pulling again when I heard Tehara honking her horn. But my mother held fast.

'Google Position Checker! Yes, that's it!' she said, triumphantly. 'So, when you and the boy are near each other, he gets an SMS to say that you are nearby and can talk to you. Apparently, it is very popular in Japan.'

'Don't I get a text too?' I asked horrified.

'No, because I thought you'd run away if you knew someone was trying to talk to you.'

Too bloody right I would!

Tehara honked her horn furiously and revved her turbo-charged engine. 'I'd better go,' I said, finally shaking myself free from her grasp.

'Take this,' she replied, thrusting the box of potential groom profiles into my hands.

It took us all of two minutes to get to a supermarket from Amani's place. Amani swung between incandescent rage and tears all the way in the car. And through the rage and the tears, she was looking increasingly uncomfortable.

'Amani, are you okay?' Tehara asked, as we followed Amani into the supermarket like a string of paper dolls, all dressed in white.

'Yeah, just a little back ache,' Amani snapped. 'What gets me is all my mother's self-righteous, sanctimonious crap, you know? She's all about doing everything to the letter of the law, but she never thinks of the trouble she puts people through to do it!'

'I know honey, I know. You mustn't get upset by her, she has her heart in the right place,' Tehara defended.

'Where is her heart? It's certainly not with me! It's all about showing to the world how pious she is,' Amani snapped, waddling as fast as she could to the mineral water aisle.

'Honey, you have got to calm down. You've got to think of the baby,' I said witlessly, trying to calm the situation.

Tehara, Una and Amani all turned on me, giving me withering glares. Clearly, I must have left my brains at the pub yesterday.

'I know you are thinking of the baby, love. She is the one with issues not you,' Tehara placated. Did I tell you that Tehara is a fantastic suicide negotiator?

'The thing that gets me most is that it is unending. She is *never* happy with me. Nothing I do is good enough. Remember when we were at school, she wanted me to do Law when

Aunty Sonali's cousin's daughter did Law. So, I did Law. And when you got into Medicine, she wanted me to do Medicine. Then she wanted me to get married. Rohan and I rushed our wedding just to please her. She has nagged me for the last five years to have a grandchild and now that I am pregnant, all she sees are disasters around every corner. She simply does not help,' Amani said, with a sob as she reached to grab a bottle of Fiji water.

'You know she'll help when the baby arrives ...' Una said.

'Not a chance. Apparently she had me by herself, all alone, so I should do the same too,' Amani said with a grimace as she reached for a bottle of Perrier. 'Did she say still or sparkling? I'll get both. No, she won't help. She said to me the other day that I would have to do it alone 'cause she had to do it alone here in Australia! '

'But you have us. Not that any one of us know how to change a nappy. As I recall, Tehara got banned from her obstetrics/gynaecology rotation for barfing every time she saw a vagina, and I think Una dropped a baby while on her midwifery rotation. I am therefore the only one you should seriously consider as good babysitting material.'

'How hard can a baby be anyway? You feed one end and you wipe the other,' Una pointed out.

'If nothing else, we can show it these groom profiles,' I said, holding up the box in my hand.

Amani finally started giggling at that.

'You guys are really the best, you know,' she said, gasping a little, putting her hand to her stomach. 'Oh, oh, what is that?' she exclaimed. 'Oh my god, oh my god, I think ... I think ... I think my waters are about to break!'

Una, Tehara and I looked at each other in complete shock. This is *not* how it's supposed to happen!

'Quick, someone help me!' Amani cried as she pressed her hand between her legs.

'Does anyone have towels?' Tehara called out, shocked out of her normal calm.

'The waters are coming!'

'Here, catch it with this,' I said, thrusting the document box at her, whipping the cover off in one swift motion.

Amani shoved the box between her legs as a flood of water poured out.

Crap! Not only was the baby really coming, but my box of groom profiles was now drenched in amniotic fluid.

CHAPTER 14

Suitcases

'Okay, Amani, we'll get you home first and once Rohan gets back, we'll go to the hospital,' Tehara said, recovering her sense of authority.

'No bloody way am I going home! Especially not with my mum there!'

'Okay, okay, we'll call Rohan and ask him to meet us. Let's just get out of here!'

As the four of us waddled in a curious-looking huddle out of the supermarket, an over-officious shop person confronted us. 'What are you girls doing?' she asked aggressively.

I suppose we did look a bit odd, but there was no need for her to be rude.

'We are leaving because this lady is in labour,' Una answered.

'I don't think so!' she replied tartly. 'I've had enough of you international students nicking stuff from this shop. Enough is enough! I'm going to call the police.'

Surely, the woman wasn't blind. How could Amani be anything but pregnant? And how could any one of us be mistaken for students? Though I must confess, I felt momentarily pleased at being able to pass myself off as an eighteen year-old.

'Excuse me, this woman is in labour and needs to reach a hospital as soon as possible,' Tehara said, drawing herself to her full miniscule height and donning her cut-glass, private-school accent and 'I-grew-up-in-Toorak-so-you-can-kiss-my-arse-and-still-not-be-good-enough' tone. 'I am a doctor, trust me!'

This almost put a spanner in the woman's argument, but something about a disenfranchised person being given even a modicum of power steeled her spine. 'I don't think so. I'm going to call the police now, and if you don't shut up, I'm going to tell them that you abused me as well.'

This roused Amani who should have been breathing through a contraction.

'Look, love …' Amani said through clenched teeth. 'Where is your proof of theft? We have to leave the premises with stolen goods in our possession for an act of theft to have occurred. All you have at the moment is a suspicion of theft and no proof.'

'Says who?'

'Says me! Call the police and find out for yourself,' Amani challenged. 'I know quite a few of them. And while you drag them away from their official policing duties, I will wait for them in the car park.'

'But you can't leave the store,' the girl cried. 'Look, your proof or whatever is in that box. Give it to me,' she demanded, pointing to the soggy document box in my hands. 'I bet you you've pinched a few packets of smoked salmon and stuck 'em in there.'

I must confess to feeling a sense of unholy joy as I handed

the document box over to her. There must have been a divine purpose for me to still cling to it like an octopus with tetanus.

'It's all yours, darl,' I drawled, trying not to smirk too broadly as she lifted the lid.

'What is this?' she asked, looking at the sodden mess of papers.

'Groom profiles for an arranged marriage!'

'Why are they wet?'

'Because she used the box to catch her waters.'

'Yuuuck!' the girl squealed and dropped the box on the floor.

'Make sure you clean that up. It could be an occupational health and safety hazard!' I called as we walked out the store.

'I'm calling the police!' she screamed.

We ignored her and kept walking. It's such a pity that there is no medication for stupidity – GlaxoSmithKline would make a packet if it could produce a pill containing commonsense and average intelligence.

By the time we made it to the car, it was clear that Amani was actually in a great deal of pain.

'Hasn't anyone rung Rohan yet?' Amani gasped between pants.

I grabbed my mobile and stood a little away from the car as I put the call through. But I could still hear the three of them. Amani was sitting sideways in the backseat with her legs sticking out of the car and Una supporting her back. Tehara was crouched on her knees near Amani's legs with the passenger side door wide open.

Rohan picked up the call immediately.

'Hey Shani, has Amani's mum driven you all mad?' he asked cheerfully, then realised that the monks in his car could hear everything he said through the hands-free phone. 'Mad with anticipation, that is ...'

'Err ... Rohan ... Amani is in labour.'

'Holy shit, but the baby is not due for another two weeks! Oh, sorry *Swarminwahansa*, but I think my wife is in labour.'

'There is no "thinking" about it, Rohan. Her waters just broke.'

'I'll be there in about ten minutes. Just keep Amani quiet and start packing her bag.'

'Rohan, we're not at your house.'

'Where the fuck are you then?'

Finding out that his baby was on its way had temporarily made him forget about the monks and their delicate ears.

'Don't get your knickers in a knot, we're at the super-market.'

'What are you doing there? I only went about a dozen times this morning ... Actually, don't answer that question,' Rohan said wearily. He knew his mother-in-law only too well.

'Here's the plan, *machang*. Just drop the monks off at your house for the *Dhanay* and pick Amani up here. She wants you with her right now,' I explained quickly.

'Okay.'

As I turned back to the car I heard Amani screech as another contraction hit.

'How far apart are the contractions?' I heard Tehara ask Una urgently as she gently massaged Amani's contracting belly. I sent up a silent prayer of thanks that we were in the company of both a doctor and a nurse.

'Three or two minutes apart,' Una replied. Had I really missed that much while I was on the phone?

'Rohan will be here in fifteen minutes. You can't go from breaking your waters to instant childbirth, can you?' I asked, trying not to panic. Everything I'd heard about childbirth had painted a picture of a long, protracted and messy affair. And as Amani nodded her head vigorously, I could see she'd thought the same too.

'It sometimes happens,' Una replied, looking worried as

Amani bit down hard on her change purse to stifle a scream of pain. 'Didn't they tell you all of this in childbirth class?'

'Err, well ... we didn't go 'cause I thought it'd be really stupid to sit around and talk about breathing and shit. Besides, it was on the weekend of Gayani's wedding and I really needed a facial,' Amani said in a rush as she chomped down again on the soft leather.

'They don't just talk about breathing! They mainly talk about the stages of labour and what to do when.'

'Well, I am reading a book on it!'

'There is only one way to find out how far along she is,' Una said, looking Tehara straight in the eye as another contraction hit. 'Besides, the contractions are getting closer and closer together.'

'Find out what?'

'How close you are to delivering the baby,' Una said in a soothing voice.

'Okay, just call my obstetrician,' Amani semi-screamed as another contraction hit hard.

'Honey, we'll do that too. But we need to know how far along you are,' Una reassured her.

'Call Samantha McNally!'

I fished around in Amani's handbag and found her phone. Samantha McNally's phone number was in her list of contacts so I was able to leave a detailed message on her answering service before coming back to the car.

'All done,' I said as I squatted next to Tehara at the open car door. The debate about how far along Amani really was still raging.

'Okay, okay ... we need to know when the baby will come,' Amani finally conceded. 'But can't Tehara tell by feeling my tummy?'

'No honey, she would really need to do an internal examination for that,' Una replied gently.

Was that what I really thought it was? Clearly, there is no dignity in childbirth. And, considering the very public car park we were in, in the inner-city suburb of Hawthorn, very little privacy either.

'But honey, you know we have to do it or we could all get into trouble,' Una said in a soothing voice.

'Shani, could you grab my medical bag from the boot?' Tehara asked, sounding very resolute even if she didn't look it. The reason why Tehara had taken up psychiatry really had as much to do with her distaste of icky stuff as it did from a need to emulate her emotionally bankrupt father. Sticking one's fingers up another woman's privates definitely fell into the icky category.

'Call the ambulance!' Amani protested.

'No point. They often don't bother to come for obstetric calls,' Tehara said. 'Besides, you could be hours away.'

'Then there is no reason for an internal examination!' Amani snapped back.

'Fine by me. Sticking my fingers up your hoo haa is the last thing I want to do,' Tehara said, snapping off the surgical gloves I'd just handed to her. 'But don't blame me if your child is born in the back seat of this car.'

Conceived in the back seat of a car, delivered in the back seat of a car; this child's destiny *really did* have bogan written all over it. I wonder what the Vedic astrological sign for a bogan baby is.

'Tehara, it *hurts*!' Amani screamed. 'Give me some drugs. I know you have bloody drugs in that bag of yours.'

'Anti-psychotic drugs. I can help out if you are having a psychotic breakdown but not much else!'

'Don't lie, you must have some pain killers in there.' Amani pushed herself forward, almost getting out of the car to reach for the medical bag I clutched in my hands.

'For God's sake, Amani, be reasonable. I can't give you any

pain medication without knowing how far along you are. I am not your attending physician, and I could put both you and the baby in danger,' Tehara said whipping the medical bag out my hands and holding it aloft. I couldn't believe they were about to have a bitch fight over the medical bag.

I was getting ready to intercept the bag myself when the police turned up, sirens wailing and lights flashing. The officious girl from the supermarket rushed out to join the men in blue, probably thinking there'd be safety in numbers.

'There they are,' the girl pointed us out to the officers. 'They abused me and nicked stuff from the supermarket.'

By now, we'd accumulated a horde of onlookers, fascinated by what was happening in front of them. We were a full-blown drama starring a carload full of girls, a screaming check-out chick and the boys in blue.

'We didn't steal anything, officers,' I said, opting to deal with Victoria Police rather than Amani. Trust me when I say it was the safer option, their reputation with guns notwithstanding.

'Prove it!' the check-out operator screamed.

Now, I do have a degree in law for what it's worth, and I can still remember some of my basics from first year, even though the vast bulk of it is lost in a beer-coloured haze.

'Actually, you have to prove we've stolen something. The basic tenet of the adversarial legal system in Australia means that a person is innocent until proven guilty.'

'Well, well … well, that's not how they treat terrorists,' the girl countered.

'This is exactly why lawyers have been protesting against those stupid laws ever since Phillip Ruddock drafted them. They are unconstitutional.'

'You must be terrorists, then!'

'Oh, for fuck sake. I am an accountant, that girl fighting with that pregnant woman is a doctor …' Amani had her back to us; somehow she had managed to get hold of Tehara's medical bag and a fierce struggle was taking place with Una trying in vain to referee.

'The guy who helped those terrorists in the UK was a doctor!'

'Dr Mohamed Haneef, you mean?'

'Yeah, whatever! '

'He was innocent! They released him!'

'But he can't come back to Australia!'

'And since when has DIMIA … oops, sorry, it's now the Department of Immigration and Citizenship, ever been unfailingly right? Just ask Vivian Salon and Cornelia Rau,' I said witheringly. Could people this stupid really walk the earth?

I was distracted by a groan from the car. Amani was gripped by another hard contraction as she crumpled back into the car. The already exhausted police officers were finally able to get a word in.

'Miss … Natalie …' the police officer paused to check the name badge on the woman's uniform. 'The lady here is right. You cannot accuse them of shoplifting unless you have proof of the crime. And making an allegation of terrorism is a serious charge.'

'What about being alert and aware? I still have my fridge magnet!'

'I returned mine,' I quipped. The officer gave me a silencing glare.

Amani gave another scream of pain and the police officers finally looked at her.

'Oh my God,' the second police officer yelped and rushed over to the car. 'I know this lady! It's Amani Wickramasinghe. She's a Prosecutor with the DPP. I think I can safely say she's not going to nick anything.'

'Please Tehara, give me some drugs,' implored Amani. 'I've been one of your best friends for nearly twenty years.'

'Honey, I can't give you any meds unless I know how far along you are,' Tehara replied, again holding the medical bag out of Amani's reach.

The other police officer looked over now and recognition dawned on his face. 'Dr Jayasuriya!'

'You mean she really is a doctor?' the worrisome check-out chick asked incredulously.

'Yes, and a suicide negotiator. One of the best. I worked with her a few weeks ago when there was a jumper in the city,' the first police officer confirmed.

Both police officers knelt beside Tehara, talking to Amani who was again chewing on her coin purse.

'Should we call the ambulance?' the police officer asked Tehara.

'Well, we don't know how far along she is and the length of the time between contractions is fluctuating. Her husband will be here any minute, and she wants to go to the hospital with him.'

I was so engrossed in the conversation between Tehara and the police officers, and watching Amani's face writhe in pain that I didn't notice a Sri Lankan man now standing beside me. He tapped me gently on the shoulder.

'Hi, is there a Shani Devapura here somewhere?' he asked politely.

I knew I was in trouble.

He was reasonably tall, wore a baseball cap and carried a man bag. As my eyes travelled further south I shuddered as I saw the gold-buckled belt holding up his chinos and the white New Balance shoes. Jerry Seinfeld *may* have been able to carry off wearing sneakers with casual pants, but that was a long time ago.

'I'm Shani Devapura.'

'Hi, I'm Chathu Gunadasa. I just got an SMS saying that you were interested in meeting me,' he said with a polite smile.

On the surface, this seemed to tick all the boxes. I was meeting a guy in a natural setting, surrounded by my friends and probably not looking my best. Any guy who could see past these things ought to be a worthy catch. Maybe my mother had picked a good one, for once.

'Shani!' Amani screamed from inside the car. 'Where the fuck is Rohan?'

Nothing like my foul-mouthed friends to show a man my best side.

'He's on his way,' I yelled back. Just like trailer trash. Chathu looked at me like the bottom had fallen out of his world. Sri Lankan women weren't supposed to yell. I guessed I wasn't making a good impression.

'Look Chathu, I don't think now is really a good time for us to catch up. My best friend is kinda in labour and my head's not really in the "meeting people" space,' I said.

'Yeah, yeah, I understand. But why isn't she in hospital?' Chathu asked, looking a little perplexed.

'Well … we're waiting for her husband to come and take her?'

'Why don't you guys take her?'

'She doesn't want to go with us, she wants to go there with her husband.'

'Well, that's just stupid. Stupid women irritate me.'

Okay. I did fundamentally agree with him. We ought to have rushed Amani straight to the hospital without letting the whole thing degrade into a spectacle worthy of the Calder Park Thunder Dome, but he was breaking Rule # 1. *Don't call my friends stupid.* Just don't. No man will ever understand a woman's psyche. Deal with it and move on. Don't question. Don't look for answers. And never look for logic. Accept that it is a limitation imposed by the Y chromosome and just move on.

I tried to be as tactful as possible. 'Look Chathu …'

'Shani, can you please find where the fuck my arsehole of a husband is?' Amani screamed between contractions.

'Hang ten,' I said to Amani, turning to call Rohan again. From what I could overhear, the contractions were getting close together and someone (Tehara) was about to duck in and have a look whether the baby was crowning because Amani certainly looked – and sounded – like she was about to deliver the baby immediately.

The police officers had politely draped a blue cloth over the car door now, shielding Amani from most of the small crowd of interested bystanders. Or maybe protecting them from the sight of Amani giving birth ... whichever.

I dialled Rohan's number and he picked up straight away.

'Where *are* you Rohan?' I asked grumpily, trying to keep my voice down to a quiet screech.

'I'm trying to turn into the bloody car park but there is a huge crowd here gawking at something,' he replied.

'Just give me a sec and I'll get that sorted for you,' I said triumphantly. For the first time in a very long time, I was actually glad to have a member of the Victorian Police Force at hand.

'Officer Jones!' I called out to the young constable who was trying to contain the growing crowd. 'The father of the baby is trying to turn into the carpark and can't get in. He drives a blue Saab convertible. Do you think you could get him in here?'

'Of course, madam,' he said politely and walked off authoritatively, all six foot four inches of him, to sort out the fracas. Normally I am not attracted to men in uniform, but that whole 'taking charge thing' can be dead sexy when you need something done.

'Honey, honey ... how are you?' Rohan asked as the police officer ushered him through the crowd.

Tehara emerged from wherever she was, looking a little ashen. I wasn't really surprised. The girl had developed such a reputation for passing out regularly throughout her obstetric rotation, she'd ended up being excused from it because it'd been too resource-intensive for the teaching hospital to have doctors tending to both a labouring mother and a fainting student.

'Okay,' Tehara said, swallowing convulsively. 'The baby has progressed a fair way down the birth canal, but you are not in transition.'

'What next?' Rohan asked breathlessly, clutching his wife's hand, interlinking her fingers with in his.

'Get Amani to the hospital now, and Sam McNally will look after you. Rohan, jump in the back seat with Amani, I'll drive you guys to hospital. Shani, you and Una take Rohan's car back to their house and sort out the mess there. Then come to the hospital with Amani's bag.'

'Shani, make sure you pack both pink and blue rompers,' Amani told me between contractions. *Now*, she was thinking about rompers? Sometimes I'll never understand that girl.

As Tehara reversed the car, the window rolled down.

'And don't forget to put in some singlets, sizes 0000, 000 and 00,' Amani yelled out.

She was still yelling instructions as Tehara's Mercedes Benz finally revved up to go past us, complete with police escort.

'And don't forget the maternity pads!'

Was nothing sacred in this world?

CHAPTER 15

A Crack in the Wall

It was Wednesday and I was back at work after taking the previous day off. As it happened, Rohan and Amani's daughter wasn't born in the back seat of Tehara's car en route to hospital. Maybe she wouldn't be a bogan after all, but I was secretly clinging to the hope that one day she will get a tattoo and multiple piercings.

The drama surrounding our little princess's arrival hadn't stopped when Amani and Rohan arrived at the hospital. Once Amani had been comfortably ensconced in a dimmed birth suite (complete with relaxing mood music, aromatherapy oils burning in the corner and Vichy shower) the two to three minute apart contractions stopped. Completely. It was as if the baby didn't want to be born in a hospital and would rather arrive in the back seat of a car.

The stop-start labour had gone on for a full day, until there were signs of foetal distress the following day. At that point, Amani was prepped for surgery, given an epidural and Princess arrived much in the style of Julius Caesar. See, her claims to royalty don't just come from three doting *punchi-ammas*, but also in her manner of delivery.

The next day the new *ammi* and *thathi* named their little angel Maya (after the mother of the Buddha) and second name Kumari (meaning princess). We, the Four Musketeers, had spent the third day together after the baby had been born, supposedly chasing away the baby blues, but in actual fact bonding with the littlest musketeer.

Maya was blessed with Amani's traffic stopping beauty and Rohan's laid back disposition. We were all completely in love with her. Una hadn't even dropped her. Yet.

But life rolls along and I needed to go back to work to pay off the mortgage. Debt can be such a burden. Especially if you're not enjoying your job the way I wasn't at the time. The first thing I saw when I logged into my computer was a string of about fifteen emails from Max asking all manner of inane questions. Oh, what fun!

Once I'd finished dealing with him via email, I got stuck into cleaning up the data mess before me, reassigning the right values and correcting double entries. I didn't want one of my direct reports doing it because I wanted to personally get close to the information.

So by the time I made my way to the office kitchenette for morning tea, I felt as if I'd already put in a day's work, not just a couple of hours!

'Hey, Shani,' Max greeted me with an evil grin. 'How's your part of the report going?'

'Fine, just fine,' I replied airly, though a more observant person would have noticed that there was undue force applied to the fridge door when I shut it after returning the milk.

'It must be going really well 'cause I heard you had a long weekend!'

'Excuse me?'

'Well, a little birdie told me that someone was out in South Melbourne having drinkie-poos all afternoon ...'

Obviously someone had seen me with Amani. Clearly a rumour was making the rounds that I had skived off work.

'Yes, I rang John and took the rest of the afternoon off as half-day leave to spend some time with my friend.'

'I'm sure it was all legit ...' Max replied with a wink, before swanning off.

The next eight hours of my work day had to be some of the worst of my life. I realised that producing the board report with the data that Max had given me would be near impossible, even if the deadline were to be extended. I debated as to whether to call in the forensic accountants to find out if there was any shonky business going on. However, as I worked the information, I didn't get any hard evidence to substantiate such as drastic action; just a hardening hunch. A hunch I could not go to John with without substantial proof.

Anyway, I was definitely feeling queasy when I drove back home that evening. I'd worked through lunch, munching on some stale sandwiches from the milkbar around the corner. And staring at the computer screen for nearly ten hours straight, had given me a thumping migraine. I had already tried Panadeine and failed miserably.

I was halfway home that evening when my phone rang. It was Amani.

'Hey honey, how is my little *kumari*? I asked, my voice getting a little mushy and gooey. I'd never really been one for babies before. I'd always thought they looked a little alien, especially newborns with their squished faces, misshapen heads and floppy bodies; but Amani's little girl had me twisted around her little finger. Already.

'Yeah, she is good ...' Amani said with a little happy sigh. 'Honey ... Rohan found a bag in the back seat of the car with a couple of articles from Lord Monckton. Apparently, it belongs to a guy called Chathu Gunadasa. Do you know who he is?'

'Yeah, I know who he is,' I replied ominously. 'He's this guy *Ammi* set me up with. You kinda missed seeing him at the car park. I think you were a bit busy ...'

'Please, please tell me he didn't see my C U Next Tuesday?'

'Of course not! Tehara was very careful about the whole thing and the police officers had draped a blue cloth around the car anyway.'

'Spill, then,' Amani said gleefully, relieved to hear her modesty was still intact. 'Tell me what happened with this guy!'

'Una and I found him in the back seat when we were halfway to your place,' I reminisced, painfully ...

'Who are *you*?' Una had asked abruptly when she'd finally noticed a strange man in the car. It nearly gave me a heart attack. Somehow, I hadn't even realised he was there.

'Hi, I'm Chathu. I thought I'd come along and get to know Shani a little better!'

I should have pulled over and demanded he get out immediately, but I was so astonished I didn't know what to say.

As soon as we got to the *Dhanay*, he tried taking over. He took it upon himself to tell everybody what had happened. To hear him describe it, you'd think he had been the one who'd called the police, determined how far along Amani was *and* driven them to hospital.

I should have put a stop to it when he started describing the crowd that gathered around the car. Aunty Chandra screamed with embarrassment when he started to tell everybody that the police had had to drape a cloth around the car so that the baby could be born with a modicum of privacy.

'Actually, Chathu,' Una had interjected furiously once Aunty Chandra had a fit of hysterics at the thought of her grand-daughter being born in a public car park, '... the baby probably won't be born for a couple of hours yet!'

'How would you know? It's not like you are a doctor!'

'Actually, I'm a nurse!'

'Hadn't both of you better start packing?' he had returned, clearly unwilling to share the limelight.

Not wanting to spend another second in his obnoxious company galvanised us into action. We started throwing baby gear into a suitcase willy-nilly. And while Una and I made our way through the house like two little whirlwinds, piling enough stuff into a suitcase to shame Victoria Beckham, the *Dhanay* guests and the monks watched us, standing around doing nothing.

That was until the old grandfather clock that Rohan had salvaged from an antique shop struck midday. And pandemonium broke out.

Why? Tradition has it that monks can't start their meal after midday. If somebody didn't offer them food straightaway, they weren't going to be able to eat until the next day. A few of them were diabetic, so a drop in their glucose level could literally end up killing them.

You can bet your bottom dollar that causing a monk to go into coma is high on the list of things that'll get you into heavy karmic debt. And we all know that karmic debt has a higher interest rate than Amex.

Chathu added to the mayhem by trying to order people around, but nobody knew him, so nobody really listened to him.

'Get the rice,' he commanded my mother, rudely.

'And who are you?' my mother had returned, equally rude.

'I am Chathu. I am Shani's intended,' he said with a smarmy smile. How the hell did he go from being a guy who I'd just met in a carpark, to being the man I was about to marry?

Again, I should have stopped him at that point. I should have got my six foot tall younger brother to twist his ear and push him out the door. But the opportunity was lost the moment my mother made the move from being confrontational to deferential within a nanosecond.

'Hello, I am Shani's *Ammi*,' she simpered, with an ingratiating smile.

'Yes, yes, Aunty. *Aiyubowan*. We'd better serve the monks before they collapse,' he said hurriedly, grabbing the steaming dish of rice someone had just handed my mother, and leaping to the task of serving the monks like a paramedic applying resuscitation paddles.

My mother got into the queue to start serving *paripu* when Chathu made another fatal blunder. He'd turned around to watch my mother place a spoonful of curry into the head monk's alms bowl.

'Aunty, I have been reading a Dharma book and it says that monks should first be served by men and women should serve only if there aren't men available ...' he intoned piously.

Now, that is just bullshit. I knew it. My mother knew it. And everybody around, including the monks who'd heard his crass remark knew it. Only, being Sri Lankan, we were too polite to call him a fuckwit and ask him to leave the house. Trust me, we are all far too polite for our own good. Sometimes.

Fortunately for my future marriage prospects, Chathu didn't know when to stop. The final straw was when he went on to say: 'You know the reason why monks get diabetes? It's because of Sri Lankan ladies ...'

I could see the thought bubbles in my mother's head. They were very similar to mine. *Why? How? Was he off his rocker?*

'It's because our women cook such rich food for them. They cook and cook for the monks and kill them with diabetes ...'

My mother's sense of hospitality and courtesy was cast to the wind. 'Now look here, Chathu, I don't know where you get this *bullshit* from, but we offer the monks the best, and nothing else. Because that is in the spirit of charity. And if you can't understand that, you don't belong in this family. In fact, you'd better leave!'

As Una and I hurried out the door with two suitcases, Chathu was sitting on the veranda next to my father who was listening to the cricket on his mobile phone radio. Having put my mother thoroughly offside, Chathu had continued in his tactless way by making the cardinal error of attempting to converse with my father while the cricket was on. Then he added insult to injury. I only heard this bit as we drove off.

'Uncle, Kumar Sangakarra is a second-rate cricketer …'

Amani was laughing so hard by the time I finished telling her all this that she was clinging to her stitched belly for dear life.

'But your father thinks Sangakarra is a living god!' she said between gasps of laughter.

'Oh yes, he even put a picture of Sangakarra in *Ammi*'s shrine room last World Cup. And *Ammi* was so caught up with the whole World Cup hype that she didn't care about potential blasphemy,' I said, as I climbed out of my car and walked up the driveway to the mailbox.

'I gather I won't get an invitation to Shani and Chathu's wedding then?'

'You gather right. But on the upside, I only have 100 more guys to meet.'

'Will we see you on Sunday?'

'Yes, I'll be there to welcome little Maya home.'

'Okay. See you then! And don't forget to bring a man from your list,' she added with a heavy dose of sarcasm just before she hung up.

As I looked up from my mail, I noticed that my brick mail box was cracked. Actually, the crack in the mail box ran down the centre of the mail box all the way to the drive. Strange. And as my eyes followed the crack, I realised the crack ran all the way to the house.

CHAPTER 16

Traditions

Una and I have had a tradition running for the last few years, ever since Tehara and Amani hooked up with men and dumped us. We catch up for a drink on a Friday evening after work. After my shiteful week, I was really looking forward to our weekly date.

The bloody awful start to my week had only been the tip of an iceberg akin to the one that sank the *Titanic*. I was certainly feeling as desperate as the doomed band that played as the ship sank.

So, I was at a nice little café-bar in South Yarra nursing a lovely glass of Chardy, watching the beautiful people and the trying-hard-to-be beautiful people parading by, when I was, again, accosted by a Sri Lankan man.

The most annoying thing about my mother having given out my mobile number to a stalker service is that I can't have my phone on when I really need it. Like now, when I wanted to find out why Una was running late.

However, I was beginning to gain some experience in dealing with strange Sri Lankan men talking to me in odd places. In the last week, I'd despatched four of them to the far reaches of bachelorhood, in addition to Chathu the Pest.

First there was the guy who tried to chat me up at the coffee shop yesterday morning. It was nothing personal, but I am just not a morning person. People who know and love me know not to talk to me until I've had my latte to start the day. Especially if I've spent the night before terrified that my house was going to collapse around me because I had finally noticed the zillion cracks in the brickwork and plasterboard.

'Hey, are you Shani Devapura?' an unnaturally cheerful young man asked me as he smacked his bike helmet on the counter just as the waitress put my latte down. Not a good start, spilling half my morning bevvie.

'Shani, I'll get you another one,' the waitress said kindly, as she mopped the spill.

Damn! Guess I can't lie and say my name is Tehara now.

'Yes, I'm Shani' I said with a deep, calming breath, turning around with a bright smile to greet him.

'Hey, wassup sista,' he quipped as he did a little gangsta rap move, moving his arms sideways with his hands clenched into the sign of the horns.

Okay. I dig rap music. I really do. I have no problem with Akon, 50 cent or Kanye West. Other than their depiction of all women as slappers.

'I'm about to go to work, is what's up. And you are?' I was still a little too soft hearted to completely dismiss a man before asking his name. Time for that the next day.

'My name is Shan.'

Shan and Shani. How was this going to work? And what

were we going call each other in the throes of passion? It'd all be too much like masturbation only with sound effects.

On the surface, this guy, unlike Chathu, was very appealing. He obviously rode his bike to work, so he was fit. He looked quite cute in his riding gear, no mean feat since skin-tight leggings usually do no one any favours. He had nice hands and a roguish grin.

'Okay, Shan,' I said as I reached for my fresh latte that the waitress kindly handed to me. 'I'm running late for work. You've got my mobile number, why don't you text me later?'

'I'll do that. But why don't I walk you to your office?'

Might as well get it over with. 'Sure, sure. So, tell me about yourself?' I asked as we stepped into the brisk autumn Melbourne day. The ominous bite of winter was tempered by the bright sunlight.

'I am an IT nerd,' he said with an apologetic grin.

'Oh, yeah? Plenty of those around. Especially of the Sri Lankan variety ...'

'Yeah. Hey, from the information I got, I gather your mother put you up to this, yeah?'

'Yeah, apparently I'm in *Mangala Yoga* and my mother must marry me off!'

'Same here. Which is why my mother signed me up for this stupid service!'

'Are you close to your mum?'

'Hell, no. She's a bitch. She left my father once for Step Dad Number One. Then she left him for Step Dad Number Two and then she left *him* for my dad,' he said with a smile. 'Hate to say it, but she's a bit of a gold digger, my mother!'

A bit too much information for a first conversation. A simple *No, we aren't close* would have sufficed.

'Oh. Any brothers or sisters?' I asked as there was at least another fifty metres to my office. I was hoping against hope that this would elicit a halfway-normal response.

'Yeah, I have two half-brothers that Dad had with his second wife, and I have a full sister. But, she's a skanky ho. Screws anything with a dick. She's slept with my two best friends ...'

Did I fall asleep and wake up on The Jerry Springer Show?

'This is me,' I said in a perky voice as we reached the sliding glass doors of my office building.

'Hey, I like you,' he said. 'You aren't one of those women who talks a lot. I dig that about you. When I saw you had studied law, I thought you'd be a feisty bitch. You're nice and quiet, like a good woman should be. Wanna have lunch?'

I seriously considered pouring my hot coffee over his crotch to jolt him out of the time warp he was in. Only, it'd be a complete waste of a good coffee. I did think, however, that I should set him straight, if only for the sake of the next girl he met.

'Look, pet, the only reason I have been quiet is because I'm half asleep. Second, don't ever, ever call your mother a "bitch" 'cause you know what? Unlike a female canine, she had the choice to terminate her pregnancy when she was carrying you. And, unfortunately for the rest of the world, she didn't. Also, your sister's sex life is none of your business. If you want a quiet, malleable chick, I suggest you look in the morgue because I doubt you'll find a willing live one. And, no, I won't have lunch with you,' I spat out before striding into my office.

'Oooo, feisty, come fuck me,' he jeered, as he did a geeky little dance move.

'Who's that?' Max asked as he held the lift door open for me.

'A person who has just proved the case for the use of abortion as a legitimate and humane means of contraception.'

'Look at you, Shani,' Max suddenly exclaimed when he finally got a good look at my bloodshot eyes. 'I knew you were lying when you said that you were breezing through the board report. You don't look like you've slept at all. Pulled an all-nighter, did you?' he snorted.

'Actually Max, I saw a million cracks in the brickwork and plaster in my unit last night, that's why I could not sleep. I'm on my way to call the people from whom I bought my unit to find out what the hell's happening!'

To put you in the picture, I need to fill in a few details about my dwelling, and why I was so upset about it. I'd bought my unit from a reputable builder a couple of years ago. It was the last unit to be sold in that housing development and as a result, I got a nice little discount even though it was located in the family-oriented, publess suburb of Blackburn. I had consoled myself with the thought that at least I wasn't living in a shoebox!

'You'll need to shelve your plans for chasing shonky builders for another day. John wants to meet with us in about ten minutes.'

'Excuse me? I'm pretty sure I don't have any meetings booked this morning.'

'Check your inbox. I booked a meeting with the three of us this morning,' he chirruped as he breezed past me out of the lift. I checked my iPhone, and yup, there it was. A meeting set up at 7.30 am – right when I was driving to work and couldn't check my email!

So I walked into the meeting with John and Max and got ambushed. Yet again!

'Brilliant game of tennis yesterday,' Max complimented John as both men sat down. 'How come I have never seen you at Tooronga before?'

'I usually get a game or two in before I come to work. But I never knew you played tennis ...'

'Was the tennis captain at St Kevins in my day ...' Max laughed, patting his too rounded tummy.

St Kevin's boys were known tosspots. St Cath's girls would not be caught dead going out with a wanker from St Kevs.

'Are you into rugby?

'Of course! My brother-in-law has a box at Etihad Stadium. I am sure we can squeeze you into the game this Friday. Beer and meat pies all provided!'

'Excellent. I'll come in my Wallabies gear.'

So, they were best friends now, were they? Were they going to start gushing too – complimenting each other on their cleats?

'By the way, I also have connections at the AFL. Been getting tickets to every grand final for the last five years!'

'Even the Magpies and Geelong games?'

'Yes, even those.'

'But those tickets are rare as hen's teeth.'

'I even get tickets to the Grand Final Breakfast.'

'Oh wow … I went to the Grand Final Breakfast with the CEO last year of course … but it was all business talk. Didn't get to meet any of the players. I'd love to meet some of them though.'

'Actually, I know a couple of Geelong players personally,' Max replied in a mock whisper.

That was it. I was not putting up with any more jock talk!

'Excuse, me …' I interjected, giving them a meaningful look. I was sure they were both going to start scratching their balls and chugging on a beer in a few moments.

'Sorry Shani,' John apologised with a wry grin.

'I'd invite you to shoe shopping,' I offered John with a smile. 'But no one makes any bones about that being a non-contact sport, so you'll have to get your protective gear sorted out first.'

John roared with laughter, 'I am sure I'd get to finally under-stand our largest customer base if I hung out with you, Shani!'

'Here's my first draft of the report for Shani's side of the business,' Max interjected, pompously handing over the documents. 'I commend you for your meticulous attention to detail. Why, it was hardly any work to pull this together.'

I smiled weakly.

'And how are you going on the report?' John asked, looking at my empty hands.

'I … I … should have something for you by the end of the week …'

'Shani, please let me know if I can help in anyway – I am more than happy to run through the basics with you if you are having any issues,' Max chimed in an earnest voice. 'I was sure you'd have no problems with the data, especially since you've had it for two weeks now!'

'Excuse me? I only got a cut of the data …'

'Remember I told you that there was a CD of the data in the stack of files I dropped off at your desk the very day after John spoke to us? Maybe you were too busy speaking with one of your friends …'

'I … I …' I mumbled. This man was pure evil.

'Maybe it's all this stress about your house,' Max said facetiously.

'Shani, what's going on with your house?' John asked, looking concerned.

'Oh nothing really …' I fibbed. I didn't want to appear like a drama queen. 'Just a few issues I need to iron out with the builder.'

'So soon? You only moved in a few months ago, didn't you?'

'Couple of years ago actually …'

'Make sure you don't let anything slip by,' John advised. 'You don't want to be out of pocket for anything!'

Easier said than done.

I grabbed the half-hour window of opportunity between back-to-back meetings to try to hunt down an answer as to why my house was becoming as fragile as a porcelain vase found at an archaeological dig. And I got nowhere fast. The whole process was like walking into a Swiss Bank vault with the ominous hissing as each door slammed shut in my face.

Firstly, I called the builder and was put on hold for a good twenty minutes. When I finally got through, it was to a call centre in Mumbai!

I am not racist by any stretch of the imagination – for obvious reasons – but I'll be damned if I am going to explain to Vivek from Uttrapradesh what plasterboard is when he's a) supposed to work for a construction company and b) when every second syllable I said had to be repeated because of the poor VOIP quality. Damnit – how can Elastoplast be in anyway confused with plasterboards! And no, I am not calling to complain about being injured while I was in a property built by you!

Anyway, after arguing with Vivek and then his boss Madame Padma and then her boss the Senior Vice President of Customer Service, Mr K.M.K. Poolisamy, my call was finally transferred back to Australia.

Not that I had much luck dealing with young lass who I knew to be sitting only a suburb and a half away.

'Where's your house?' she asked curtly.

'Blackburn, the Oakridge Development.'

'Not even sure that is one of our developments.'

'Yes, it is one of your developments. I have the contract of sale right in front of me.'

'You sure it's from ConMore Homes and not ConMore Developments? Because they are two different companies, you know.'

'Yes, I am sure I bought my house from ConMore Homes.'

'Okay, have you done any modifications to the property?'

'Barring changing the odd light bulb or two, no.'

'No new hot water service, air-conditioning or decking?'

'No.'

'No modifications to any of your bathrooms?'

'No!'

'No changes to your kitchen?'

'I hardly cook in my kitchen. Surely using a microwave cannot null and void a five-year warranty.'

'Okay then, let me take down your name and number and we'll call you.'

And she hung up no sooner had she typed in the last digit.

So, I was in an understandably foul mood when I met the second potential groom for the day as I ducked out for coffee mid-morning. I didn't even bother with niceties. When he asked the ubiquitous question 'Are you Shani?' I had no issue in turning around and telling him I was a lesbian. I knew I'd have to start coming up with more creative excuses once they started comparing notes down the track, but right then, my mind was frazzled. I despatched the next guy later in the day using the same excuse.

By the end of the day, I was no closer to getting an answer for the fragile state of my home nor had Max's 'correct' data turned out to be useful. If possible, it'd turned out to be worse! I had spent the rest of the day 'fixing' it, stifling a dreadful sense of déjà vu as I spent hours adjusting the anomalies – and getting another migrane for my efforts.

So when I was once more accosted by a Sri Lankan man – this one was loitering by the milk fridge in Woolies – on my way home, I snapped.

'Hey, you must be Shani,' the hapless guy said with an engaging smile.

I am not quite sure what scared him, but he took a hasty step back when I turned around. Most likely it was the manic glint in my eye, or it could have been the fact that my normal sartorial elegance had given way to the bedraggled state worthy of a bag lady. My silk blouse was spotted with coffee and my hair was out of its customarily elegant chignon, I had chewed off my lipstick and smudged my eyeliner, giving me the air of a feral panda. I managed not to snarl words to the effect of 'Who the fuck wants to know?'

'Yeah, I'm Shani.'

'How are you? My name is Suresh,' the guy said, cautiously.

Maybe he'd got the hint, but I wanted to make sure there was no mistake.

'Look mate, I've had a fucking awful day. I am not in the mood to talk to anyone. You've got my mobile number, so why don't you text me tomorrow?' I was close to tears. In fact, a stray tear may actually have slipped down my face.

'Err, yeah … Look, I don't think you are for me,' he said, furtively looking for a quick getaway. Smart guy. 'I mean, I don't want to get your hopes up or anything.'

To my surprise, the rejection actually stung. Badly. Normally, I did the rejecting. Not the other way around.

'Okay,' I said, crying in earnest now.

'Look, should I call anybody?' he asked, a little concerned.

'No, no, I'll be fine,' I sniffled back.

And with his duty done, he ran out the supermarket doors.

***

'Yes, I am Shani,' I said aggressively to the guy who dared to interrupt me while I waited for Una at our usual bar. I had handed John the first draft of my report though I was very uncomfortable with its quality. And I was even more on edge after I had noticed cracks in my floorboards this morning as well. 'What's it to you?'

'My name is Darshan,' the guy said a little apprehensively. 'I am so sorry to bug you, but I am a friend of Rohan's.'

'Oh, I am so sorry,' I said, truly contrite. I was turning into such a bitch. 'I was waiting for a friend …'

'Look, I'm really sorry to bug you, but I just got a call from Rohan. They've been trying to call you for a while,' he said.

'I just switched on my phone …'

'They didn't want to leave you a message. Apparently, your friend Una already knows and is on her way to the hospital. Maya has got a high fever and has been rushed to the Royal Children's Hospital.'

CHAPTER 17

Homecomings!

Maya's short but eventful trip to the Royal Children's Hospital turned out to be the result of a little overreaction. Amani had noticed that Maya was feeling a little warm and had told the nurse. While the nurse was checking the baby's temperature and calling the paediatrician, Aunty Chandra had got in on the act.

'Amani,' Aunty Chandra had said gravely, 'newborn babies need to be watched all the time. She could have an infection. My sister's second child, your cousin HemaMali, died from high fever when she was only two days old. My cousin Priyanthi, her brother's sister-in-law's child became a vegetable after the fever she had went to her head.' On and on Aunty Chandra droned, with a seemingly endless list of children who had died as a result of supposedly minor illnesses.

Under normal circumstances, Amani would have just ignored Aunty Chandra and told her to take a chill pill; but

Amani was new to the whole motherhood gig and wanted to do it right. By the time the paediatrician had checked little Maya out, Amani had been concerned but not alarmed. A dose of paracetamol had been ordered and administered to the baby. Unfortunately, that had not brought the temperature down as expected and Maya had been taken to the nurses' station for observation.

Aunty Chandra, of course, took this as a sign to start recounting all manner of rumours and half-truths about children's illnesses and how tenuous their grasp on life was. By the time Amani had been treated to two hours of unending horror about how easily a child could die, she was understandably agitated and nervous. She'd struggled through watching the nurses do a heel prick to draw blood for a blood test.

'Look, it's taken the nurse two tries to get a blood sample,' Aunty Chandra had complained, while Amani's heart clenched as her little daughter's little foot was being firmly held down to draw a sample of blood, while Maya screamed at the top of her lungs at the outrage done to her small body.

'Is this a good hospital?'

'We are in one of the best hospitals in the state,' Amani had responded with a little wobble to her voice. She rushed forward to comfort Maya, who was still wailing pitifully some time after the needle had been withdrawn.

When the paediatrician came to deliver the results of the blood test, Amani turned on him, convinced there was something dangerously wrong with her daughter. She did what came to her naturally when she was under stress. She cross-examined him as if he were a witness on the stand. A hostile witness.

After a forty-five minute, nerve-racking interview (for the doctor), he had suggested that the baby be transferred to the Royal Children's Hospital for observation. The private, five star hotel-like hospital that Amani had been taken to was not equipped to handle anything beyond the ordinary.

So Rohan got a hysterical call from Amani while she was riding in the back seat of the ambulance, commanding him to meet her and their child at the Royal Children's Hospital. Of course within hours of Maya being admitted to the Kids her temperature dropped and she was right as rain. Amani and Maya came home on Sunday as planned and Rohan had a couple of shots of whisky to calm himself down.

'Here's the happy family,' Tehara called out as Rohan carefully pulled up in front of their house. I don't think anybody had ever seen Rohan drive so slowly. It had taken him a good five minutes to come down the street; he could not have broken the forty kilometres per hour speed limit during the entire journey.

'Gehani, quick! Bring the video camera,' Una commanded.

We made a huge production of welcoming the new family home. Una, Tehara and I had decorated the whole house with pink balloons and pink crepe paper garlands. We even had pink champagne on hand!

'Get her out of the cold quickly,' Aunty Chandra commanded as we group-hugged our way up the path.

Amani settled the sleeping infant in her crib and then joined us in the lounge room. My parents were there, as well Gehani and Aunty Chandra. Muthu was hiding around the corner in his car. Once my parents and Aunty Chandra left, Tehara would let him know the coast was clear.

'I propose a toast,' my suddenly articulate brother said as he handed around the glasses of pink fizz. 'To the happy family!'

'To the happy family,' we all echoed, holding up our glasses.

'Isn't it strange,' Aunty Chandra quipped.

'What's strange?'

'You are celebrating, but someone somewhere else is crying,' she said with a superior smirk.

'Huh?'

'Well, Maya has just been born and you are celebrating her

birth. But someone somewhere else is crying because someone else had to die for her to be born. There cannot be birth without death, so spare a thought for those in tears,' she said with a piety bordering on the sanctimonious.

Of all the insensitive, stupid comments to make about reincarnation theory, that surely had to take the cake. The fact that she'd upset Amani, who was looking stricken and dismayed, did not seem to register with Aunty Chandra, who was too caught up in the wonder of connecting the dots in the cosmic recycling process to realise the effect her words had on her daughter.

Una, Tehara and I all started babbling simultaneously to break the awful silence that descended.

'So, was the food in hospital good?' I asked inanely, pulling Amani along into the kitchen.

'Yeah,' Amani said with a small giggle. 'I am not upset by her. Honestly, I'm not.'

'Well, if you are all settled, I'd better go,' Aunty Chandra called out as everybody started to settle in.

'*Amma*, why don't you stay?' Rohan asked perfunctorily.

'No, no. I had better go home and meditate. My meditation practice is in such an advanced state that I do not like to be with groups of people anymore. Jayanthi, can you drop me off?' she asked my mother.

My *Ammi* clearly wanted to stay and maybe even have a hand in cuddling the baby. Even my *Thathi* had put his iPod with his downloaded cricket game away and was looking expectantly towards the nursery door.

'But I don't want to trouble you, Jayanthi,' Aunty Chandra said. She turned away with her handbag and a sudden exaggerated limp that had not been there moments ago.

'Chandra, is your leg giving you pain again?'

'*Anay* yes, Jayanthi. Amani used to take me to see an acupuncturist, but now she doesn't.'

'*Ammi*, I just don't have the time or the energy to drive you all the way out to Berwick!'

'Well, women in Sri Lanka catch crowded buses to work. All this complaining about having to drive somewhere, Amani. You are just too lazy to bother!'

'But why can't you find an acupuncturist who lives nearby?'

'Because Hema Balasuriya is Sri Lankan and she is good!'

'I don't even think Hema Balasuriya is actually a qualified acupuncturist. Didn't she just learn the trade from her husband?'

'*Chee chee chee*, Amani, don't make up stories about a woman you've known since you were a baby. She went to TAFE and everything.'

'She went to TAFE to study horticulture, not acupuncture!'

'*Haa haa*, Chandra, Mahinda and I will drop you off,' my mother intervened hastily. Blind Freddy could see that Aunty Chandra and Amani were about to start a nuclear war.

'I am sure there are good acupuncturists who aren't Sri Lankan,' Amani shot back, wanting to have the last word.

'Not ones who are as cheap as Hema,' Aunty Chandra retorted, crankily.

'Okay, we're ready to go,' my *Ammi* called out as my father stood at the door jiggling his car keys as loudly as he dared. 'Gehani, make sure you come home at a decent hour. I'm making *pittu* and *pol kiri hodi* for dinner and it's best had warm,' she said, reaching to tuck his T-shirt into his pants.

Gehani, who towered over her by half a body length, looked aghast. He cast an embarrassed look Una's way and jerked out of my mother's reach. Una tactfully pretended not to notice.

'Amani, look after the baby well. Make sure she has plenty to drink,' Aunty Chandra counselled from the door as they finally left.

Everybody breathed a sigh of relief as the parental units left.

'I hope to God our children like us more than we like our parents,' Rohan said with a relieved droop of his shoulders.

'I think we may safely say they will,' Amani returned as she sank into the armchair.

'Muthu,' Tehara had called him on his mobile as soon the door had clicked shut on my parents. 'Come on in.'

We all sat in our familiar seats at Amani and Rohan's. Gehani, who was new to the scene, was an acceptable addition now that he was in on the Tehara/Muthu secret. He sidled up to Una and perched on the arm of her couch she was sitting on.

It took Muthu all of about a minute to walk through the back door. He must have parked in the laneway behind the house.

'Hey guys,' he began, stopping in alarm when he saw Gehani.

'Hey, *machang*! It's all good. I'm in on the secret,' Gehani said, affably.

'Can we trust him?'

'Yes, we can trust him,' Una smiled. 'Besides, we all know where he lives and how he likes his *paripu*. We can do him unspeakable damage if he crosses us.'

Even while she threatened him, Gehani looked on Una with unwavering adoration.

'Where's the pretty little girl?' asked Muthu.

'Sleeping, but we can have a peek,' Rohan said with a slightly cheeky grin. And the boys, including Gehani, trooped off to have a look.

'I hope she sleeps through the night,' Amani said, giving a little stretch. 'I could do with a good night's sleep. I just couldn't sleep in hospital.'

'What? You couldn't sleep in that five-star excuse for a hospital?'

'No, my back was killing me.'

'You should get that checked out. You don't want a bad back when you're carting around a toddler.'

'Too right,' Tehara seconded as the boys trooped back out.

'She is just gorgeous,' Muthu enthused. 'She looks exactly like you, Amani, but she has Rohan's hair.'

'Don't you just love her hair? All curly and long. I'm so used to seeing bald babies.'

'Aunty Sonali says that curly hair is a lucky sign for a little girl,' Una piped up.

'Are you still hanging out with that old bat?' Gehani asked with exasperation.

'She's not an old bat,' Una defended automatically. To which my brother raised a cocky eyebrow. 'Okay, she's old,' Una conceded. Gehani raised his eyebrow even higher. My brother, the amazing eyebrow man. Who would have thought it?

'Okay, I suppose she's a little batty,' Una conceded, grudgingly.

'Didn't she convince you not to buy a house in Malvern once?' Amani asked. 'Back when normal people could afford to buy houses in Malvern? I thought she said your *Kethu* conjuncted with your *Rahu* so buying a house that year was a bad idea.'

'Wasn't that, like, in 1999? Before the property boom,' Tehara reminded all present.

'Okay, she's a lot batty,' Una conceded with little grace. 'But she has a heart of pure gold ...'

'You would have had a bank vault full of gold if you'd bought that old worker's cottage off Kooyong Road,' I added. 'A place similar to that went for $1.5 million last week. You were only going to pay $95,000 for that place.'

'We who live in the mystical world have little care for such materialistic concerns,' Una replied in an airy-fairy tone.

'Yeah, but have you ever tried sneaking a spare biscuit at Aunty Sonali's? I still have a divot on my knuckles from when she rapped me over the hand for taking more than my regulation two Marie biscuits,' Gehani complained, holding his knuckles out for all to see.

'She *is* a bit of terror with her cane,' Una admitted.

'Hey girls, now that we are all together, was there a good reason why you thought I needed my French lingerie in a maternity ward? I haven't fitted into those bras for months,' Amani asked with a wry smile.

'Well, we didn't know what to pack,' I defended. 'It seemed wiser to pack everything rather than leave anything out.'

'I could have gone travelling for a year without doing laundry with all the stuff you packed for me!'

'I thought the neck pillow was inspired,' Rohan said as he settled himself next to Amani, giving his wife a cuddle. 'Did you think we could use it as a feeding pillow?'

'More seemed to be a better option than less,' Una added.

'Could you blame us after the last time?' I asked.

'Thank God I didn't need to do anything this time,' Gehani added with a delicate wince and a fierce blush. Yes, we Sri Lankans blush. Our ears go red.

'What gives, guys?' Muthu asked, scenting a mystery.

'You've never told him?' Amani asked Tehara.

'Some things are best forgotten,' Tehara admitted with a shudder.

'Come on, spill. I feel a good story coming on!'

'Let Shani tell the story, she does it best,' Amani pointed out.

'Strap yourself in, Muthu, 'cause you may ditch all of us as friends by the time Shani finishes,' Rohan warned.

CHAPTER 18

The Importance of Being Earnest

When Amani and Rohan got married five years ago, they did so in Sri Lanka. Why? It was not because Rohan's parents lived there. They lived in Dubai, where his father has worked for an oil company for the last twenty years, and they were happy for Rohan to get married anywhere.

It wasn't because all of Amani and Rohan's friends were in Sri Lanka either. We were all here in Australia. And it wasn't because all of the extended families were back in Sri Lanka. All of Aunty Chandra's siblings and late Uncle Presantha's family lived in Australia.

No, Amani and Rohan got married in Sri Lanka because Aunty Chandra nagged and nagged and nagged until she got her way. She wanted to invite *all* the family to Amani's wedding. And her family has as many members as a moderate-sized termite mound.

So, in Sri Lanka, Aunty Chandra invited not just immediate family and extended family, but the in-laws, out-laws and their neighbours. Their dogs came as well along with their fleas. The final count of guests at the wedding reception was 500. Yes, 500. Give or take a few fleas ...

In the end, one could have been thankful for having the wedding there, because without converting Australian dollars to rupees, nobody other than the late Kerry Packer could have afforded to pay for it.

So three weeks before the accurately calculated *nekath* day, we all trooped to Sri Lanka in a pageant worthy of a royal procession of a bygone era. Imagine the opening sequence of the movie *Titanic* where they load the car onto the boat, only in our case the spectacle took place at Tullamarine Airport with a seriously disgruntled Customs officer. Each one of us took at least five pieces of luggage because we had to take everything from Australia, including our *sarees* (three each because we had three separate functions we needed to dress for), wedding cakes (Sri Lankan cakes were apparently not up to scratch) and enough clothes for any possible occasion that may arise.

We ended paying as much money to transport our excess luggage as we did for our plane tickets.

Once we got to Sri Lanka, the real mayhem descended upon us. Una, Tehara and I had decided very early on that we were going to bunk together at Tehara's father's house in Colombo 7. It was quiet, it was private, and it was close to all the night-clubs. My mother was cool with this because she hoped I'd meet a nice, rich Colombo 7 guy.

We were halfway to Tehara's father's glorious mansion, complete with swimming pool, air-conditioning, maid service and chauffeured car, when Aunty Chandra dropped a cluster bomb.

'*Anay* Jayanthi, who's to be looking after these girls?

You don't know the things that happen in Sri Lanka these days!'

'Aunty Chandra, *Thathi* has a security guard at the house.'

'All the same, last week Sonali told me that a woman was murdered in her Colombo 7 apartment and fed as ground meat to her dogs!'

'Oh yes, I heard that on the *Rupavahini*. I also read in *Divaina* about four girls who were raped and abducted here in Colombo,' my mother added to our horror. We could see where this was going to end up.

'Yes, and did you also hear about that lady who was abducted when she was on her way to pay her phone bill? Apparently, the three-wheel driver knew she had money in her purse and cut her arm off to get the money!' Aunty Chandra then threw herself into recounting the graphic details with enthusiastic abandon. 'It took five policemen and a whole squad of police dogs to find all her body parts.'

'Probably 'cause the dogs made off with the bones,' I muttered.

'Very funny to you, but think of the poor woman's family. Apparently they had to make a dummy for the casket,' Aunty Chandra continued.

It's a tradition in Sri Lanka to have open caskets at funerals. Don't get me wrong, I've heard the logic that it makes the bereaved confront death. But every time I see someone kiss a corpse, I feel like barfing up breakfast.

'Last month I heard that one old lady was murdered in her bed for a radio,' my *ammi* said, continuing the house of horrors stories. 'Look, I think it's better if the girls stay with a proper family.'

'Yes, yes,' Aunty Chandra agreed while Una, Tehara and I were vigorously shaking our heads in the negative.

'But *Ammi* …' I started.

'But nothing, Shani. You and Una can stay with us in Mount Lavinia and Tehara can stay with Chandra and Amani in Nugegoda,' *Ammi* directed us, much to Gehani's delight.

'But Tehara and I are free agents,' Una cut across urgently.

'*Anay* Chandra, explain to this poor white girl why she can't stay by herself in Colombo.'

'Darling Una *patiyo*, it is not safe for young girls like you to stay by yourselves here!' Aunty Chandra explained as if she were speaking to a five-year old.

'But we want to stay together!'

'I don't have the room,' *Ammi* fretted.

'Oh but ...' Aunty Chandra looked crestfallen. For all her concern about propriety, she was a cheapskate and didn't want us eating at her house the whole time.

'They can stay with us at night and spend the day at the house in Colombo 7,' Amani compromised. That way, Amani could escape her mother with regular frequency as well.

So that was how Una, Amani, Tehara and I ended up rooming together in a tiny bedroom in a poorly ventilated house in Nugegoda before Amani's wedding. Aunty Chandra's mortal fear of thieves meant that we could not open the windows at night either; it was a miracle that we didn't die of suffocation.

By the end of three weeks, even such lifelong friends as us four were ready to kill each other. Actually, we were ready to kill Aunty Chandra, but matricide has such a heavy karmic debt. It'd be like buying a Ferrari on Amex card and not being able to keep up with the minimum repayments.

As the wedding day dawned, Aunty Chandra almost had a meltdown from excitement, anxiety and panic. She ran around, getting in our way as we were preparing.

The *saree* dresser appeared at the house at 9 am to dress us for the wedding in the afternoon. Each time she started doing our hair, makeup or even dressing the bride, Aunty Chandra would interrupt her, concerned about her own *saree*, hair or makeup. By the time the bridal party had finished dressing, I could have sworn that dresser had downed a valium with her can of Coke. She richly deserved it.

As we waited for the car, Aunty Chandra came in to chat with Amani. She hurriedly shooed us from the room, wheeling in the little carry case Amani had packed for her honeymoon. Aunty Chandra came back out after only a couple of minutes, looking even more flustered and panicky as the driver in the car honked his horn.

'What did your mother say to you?' Una asked as we sat in the interminable Colombo traffic.

'She tried to tell me all about sex,' Amani said with an infectious giggle, which gave way to an insane bout of laughing.

'What exactly did she tell you?'

'She told me that Rohan would know what to do tonight.' She puffed as she struggled to regain breath from laughing.

'What? That was it? That was your sex talk? Your *entire* sex talk?' Una asked, as she fell off the car seat laughing.

'Yup, and she said she'd re-packed my overnight bag. Could you have a look and re-pack it again?'

'Yeah, sure,' Tehara promised with an evil grin.

After the official wedding business (the *poruwa* procession had been blessedly short because Amani had point blank refused to be part of something that resembled a mardi gras parade), Tehara, Una and I went into the bridal suite to look through Amani's suitcase. It was not like Amani needed us; she and Rohan were occupied in a greeting line that stretched out the doors of the reception venue into the hotel lobby.

Aunty Chandra had re-packed the suitcase, alright; it was full of gowns worthy of a chaste Victorian maiden. And one intent on remaining that way.

'What the bleeding hell is this?' Tehara asked, holding up a voluminous cotton nightgown complete with a lace button-up collar, long sleeves with buttoned cuffs, and a ruffle down the middle. 'This suitcase is full of these things.'

'Hey, I know what it is!' Una said with an excited shout. 'I saw something exactly like that in *A Room with a View*.'

'Bloody hell, Aunty Chandra has even packed grandma knickers,' I said, holding up a massive pair of panties.

'Thank goodness, we are here to save the day!'

Aunty Chandra had also packed a bed sheet. It was not like they were honeymooning in a caravan park. They were going on a tour of Nuwara Eliya and staying at some of the finest highland five-star resorts.

So, Tehara, Una and I decided we'd go for a quick shop at the French lingerie shop in the lobby of the Colombo Hilton. We didn't need to worry about sizes; Amani and I had been borrowing each other's bras since Year 10.

We tossed out all the stuff Aunty Chandra had packed and replaced it with kinky nighties, teddies and a nice little French maid's outfit. The only thing of Aunty Chandra's contributions we left in the suitcase was the bed sheet, which we cut up with a pair of nail scissors and plaited it into a cotton dominatrix whip. We placed that on top of all the other clothes.

'Hoocha!' Una said as she snapped the whip around her head. 'Amani will have fun with this.'

We really felt that we'd finally got one over Aunty Chandra when we waved the happy couple goodbye. Actually, that was the last we saw of Aunty Chandra until the official 'Homecoming', because she abandoned us and went to stay with some relative who was living near a local monastery. So much for ensuring the security of unmarried girls!

The official 'Homecoming' for the happy couple was held at Rohan's parents' house in the mountain city of Kandy. Tehara, Una and I had caught the train up the night before. We were all in really good form because we'd spent the intervening days between the wedding and homecoming partying at the many nightclubs in Colombo and staying at Tehara's luxurious mansion. God bless maid service! Nothing quite like getting breakfast in bed and having your bed made while you shower.

The couple were supposed to arrive at the correct *nekath* time late in the afternoon. Tehara, Una and I had arrived at Rohan's parents' home in the morning to help them set up.

We were helping Aunty Pooja, Rohan's mother, with decorations when we overheard a conversation between my *ammi* and Aunty Chandra.

'You know, I have the utmost confidence in my girl's purity,' Aunty Chandra had intoned sanctimoniously to my mother.

'Really?' my mother asked sceptically. My mother can be many things, but naive she most certainly is not.

'Why yes, she could not even speak properly when I had our mother–daughter chat right before the wedding,' Aunty Chandra said loftily. 'She is such a decent girl. I put a white bed sheet in her suitcase so that she can prove her purity this afternoon.'

Una, Tehara and I looked at each other in abject horror. Surely that was not the sheet Tehara, Una and I had ripped up and plaited into the whip?

'Would she know what the sheet was for?' my *Ammi* asked.

'Rohan will tell her,' Aunty Chandra replied. 'Besides, I've already invited the *dhobi* woman, Rohan's *Loku Amma* and Rohan's amma to inspect the sheets later this afternoon. Pooja wasn't very keen on the idea, but I insisted. My daughter has nothing to hide.' Aunty Chandra pointed out a wizened old *dhobi* woman whose job would be to wash the soiled bedclothes and Rohan's *Loku Amma*, a stern, matronly looking woman who looked more like a jail warden than a kindly aunt.

Shit.

'If anything, she has to prove her son is up for the job. As you know, blood stains aren't the only thing they need to look for,' Aunty Chandra continued.

'The Kandyans are well known for chasing out brides who

are not pure. Why, Sonali told me a girl was divorced just last year on the grounds of insufficient proof of purity. It turned out the poor girl was born without a hymen!'

Holy shit!

Una, Tehara and I slowly backed out of Rohan's parents' lounge room and convened a hasty meeting in the driveway. We had to save Amani's marriage! Who knew it would all be about about purity and shit?

'What the fuck are we going to do?' Una asked in a panic.

'We need to get a soiled sheet to her is what we need to do,' Tehara pointed out bluntly.

'How are we going to soil it?' I asked as Tehara signalled to the chauffeur who was having a cigarette around the corner of the house to come with the car.

'We'll prick a finger and squirt some blood on it!'

'I hate needles,' I squirmed.

'You are such a girl, Shani! Fine, I'll prick my own fucking finger.'

'We also need some snot,' Tehara said. 'Remember they said they don't just look for blood, they also look for semen stains?'

How were we going to get a semen-looking stain? Everybody around us looked the picture of health; there was not a snotty hanky in sight.

'We'll worry about that later,' Una said as we all climbed into Rohan's father's car. 'Take us into town,' Una commanded the driver who took off down the windy, mountainous roads like Michael Schumacher, only with a tiny fraction of the Formula 1 driver's exceptional motoring skills.

We quickly ducked into the first manchester shop in Kandy. Something about our extreme panic must have tipped off the sales assistant because we paid a ridiculous amount of money for a simple bed sheet.

Once we got the sheet back to the house, we needed to find something to get some blood out of one of us.

'Aunty Pooja,' I gently nudged, 'may I have a needle and some cotton? A hook came off my *saree* blouse.'

We sent the poor harassed woman off to find a needle and she came back with one that had definitely seen better days.

'Okay,' Una said stoically, 'I've had my tetanus shot recently. All we need to do is hold the needle to a flame and burn off any germs that may be on it.'

'Okay.' Tehara, squeamish as ever, looked like she was about to pass out.

We were in Rohan's parents' kitchen, holding out a needle to be sterilised when we were sprung. By my brother, Gehani.

'What the hell are you doing?' he yelled as I held a flaming hot needle that Una was about to puncture her finger with. Una was already grimacing for the pain that was about to come. Tehara had stuffed her fist in her mouth. And I was trying my hardest not to barf.

Una broke down and we confessed everything to Gehani. Having an additional conspirator ended up not being such a bad thing because Gehani remembered that Rohan's father was diabetic (like all Sri Lankan men over fifty seem to be these days), but more importantly, he knew where Rohan's father kept his glucose testing kit.

Keen to show off his James Bond-like stealth to Una, Gehani scaled the side of the house into the study and nicked the glucose testing kit. He even volunteered to donate a sample of blood to smear on the sheet.

'Is that all you need me to do?' Gehani asked, as we theatrically smeared the blood from his bleeding finger all over the bed sheet.

'Well actually Gehani …' Una said, blushing fiercely as she pulled Gehani aside. I wasn't going to ask my brother. 'We actually need some …'

'No fucking way!' he yelled as soon as Una was able to gargle out the word semen.

'But please ...' Una pleaded with wide eyes. 'She's like a sister to you. You wouldn't want Amani's marriage to start off on the wrong foot?'

'But she and Rohan have been at it for years!'

'Yeah, but appearances matter, you know that.'

Gehani turned back to see Tehara and me looking on worriedly. We all knew that the stakes were high. Things like this could make or break a Sri Lankan marriage. We had visions of overturned tables of food, relatives storming off in a huff as Amani was cruelly thrown out into the rain for not being a virgin. Rohan would then be forced to marry a picture-perfect boring Lankan girl and Amani would die of misery. We all loved Amani and Rohan too much to allow that to happen.

'Okay, fine!' Gehani said without much grace as he grabbed the sheet and stomped away to scale the side of the house again. He went back the study where the computer was, complete with internet access.

'At least we didn't have to look for a stash of *Playboy* magazines,' Tehara consoled.

'Well, I never thought I'd be thankful for internet porn ...' I added as Gehani came back down about twenty minutes later, gingerly holding out the neatly folded bed sheet.

The task of getting the soiled sheet into Amani's suitcase was relatively easy. As the happy couple drove up, we were at the forefront of the welcoming committee. We didn't so much as greet Amani and Rohan as we leapt to the boot and wrestled to get to her luggage. We stuffed the sheet into the Louis Vuitton suitcase before the driver had even cut the engine, our erratic behaviour hopefully masked by the hordes of people swarming around the newlyweds.

Things nearly went pear-shaped again when Amani was ceremoniously ushered away to present the sheet to the inspection panel consisting of Aunty Pooja, Aunty Chandra, Rohan's aunt and the old *dhobi* woman.

'Daughter, it's time to show us,' Aunty Chandra cajoled as she tried to whisk Amani into the nearest bedroom as the couple entered Rohan's parents' home as man and wife for the first time.

'Show you what?'

'Oh, come on, Amani, no need to be shy now.'

'I am serious, show you what exactly?' Amani queried, in evident frustration, while Una, Tehara and I were furiously gesturing to her from behind Aunty Chandra.

'Now, you unmarried girls should go away. There is nothing you need to know here,' Aunty Chandra said, tersely shooing the three of us away.

Quick-thinking Una saved the day by pretending to trip over her *saree* hem as we were pushed away.

'Don't worry about anything,' Una had whispered urgently as Amani helped her back up to her feet. 'We've taken care of everything. Just go with her …'

And that was it. By the time I'd finished telling the story Muthu was rolling on the lounge room floor, doubled over with laughter.

'Imagine my surprise when I pulled out a damp bed sheet from my suitcase,' Amani said, wiping tears of laughter from her eyes. 'The thing was so bloody and soiled that you'd have thought Rohan had murdered me!'

'Well, that's gratitude for you. We didn't want the two of you to be forced into a divorce, that's all,' Tehara snapped.

'See, you can trust me,' Gehani said to Muthu. 'I'll be taking that story to my grave.'

Just as everybody was settling down from their laughter, little Maya gave a wail indicating that she was hungry. 'Time for lunch,' said Amani, getting up.

As the afternoon progressed, however, it became clear that Maya was rather unsettled. She kept crying and fussing even though she'd been well fed, changed and comforted. Nothing seemed to soothe her.

'Young babies can be a little fussy,' Una dismissed.

'Yeah, they can cry buckets,' both Tehara and Muthu seconded Una.

Amani and Rohan took to walking the little girl up and down the long corridor between the nursery and the lounge room. They barely paid us any attention as they focused their attention wholly on their child.

'Look, I'd better go,' I said over Maya's near deafening screams.

'Hey, Una, fancy a drink before you turn in tonight?' Gehani asked casually while swallowing convulsively.

'No, pet, I need to get home and do a ton of laundry.'

'Yeah, yeah …' Gehani said, trying not to look crushed.

Amani, however, was looking completely devastated by her daughter's uncontrollable crying.

'Yeah, we'd better go too,' Muthu and Tehara added as we flocked to the front door like people bolting out of the way of a tsunami.

'Yeah, see you later.'

As the door closed behind us, we could hear the sheer hell little Maya was raising. 'There's nothing wrong with that girl's lungs,' Muthu commented.

'They're parents,' Gehani said, with the cheerful heartlessness of someone who hadn't experienced fatherhood. 'They'll figure it out.'

Looking back, I can see with blinding clarity that Amani and Rohan were about as clueless with babies as we were. The young of our species were completely alien to those of us who'd grown up in nuclear families. I had never changed a nappy and I was pretty sure Amani hadn't either.

As I drove away in the blessed quietness of my car, I spied Amani through the window. Maya was screaming while Amani paced up and down the hallway, limping from her bad back. Parenting sure involved a steep learning curve!

CHAPTER 19

Does the Roof Need to Fall in for Someone to Take Me Seriously?

I love the Yarra River. I love how it meanders through Melbourne, providing a safe haven for water birds and duck-billed platypuses. I also love the parks that dot the Yarra along the way, like tinsel hung with Christmas ornaments – especially since I'd taken to spending copious amounts of time in those parks like some homeless juvenile delinquent. Why? Because I didn't feel safe. In my own home, that is.

'Hmm ...' the middle-aged building inspector said as he walked slowly around my house early that Saturday morning.

'Hmm?' I asked, cocking my head to the side, hoping he would take the hint to elaborate further. When he didn't take the hint, I asked him. 'So, what do you think?'

'Hmm ... very interesting ...'

He poked here and he poked there. He shone his light into crevices; he crawled in the roof cavity and dug around the foundations as if he were lost in some sort of primitive treasure hunt. He took copious notes, none of which I could decipher when I tried reading them over his shoulder.

'Can I get you a cup of tea?'

'No. I don't drink tea.'

'How about a cup of coffee then?'

'Don't drink coffee either.'

'A stubbie? I have couple of Crownies in the fridge.'

Damn it, I *needed* to find out what was wrong with my house. It wasn't like I was getting answers from the shonky bastards who had built it. Every day last week I'd queued behind 300 other people at the offices of ConMore trying to get to the bottom of why my previously sound house had started disintegrating like an alcoholic party queen at the Spring Racing Carnival. Then I would rush back to work to spend the evenings and nights polishing up the final draft of my board report.

'I wouldn't mind a glass of water, though,' the building inspector said after he'd spent another twenty minutes crawling around the roof space for the second time.

I jumped at the chance to do something that might get a word out of this man about the state of my house. As I poured a glass of bottled water from the fridge, he walked in through the back door, carefully removing his steel-capped work boots first.

'Here you go! So can I have the verdict? Should I be moving out?'

'Hmmm ...'

What was I going to do? It was going to kill me if I had to move back in with my parents, but even that would be preferable to certain death I would face if my roof caved in.

'Hmm ...' he said, draining his glass. He slowly walked toward the table and sat down, massaging his head. 'This is what I think ... I don't think you need to move out just yet. I'm going to put everything in my report ...'

'When can I expect the report?'

'Tuesday.'

'Is the house safe to live in until then?'

'It depends ...' he said, as he drifted off again. He had come highly recommended by Rohan, so I swallowed my frustration.

'On what?'

'On a few things.'

'Such as?'

'Do you cook?'

'No.'

'Good. Then I reckon you ought to be fine until all the testing is done.'

I should tell my mother that my lack of cooking skills had finally netted some benefits.

'What testing?' I asked.

I so needed Rohan here. He would have come, but I think the new parents were having a bit of a meltdown. From the rather hysterical call I had from Amani last night, I gathered little Maya didn't believe in sleep. I'd even had a long chat with Rohan later, supposedly about my house, but he was desperately worried and wanted to talk about Amani and Maya – apparently sleep deprivation and exhaustion were making Amani's moods swing faster than a pair of hips in a hula-hula competition.

'You'll need to get the pressures on the joists re-tested,' the inspector continued, in a matter-of-fact way that was beginning to get on my nerves.

'Is that it?'

'No ... you need to get soil testing done too.'

'Do you know how much that will cost?'

'A couple of grand,' he replied vaguely, then went over and shook a door.

'Hey!' I protested as cracked plaster started falling on my polished wooden floors.

'You'll need to get someone to have a look at the concrete slab.'

'How much will that cost?'

'A bit.' It was truly like pulling teeth.

'And you'll need to get the plumbing looked at as well. And the electrical.'

I gritted my teeth and asked the question that needed to be asked, 'How much do you think that'll cost?'

'A fair bit.'

'But is it safe to live here?'

'Just don't knock into anything,' he advised as he walked out the door.

I wanted to cry. Not a sniffling sob, but a good kicking-my-legs-while-pounding-the-floor-with-my-fists kind of cry. But the crying would make my eyes red and my nose snotty, and the drumming of my heels on the floor might possibly cause my house to collapse. So I held myself back.

Instead, to work off the anxiety I was running alongside the Yarra near Dight's Falls as if the hounds of hell were at my heels. It was late in the afternoon and soon it'd be too dark to run. I had switched on my phone for safety.

I stopped briefly to stretch and started running again. I had been on the Monash University cross-country team and I still could run ten kilometres in under an hour.

Breathe … breathe … everything will be alright … breathe … breathe … I kept repeating the mantra to myself.

Things weren't really all that bad. Sure, I could be homeless very soon. But what's in a house, anyway? It's only bricks and mortar. And the greatest sum of money I had ever spent. Not to mention the months I had spent decorating!

I felt a panic attack coming on so I went back to my mantra. Breathe … breathe … everything will be alright … breathe … breathe …

I felt another panic attack approaching when I realised that another runner had joined me on the walking track. Though he didn't look like a regular runner; he was greying and quite overweight. Suppose everyone has to start somewhere.

I kept doing laps of the walking circuit and he kept following behind. I was very aware of him, not because I thought he could hurt me, but because he was seriously out of breath. After a while, I had run fast enough to do an extra lap and had managed to overtake him. He was leaning against a gum tree trying to catch his breath when I did a second run past. He was trying to say something, so I stopped.

'Are ... you ... Shani?' the man gasped between breaths.

'Yes,' I replied, quite alarmed because the man was shaking visibly.

'My name is ... Karu ...' he gasped. 'I got a text message that you wanted to meet with me.'

He sat heavily down on the ground and started to pant.

'Look, my mother put me up to it ...' my voice trailed off as soon as I noticed his lips were turning blue. Holy crap!

'You're not feeling well! Do you want me to call someone?'

'... ambulance?' he gasped before his eyes started rolling in his head.

And that was how I got to meet the tenth man on my mother's list of potential grooms. It was quite romantic, really. I held his hand in the twilight of a cold autumn evening by Dight's Falls as water birds nested in the nearby reeds. I waited patiently, hoping, as the ambulance turned up, sirens wailing and all, that he would not die.

CHAPTER 20

'Please Explain ...?' Yes, it's Me Shani –NOT Pauline Hanson

Okay, so I finally got the construction report from the building inspector that Rohan recommended, all 100 pages of it, excluding pictures. It was meticulous in its details, complete with diagrams, complex calculations and mathematical formulae worthy of Albert Einstein.

And I could not understand a word of it. Don't get me wrong, I am not dumb. I work with mathematical formulae all the time. But rarely with quadratic equations or integrals that stretch over five pages! I am an accountant for god's sake.

I felt like I was in high school reading Dostoyevsky – reading and re-reading the same sentence over and over again! And no matter how many times I tried to re-arrange the verb–noun–adverb combination – it did not make a skerrick of sense!

So I called in the reinforcements. Rohan. I knew he and Amani were completely stressed out by the baby – so I made it easy by popping into the café next to his offices in the Docklands.

'What have you done now?' he asked with a wry grin when he spotted me sitting at the café, chugging on a macchiato for dear life. 'If you don't chill, Shani, you're going to snap in two,' he teased as I handed the report over to him.

'So, what does it mean?'

'Hang ten … deep breaths, Shani. Deep breaths. Let me read this,' he advised as he perched his reading glasses on the end of his nose. 'Nothing is ever as bad as it seems. It's the same thing I keep telling Amani. The woman is running herself into the ground trying to be the perfect mum!'

'Isn't it a bit early to be starting the "perfect mum" thing? Maya is only five weeks old!'

'Yeah, well tell Amani that. Maya has already started Music Appreciation for Newborns twice a week and Amani hit the roof yesterday when Maya dropped from being in the seventy-fifth percentile for height and weight to the sixty-fifth!'

'She facebooked that last week. And then she spoke to me at length about some research from the University of Shinchua in China which had correlated rapid decline in percentile growth with intellectual impairment.'

'Where's the University of Shinchua anyway?'

'Rohan, I was so worried that I looked it up. It's on the border between China and Tibet. And the original research was published in Mongolian so who knows what it actually said! I think you need to restrict internet access in your house, Rohan. For your own sanity!'

'I know, Shani, I know. But Amani loses the plot every time she can't cross-check the developmental milestones on parenting websites! She was positively livid with the Maternal Child Health nurse when she told Amani that there was an age range for developmental milestones and some other expert had said something else. She wants Maya to be in ninety-ninth percentile for everything!'

'Oh my god! Amani has turned into her mother!'

Rohan looked up from the report, completely horrified.

'Don't worry, we'll do something about this. We'll get her a brain transplant or something if we need to. We'll smack Aunty Chandra out of Amani if it is the last thing we do!'

'Oh don't worry about Amani and Maya. You've bought a lemon!'

'What exactly do you mean?' I shrieked, but Rohan put a calming hand over mine to stop me from jumping out of my chair.

'It's all here in the report. Nothing about the house is right. The electricals are shoddy, the foundation block was not properly set and they have used sub-standard timber for the roof ... that's why it looked fine to begin with and then started to deteriorate. Look!' he said, pointing to an obscure mathematical equation.

'What does it mean?'

'It means that unless the company that built your house is willing to put some serious dough into remediation, they will need to demolish and rebuild it! And that might just well end up being cheaper!'

I started to hyperventilate. Something I haven't done since Tehara, Amani, Una and I accidentally smuggled hash cookies out of Amsterdam in our backpacks on Eurorail. Una spotted the uneaten packet as we reached the border with Germany. As the ticket checker came past quick-thinking Amani tossed it out the open window.

Rohan instantly sprang into action, getting me a bag to breathe into and a glass of water. 'Okay now?' he asked, sitting down as soon as I could breathe normally. I nodded, though my eyes were glazed over.

'From what I can see, you'll need to move out some time in the next six months so that the remediation work can begin.'

'But where will I move to?'

'How about your parents'?'

'Surely you jest! I wouldn't escape my mother's clutches with my name intact, much less my sanity.'

'Una or Tehara?'

'Yes, I guess it will have to be either one of them,' I conceded, tears pouring down my face.

Rohan came around and gave me a warm hug and gently rubbed my back. And for a psychotic moment, the intense pain that had once pierced me when Rohan and Amani got together came to the fore. I had long since stopped wondering what my life would have been like if I hadn't unwittingly introduced them to each other. It must have been the shock of the news about my house that led me down this unconscionable train of thoughts.

'Look Shani, it's not all that bad. They'll probably have to demolish your house, but I will make sure what they re-build for you is rock solid, hmm?'

Rohan walked me to the tram stop and waited till I got on the tram back to work.

When I got back to my office, the red light on my phone answering service was flashing like that on a police car. I was sure they'd all be calls from my mother so I ignored them. I really did not want to have a discussion about Karu, the man who was undergoing a quadruple bypass because of me. I so did not want to dwell on the karmic debt I had just signed up for thanks to that incident.

But I really needed to talk to *someone*, or my brain would explode. It was nearly mid-afternoon so I knew it would be pointless to call Tehara; she'd be on rounds. I couldn't call Una because she'd been on night shift. That left Amani, to whom I'd normally have no qualms about putting in a call, but I was worried about waking the baby and such. So, I texted her to call me back urgently if it were possible.

I was about to the switch off my mobile (it was semi-permanently off now as a matter of precaution) when Amani rang back.

'Hey,' she said in a tiny voice. 'Just spoke to Rohan. I was going to call you just before you texted me.'

'What's up?' I asked. This wasn't the normally upbeat and chirpy Amani I knew and loved.

'Nuttin',' she replied in an even smaller whisper.

'*Machang*, where are you talking from? You sound like you're in a tunnel somewhere.' The call dropped out for a second or so. Amani lived in inner-city Melbourne and her reception ought to be crystal clear.

'I'm hiding in a wardrobe.'

'Why?'

'Because I don't want *her* to wake up.'

'Why not go outside and speak?'

'The baby monitor doesn't work outside the house 'cause of all the wireless networks. And I really need her to sleep. Hell, *I* need to sleep!'

'Why don't you, then?' I asked, before realising it mightn't have been the most intelligent thing to say.

'Because I *can't* fall asleep! My back is still very sore and I can't stop thinking.'

'What about?'

'Everything and anything. It's like my mind has gone into overdrive. I think of a million things I need to do, like booking Maya into Gymbaroo, doing the cleaning, doing the washing, doing the vacuuming, reading a book. I just can't stop. Even when I close my eyes, I can't *relax*,' Amani said, her voice rising on a sob.

'Have you tried taking a bath?' It was the first thing that popped into my head.

'No, Maya might wake up and I am not moving well.'

'Could your mum come over and help?'

'No,' Amani snapped, venomously. 'She came over yesterday and did enough damage.'

'What did she do?'

'Well, I was sitting on the couch feeding Maya when she came in. The poor child was really hungry so she was really tucking in. So *Ammi* leant over her, I thought she was going to kiss her but she said, "Maya, you owe your mother for every single drop of milk you drink."'

Amani was crying in earnest now. As I have said before, the Sri Lankan mother-guilt thing starts *very* early. Amani swallowed a sob, and continued:

'But I don't want Maya to grow up like that. You know, being constantly dragged down by her parents.'

'You and Rohan would never do that.'

'But what if I do it accidentally?' Amani asked. 'I am not holding things together. I nearly lost it with *Ammi* yesterday when she said that Maya was a bad child for giving her parents so much grief.'

'Honey, some day you, Rohan or I are going to snap at your mum and try to rip her head off. It may be Tehara. She even drives Una to distraction. Your mother could do well with a reality check. Seriously, the woman lives in a planet of her own.'

'But ... what if I'm secretly just like her?'

We'd reached the unspoken fear we all shared, with the possible exception of Una. Each of us lived in perpetual fear that one day we might turn into our mother.

'You are not like her, *machang*, and you know it,' I lied effortlessly, making a mental note to talk to her about her Aunty Chandra tendencies another time.

'I am just so ... I can understand why parents snap at their children now.'

'Have you snapped at Maya?'

'No, I yelled at Rohan instead for leaving the toilet seat up.'

'Oh come on!' I tried to cheer her up with an attempt at humour. 'A man who leaves the toilet seat up is always fair game.'

'I suppose …'

'How can we make you feel better, *machang*?'

'I just need some sleep. And maybe you could book me a massage? One of those people who come over to your house and do it? My back is just killing me.'

'Consider it done!'

I overheard Maya give a grunt in the background.

'Look, Bessy the milk cow is wanted, I had better go,' Amani said as she hung up, even before I could say goodbye.

It felt good to help Amani with her crisis. All the same, I felt as if all of the building blocks of my life were being slowly dismantled; I was certainly in no doubt that my house was in jeopardy. And I had narky feeling that Max had been bitching to John behind my back too. Over the last few weeks, I'd found myself more and more on the outer, being left out of meeting and things. Not only that, Max and his platypus-faced wife had had John and his wife over for dinner and bridge – like a really bad 1950s soap opera!

I mean WTF? I'd gladly invite John and his wife over for dinner – only I didn't cook and my house was falling apart. I wasn't in a relationship so I'd ask one of my friends to co-host, which *could* cast doubts to my sexual orientation. Not that that would bother me – but damn it, being a single woman was difficult.

And I was angry. Not quite sure whom I was angry with but the life I had worked so hard to build from scratch was coming apart at the seams. It's hard work fitting yourself into a brand new country where your welcome is often, at best, a little grudging. I had worked hard to establish my career and achieve those milestones, tangible and intangible, that said I belonged. So why did it all feel so tenuous now?

CHAPTER 21

It Must Be a Full Moon ... or There Must Be Something in the Water!

When my family first immigrated to Australia twenty-one years ago, there was one shop in the whole of Melbourne where you could buy your spices: Hindustani Imports. The only one in the entire city. No Indian/Sri Lankan grocers on every street corner. They are newer additions to the suburban streetscape.

In the early years, each month would see us making the trip out to Dandenong where spices and Sri Lankan groceries were shipped in by the container load. The 'shop', as such, was the tiny office that was attached to the warehouse. As kids, my brothers and I used to have a wonderful time running around the mountains of stacked groceries, completely oblivious to the occupational health and safety risks associated with teetering stacks of pallets and shipping crates. The warehouse was bitterly cold in winter and stinking hot in summer. Looking back, I am amazed that nobody died during summer from the combined heat and vapours rising off the sacks of chillies and black peppers.

Some traditions never change. My mother and I still make a monthly trip out to Dandenong to buy our spices. The warehouse and tiny office have now given way to a supermarket worthy of any suburban mall, while still retaining some elements of being 'charmingly' ethnic. Somehow I can't see Woolworths or Coles stocking Ganesh sculptures, incense and spittoons alongside their usual offerings of bread and milk.

'Shani, I am really worried,' my mother started, with a deepening furrow between her eyebrows as we got into my father's car. Contrary to what Amani said, the real reason why I usually drove my dad's car to Dandenong was because I can never get the stench of hundreds of kilos of spices out of my plush leather upholstery. And the suggestion that I was afraid of the hordes of ethnic drivers that populated that suburb was just absurd. I have done a course in defensive driving.

'What about, *Ammi*?'

'It's Gehani!'

'What's he done?'

My mother turned her head away and wiped a tear from her eye. For all her histrionics, she didn't usually resort to tears unless it was serious. I began worry.

'He is alright, isn't he? He isn't sick?' I asked. I was still rattled by the news of my house (which I hadn't discussed with my mother just yet), and by that guy in the park – who, by the way, was now recovering from his bypass, thank you very much.

'He ... he's doing his own laundry!'

Only a Lankan mother would greet the news of their child doing their own laundry with the worry normally reserved for finding out he or she was doing crack-cocaine.

'Maybe he is just growing up,' I said, trying not to laugh.

'It gets worse. He is *looking for houses* as well,' my mother whispered urgently. You'd think she'd discovered he was an undercover ASIO agent.

'Maybe he just wants to a buy a house.'

'What for? He already has two investment properties. Why should he buy more? Besides, he said he was looking for a family house. Do you think he has a girlfriend?'

'I'm pretty sure he doesn't,' I responded, unless my brother had fallen out of love with Una in the last two weeks and fallen in love with someone else.

'But I am really worried about him. He has changed. He is not like he used to be ...' my mother continued anxiously. As I parked the car I couldn't resist an opportunity to tease her a little.

'Maybe he's getting ready to ask you to arrange a marriage for him,' I suggested.

'No. I asked him, but he said that if I ever did to him what I did to you, he'd tell everybody that I dye my hair,' she huffed indignantly. The fact that my mother dyes her hair is a close-kept family secret. She has everybody in the Sri Lankan community convinced her ebony locks are natural. She even peddles advice on how to stop your hair from going grey.

'If only I'd known that's all it would have taken for you to stop sending mad men my way, I would have used that threat myself.'

'So, he must have a girlfriend. I wish he'd bring her home for us to meet her.'

'If he does have a girlfriend he'll bring her home when he is well and ready, not before.'

'I hope she is nice. It must be serious because he actually asked for Sonali's phone number the other day. When I asked him why he wanted to know, he said it was to ask for some advice. Why can't my children ask me for advice?'

'I dunno.'

'I am smart, you know. I used to be able to do things. You kids used to come to me all the time. Sometimes I wish we had never come to Australia!' she said fiercely, as I disentangled a shopping cart from the trolley bay.

What had brought this on? Maybe she was moving into the second stage of menopause.

'*Ammi*, I don't understand. Weren't you dying to come out here? Didn't you hate the fact that people never treated you with respect because you were married to a mechanic?'

'Yes, but I feel we would have been better off had we stayed in Sri Lanka.'

'Why?' I was genuinely perplexed. Turning to face her, I came to a dead stop in the religious aisle of the supermarket, but moved along quickly as I realised I had stopped at the phallic-shaped Shiva Lingam section where a few young girls stood giggling, pointing at the improbably sized statues.

'Because of you kids …'

She must definitely be menopausal. Women go strange when the change comes. In my opinion, you only have to look at Hillary Clinton. No, scotch that; she has always been strange.

'How so? All three of your kids are educated professionals who aren't in any way criminals. We don't smoke, do drugs or have any illegitimate children. What more do you want?'

'You are not married,' my mother started. Here we go again, I thought with frustration. It's only been a day or so …
'… Gamini lives so far away …'

'*Ammi*,' I interrupted, picking up a sack of dried chillies, 'it makes sense that Gamini lives in Sydney. He works there.'

'But he never calls me to find out how I am going,' my mother retorted, picking up a large bag of cloves. 'See, it's only $10 here. A handful of cloves are $4.99 at normal supermarkets.'

'Not many men his age call their mothers. Besides, you have Gehani at home to look after you.'

'Not for long,' she snapped, picking out some brinjals. 'He'll find some girl and then he'll get married.'

'But isn't that what you've always wanted. For all of us to get married and move on with our lives?'

'Yes, but in Sri Lanka I would have still had *you*,' she said in exasperation as she selected the rest of the spices. Cardamom, nutmeg, coriander, cumin and pepper.

'I don't understand. What do you mean by "have us"?'

'Have you. Yes, I had you. Look at Amani. Look at how hard it is to raise a child,' my mother said, as the checkout operator started scanning the groceries.

Maybe she had a point. I had never paid much attention to how hard it was to raise a baby, but going by little Maya's example, it wasn't easy. I doubted Amani had had a night of sleep since that little girl was born.

I had dropped in yesterday to thank Rohan, but things had gone pear-shaped very quickly. Amani looked like she was about to have a nervous breakdown and Aunty Chandra stood around gloating. The more Maya had screamed and the more frantic Amani became while trying to soothe her, the more smug Aunty Chandra's expression had become.

'See, daughter? I told you it was not easy to raise a child. Children are all about *dukka*. Look at the *dukka* this child is giving her parents,' Aunty Chandra had intoned as Amani limped up and down the corridor desperately trying to settle the screaming baby.

Meanwhile, in the supermarket, my mother was echoing Aunty Chandra. I could see her point.

'Yes, raising a child is bloody hard, *Ammi*, I'll give you that. How did you manage with three children?' I asked as she paid for the groceries and we made our way back to the car.

'It wasn't so bad. You forget I had lots of help back in Sri Lanka. But the thing is that it does not matter about all the hard work you put in, they always leave you …'

'But that's just the natural order of families, isn't it? Besides, that's how it's done here in Australia.'

'That may be the case. But you are Sinhalese, don't ever forget where you are from,' my mother reminded me firmly.

'So, this is all about me not behaving like a Sri Lankan should?'

'No, it about you and your brother not being a part of our family,' she said tersely.

'*Ammi*, in case you haven't realised, Gehani is still at home living with you and I am out shopping with you as we speak!'

'But you don't want to be here!'

'How do you know that?'

'Don't you think I know that you ignore my calls? Don't you think I know how you avoid me? Don't you think I know how you'd rather not be seen with me?' my mother yelled. And then she started crying. Not silent tears, but great big sobbing cries. Yup, my mother sure picked the best place to go completely postal. In the carpark of Hindustani Imports!

'What did you expect, *Ammi*? That I'd like your interference in my life? That I'd like the fact that you have sicced a million mad men onto me? Why can't you be a normal mother?' I yelled as I bundled her into the car and sped off.

And there it was, the heart of the problem. All my life, I'd just wanted to fit in. To be normal. How do you think people would react if they knew about the insanity I lived with at home? The nutty mother who had an obsession with marrying off her children? The father with a cricket addiction?

'I am a normal mother! I am as normal as I know how to be. I cannot be something I am not.'

'Well, I cannot be something I am not either!'

'Pull the car over,' my mother screamed.

I pulled over into a side street. My mother and I were having a complete meltdown. And in many ways it felt good. Usually we skirt around issues. We never really talk about things fully.

We hide behind what is appropriate and traditional codes of politeness. And nothing ever really gets resolved. Things are just swept under the carpet – until the next time. But not, apparently, this time.

'All I ask is that you let me be a part of your life,' my mother cried.

'But you are a part of my life. What is this really about, *Ammi*? The stupid arranged marriages?'

'I mean letting me be a part of your life willingly, instead of just tolerating me.'

'Then change. Be normal,' I replied in frustration.

'How?'

'Be more like Una's mum,' I said, at last giving voice to my most fundamental desire. Una's mum was cool. She mainly left Una to her own devices, parachuting in occasionally with sane advice, good food and loads of presents. A perfect mother, really.

'You want me to be like that white woman? You want me to be white?' my mother screeched in response.

'Weeelll …' I drawled. 'You could try to be less interfering, more supportive.'

'I *am* supporting you. I want you to get married!'

'But that's exactly the point. It's what you want. It's not what *I* want!'

'You don't know what you want,' my mother shouted back.

I threw my hands up in the air in frustration. As usual, I might as well have been talking to myself.

'Oh, forget it, just take me home. Imagine if someone saw us,' she said, wiping her snotty nose and drying her eyes.

I gladly put the car back into gear and headed home.

My mother and I drove back in a silence frigid enough to freeze nitrogen. Neither one of us was willing to give an inch. I knew her well enough to know that I would need to deliver a grovelling apology at some stage to even have a halfway decent relationship with her in the future. But definitely not today. She could wait. Maybe until next month. Hopefully, this would finally put the kibosh on the whole arranged marriage mission, though. I was dying to bring it up, but I didn't want to appear as if I were asking her for something.

I would have given my right arm to be able to drive off in a huff once I dropped my mother off without deigning to say goodbye, but I had to change cars. My mother jumped out of the car just as I put it into park. I didn't even look at her as I stomped off to my car parked on the street.

'Shani!'

'What?'

I turned to face my mother across my parents' driveway like a cowboy from a bad Western movie.

'I hope you never have the grief of just being *tolerated* by your child ...'

'I don't just ...'

My mother stopped my denials by raising a hand.

'Just listen to me. From the day you met Amani ...'

Again I tried interrupting her, but again she stopped me by raising her hand.

'From the day you met Amani, you never came to me for anything. She became your guide ...'

'But she knew more about living in Australia ...' I interrupted.

'Yes, and I was happy for you. I was happy you'd found someone. A friend. But you never came back. Suddenly I became the stupid one. I became someone you were embarrassed by. I did not fit into your new world. Did you ever think what it was like for me?'

'No. You had your friends too! You started working,' I answered back.

'Yes, that mad Sonali! Do you have any idea of what it's

like to sacrifice everything, your home, your family, your life, all for the future of your children and then they ignore you? Do you *know* what that feels like?'

Of course I didn't. I actually started to feel a little guilty, but I crushed that tenuous shoot of emotion. After all, nobody had asked her to immigrate here. I had wanted to go back to Sri Lanka every day of the first two years I was in Australia. Nobody had listened to me. Everybody had been too excited by simple things like free-flowing traffic and piped hot water to consider the feelings of a young girl.

'Ever since you met your *kara* friends, I have been nothing but an annoyance. Had we been in Sri Lanka, I would have been something to you. There would have been none of this moving out, going away with friends or ignoring your mother. I need to be needed, too,' she said emphatically.

'Well, I don't need you,' I said mutinously, knowing I was lying before the words even left my mouth.

'Well, if you feel that way, there is no need for you to come back,' she yelled. I could hear the quiver of doubt in her voice.

'Fine,' I said as I turned my back to her and stomped away to my car. In the distance, I heard my mother, very uncharacteristically, slam her own front door.

I was shaking with rage as I sped back home. Not that home would be much of a comfort at the moment. I lived in perpetual fear that the roof was going to fall on my head.

I was almost halfway home when I received a frantic phone call from Rohan. Apparently, Amani had completely lost it, screaming hysterically at her mother as well.

'Rohan, don't you think Tehara is a better peace negotiator than me?'

'Tehara is here, but that coconut can't understand Sinhala.'

'Can't you do it?'

'I tried but Amani's *amma* wants an impartial translator. She asked for you,' he pleaded.

Me? Impartial?

I turned my car around and headed off to Hawthorn.

The scene I walked in on was akin to a war zone. Amani was cradling a screaming baby while trying to shout down her mother.

'Amani, I don't know what all this fuss is about!' Aunty Chandra shouted at her while Amani was desperately trying to get Maya to latch on to her breast.

'*Ammi*, I just want you to stop. I want you to stop comparing me to all your friend's daughters,' Amani said, in tears. 'I am not like them. Okay, so I am crap at being a mother. But I am trying the best I can.'

'Of course, you are a bad mother,' Aunty Chandra said matter of factly, 'you only ever think about yourself.'

'*Amma*, you know that is not fair,' Rohan interrupted.

'What is not fair is that I am not being allowed to see my grand-daughter!'

'Okay,' I said as Tehara and I confronted the warring factions like members of a UN peacekeeping force. 'What started this?'

'Amani won't let me see Maya,' Aunty Chandra yelled in Singhalese. 'And she is poisoning her against me!'

I could see why Rohan had called in a translator. Tehara had no hope in hell of understanding Aunty Chandra when she screeched at the top of her voice. Even I could only pick out one word in every two of her diatribe.

'I am not!' Amani hotly defended herself. 'All I said was that it would be better if you came tomorrow. I am tired and I need to get some sleep.'

'Tired? Tired! You are always tired. It's all in your mind. Mind over matter! That is what the Buddha said.'

I am also sure the Buddha preached patience, tolerance and kindness. Traits that seemed to be in short supply at the moment.

'All I said, *Ammi*, was that I needed some rest!' Amani said, crying in earnest now.

'What do you think about those poor women in Sri Lanka? Do you think they get rest? Do you think I got a rest when you were young? Amani, you disgust me. You are teaching your daughter to hate me.'

She then turned to me, and I took a quick step back in fear.

'*Puthay*, please explain to Amani that I have every right to see Maya.'

'Aunty Chandra,' Tehara interrupted cautiously.

'Look, I don't take advice from a girl whose mother could not keep her legs crossed. You will probably end up a prostitute just like her!' Aunty Chandra spat.

Tehara flinched. It was, even for Aunty Chandra, a very low blow.

'*Puthay!*' Aunty Chandra commanded me again. Her command snapped me out of my horrified trance.

'Amani, of course you are a bad mother. How could you be anything else with the example of motherhood you've had to follow?' I said quickly, bringing a tiny smile from Amani.

I turned to Aunty Chandra, who was a little slow on the uptake but whose smile was fading as the semantics of my back-handed insult finally started sinking in.

'Aunty Chandra,' I said fiercely with my hands on my hips. 'Amani is a fabulous mother. Maybe she and Maya are off to a rocky start, but she'll get better. Maya is only weeks old. It will not kill you to be a little supportive. When Amani said it'd be better for you to come tomorrow, she meant exactly that. Nothing more, nothing less. Yes, Amani needs her rest. Maybe you didn't. And frankly, I don't give a damn about the poor women in Sri Lanka who probably have tons of relatives sharing in looking after their children. I care about Amani and you've been upsetting her all her life.'

'How would you know?' Aunty Chandra said scornfully and turned around.

Nobody had noticed, but Una had slipped into the house.

'Actually, Aunty Chandra,' Una said firmly, 'I think you'd better listen to Shani. She has a point. We've all stood back while you've torn strips off Amani for years. You have never appreciated the lovely daughter you have. She is kind, loyal, giving, intelligent and incredibly beautiful. You should learn to love her before you lose her completely.'

'And I'm supposed to take the opinion of a white girl? Whatever you say is of no relevance.'

'But what I say is,' Amani said quietly, as Maya had, amazingly, settled down to suckling. '*Amma*, please do not call me until you are able to talk to me without using guilt trips or comparing me to someone else. I am me and I cannot be something I am not.'

'Is this how you treat your widowed, elderly mother? The mother who has sacrificed everything for you?'

'Yes. And if you don't like it, you don't have to be my mother anymore,' Amani said calmly.

'Fine,' Aunty Chandra said huffily. She looked pointedly at Rohan, hoping that he'd take her side. But he looked away. He was at the end of his patience.

'Fine,' Aunty Chandra huffed again and limped towards the door. Her limp that had been noticeably absent before.

'I am going and I won't come back!' she called as she slammed the door shut.

CHAPTER 22

I Am a Republican ... Except on the Queen's Birthday!

I breathed in a deep breath of fresh mountain air high in the Grampians and let the serenity fill me. The night before Una and I had left the bright lights of the big city and headed out west to the craggy sandstone of the national park two hours west of Melbourne. We were spending the Queen's Birthday weekend exploring the mysterious caves and dramatic rock art at the ancient Aboriginal prayer ground of the Gariwerd. Just as the doctor had ordered.

After Aunty Chandra's rather dramatic exit, Amani and I had been read the riot act by both Tehara and Una. Tehara had booked Amani in to see a post-natal depression specialist and both she and Maya were in a mother–baby unit in a swanky private hospital right now. I was told to relax and take a chill pill.

Tehara was right. I had lost a worrisome amount of weight over the whole house business.

'Have you rung your mother yet?' Una asked as we started hiking up to the Pinnacles, the iridescent peak of one of the mountains with awe-inspiring views of the valley below.

'Er ... no,' I mumbled.

I wished I could say I had made peace with my mother. I really did. I wished I could say that I had rung her as soon as I had got back from Rohan and Amani's. But things kept getting in the way.

'Things' being a major migraine that literally grounded me for the whole of the next day. I could have rung her on Monday, but I felt the apology needed to be in person. And as each day passed, it became harder and harder to eat humble pie. Paradoxically, the harder it became to apologise, the more I wanted to mend bridges with her. Lord knows, my mother was nowhere near as bad as Aunty Chandra and I wanted her to know I appreciated it.

'You'll want to do it sooner rather than later ...' Una said as we wriggled through a tight crevice.

'I know, I know ...'

'Gehani said that she's not been feeling well this last week and your dad has been doing the cooking ...'

'What? *Thathi* doing the cooking. Things must be really bad!' I think it may have been the second time in my parents' entire married life that my father has done the cooking. The first being when my mum had to rush off to Sri Lanka for my grandmother's funeral.

'Before you tell me what's wrong with her, can you tell me when you started hanging out with Gehani?' I asked, trying to deflect her questions. We were going through an echoey section of the tight mountain pass, so my question came back to me a full ten seconds later.

'We are not hanging out. I ran into him at the hospital. He was working with some cardiac patients and we had coffee. Is that a crime?'

'Fine,' I said, a little taken back by her vehemence. 'You can hang out with whomever you want.'

'You know Shani, Gehani is a really nice guy. We've always treated him like a little pest, but he's never let us down. I know, it's a pity he's got a crush on me.'

'Yeah, I mean, that much is obvious …'

'Remember the Valentine's Day card he made for me in Year 9? He'd saved up his weekly allowance to buy that gold paper. He caught the train to South Yarra and cycled up to the school and gave it to me at the gate.'

'Yeah, and he got into trouble for wagging school,' I remembered, still reeling from the tongue-lashing my parents had given Gehani after the call came through from the Year 9 coordinator. You'd think he'd been caught stealing a car or something for all the drama my parents created over the incident.

'Remember when we were in Year 12, he brought us coffees and sandwiches while we were doing exams?'

'Yeah, and he got his vocation as a physio after he massaged your headaches and backaches away. Wasn't he trying to feel you up?'

'He was young! And a boy! And he always tried his best,' Una defended. 'It was like me and Hugh, only in reverse.'

'Does that mean you are finally over that bloody man?' I puffed, as we commenced climbing a steep part of the mountain.

'Ummm … maybe … no … Oh, I don't know,' Una mumbled, as I helped her climb through a crevice. 'And do you remember the time Gehani bought us all Maccas by riding his BMX through the drive through when we were all hungover?'

Una was pretty intent on reminiscing on all the old Gehani stories. Admittedly they were generally funny. There was the time Gehani drove all the way to Ocean Grove to buy Una fish and chips because they were her favourite. Then there was the time he spent four hours fanning Una with a paper fan to keep the mozzies off her when she'd fallen asleep in a hammock by the beach in Port Douglas. And there was also the time he had saved up a year's wages from his paper run to buy Una a gold bracelet for her twenty-first birthday. Then he'd saved up another year's wages the following year to buy her the matching earrings.

You had to admire his persistence. A weaker man would have given up years ago.

By the time we'd reached the top of the Pinnacles, we'd run out of Gehani stories. Which meant it was time we dealt with my mum.

'Shani, I think you ought to ring your mum and say sorry,' Una stated emphatically.

'I suppose so ...'

'You know your mum is lovely ...'

'You can say that. She's not your mother and you are not lumbered with her for life. You have no idea what it's like to have strange parents.'

'Me? Not know about strange parents? You have got to be kidding me! My mother nearly caused my primary school to close by serving us tofu burgers when she was on tuckshop duty.' Una cried.

'Honey, you don't know the meaning of strange. Remember when *Ammi* rocked up to my parent–teacher interview in a *saree*?'

'And she looked gorgeous!'

'But so out of place!'

'And since when have my parents ever blended in?' Una asked. 'Remember the time my mum came to my room in Year 11 and smudged it with lavender and sage?'

'Yeah, didn't one of the pastoral care teachers try to get you chucked out for being a witch?'

'Honey, your mother is lovely. Would you rather have

Aunty Chandra? Or Tehara's mother? She has not once tried to contact Tehara in the last twenty years.'

'Okay, okay …'

'Shani, parents aren't perfect. I suppose we always expect them to be further ahead in the game than we are, but don't forget, our folks had us when they were young. They didn't have time to ponder the meaning of life before they started a family. Of course they are going to stuff up. We all stuff up.'

Una had made a really good point. I knew I had a lot to be thankful for. Our parents had set aside their self-obsession to raise our ungrateful arses and there was much to be said for that.

'I'll give her a call tomorrow from Halls Gap,' I said as we sat down to rest and chew on a muesli bar apiece.

'Why don't you do it now?' Una asked, reaching for my iPhone and switching it on.

'Don't do that!' I said reaching for my phone. It would be just my luck that one of my mother's would-be grooms would be in the vicinity and I didn't want to be caught by a stalker in this magnificent place.

'What's the problem?' Una teased, sensing my alarm. 'If they can make it up here, they'll survive you!'

'Okay, okay,' I said moving away from where all the hikers were milling to call my parents. The first time I called, it went to voicemail. So I tried my dad's mobile.

'*Thathi* … it's Shani. Where's *Ammi*?'

I was answered by a burst of static.

'We're … at … '

'*Thathi*, speak up! I can't hear you.'

'*Ammi* … Alfred …'

'Who's Alfred?' I asked in frustration. I could barely make out what he was saying.

Another burst of static.

'Look, I'll call you back,' I said, hanging up. Which was when I noticed a rather delicious young man standing back a little and looking enquiringly at me.

'Are you Shani Devapura?'

'Yes, I am.'

This guy looked as if he'd just walked off a photo shoot for *GQ*. He was tall, lightly tanned and oh so handsome. He had wide, chiselled features and beautiful eyes. His short, well-trimmed hair was rakishly ruffled and his professional hiking gear screamed that being outdoors was more than an occasional pastime for him.

'Hi, my name is Ruwan,' came his deep gravelly voice with a slight American accent.

'American?' I asked, flipping my ponytail. I am a sucker for an accent.

'Oh no, I just got back from spending the last two years there. I suppose working there for such a long time, the accent does rub off.'

'My friend and I were hiking when I got your text message,' Ruwan said, pointing to another man who was sitting on a rock some distance away scowling at me.

'Oh …'

I could speak to my mother later, I suppose. I could even give her some good news!

'Are you up here alone?'

'No … I am here with a friend too,' I said, pointing to Una who was staring at us with interest.

Ruwan turned out to be an intelligent, articulate management consultant with an MBA from a prestigious Sydney university. He'd just spent two years working in Boston. He was well read, well travelled and really, really funny.

On the other hand Andrew, his companion, was a bore. He barely spoke and pretended to be more interested in the scenery. He just grunted replies to questions Una and I put to him, before he raced ahead of us, hiking at a furious pace down the mountain.

And what a lovely hike we had too! Una, Ruwan and I seemed to all like the same music, the same food and he was even a fan of *Eat, Pray, Love*! Imagine that, a bloke who was into spiritual chick lit.

'Shani, Shani, Shani,' Ruwan said, leaning flirtatiously against the passenger side door of Una's car once we'd made it down the mountain safely.

'Ruwan, Ruwan, Ruwan …' I flirted back, twirling a lock of my hair.

'I think we've got some potential here.'

'Potential? Is that what you call it?'

'I think it could be described as potential.' He smiled a little lopsided smile.

'So what do you suggest we do with this potential?'

'I say we take it to the Halls Gap pub tonight and see where it goes.'

'I think could be a good idea … but …' I hesitated. I never put dates before mates.

'Bring Una along. Andrew and Una can double date … chaperone us, if you will. You know, like in the olden days.' His grin sealed it for me.

'Okay then.'

'I'll be the guy waiting for you at the bar,' he said with a little wink before he sauntered away to his Subaru Outback.

Una held it in until we neared the exit of the carpark, then screamed, almost deafening me in the process, 'Oh my *God*!' 'He is so *hot*. I mean Code Red Hot! You guys are *so* going to have to get married at …'

'Whoa! Hang on, there, Road Runner! I need to get to know the man first!'

'You know what your problem is, Shani? You haven't an ounce of romance in you. You are such a bloody accountant.'

I wasn't really listening. As we'd turned and driven back past the carpark, I saw Ruwan and his mate having a rather spirited argument. Ruwan was perched on the boot of his car while the taciturn Andrew was railing at him. What was that all about?

CHAPTER 23

Can Someone Please Fix Mobile Reception in the Bush?

Una and I hadn't planned for 'dates' when we'd packed for our impromptu break in the Grampians. We'd planned for yoga and back-to-back episodes of *Grey's Anatomy*, so there were no slinky Jigsaw numbers packed into our MacPacs. Una made do by wearing a tight lycra scoop neck top teamed with a red polar fleece vest and a pair of Bettina Liano jeans. I was able to pull together a grey top with black tights and a pair of calf-length black high-heeled boots. I also wore a short sheer *saree* print skirt over my tights to give the whole ensemble a splash of glamour.

'Hey, girls!' Ruwan had greeted us loudly, pecking us both on the cheek. 'What will you have? You'll find this place somewhat backward, they don't even have Coronas!'

'Well, I'll have the house Chardonnay, then,' Una replied while I settled for a Boag's.

'Do you know who James is?' Ruwan teased me lightly as I took deep swig of my beer.

'No, do you?' Where's Andrew?'

'He said he'll join us later,' Ruwan breezed. 'So, girls, what did you think of … ?'

It turned out to be one of the best nights I'd had in a long time. Ruwan was not only into chick lit, he was also into chick movies and he'd read the classics. What a guy! Over dinner, Una, Ruwan and I even had a lengthy debate over whether Harry Potter was a better role model for young boys than Bart Simpson.

'I think Harry is too much of a goody-goody,' I protested. 'Young boys just can't relate to him – he's too perfect.'

'He's flawed, alright. Didn't he use the *Cruciatus* curse on what's his name?' Una slurred. She and Ruwan had been getting stuck into vodka and Red Bull shots over dinner.

'I agree with you but I think …' Ruwan was about to say something, but stopped abruptly when Andrew joined us.

'I thought you were never going to come!' I giggled. Alcohol had definitely loosened my tongue. And Andrew seemed like he was in a better mood too.

'Oh, I can come, darling! I can come!' he laughed back, camping it up for good measure.

'Careful, sweetheart. We're in the bush and you don't want to be mistaken for gay … not with bogans like that around,' Una cautioned drunkenly, pointing to a few feral blokes hogging the fire.

'You know what, they've been staring at us for while,' I pointed out.

'That's because they're jealous. Both you girls look hot tonight,' Ruwan teased, pouring me another glass of white wine.

'And where have you been, Andrew?'

'Believe it or not, I have been on a call with work.'

'So what do you do?'

'I work for Telstra and I have a project going live in a few days.'

'Speaking of Telstra, I have been trying to ring my parents and I've had no luck with my mobile signal.'

'Why don't you try this?' Andrew said, offering me his phone.

'Why is your phone better than hers?' Una asked, with a silly giggle.

'Because it is a satellite phone.'

I took Andrew's offered mobile and walked out of the noisy pub. It was freezing outside, so I bundled myself tightly in my ski jacket and stood next to the brickwork of the chimney around the corner. First I called my parents' house. There was no answer. Then I tried my father's mobile, but it was switched off. I tried Aunty Sonali next. Again, no answer. I tried a few more family friends, but no one was picking up. Finally, in desperation I tried Gehani.

'Gehani, where the bloody hell are the parental units?'

'Shani, *Ammi* is in hospital. I've been trying to call you all day.'

Oh. My. God.

In my mad rush to get back to Melbourne and see my mother, I almost didn't notice Ruwan standing in the distance under a tree across the carpark from me. Was he looking for me? Bless him.

But why was he bent over like that? Who was he holding? Surely he wasn't ... He *was!*

He was pashing someone!

Surely Una wouldn't ... And then I froze. It was Andrew!

CHAPTER 24

Humble Pie

If humble pie is a dish best eaten cold, surely the same can't be said for curried humble pie? Because, right this moment, I was eating plenty of cold curried humble pie and it ain't nice.

'Shani? Are you ready?' my mother called in a joyful voice from her lounge room.

Of course I was ready. Trussed up like a Christmas chook, what else could I be?

I was sitting in my old bedroom in my parents' house dressed in a *saree* waiting to meet a potential groom. I wasn't dressed in one of my skimpy, Bollywood hipster numbers. No, that would not appeal to a potential mother-in-law. I was dressed in a silk *saree* given to me by my grandmother when I was thirteen. It was of heavy grey silk brocade with ugly silver embroidery in a floral motif.

The blouse was also cut so conservatively that I barely showed any midriff. Added to the humiliation of such a frumpy outfit, it was too tight; I could barely breathe and didn't dare lift my arms.

The whole point of me looking like a geriatric sushi roll? Supposedly, to bump up my appeal to men. According to my mother, men did not marry strumpets. I even had my hair in a conservative bun and was wearing no makeup.

So, why was I going through the whole farce of meeting proposed grooms in the traditional way? Because I had finally mended those bridges with my mother.

Una and I hadn't driven back to Melbourne that night. We'd been too drunk. I spent an awful night worrying about my mum and we drove out early the next morning. Gehani told me not to bother going to the hospital but to meet Mum at home; they were discharging her early the next day.

But before I rocked up to my parents' house, I had made a quick pit stop at Hindustani Imports. I bought seven betel leaves, a coconut and some camphor. If I was going to beg for forgiveness from my mother, I was going to do it right.

Yes, I had begged for forgiveness. Not because I thought I did anything particularly wrong. Not because I thought that she had magically re-modelled herself into the perfect mother during our two-week cold war. And definitely not because I thought she was at death's door. I begged for my mother's forgiveness simply because I loved her. I begged for my mother's forgiveness because I needed her. And I missed her. I missed her neurotic ramblings. I missed organising her. I missed being around at my parents' house averting disasters. I understood what my mother said when she said she needed to be needed. I needed her to need me too.

So, I balanced the coconut on the seven betel leaves, lit the camphor on my parents' doorstep, knocked on the door and got down on my knees with my head bent low. Sure I could have used my keys, but I wanted to give my mother the impression of complete dominance over me. I was hoping for a quick and painless forgiveness process. Then we could all get on with our lives as soon as possible.

Only my plan was scuppered from the start. My father answered the door. This was such an unusual occurrence that I nearly set my hair on fire with the flaming camphor.

'Where's *Ammi*?' I asked, anxiety making my voice unnaturally high. Gehani had assured me that it'd all been a false alarm.

'She's in there,' my dad said, pointing to the lounge room.

And there my mother was. Sitting in the lounge room. Having a snooze on the couch.

'Is that you, Shani?' my mother called back when she heard the commotion at the door, barely lifting her eyelids. 'What do you want?' she asked coldly.

Okay, my dramatic gesture was a little out on its timing but I knew I needed to make peace. Quick. Before the screaming started.

So I relit the camphor, careful to keep my hair out of the way, and dropped to my knees in front of my mother. '*Ammi*, I am very sorry for all the horrible things I said to you. I am a horrible, ungrateful daughter and I am very ashamed of my selfish and wilful behaviour. I have dishonoured you and our family. Please forgive me,' I pleaded. Okay, I really didn't mean the *whole* thing, particularly the wilful bit, but I had to concede that I had been ungrateful and slightly horrible.

Silence. It was as if she hadn't heard a word I'd said. I snuck a quick peek at her. Yes, she was breathing and clearly alive.

'Oh *Ammi*, I am really sorry. Please, please forgive me!'

Still silence.

'I am really sorry. I need you to need me too,' I cried. 'I understand what it's like to sacrifice everything. I think you are the best mother. Of course I look up to you and admire you.'

Silence.

'*Ammi*, *Buddhu Ammi* … please. I really miss you!'

Silence.

'Please *Ammi*?' I begged. 'I'll do anything you want!'

The enormity of what I had said hit me nanoseconds after the words had left my mouth, and I realised with a sinking feeling that once more I had been outwitted.

'Anything?' *Uh, oh!*

But I'd got this far, there was no going back. 'Anything,' I repeated in a broken voice.

'Will you meet the remaining boys properly?'

'Yes,' I conceded glumly.

'Not just meet them, but talk with them and make an effort to get to know them?'

'Yes.'

'If you meet someone you like, will you make an honest effort at liking them and thinking of them as a potential partner?'

'Yes.'

'Good. Now get up off your knees, your jeans will go saggy. And put out that silly fire before you hair goes up. If that happens, I'll have no chance of marrying you off,' she commanded.

'What landed you in hospital?' I asked as I helped her off the couch.

'Indigestion. *Thathi* did the cooking and he panicked when I said I was in pain and called the ambulance,' she confessed, shame-faced.

'So, how many boys are remaining?'

'Seventy-five. I checked the service last night and it said there'd been an introduction yesterday. How did that go?'

I shook my head and pointed my thumbs down.

'That boy Ruwan's profile was so promising too. Shani, it must have been your fault. You're far too picky.'

I really didn't want to go into the whole gay-boy thing with Mum so I kept silent. And any hope that I may have clung to that my mother could not possibly organise for me to meet seventy-five men in three weeks was dispelled when I turned up for dinner the next night.

She'd organised for two to come in one evening. One was invited for drinks and nibbles at 6.30 pm and despatched at 7.30 pm with the excuse that we had to visit an elderly relative later in the evening.

The other was invited for dinner at 8 pm and stayed the rest of the evening. This became the pattern for the rest of my week nights. Forget catching up with friends or having a night off or anything. My mother meant business.

And weekends were even more intense. My mother had held off on the really good prospects until then when I would meet four in a day, plus a few more in between. One for brunch. One for lunch. One for afternoon tea and one for dinner. A blur of dark faces swam before my eyes at the breakfast table, which was the only time I got to have to myself. At least I didn't have to 'make nice' to anyone over a bowl of muesli.

'If you are ready, come then, *Puthay*' my mother called lightly, though I could hear the steel in her voice that ensured I would fall in with her orders.

She was standing at the entrance to the lounge room, dressed in a *saree* too, with her arm extended out. She gestured for me to come forth. Quickly. The next groom was sure to be there on the dot.

I nodded vigorously to indicate that I was coming as fast as I could. Only it's damned hard to stride wrapped in six yards of tightly pleated silk.

She waved at me even more furiously. What did she want me to do? Sprint into the lounge room in *saree*? I'd kill myself tripping over my *saree* hem.

But no. She didn't want me to come faster. She wanted me to … oh, I got it now. She wanted me to bow my head. Like a subservient wife.

'Don't talk too much, men don't like women who talk,' my

mother hissed as she handed me a tray complete with bananas, milky tea and sweets. She had gone all out on the sweets. We had *kokis* (crispy deep fried biscuits made from rice flour and coconut milk), *kaun* (little oil cakes made from treacle and rice flour), milk toffee and *mung kaun* (sweet pastries made of mung bean flour and treacle).

And then we spent an hour making small talk. Talk calculated to reveal the true nature of my potential mate and his family. Especially the family.

Let's just take one example. This was one of the funnier exchanges. It left me in tears.

'So, what do you do?' the mother of one of the potential grooms, who wore far too much foundation and no deodorant, asked me.

'I am an accountant,' I responded solemnly, remembering not to smile. Aunty Sonali had worded up my mother that being cheerful was not a positive trait in the Sri Lankan marriage mart.

'That's good. Not a real career like being a doctor or lawyer. It will be good when the children come. You can stay home and look after them.'

At which point I looked up and opened my mouth to give her a serve, only my mother kicked me on the ankle with her pointy shoe. Hard.

'Oh, so very true!' my mother said, while I simpered, massaging my ankle as discreetly as I could. 'These career women never look after their families. And we are a traditional Lankan family. We look after our children,' she finished, offering a fake smile.

'That boy is not for you, Shani,' my mother said as soon as they had left. 'You want a man who respects you for your education.'

'Then why didn't you let me say it?'

'Why confront people unnecessarily? You can't change them. Pick your battles, Shani! At least those people now think you're a nice girl.'

And here's another scintillating snippet of 'conversation' between myself and a man the astrological charts deemed to be my perfect match.

'Hi,' I greeted the stolid young man who sat wedged in between his sister and brother-in-law on my parents' couch.

Silence.

More silence. Was I meant to make the next move?

'*Anay*, did you read about that awful murder in Colombo the other day? Three people killed for a gold necklace?' The sister of the groom asked my mother.

'*Anay*, yes. That was very close to our house in Mount,' my mother said in the hushed tone she used to convey genteel horror.

The wonderful thing about the immediacy of the internet means that my mother not only worries about crime in Melbourne, she worries about crime in Colombo simultaneously.

Silence prevailed between myself and my astrological soul mate, while the relatives continued blithely.

'But things are not good in Melbourne either,' the sister continued. She wore no makeup but too much perfume which smelled suspiciously like fake Chanel No. 5. The kind you buy from those Chinese stalls at the market.

'So what do you do?' I asked the man. He was almost being crushed by his sister and brother-in-law.

Silence.

I quickly snuck a peek around at my father. He was looking as bored as I felt. I saw him glance up at the wall clock and a faint look of disgust crossed his patrician features. Yup, he'd just missed another IPL game on Foxtel.

'Crime is very bad here too,' the sister added.

Then we'd all lapsed into an uncomfortable silence. This continued for a good few minutes before my mother turned to the groom.

'*Puthay*, tell us a little about yourself?'

Again silence.

'*Anay*, Mrs Devapura, my brother is a quiet man. But I always say a quiet man is a good man. He won't interfere in the running of a house or family,' the sister spoke for him.

After another twenty minutes punctuated by awkward silence, the family mercifully made their excuses and left.

'I don't think he's for you,' my mother conceded as we washed the tea cups. 'I think you need a man who will at least have an opinion on crime for a marriage to succeed.'

'Is that it, Jayanthi?' my father asked my mother. It was nearly 9 pm on Saturday and we were exhausted. We'd been at it non-stop for the last two weeks. My days and nights had blurred into one gigantic blind date.

'No, that is not it, there are twenty-five more grooms to see,' my mother protested.

'Not tonight, though?'

This whole arranged marriage business was putting a serious dent into my father's cricket-watching schedule. Not that he was an active participant in any of the marriage shenanigans. He just sat in the corner and nodded. But it was beginning to get to him.

While my mother counted the number of times a potential groom smiled at me, my father counted the minutes between visits so he could watch the cricket games he'd recorded on Foxtel IQ. At the moment, he was about ten hours behind on knowing what had happened in some test match between Kenya and South Africa. Did they even play cricket in Kenya? Who knew? I thought it was all roasted coffee there.

'No, not tonight,' my mother said grumpily. 'I thought we could take a little break. Besides, next week is going to be busy. Shani comes out of *Mangala Yoga* next Saturday night.'

'But I thought the whole wedding season corresponded with my *Mangala Yoga*' I said, confused. 'The Kohanagoda wedding is on Sunday night.'

'No, *Puthay*. I had a look at the reading that was done by Mr Kapulitiphanagoda. He says you come out of *Mangala Yoga* at midnight next Saturday. And there have been no good prospects!' My mother was sounding genuinely worried.

'Is the coast clear?' my brother asked as he descended the stairs, looking furtively around the family room.

'Yes, come on down. Dinner is in the kitchen. Oh, how are we going to get you to see the rest of the grooms?' *Ammi* fretted. 'I have to find someone for you.'

'Thanks, but I've already had dinner,' Gehani said as he settled himself down next to me.

'I heard you come in about half an hour ago, where have you been?' I asked Gehani.

'Nowhere …'

'Nowhere, where you could get dinner?'

'Yes, nowhere, where you could get dinner,' he retorted.

I leant over and sniffed him. He carried the distinctive pong of curried cabbage and over-brewed tea.

'You've been at Aunty Sonali's.'

'So what if I have been there? She is an older lady and her neck has been giving her trouble. I just don't like to advertise the fact that I do freebies.'

I immediately felt guilty. Una was the only other person I knew who hung out with Aunty Sonali voluntarily.

'Una said that you girls will be busy next week,' Gehani added.

'When did you see Una?'

'I ran into her at Aunty Sonali's. She was there to check Aunty's blood pressure and make sure she was taking her cholesterol medication.' Gehani sounded defensive. 'Una said that you were going to have to practise the dance next week and there'd be no time for you to meet grooms.'

'I've got an idea,' my mother interrupted excitedly. 'Why don't we invite the remaining grooms to a dinner here on Saturday night? Like one of those speed dating things I read about in *New Idea*.'

'Those speed dating things usually involve an equal number of single women!'

'Invite your friends then! Una and Tehara ...'

'But that's still not anywhere near an equal number. Besides, aren't Gayani and Sarath coming over for their wedding visit that night?'

'Oh, we'll make a real party of it then,' my mother enthused. 'Like a mixer. Invite Amani, Rohan and Maya, Una and Tehara, and we'll even invite Sonali. It will be a natural setting for you to meet all those boys.'

Natural? Was she for real? I looked carefully at my mother. I wondered whether the drugs she'd been given for her indigestion had somehow short-circuited her brain.

We all stopped talking when we heard doors slam in the driveway.

'Jayanthi! If that is a groom, please tell him that Shani's father is unavailable,' my father called out from his recliner as he determinedly unbuckled his pants and turned up the volume on the cricket. No man messes with my father in his underwear!

Gehani was almost at the door when whoever was on the other side raised their hand to knock on it.

'Yes, is Shani Devapura here?' a deep booming voice called.

'Yes, I'm here,' I replied, exchanging a meaningful glance with Mum. She'd told me she'd pulled my name off the stalker service.

Two tall, lean constables strolled into my parents' family room as my father hurriedly buckled up his pants again.

'Ms Devapura, we're sorry to have to inform you, but your unit collapsed about two hours ago. Can you confirm that no one was in residence at that time?'

CHAPTER 25

The Invitation

I wished Amani would pick up the phone. I'd tried calling her about a gazillion times since Sunday to invite her to my mother's 'mixer' without much luck. I had stopped trying to convince *Ammi* that inviting all the remaining grooms to the house at the one time was a stupid idea. Let her do it. I just didn't have the energy anymore.

Now I knew what my mother felt like when I ignore her calls. Ignored!

Finally Amani picked up. 'Yes, Shani. I was going to return your call. I just had to see Una out the door.'

'Hey how are you? I was worried about you,' I said as I settled into my seat at work. I'd finally handed over my completed, polished-up report and was taking a tiny break.

'I should say that I've been worried about you. I got your message that your unit had collapsed. I saw it on TV. How did it happen?'

Today Tonight had done a wonderful piece on 'CON More … More con jobs than anyone had realised'.

'Never mind me. Are you okay?' I knew Amani and Maya had been kept in at the mother and baby unit for an extended stay. We hadn't been allowed to visit.

'Yeah, I am okay …'

'Are you sure?' I asked, unconvinced.

'I am on anti-depressants. They just make me so groggy …'

'But are they helping you?'

'I suppose so. But it feels kinda extreme, really. They don't just stop me from feeling crap, they stop me feeling at all,' she went on listlessly. 'But I know I'll really need them since I'll be starting work again.'

'What? I thought you were going to have six months off.'

'Just don't start on me, okay?' I should have known to back off then, but something made me persist.

'Honey, is that wise? You had a c-section and Maya is not really old enough.'

'Plenty of women do it. Crèches take babies at six weeks.'

'But you've struggled a little with Maya.'

'And don't you think I feel enough of a failure without being reminded?' Amani responded with more energy than I'd heard so far.

'It's not your fault that she was difficult to settle …'

'Not my fault? Of course it was my fault. I mean, what do I know about babies?' Amani said with a sob. 'You need to get a licence to drive a car but there's no test, no qualification of any sort to take home a real live human being from hospital.'

'You've just had some teething problems and things will get better …' I tried to sound soothing, but somehow, I didn't think it was working.

'It is all so confusing, Shani. One book will tell you to let them cry it out. Another book will tell you not to. One person will tell you to feed on demand and the other person will tell you to space out the feeds. I just want to do the right thing but I don't *know* what is right,' Amani fretted. 'At least if I go back to work, I'll know what I am doing,' she said with a soft sigh. 'I mean, I am a crap mum, but I know am not a crap lawyer. Besides, the psychiatrist thought it might be a good idea. Give me a break from Maya.'

'You're not a crap mum!'

'How would you know, Shani? I can't get her to settle. I don't know what I am doing half the time. I am so tired. I see women out there who already have their pre-baby bodies back and I can't even get out bed in the morning.'

'And going back to work is going to help? How?'

'That part of my life is controllable,' Amani said with a sense of relief that was palpable. 'I just want to be a normal woman again. I want to be like those women who drop their kids off at crèche in their high heels and pick them up at the end of the day in time to put them to bed. I just want my life to go back to being perfect again.'

If going back to work was going to help Amani, I was all for it.

'How is Maya going by the way?' I asked.

'Still colicky. But she's putting on weight. That's all that matters …'

'So, how are you going to cope if you can't sleep all night and have to go to work the next day?' I asked. 'Surely, you'll need some proper rest.'

'I'll cope. The same way thousands of women cope. I mean, you don't see most women fall apart just because they have children, so why should I? Don't stress. That's what they kept telling me at the mother and baby unit. The more you stress, the worse it is for the baby. It's all about getting emotional distance, the nurses kept telling me. Practise detachment,' Amani said, lapsing back into inertia.

'When do you start?'

'Monday.'

That didn't sound wise to me, but I thought it better to change the subject.

'What are you guys doing this Saturday night?'

'A big fat nothing,' Amani said.

'Well, why don't you come over to my parents' place?'

'Why, are you having a house warming for moving back in with your folks?' Amani asked with a ghost of her former humour.

'No, my parents are having Gayani and her new hubby over for their wedding visit and they thought they'd make a party of it by inviting twenty-five potential suitors along to the soirée as well. *Ammi* needs to pad it out by having a few more girls there, as long they are married, of course,' I drawled sarcastically.

'Oh yes, Una and Tehara told me how your *Ammi* conned you into this … you were so suckered.'

'Yeah, I know,' I said. 'But it had to be done. I can't stay angry with my mother forever. Speaking of which …'

'Yes, I made peace with her,' Amani affirmed sourly.

'Huh? I thought things were pretty final the other day.'

'But in group therapy at the unit, I agreed to make peace with her. I called her. She came. She hugged me. She gave everybody there a lecture on meditation. The nurses wondered why I had so many problems with my mother since she was "so lovely". We all had a group hug and everything is good …' Amani finished in a faux chirpy voice.

'Did you guys really sort things out, though? Did she agree to stop doing the guilt trip on you?'

'Of course not! We agreed that I was having a bad time and I should be more sensitive to my mother's needs.'

That made no sense to me at all, but I couldn't see the point in going further. 'Oh, okay then. It's just that *Ammi* wanted to know whether it'd be alright to invite her, too.'

'Of course, go for it. Besides, your mum really needs to pad out the party. Why are you seeing more grooms anyway? Una told me about that hot guy you met at the Grampians.'

'But …'

'But what?'

'Nothing,' I parried absently as I spied Max going into a meeting room with the Head of Human Resources. Wonder what he's up to?

'Shani, you there?'

'Yes, I am,' I replied as soon as the door closed on the meeting room.

'Una didn't finish the story about your double date. Did you do something to that poor man like you did to that guy who ended up in hospital?'

'I didn't do anything to him!' I defended myself indignantly.

'Then why aren't you seeing him again?'

'Because he's gay.' And that, was that.

CHAPTER 26

The Wedding Visit

One of the many bad things about losing my house and all my possessions was that I only had one *saree* to my name. The *saree* that I wore the day the cops called at my parents' front door. The thick grey silk number that my grandmother had given me when I was thirteen. The only silver lining I could see in the whole disaster was that no man was ever going to give me a sideways glance with me looking like a Sri Lankan nanna.

When Gehani, Una and I had picked through the debris of my collapsed unit we'd managed to salvage some things, like a few photo albums and a couple of my favourite pieces of jewellery. But all my delicate silk *sarees*, georgettes with beadings and gold embroidery were ruined. Delicate handwoven fabrics were pretty defenceless against ConMore's shoddy building practices.

'*Puthay*, why don't you take this tray of *patis* to the boys?' my mother said, shoving a tray full of spicy pastries into my hands, shocking me out of my reverie. I had been looking at my reflection in her gleaming stainless steel oven. It was official. In this *saree*, even *I* thought I was unattractive. It was a bona fide romance killer.

The party was in full swing, though things were pretty quiet. There were about thirty people at my parents' house. Mainly men or 'boys', as my mother liked to call them. They were all sitting around in the family room. In front of the TV. Watching cricket. Sri Lanka was playing England for some championship trophy in some obscure country. You'd be fooled into thinking that the fate of the world hinged on who won the game.

Occasionally one boy/man would dash into the kitchen to pick up a plate of food, then return to the cave to share the fruits of his hunt with his fellow Neanderthals. My mother was trying to entice the savages out of their den by alternating between giving my father the look of death and wilding gesticulating at him switch off the TV, and sending me in with trays of food. Neither tactic had yielded any results. My father, deprived of cricket for nearly three weeks, was determinedly ignoring my mother. And none of the 'boys' were looking at me.

Not that I blamed them. Dressed as I was, Kevin Peitersen was probably a more attractive proposition. I shouldn't complain, though. Cricket saved me from making conversation with any of them.

'Hey, is Aunty Sonali here?' Una asked as she bounded down the stairs from my old bedroom like a hyped-up spaniel. She looked spectacular. Her hair was all done up and she wore a white *gagra choli* with green beading that highlighted her emerald eyes.

'No,' I said as I returned from the family room with an empty tray.

'She said she was going to try to come a bit early. She is going to the astrologer in Keysborough then coming straight here.'

'Why was she going to see the astrologer?'

'Because I asked her to,' my mother replied.

'*Ammi*, you aren't hoping to get my *Mangala Yoga* extended, are you? I mean, astrology is pretty immutable,' I said in exasperation, as Tehara joined us.

'No, I wasn't looking at getting your *Mangala Yoga* extended. But since your house collapsed, I thought it best to get him to have better look at your horoscope.'

'Why? Is there a specific Vedic astrological combination for shoddy building?'

'No, but you may be having a *Rahu Apala*,' Una said seriously.

'A what?' Tehara asked incredulously. 'Is that a skin disease?'

'*Rahu Apala*, darling. Or Mars return. It's when everything in your life goes to pot.'

'Ya don't say,' I muttered.

'I mean, look at your life at the moment. Your house collapsed. All you need is someone close to you to die and I won't even need to look at your horoscope to know you have *Rahu Apala!*'

'How did the astrologer not see this the first time round?' I demanded.

'We don't know for sure that Shani has *Rahu Apala* yet, Aunty, but that is one of the many things about it. It disguises itself and causes untold problems,' Una continued mysteriously.

'Well, it's all academic now anyway. I am officially out of *Mangala Yoga* as of tomorrow and I see freedom beckoning,' I said as Gehani came out of the family room. He did a dramatic start when he saw Una.

'Hey, Una,' Gehani gushed, visibly salivating. 'You look great tonight.'

'Thanks, Gehani,' Una said with a saucy little curtsy. 'I thought I might pick up one of Shani's cast-offs if I'm lucky. That last guy was completely hot. Gay, but hot.'

Gehani looked as if he'd just taken a bullet. A mortal bullet. He lapsed into injured silence, which was broken by a knock at the door.

'Oh, here's the happy couple!' my mother called as Gayani and Sarath walked in.

Gayani literally glowed with joy. Her skin sparkled with an inner radiance that took my breath away. She looked soul-deep happy, with a vivacity that was both infectious and awe inspiring. And Sarath ...

Sarath looked like a man well pleased with himself. In that instant, I must confess, I felt a little wistful. I desperately wanted some peace, and even a little joy in my life. And I wondered whether my views on marriage were just the ramblings of a jaded cynic. I mean, surely marriage was worth it if it afforded us brief glimpses of happiness such as these two were clearly enjoying?

'Oh, she looks so happy,' Una enthused.

'She must be getting plenty of sex,' Tehara muttered cynically.

Was it a sign of the times we lived in that we truly question the source of joy?

'Hey girls! How are you?' Gayani called as she strolled to greet us. She'd lost her customary smirk of superiority that had infuriated us for decades.

'We're good.'

'Where's Amani? Is Maya as gorgeous as Amani?'

'She is. They should be here any minute,' I said as I saw more people come through the front door.

My mother had not pulled any punches organising this little party. She'd invited dozens of people, all of whom decided that they'd appear at the same time.

'How's the man hunt going?' Mrs Peiris, Gayani's mother asked as she joined our little group anchored between the kitchen and the family room.

'*Ammi*, leave the girl alone,' Gayani defended hotly.

'Why? Why should I leave her alone? It's for her own good. *Anay*, I know exactly what your mother feels. It is so stressful having unmarried daughters,' Mrs Peiris said as she stuffed her mouth full of fish cutlets, small peppery balls of mashed tuna flavoured with curry leaves and aniseed.

'Ignore her, Shani,' Gayani said. 'Don't marry because it's the right time or because his horoscope tallies with yours. Marry a man if you love him and for no other reason.'

I could not believe I was having this conversation, and with Gayani of all people. I had always thought she toed the Sri Lankan party line down to a T. She'd always appeared scathing of our antics. Turning up her nose when we'd crashed temple fetes, got drunk at Mrs Peiris's silver anniversary and especially when the four of us were caught skinny dipping at the Kohanagoda pool about six years ago after a really raucous party.

'Well, that was my initial plan. But I thought it best to go through the motions of meeting guys anyway. You never know your luck in the big city.'

Gayani peaked around the corner into the family room and faced me abruptly.

'In that mob? You've got to be kidding me, right? Some of them have been on the arranged marriage circuit for such a long time I'm sure their proposals have been recycled. My sister and I used to have a name for them. TDB. Tea Drinking Bachelors,' Gayani said with a muffled giggle. 'They go from house to house every weekend drinking tea and meeting girls.

We thought they only did it so they didn't have to cook all weekend.'

'What? You mean they aren't a perfect astrological match for Shani?' Una asked in scandalised tones.

'Of course not. You know ninety-nine per cent of this horoscope business is complete horse poo, right?'

'No!' Una cried, horrified. It's hard to have your illusions shattered, I know.

Gayani marched Una, Tehara and me up the stairs so we could covertly spy on the group of guys watching the cricket. They were getting increasingly irate when a few guests had the audacity to walk in front of the TV.

'See that guy there with the glasses? The one in the cream polo T-shirt and cream pants and patent leather shoes? He was over at my parents' house last weekend to see my sister. Two years ago, he came to see me. Three months before I met Sarath, he forgot and he came to see me again. I only remembered who he was when I saw those shoes. He never changes them.'

Una, Tehara and I looked at the shoes. They were truly hideous. Nobody could forget a pair like that.

'See the one who is sitting in the corner by himself? The one in the red *batik* shirt? Don't ever go out for a meal with him because he pretends to have lost his wallet when the bill comes. He did it to me, Tani Kaluarchachie, Metha Fernando and to Anjula Hemaratne.'

'But Anjula is still a student!' I said aghast.

'Yeah, she had to ring her dad for his credit card number to pay for dinner and then they legged it out of the restaurant,' Gayani said in disgust. 'Oh Shani, you've got the standard bunch, alright. There's barnacle Banda, don't ever get into a car with him, he sticks to you like you wouldn't believe. Then there's Sissy Suresh, he screamed and screamed on a date with my sister when he saw a spider crawl across his windscreen. Over there, wedged between Happy Herath – laughs uncontrollably at his own stupid jokes – and Lazy Lasanga – I dated him for two weeks, he wanted me to do his laundry, so I dumped him – is Insane …'

'Imantha,' Tehara added. 'He's been in and out of psych wards for the last five years. I've seen him on rounds.'

'Please tell me your mum does not use that idiot astrologer in Keysborough,' begged Gayani.

Una nodded. And she would bloody know; she, Aunty Sonali and my mum have permanent parking spots in front of the shyster's house.

'He tells our mothers every year that *Mangala Yoga* will come around *nekath* time for their daughters. He then hands over all these proposals he's been given to match up. They don't. He just gets paid $10 every time he hands out a proposal,' she explained.

'But *Ammi* said she used an online service this time,' I protested. Not that I actually wanted to get matched up with anybody but I hated the thought of my mum getting ripped off.

'Yes, but he runs the online service too. My nephew, Tilak, did the software for it and he's only in Year 9!'

'Think of it this way, Shani,' Tehara consoled. 'At least you won't have to meet these guys the next time your mother decides it's *Mangala Yoga*. You've done your dash. Your mum can't ask any more of you.'

'But I always thought that astrologer was so legit,' Una wailed.

'Appearances can be *so* deceptive.'

Someone had pulled the plug on the TV (methinks it might have been Mum!) forcing everybody to mingle. I saw the guy in the red *batik* shirt furtively stuff his pockets full of *patis*, cutlets and pan rolls. Yep, another weirdo!

'Hey girls!' Amani called as she and Rohan came through the door. Rohan had Maya in her capsule. And Amani looked simply amazing in a slinky grey Scanlan and Theodore dress.

'Hey, Amani,' we all chorused as we all crowded around to have a look at Maya. She'd grown out of her newborn alien look and looked ... like the gorgeous baby she was.

'How are things going? I so want one,' Gayani enthused, cooing at Maya.

'Yeah, good,' Amani said as she freed the baby from the capsule and expertly held the sleeping infant in the crook of her arm. 'How are things going with you?'

'I've just given these girls here the run down on the arranged marriage losers,' Gayani said conspiratorially.

Amani ducked her head around the corner to check them out. 'I can't believe it, Smartarse Senerath is still doing the rounds. My mum made me meet him before I started dating Rohan.'

I had to acknowledge that Mother had been royally had.

As people started mingling more, Una was distracted by a good looking guy who'd just walked in the door.

'I hope that's not one of the losers,' Una hissed as Sarath greeted him at the door.

'Nope. That's Aunty Sonali's nephew, Bhatiya. He's over here from the UK on holiday,' Gayani said.

Bhatiya was handsome. Not in the gay-boy-action-man way Ruwan had been gorgeous, but more the Gregory Peck handsome. Almost like a Sri Lankan Jude Law. Tall, tanned, high cheek bones and even a little cleft in his chin. He was dressed beautifully in an Armani knit top and matching casual trousers. Blind Freddy could see this man was straight.

And I was dressed like a Lankan nanna. There was no justice in the world. None at all.

'Ooo, he'll even have a cute accent. Gayani, can you intro-duce us?' Una asked.

Gehani heard Una ask for the introduction and mistook its intent. As always, he was devastated. He turned on his heel determinedly and hurried upstairs to his bedroom, to sulk no doubt. I made a mental note to have a chat with him later and put him out of his misery – the conversation was long overdue.

'Shani! Shani!' Aunty Chandra called as more people filed into our house, interrupting my train of thought.

'Hello, Aunty Chandra,' I mumbled sheepishly.

'I was just telling Jayanthi what a lovely daughter you are. You have done right by your parents, Shani. Meeting all these boys, you're sure to meet the right one for you because making your parents happy is such good karma.'

'And, Tehara, how are you?' Aunty Chandra asked frostily.

'I am well and you, Aunty? How are you?'

'*Anay*, my arthritis is giving so much trouble. Do you think you could get me a referral to see a specialist?'

'Aunty, I am not your doctor. You need to see your GP for that,' Tehara explained patiently.

'How can I see my GP? Who'll take me?'

'*Ammi*, I start work next week,' Amani chided. 'Why don't you catch a cab to see Dr Jayasuriya. I'll pay for it.'

'But I hate catching cabs. It's such a waste of money,' Aunty Chandra replied scathingly. 'I suppose you think you can waste money now that you are going to work and neglecting your daughter.'

We all stifled groans of despair.

'I am not neglecting my daughter,' Amani said through gritted teeth. 'I am getting some balance in my life.'

'Of course you are. What other mother would go to work and leave her only daughter to be taken care of by strangers? You have no heart, Amani.'

'*Ammi*, as I have said, I am not coping well with motherhood. A little break is just what I need to be able to cope better.'

Tehara, Gayani and I exchanged panicked glances. We

needed to diffuse the situation quickly before it went nuclear. But just then, Mrs Peiris came bustling up.

'*Anay* Amani *Puthay*, I was going to call you,' Mrs Peiris gushed. 'Chandrika Beneragama told me she saw you leave a psychiatrist's clinic the other day. I hope you are okay?'

'Aunty, Chandrika had no right to tell you that!' Tehara protested.

'Why are you seeing a psychiatrist?' Aunty Chandra demanded furiously.

I saw Gehani bound down the stairs with a determined look on his face. I hadn't seen that look since he'd smuggled a puppy into our flat in Springvale when he was ten. When my parents took the puppy to the RSPCA, he spent an entire winter's night out in the cold in protest. In the end, they couldn't bear his mute pleading and relented, adopted the puppy and bought a new house within weeks. Rex (a Maltese x Shih Tzu) died five years ago and the family still mourned the absence of his small furry self.

Gehani was holding something in his trousers pocket and grabbed a couple of glasses of wine from the kitchen. He jiggled whatever he had in his pocket and made a beeline to Una who was chatting with Bhatiya. For all of Una's efforts at engaging him, he was determinedly looking at me and smiling.

'I am waiting for an answer, Amani,' Aunty Chandra persisted when Amani remained mute.

'Aunty, would you like a cutlet or *patis*?' Tehara offered.

'Amani! Answer me,' Aunty Chandra demanded, talking to Amani as if she were four again.

'Okay, I am seeing a psychiatrist.'

'But *why* are you seeing a psychiatrist?' Aunty Chandra demanded loudly. 'All you need is Buddhism. You know how it works. Pray and your problems will go away.'

'Aunty Chandra, I am not quite sure this is the right place to be having this discussion,' Tehara interrupted.

'Do not tell me what to do!'

'*Ammi*, we can talk about this later,' Amani said, and made to leave with Maya in her arms.

Aunty Chandra quickly shot her hand out and grabbed her daughter's arm with the same lightning speed as one of those venomous sea creatures you see in those underwater documentaries on the ABC.

'No! Tell me now!'

Across the room, Gehani had been waylaid by a few guests who wanted directions to the 'ladies'. He took his hand out of his pocket with something gripped in his palm to wave them towards us. That got my attention.

One of the ladies who asked for directions was little elderly, so Gehani took a moment to point out the way again. This gave me a good look at what he had his hand. It was a small vial of water.

'*Ammi*, I really don't want to talk about it,' Amani said as she tried to untangle her herself from her mother's grip, trying to juggle the baby as well.

I had seen a vial of water similar to that before.

'Tell me, Amani, I am your mother!'

I'd seen it about fourteen years ago. In Sydney. When Una and I had visited that dodgy *tho-il karaya*.

Gehani covertly poured half the vial into one glass of wine and the other half into the glass of wine he'd already been sipping. He looked at Una and walked straight to her.

Oh my god, Gehani was about to slip Una a *guliyak*!

As you know, I think astrology is a lot of hooey, but I had to stop this insanity from proceeding any further.

'Shani, tell Amani what to do.' Aunty Chandra said, grabbing me.

'Aunty, let me go. I need to speak to Gehani,' I said urgently as I saw him tap Una on the shoulder. They walked a little away to stand in the alcove of a doorway.

'*Anay*, please *Puthay*, tell Amani to talk to me,' Aunty Chandra said, gripping my arm even more fiercely.

'Aunty, just give me ten seconds.'

'*Puthay* do the right thing. Tell Amani what to do!'

'Aunty, let me go!' I said furiously and ripped my arm out of her grasp.

'*Ammi*, I am seeing a psychiatrist for help,' I heard Amani concede as I tried to make it across the crowded room. Gehani had given Una the glass of wine and was smiling at her. A determined smile. The idiot was going to go through with it. And it was not like Una to refuse a glass of wine.

I tried parting the crowds but all of a sudden it seemed like a sea of people were choosing to head towards me, or rather, towards the kitchen to find food.

'Are you taking any medication?' I heard Aunty Chandra quiz hotly.

'It's none of your business!'

'Of course it's my business!'

Una had lifted the glass up to her lips and I was still a good half a room away from her. As I pushed my way through the crowd, I came up right in front of Bhatiya.

'Hi, you're Shani right?' he asked brightly.

'Yes … could you excuse me for a second?' I asked desperately as I saw Una lift her glass.

'Sure … sure …' he said, noticing how distracted I was. But he momentarily grabbed my hand, looked deep into my eyes and said, 'Come back and we'll have a drink.'

And then my mother confronted me.

'Shani, you have to stop this,' she said, her arms akimbo.

I started briefly. She looked sick.

'I'm *trying* to stop it,' I said as I tried to get around her. Una had almost taken a sip.

She moved to cut me off and then grabbed my arm.

'You can't do it. You can't meet any more men. You have *Rahu Apala!*'

'What?' I kept moving though, desperate to get to Una with my mother clinging like a limpet. What was with these older women who felt they had to hang on to you to make a point?

'I just spoke to Aunty Sonali on the phone. You have *Rahu Apala*! No more meeting men!'

I didn't even have a moment to feel relieved because I heard Aunty Chandra roar, 'My daughter is on anti-depressants,' as Una took a massive gulp of her wine.

'Why is my daughter taking anti-depressants?' she cried as if she'd just discovered Amani was a prostitute. I could hear shushing noises all around me as Tehara bodily dragged Amani and Aunty Chandra to the bedroom just beyond the laundry.

While I was momentarily distracted by the ruckus behind me, Una had drained the last of her glass of wine. Damn it, that girl could skull wine like it was mother's milk!

What the hell was I going to do? Who was I going to betray? My brother or my best friend?

CHAPTER 27

Rahu Apala

The sucky thing about people in love is that they are completely oblivious to everybody else. Trust me, I know all about it. Amani and Rohan were positively sickening when they first got together. Tehara and Muthu weren't much better either. Although at least *their* public displays of affection were severely curtailed by the fact that they had to sneak around a great deal and could not be seen in public. But they were positively nauseating at private house parties.

All things being equal, you'd expect to find Una and Gehani joined at the hip, thrashing about like a couple of fish fresh out of water. But they were nowhere to be found. They had disappeared. Completely. How was I supposed to save them if I could not find them?

Not that I could blame them though. Any sane person would be looking for some peace at this stage.

Amani and Aunty Chandra had gone into meltdown mode. And things got worse when Aunty Chandra pulled out the big guns. Amani was in this mess, she said, because she had done bad karma in a past life.

'You don't deserve to be a mother. You are wicked! You will suffer in this life and in the next.' Aunty Chandra had screamed.

Rohan had finally stepped in and parted the combatants by the simple expedient of prising his daughter out of Amani's arms and getting into the car. Amani followed where Maya went.

Not satisfied with having one of her guests creating a scene, my *Ammi* had gone into a rant of operatic scope. Because of my *Rahu Apala*. Aunty Sonali had re-done all our horoscopes by hand (using an ancient ephemeris that looked like a Sanskrit version of the Dead Sea Scrolls) and I was definitely the only one with the *Rahu Apala*. My father and I had to physically restrain my mother from going over to the astrologer's house and giving him a piece of her mind the next day.

'What really makes me want to slap that man,' my mother raged, 'is the time he has wasted.'

'I could not agree with you more. We've spent three weeks meeting men when there was no chance of anything happening.'

'Oh don't be stupid, Shani. It's not about men. I don't care if you don't get married.' Well, here was one for the books. I'd thought it was her chief mission in life. But no. 'It's about you, you silly girl! Because of that idiot astrologer, we haven't done any *Poojas* to negate the bad effects of the *Rahu Apala*,' *Ammi* cried desperately. 'How are we going to protect you? If I had known about the *Rahu Apala*, I would have got you out of that house before you could blink an eye.'

In that instant I did what every smart girl should do: I realised the bleeding obvious. My mother loved me. I mean, *really* loved me. She'd do anything to make sure I was safe and happy. And I was at last content to admit that I really loved her too. This was why she was able to get away with treating me like a prisoner from that day onwards.

I was not allowed to sleep alone. My father was ejected from his bed and my mother made me sleep in her bed with her. I wasn't quite sure how she was going to protect me from potential harm while I slept, but I wasn't going to argue with her.

We were also spending every spare moment either at the Buddhist temple or the Hindu temple, doing *Poojas*.

'*Ammi*, isn't it kind of traitorous to go to a Hindu temple?'

'The Buddha was a Hindu,' my mother ground out as she frogmarched me up the stairs of the temple to pray at the feet of my all-time favourite Hindu god, Lord Ganesh. Gotta love a bloke with an elephant head.

The only thing I refused to capitulate on was driving. My mother had wanted my dad to drive me to and from work, like some geriatric primary school kid. I was already living with my parents and sleeping with my mum; relinquishing my driver's licence seemed just a wee bit extreme, I felt.

Which brings me back to my brother and my erstwhile best friend. I knew they were alive. Gehani periodically came home late at night to change his clothes. I knew this because I helped *Ammi* do the laundry and I had spotted his Mr Happy boxers. I also knew Una was quite well and alive because she was doing all her shifts as usual. I tried calling her at work, but she always seemed to have a patient who needed her.

It was plain as day that the two of them were avoiding all company like the plague. Very suspicious.

When I had settled back into my chair at work late that Friday afternoon, I was both mentally and physically exhausted. Mentally exhausted because I'd fielded a few worried phone calls during the week from Tehara who was watching Amani like a hawk as well. She was genuinely worried that Amani was having another relapse of post-natal depression.

And there was an ominous silence in the office. It was like people were waiting for something big to happen, though I wasn't quite sure what.

I fired up a file to work on my computer when John appeared at my desk with the Human Resources Manager in tow. He looked as if he was on his way to his mother's funeral! 'Shani, could you please join us in my office?'

As I stood up to follow him, my phone rang. I picked it up as it was from Tehara.

'Hey, this better be quick. I have to go to meeting,' I opened.

'Wasn't Amani going to work today?' Tehara asked worriedly.

'Yes, she said she'd be working Tuesdays, Wednesdays and Fridays.'

John was waving to me from the room to hurry me along.

'I just called her office and they said she called in sick. I rang her mobile and home and she wasn't picking up!'

'Why don't you call Rohan?'

'I don't want to worry him.'

John was now glaring at me.

'Why don't you just go over? They hide a key to the back door under the potted lemon tree in the front yard. You just have to lift the pot a little to get to it.'

'Okay' she said as she hung up.

I made a mental note to text her as soon as I got out of the meeting.

'Shani,' John said, sitting down across from me. 'We've just reviewed the board report – and your entire contribution to it has been useless. You have made several large errors of interpretation, based entirely on the fact that you used the wrong data. Even after Max pointed you in the right direction. I was willing to let that go considering your previous exemplary performance and all the pressure you have been under with your house collapsing ...'

'But John ...'

'Just hear me out, Shani. But an issue of even greater concern was brought to our attention a few weeks ago. Under Max Ferguson's meticulous scrutiny of the business units you have been accountable for, we've discovered some major anomalies – anomalies totalling in excess of $5 million dollars. I am sorry, Shani, we are going to have to terminate your employment forthwith and refer the matter to the police and forensic auditors for investigation.'

'Excuse me, John, all my business units are regularly audited by forensic accountants. There can't be any anomalies. If there are any, you need to take it up with them.'

'Shani, you are being defensive now. Considering the position you are in, it would be best if you left immediately and let the auditors take over.'

'But John ...'

'Don't John me, Shani. I would have preferred to groom you for my role than Max. But Max has proved to be not only an invaluable networker but a darn fine accountant too. Nobody would have spotted the anomalies except him. His wife and the CEO's wife are now on holiday in Paris.'

I felt sick to my stomach.

'But John ... can you tell me where the anomalies are? I am sure I can explain them.'

The Human Resources Manager interjected immediately, 'Sorry, Shani, for the protection of everybody involved George Elliot & Co cannot comment any further on this matter. I will escort you to your car and we'll courier your things to you within the next twenty-four hours.'

And so I was escorted to my car flanked by the Head of Human Resources on one side and a gargantuan security guard on the other. I'm not quite sure what they thought five feet four inch me would do to either one of them. And you can't exactly go postal in metropolitan Melbourne – guns aren't easily accessible.

It was one of those cold, wet Melbourne nights. The traffic was a nightmare and the roads were slippery; especially over tram tracks. My mind tossed between a state of blankness and howling rage at Max's betrayal. I had committed no fraud and he knew it. It was more likely that he'd committed fraud and was trying to pin it on me instead.

Maybe there *was* something to this *Rahu Apala* thing, I thought, as I was held up by yet another tram. I had sped up to get past it before the lights changed, attempting the Melbourne tango. Only this time, as I flashed through the intersection as the lights turned from amber to red, an idiot from the other direction ran the red light.

***

'Hey, which hospital did they bring me to?' I asked the nurse groggily as I woke up on a gurney in an emergency room. I knew I was not going to die. I had got out of my car (which looked more like a twisted pretzel now), dealt with the driver of the other car and organised the towing; but someone had called an ambulance and I had agreed to go to the emergency room.

'The Alfred.'

Finally, some good news. Maybe I could get Tehara to drive me home and I could spin some lie to my mother. At the rate my *Rahu Apala* was going, my mother would have me under house arrest for the rest of my life.

'Could you page Dr Tehara Jayasuriya? I know she's on duty tonight.'

'Sure,' he said and went away.

I drifted off to sleep yet again. I woke up a couple of hours later. But there was no Tehara at my bedside.

The nurse came back in and said, 'If you are feeling better, you may go now.'

'Did you page Dr Jayasuriya?'

'No. Why, do you need a psych referral?'

'She's a friend and I was hoping she'd drive me home,' I replied groggily. I hate hospitals, the awful smell of bleach and rubbing alcohol, and the constant din of monitors. How did Una and Tehara work in a place like this?

'Actually, I saw her down the corridor about an hour ago. She was with a red-haired girl.'

'Short with green eyes?'

He nodded an affirmative.

Una was here, too. What was going on? I decided to find out.

My whole body jarred with pain when I swung my legs off the gurney and took my first step. Maybe house arrest at my parents' house was what I needed.

'Which way?'

He pointed left.

I limped like an old woman down the corridor. I peeked in every room I passed until I came to the last one and was jolted with surprise. Almost everybody I knew was in there.

I opened the door and stepped in. Aunty Chandra was lying on a gurney. Rohan didn't even look up as he stared fixedly at Maya in her capsule. Amani was probably out getting people coffees and sorting out the doctors for Aunty Chandra.

Gehani and Tehara were hugging a hysterically sobbing Una; it was as if they were holding her together by their joint efforts. Strange! I never knew Una had any tender feelings for Aunty Chandra.

Tehara looked up when I limped in the room.

She disentangled herself from Una and reached out for me. She looked devastated. Her eyes were red-rimmed and hollow. I had never seen her like this.

'What's going on?'

'Amani is dead,' Tehara told me softly, enfolding me in her arms.

I guess I now know what it's like to be in the middle of a bomb explosion.

PART TWO

Three Years Later

CHAPTER 28

Another Funeral

Show me a person who likes funerals and I'll show you a liar, or someone who is emotionally deranged. Yet, it never fails to amaze me, the sheer number of people who didn't even know the dearly departed or the grieving family, who turn up at Sri Lankan funerals. It seems that a funeral is a big social event that every Lankan in Melbourne feels they *must* be seen at.

'Are we ready to go?' Rohan asked grimly.

'Yes,' I said softly as I piled on a hat, scarf and gloves. Melbourne had thrown us some uncharacteristically cold weather in April. Here we were, barely in the first week of the month, and I'd had to pull on the woollies. I knew too well that the funeral parlours at Springvale Necropolis didn't believe in heating; Gehani and I had a theory that it was to give the dead body some respite before it entered the searing heat of the crematorium.

We drove in complete silence to the funeral. As we turned into the cemetery complex, I turned to Rohan and said, 'I'm glad we didn't bring Maya.'

'No ... children and funerals aren't a good mix,' he agreed.

We walked grimly to the largest funeral hall, Boyd Chapel, and made our way inside the already crowded room.

The crowds parted like the Red Sea under the hands of Moses as we walked in; urgent whispers started to sweep through the throng. Only some of the whispers were not so soft; the words carried clear as day across the large echoey hall.

'Do they know how she died?'

'Nobody will talk about it,' someone replied while mimicking someone slashing his or her wrists.

'*Anay* no, I heard she was *pisu*. Quite mad. Poor Chandra,' a third added while cocking an imaginary gun to their head and pulling the trigger.

'He is so handsome, we should try to find him a wife.'

Rohan and I walked through the crowd, stony-faced. Some things are just best left unsaid. A careful observer, however, would have seen the stiffness in our backs, the tell-tale twitch in my eye, Rohan's convulsive swallow – the only things that betrayed how close we still were to breaking down. How much we still missed her.

'Tehara, please accept my deepest condolences,' I said softly, as we reached the family at the front of the funeral parlour.

'Thank you,' she replied seriously as she reached forward to peck me on the cheek. 'No love lost between my dad and me, though.'

Rohan shook Muthu's hand and we sat behind the family. Tehara's stepmother was wailing quite loudly, which left Tehara and Muthu to do most of the 'meet and greet' work with the attendees.

Rohan and I had barely slipped into the pew behind the family when we were joined by Una and Gehani.

'Off to the South Pole, I see,' my brother teased, tugging at my scarf.

'Better than freezing to death. Why aren't *you* dressed to go to the South Pole?' I asked Una.

'Pregnancy, mate. I feel so warm all the time I rarely have the heating on,' Una said as she patted the rounded belly harbouring my nephew-to-be.

'While I freeze my arse off,' my brother said wryly. 'And I don't even get to cuddle you. You are so warm,' my brother said, making lovey-dovey eyes at Una.

'Where's the bucket?'

'Guys, cool it! And as Maya says, I'll dob you in if you don't,' Rohan quipped back with a gentle tremor to his voice.

But before we could continue acting inappropriately, the funeral service proper started. We were all then rendered comatose by the endless droning of the monk over what seemed like an interminable stretch of time. I'm sure there were nuggets of profound wisdom in the lengthy sermon. But I'd have been royally surprised if even one in ten people attending the funeral could understand it.

'Thank you all very much for coming,' Tehara said graciously on mounting the podium to deliver the eulogy.

'My father was a learned man who contributed a great deal to the community. He came to Australia, aged sixteen and studied at Scotch College before commencing his medical studies at the University of Melbourne,' Tehara opened. As she continued, I wondered whether she'd printed the Wiki stub for her dad and read it out loud. Delivered in a clear passionless voice, it sounded like she was reciting a résumé rather than delivering a eulogy.

'She's very kind.'

'That's our Tehara.'

'Even after the old bastard disowned her for marrying Muthu,' Una whispered.

'I think Tehara has her priorities right. She's letting the past go. She and Muthu have each other now. And they have little James,' I whispered. 'Besides, Muthu's parents adore Tehara.'

Amani's death had, in many ways, freed us all from much of the unimportant emotional baggage we'd clung on to. We'd all been too distraught to try to continue the charade that Tehara and Muthu weren't a couple in the days after Amani's death. Muthu, too, grieved for our lost friend.

The day after Amani's funeral, Muthu's mother had turned up at Tehara's place on Richmond Hill with seven *sarees* and seven golden necklaces, the traditional Hindu gifts from a mother-in-law to her new daughter.

'Where is little James, by the way? I thought he'd be terrorising all and sundry,' Rohan asked, looking back at the crowded room hoping to spot the terror on two feet.

'Tehara said her mother-in-law was going to look after him today while she attended to the formalities here.'

'Just as well, I wouldn't trust him not to knock over the casket,' Gehani agreed.

As the eulogy came to a quick conclusion once Tehara had detailed all of Dr Jayasuriya's philanthropic activities, we got to the pointy end of business. We all stood in silence as the casket was hefted onto the pallbearers' shoulders and set on the dais to be taken away.

I could not hold back the tears. It seemed just like yesterday that it had been Amani's casket being placed on that platform. Now, at this new funeral, I stood there sobbing as Rohan placed his arm around me and I could feel the grief racking his body. Una was crying too and Gehani was holding onto her.

'You poor child,' old Mrs Peiris said gently as we followed the family out. 'You knew Dr Jayasuriya well, didn't you? He was an angel of a man. He donated so much money to people in Sri Lanka; he built whole villages for people after the tsunami.'

I didn't have the heart to tell her that I wasn't crying for him.

'Where's Gayani?'

'She and Sarath are back there. They said they might be running late. Gayani's helping Jayani with her wedding preparations.'

Now there was a surprise. Gayani's sister was marrying Karu, the guy who ended up having a quadruple bypass after literally chasing me round the park. As it turned out, Karu met Jayani at the hospital while he was recovering from surgery and the two fell in love.

'Ah yes, the wedding … you must be very busy getting everything organised.'

'*Anay* yes,' she murmured softly. Then she eyed me very firmly and took hold of my hand. '*Puthay* … I hope to see you at Jayani's wedding.'

'*Anay* Aunty, no …' I responded with a gentle shrug, only she cut me off very quickly.

'I mean, everybody in the community understood when you and your friends didn't come to any weddings the season after Amani's funeral, but *Puthay* it has been three years now. It's over now. It should be over.'

'*Anay*, Aunty … it's just that …'

Mrs Peiris held up a hand to silence me. 'We even understood when your brother and your friend had a small wedding last year. Tehara and Muthu had a Hindu service three years ago,' Mrs Peiris said, furtively looking around for them as she whispered the words 'Hindu', as if it was in itself a sufficiently shameful reason for not having a big wedding. 'But it is time for you to come out of it now, *neh*?'

'But Aunty …'

'*Puthay*, enough is enough. Come now, you've known Jayani since she was a little girl,' Mrs Peiris insisted. And a pesky little brat she'd been too, I thought. 'It's settled, we'll see you at the wedding,' she said firmly, walking off before I could contradict her.

'What did she want?' Una asked, waddling up.

'My appearance at Jayani's wedding.'

'Oh shit, I'd forgotten it was wedding season!'

'Well, I'm not going,' I said, as we walked down the long corridor to join the boys as they stood chatting with each other.

'And why not?'

'What do you mean, why not? You know why not.'

'No, I don't,' she said, giving me a smartarse look and wiggling her butt like a rap star's back-up dancer.

'You know exactly why not. And stop acting all rap-gansta-ho on me. Just because you married brown does not make you brown, ginger!'

'Low blow, low blow,' she said, delicately touching her titian locks. 'But seriously, honey, I think you need to move on …'

'But I *have* moved on,' I protested.

'Pet, you have spent the last three years looking after Maya and Rohan. Everybody thought you were fantastic when you moved in and looked after them. But Maya is no longer a baby and you need a life of your own.'

'I had no choice. Rohan's mother was two steps from kidnapping Maya and taking her off to some Sri Lankan backwater to be raised if I hadn't stepped in,' I reminded her. After all, I had been jobless, homeless and car-less, so it made complete sense for me to move in and look after a baby who'd lost her mother. It wasn't like I had anything better to do.

'Yes, that was then and this is now. You need to find your own life now. Even – shock, horror! – meet a man.'

'Why? I am happy with my life as it is.'

'Because Maya will grow up one day and you'll have no one. Besides, people will start to talk soon.'

'They haven't talked for the last three years, why should they start now?'

'Because you, Maya and Rohan can't keep hiding in the bush like you have been doing. You – and I mean all of you – need to join the land of the living,' she said, making an expansive gesture to indicate Rohan, myself and the not-present Maya.

Clearly, the transformation of Una from best friend to sister-in-law had activated the bossiness chip in her brain.

'Warrandyte is not the bush. It's part of suburban Melbourne,' I parried, hopefully sidestepping the issue.

Rohan had sold up the villa in Hawthorn four months after Amani's funeral to buy a three-acre bush block in Warrandyte with an architect-designed mud-brick house on it. It was blissful waking up to the call of the bellbirds in the morning and watching the kangaroos bounce through the back yard while you had your morning tea. It was paradise and barely thirty minutes from Melbourne's CBD via the freeway.

'That's not the point. And stop trying to change the subject. You need to get out and meet some people. Get a life of your own. I mean, Rohan could meet someone, and where would you be then?'

'Looking for a new place to live?' I replied, giving Una a look of wide-eyed innocence.

'Be serious!'

'Does this have anything to do with the astrologer *Ammi* found in India?' I asked sceptically, as we reached the boys.

Another amazing change that had occurred in the last three years had been my mother's miraculous conversion to cricket. My parents were currently somewhere on the subcontinent following the Sri Lankan team from match to match. But old habits die hard. My mother had packed my horoscope along with the Sri Lankan flag in her luggage.

'Yes, I spoke with her last night. And, yes, you are in *Mangala Yoga*,' she finished, threading her arm through Gehani's.

'Not bloody *Mangala Yoga* again,' I said, feeling queasy.

'Well, it wasn't anyone's fault that someone had mislabelled Gehani's horoscope as yours all those years ago. And look at the proof that it works. It was his time to meet someone, fall in love and get married,' Una said in a gooey voice while I rolled my eyes.

'Darling, I've been in love with you since I was ten. I didn't need to be in *Mangala Yoga* for that to happen,' Gehani said.

'Maybe you needed to be in *Mangala Yoga* to give you licence to do something drastic about it.'

'Like slipping you a *guliyak*?' Rohan asked wryly. Gehani and Una's story was now the stuff of legend in our little circle. 'Besides, does that stuff work?'

'Hmmm ... No. I mean, I knew he'd slipped me a *guliyak* as soon as I sipped that glass of wine.'

'How?'

Rohan hadn't been a part of the drug intervention style confrontation I had staged to bring Gehani and Una to heel. A couple of months after Amani's death, Rohan had had more pressing concerns than my idiot younger brother and idiot best friend.

'The *guliyaks* are really vials of rose essence mixed with vodka.'

'And it completely ruined the glass of wine,' Una added sheepishly. 'Besides, Mr James Bond here isn't really much of a man of mystery. I saw the vial hidden in his palm when he gave me the glass of wine.'

'Did it make you feel any different?'

'Absolutely not. I knew all the reasons why I had been resisting were stupid anyway. I guess I'd always loved Gehani.'

'Why does that guy look familiar?' Gehani asked, nodding delicately at a man standing next to Gayani and Sarath.

'It's him! It's Bhatiya Fernando, Aunty Sonali's nephew.'

'The guy you were chatting up at Shani's party? He's looking at you,' my brother gritted jealously. 'Quick, turn sideways and flash him your ring,' Gehani said, grabbing Una's hand. 'Yeah, that's right, arsehole. She's taken now!'

'Oh shhh, and stop being so stupid. They're coming over.'

'Hi,' Gayani said brightly, introducing everybody.

As Rohan and Bhatiya shook hands, I couldn't help but compare the two men. Both were very attractive and self-assured, but while Rohan's face showed the maturity of having survived the hardship of the last three years, Bhatiya's was still relatively fresh and unlined.

'You remember Shani, of course,' Gayani introduced us.

'Yes, I am not sure if you remember me though. I came to a party at your parents' house a few years ago,' Bhatiya said, holding on to my hand just little bit longer than necessary. His hands were large, warm and dry, and oddly comforting.

'Yes, I do remember.'

'Una, Shani ...' Gayani said, clearing her throat a little. 'I was wondering whether I could ask a favour of you, and Tehara of course ...'

'Sure, go ahead.'

'Jayani has come a cropper with her bridesmaid's *sarees*. We were hoping we could get the ... three of you to help us.' There was an uneasy silence as we all tried not to remember there had once been four of us. Gayani continued hastily: 'You girls are so creative. I'm sure I've never seen any of you wearing the same *saree* twice. I remember the *saree*s you beaded for your brother Gamini's wedding – they were amazing!'

What could we say after such extravagant praise? 'Sure, of course. Happy to help. When would you like us to come over?'

'How about next Saturday? Why don't you come for lunch and we can all work on them together?'

'Sure, as long as I can bring Maya along,' I said with a smile.

'Of course, bring Maya.'

'I look forward to seeing you there, then,' Bhatiya said, beaming. This was a surprise.

'Oh, will you be there?'

'Yes, I have been spending my weekends with Sarath and Gayani,' he said. 'I haven't any family in Melbourne since Aunty Sonali died.'

'Are you here for long?'

'I haven't decided yet. But I'm doing a large project for my company which may be extended.'

Rohan caught my eye and looked at his watch. 'Maya,' he explained.

'We'd better go,' I said, waving an apologetic hand in Bhatiya's direction as we walked away quickly.

CHAPTER 29

The Saree Working Bee

'*Punchi*! Wake up! *Punchi*!!' Maya yelled at the top of her voice, bouncing on my stomach. When that didn't yield the result she wanted, she tried another tactic. She lifted the doona off my feet and started tickling me.

'It's morning, *Punchi*!' We need to get up and at 'em.' Maya's volume control was permanently set at loud. 'And I am hungry!' she yelled, lifting her pink paisley pyjama top and pointing to her rounded tummy with her belly button still cutely sticking out. 'See … it's empty! I'm really, really hungry.'

'Honey, I gave you a full bottle not an hour and a half ago,' I groaned, when I saw bedside clock read minutes past seven.

'Yes, but Tehara *Wokuma* says I am a growing girl and I need my food.'

I stood up and swung Maya high up into the air and into my arms, and then we rubbed noses. 'I love you more than the stars in the sky and the fish in the ocean,' I said to her softly, my forehead resting on hers.

'I wow you more than Weetbix!'

'Does that mean you want Weetbix for breakfast? It's Saturday, you know, and *Thathi* can make us some cooked breakfast,' I said as I carried her to the kitchen.

'No, I wan' Weetbix,' Maya insisted with a gorgeous pout of her rosebud lips. Dressed in her pink pyjamas, with her tumble of glossy black curls and exuding that warm husky smell of toddler, she was simply delicious.

'How about some eggs on toast?' Rohan asked as we strolled into the kitchen. There was a running track along the edge of the Yarra River that formed the southern boundary of the property. Rohan ran most weekends to the wood-fired bakery in Warrandyte and brought back fresh bread for breakfast.

'No, *Thathi*,' Maya insisted. 'Weetbix.'

'How about some porridge with some yummy, scrummy honey?' I asked as Rohan handed me my morning tea, with a little bow. Hot, sweet and milky, just the way I liked it. Maya scrambled onto the converted highchair-cum-barstool to sit at the breakfast bar. With its warm wooden panelling and Aga stove, the kitchen was my favourite room in the house.

'No. Weetbix,' she declared firmly.

Rohan grimaced, set a bowl on the counter and made up Maya's cereal with slices of banana and cold milk.

'At this rate, she's going to turn into a Weetbix,' he said.

'The nurse told me not to worry. Apparently it's called an eating jag. Toddlers do it all the time.'

'What? Weetbix for breakfast, lunch and dinner? How many weeks has it been now?'

'Two. Hopefully she'll eat something different at Gayani's house this afternoon.'

'Let's hope so,' Rohan said as he put the frying pan on to

make bacon and eggs. I popped the bread in the toaster, poured the orange juice and laid the plates out with our favourite condiments and spreads.

'What are we doin' today? Are we going to see baby James?'

'I thought you and James had a fight last week and you never wanted to see that "horrible, terrible" baby again?'

'Nah, we're good.' Maya had clearly moved on.

'I am going to Aunty Gayani's,' I said, passing Rohan the Tabasco sauce.

'Why?' Maya asked in that particularly whiny tone only three-year-olds could muster. 'I want go see baby James.'

'Because *I* am going to go make some *sarees* really pretty.'

'Why?' Maya asked again, looking bored. Rohan rolled his eyes.

'Because we want the *sarees* to be really pretty for a wedding.' Finally, a spark of interest in Maya's eyes.

'Pretty *sarees* like at a real wedding? Like at my *Ammi*'s wedding?' Maya spent hours poring over Amani and Rohan's wedding album, looking at the *sarees* we'd worn all those years ago.

'Yes,' I replied with a wink at Rohan.

'Can I come? Please, please?'

'May I come.' Rohan corrected automatically.

'Only if you promise to behave and eat whatever they offer you at Aunty Gayani's.'

'Do I have to kiss Peiris *Archie*?'

'Yes,' I responded with a 'don't care' attitude.

'Why?'

'To be polite,' Rohan responded.

'But she smells of curry.'

'Well, you don't have to go. You can help me rake up the autumn leaves after ballet,' Rohan offered, pointing at the large liquidambar tree out the window. The little girl took one look at the leaves scattered all over the back yard and promptly turned back to me. 'I'll be good and eat anything they give me. I'll even kiss stinky Peiris *Archie*.'

So, I picked Maya up from ballet. Rohan usually took her to the class while I did yoga and then I picked her up and took her out somewhere for the day, usually to the park or to visit my parents. That gave Rohan some time to himself over the weekend. Sundays were family time, though; we'd spend the day together, either at home doing the gardening or out somewhere.

'Hi Maya, Shani,' Gayani enthused when we knocked at the door. 'Don't you look pretty in that dress,' she complimented Maya as I spied my mum, Una, Tehara and James across the room.

'It's not a dress, it's a tutu,' Maya contradicted loftily, but her chin came down a fraction after she caught a very stern look from me.

So she gave Old Aunty Peiris a very enthusiastic kiss after theatrically prostrating on her knees and bowing to touch her forehead to the ground and clasping her hands together in veneration. A very proper and traditional greeting from a young child to an elder; but in Maya's hands, a piece of high drama. I had to stop myself smiling, which I knew would only encourage her.

'*Anay*, what a well brought up Sinhala girl,' Mrs Peiris complimented. '*Pau*, your *Ammi* would have been so proud of you.' Yeah, Amani would have been proud of Maya's theatrics, alright. She was a real chip off the old block. I remembered, with a pang of sorrow, that day in the principal's office when she'd saved us from expulsion at St Catherine's.

As we walked into the family room, the little girl stopped and sighed in wonder. Metres and metres of delicate dusky rose silk fabric was stretched on hand-made embroidery frames and hung from hooks on the ceiling. The frames were two metres across and a metre wide so that we could embellish the *sarees* in large blocks. They had been hung from the hooks to keep fabric from dragging on the floor, which created a magical effect of a silk tent with swags of fabric everywhere.

'Wow,' said Maya, softly.

It was quite fortunate that the mesmerising effect of the hung *sarees* distracted the eye from the over-large leather sofa stuffed into the small room and the completely inappropriate Italianate dining table wedged in the corner. The woefully tasteless furniture was matched by the jarring colour of the paintwork throughout the house. Only Gayani would paint adjoining walls ochre and lime green.

'Where's Jayani?'

'She's had to go off to a *saree* blouse fitting, so it'll just be us.'

'So, where are we up to?' I asked, looking at the *sarees*.

'We haven't really done much yet,' Gayani confessed.

'That's where we were hoping you could help. Jayani could not decide whether to do the whole *saree* or just focus on the *pallu*,' Aunty Peiris joined in.

'When's the wedding, again?' Tehara asked.

'In two months.'

'What? It'll be near impossible to bead these *sarees* in time for the wedding. Can't she buy *sarees* for the bridesmaids?'

'Actually, Jayani had everything organised. She had Mrs Perera send six *sarees* especially from India, only Vinitha Jayaskera saw them. She offered Mrs Perera three times what Jayani was going to pay, so she sold them to her instead.'

'That bitch,' my *Ammi* said with anger.

Did my mum just say bitch? *Really?*

'I agree with you, though it is not very Buddhist to say that,' Mrs Peiris commented piously, casting her eyes apologetically at the framed photo of the Lord Buddha hanging over the lintel.

'To make things worse, Mrs Perera lied to us and told us that the *sarees* had been lost, only Kumari Fonseka and Shanika Kirigoda, Vinitha's bridesmaids, put pictures of the *sarees* up on Facebook. Jayani was in tears.'

'That's it! Jayani's bridesmaid's *sarees* are going to be the best bridesmaid *sarees* this wedding season,' Una declared with a determined set to her mouth.

'Here's the plan,' I said. 'Forget working the whole *saree*, we won't have enough time to work six complete ones. We'll just have to do spectacular *pallus*.'

'But what design will we use?'

'How were you planning on draping the *sarees*?' Una asked.

'Not sure.'

'How about you get the bridesmaids to carry the *pallus* on their arms? It's more elegant that way anyway and it will hide the fact that we haven't embellished the entire *saree*,' Tehara said, authoritatively.

'What about when they dance? It will very difficult to dance carrying the *pallus* on their arms.'

'This is where we'll really triumph,' I said. 'During the *poruwa* ceremony, I'll go around and pin the falls over the girls' shoulders and fan it out behind them and tuck the ends into their waists. So, all that people will see during the dance will be the beautifully worked *pallus*.'

'Very ingenious!'

'With the added benefit of giving you two looks instead of just the one,' Una seconded.

'What about the design? my mum asked.

'What flowers are you using for the bouquets?' Tehara asked.

'Pink frangipanis. But Reychelle Obesekera used a frangipani motif on her *sarees* at her wedding last year.'

'Damn it,' I muttered under my breath. 'Do you have a theme for the decorations?'

'We are going for a European castle theme – kinda like the theme from *Kabhi Khushi Kabhie Gham*.'

'Are Jayani and her fiancé using *Shawa Shawa* as their bridal dance?'

'Yes.'

'Wow, they're brave. It's a damned tricky dance to do right,' Tehara commented. 'If it's slow, you look like you've done a joint of pot and if you do it too fast, it looks like the skeleton dance.'

'So, who's leading the bridal dance?'

'Surangani Subasinghe and her band of dancers. We didn't have much choice after you four ... er, three ... stopped dancing,' Gayani said, uncomfortably. 'It was either Surangani or Rehka. And everybody knows Rehka ...'

'... dances like a ho,' my *Ammi* finished.

I stared at her, shocked. Clearly, my mother had found time to pick up the vocabulary of a sailor while she had been on the sub-continent!

'Let us supervise a couple of the practice sessions just to make sure things go smoothly,' I offered, while glaring hard at my mum to lower her voice. I so didn't want to explain to Maya what a ho was just yet.

'But that gives me an idea,' Una said, waddling fast towards the TV and DVD player. She selected the Hindi movie from which the music came and fast forwarded it to the segment where the dancing started. (Trust me, the only way to watch Hindi movies is on DVD and with a fast forward button. That way you can skip over the melodrama and just watch the music or you just watch the bad acting and miss the music, either way, you get to decide – at a fraction of the time.)

'Look at her, the main chick,' Una said pointing to a *choli*-clad Bollywood temptress wriggling her hips seductively to the beat of the music.

'Rani Murkerji, you mean.'

'Yeah, look at the style of beading on her *choli*, it's simple and effective,' Una said. 'I reckon we could recreate that.'

I took a pen out of my handbag and did a quick sketch on the back of my phone bill. 'What do you think of this? We could do the outline of the design in silver beading and then fill in the body with tea-rose sequins.'

'That would be perfect!' Aunty Peiris enthused.

'And I think we can finish all six *sarees* in two months, which gives us a lot of time to make sure the bridal dance will be fantastic,' Tehara chimed in.

The race was on. We worked from about 10 am until midday. First, we drew the motif properly. We then carefully transferred the design onto the silk *sarees* using carbon paper, paying attention not to stain the rest of the *saree* with blue ink. I didn't remember ever having problems with this in the past, but that was before we had two toddlers running about under our feet, using the falls of silk *sarees* as feather boas for a cabaret performance.

'Maya! James, no!' I yelled at the two of them, trying to ward off disaster.

'But we want to make a sandpit in it,' Maya protested, trying to lift a *saree* frame.

'No, you can play with your toys.'

'But James and me wanna make a sandpit.'

'James can play with his Wiggles car.'

'NO!' both Maya and James chorused, stamping their feet.

'What if we played elephants and tigers?' Bhatiya asked quietly, as he and Sarath walked through the front door.

'Who are you?' Maya demanded.

'Maya!'

'Well, I'm not allowed to play with strangers,' she declared righteously.

'My name is Bhatiya, but you may call me Uncle Bhatiya.'

256

'You sound funny,' the little girl said, giving him an assessing look beyond her years.

'That's because I come from England.'

'But tigers and elephants don't come from England.'

'All the same, it's a great game. This is how we play it,' Bhatiya said as he whisked the toddlers out the back door into the garden to play for a good hour and a half. Miracles do occur, sometimes.

'I hope Maya isn't being too much of a pest,' I said as we later congregated around the dining table for lunch.

Though Gayani may be colour blind and not much of an interior decorator, she is a fabulous cook. She'd turned out a meal this afternoon fit for a king. On offer were prawns cooked in a delicate coconut sauce with fragrant ginger and tomatoes, peppery okra with butter, lentil curry with deep fried shallots and tomatoes, and the pièce de resistance, chicken curry flavoured with cloves and cardamom.

'No, she's been simply delightful,' Bhatiya said, as he served himself and my little girl some rice and curry.

'No chicken curry, Uncle Bhatiya, please.'

'I think Aunty Gayani may have made you and James some chicken without the chilli.'

And as if by magic, Gayani turned up at our elbows with a specially cooked mild curry for Maya and James.

'You are very good to us.'

'Considering you and your friends have saved Jayani's wedding it's the least I could do.'

Maya sat chirpily next to Bhatiya, tucking into her rice and curry. She kept him amused with tales from her pre-school, about Matilda the possum who lived in our roof and Sarah the wombat who lived near the river at the bottom of the property.

'Gee, your house sounds wonderful,' Bhatiya, said admiringly.

'Come and visit!'

'I am not sure whether Bhatiya would want to visit us all the way out in Warrandyte,' I said, wanting to give him an easy way out if he needed it.

'Actually, that would be nice.'

'Then you must come and feed the ducks with us,' Maya said bossily. '*Punchi* and I feed them every day.'

'How can I resist the invitation of a lovely lady like yourself?' Bhatiya asked, bowing slightly to Maya as we finished lunch and walked into the kitchen to rinse our plates.

'I like him,' Maya said, turning to me. 'He's not silly like Uncle Gehani or serious like Uncle Muthu or stuffy like *Thathi*.'

'You calling my husband silly?' Una called from across the room. Maya ran over to start arguing with Una.

'So, what have you been doing with yourself for the last three years?' Bhatiya asked, casually, leaning against the fridge.

'Well, not long after we met, as you know, my friend, Maya's mum, died, so I have been looking after her.'

'You've given up working?'

'No, actually I lost my job around that same time, so I didn't work until Maya was about eighteen months old and since then I have been working part-time,' I explained.

I now worked as the CFO for a not-for-profit organisation providing housing for the underprivileged. I knew what it was like to be homeless so I put my efforts into making sure the experience is not so soul-destroying for others. Besides, the corporate sector had left me with a very nasty taste in the mouth – even after the investigation had cleared me of any wrongdoing at George Elliot & Co. Max Ferguson had miscalculated when he'd tried to pin his fraud on me and was now having an extended vacation at Barwon prison to consider his options.

'Aunty Sonali told me that you were an accountant.'

'I still am. I just don't work the same stupid hours anymore. Between Rohan and I, we make sure one of us is at home to look after Maya when she is not at pre-school. So, what do you do?' I asked, serving us bowls of delicious, dark, gooey treacle and curd.

'I used to be an investment banker. But I now work in renewable energy.'

'You've ditched investment banking for science? Pretty impressive.'

'Not exactly. I am actually in a consortium starting up a solar energy plant here.'

'You mean the one out in Bendigo?'

'No, a smaller test farm not far from the Yarra Valley. So I come past your neck of the woods everyday.' Bhatiya hesitated for a moment before saying, 'I hope you don't think me too forward, but are you seeing anyone?'

'No ...' I replied, blushing furiously.

Somehow, over the past three years I'd got out of the habit of thinking about men in that way – the combination of being busy raising Maya, and a reluctance to risk further experiences of the sort my mother had subjected me to the year Amani died. In the end, I'd decided to shelve the whole relationship thing indefinitely; at least until Maya was a little older.

'*Punchi*, tell Aunty Una to stop tickling me,' Maya screamed across the room as she and Una tussled on the couch.

I was momentarily distracted, but Bhatiya gently tugged at my hand, drawing me back into a conversation I wasn't sure I wanted to have.

'That night three years ago, I actually came to see you. Aunty Sonali had been driving me insane for years telling me about this girl whose horoscope matched mine perfectly.'

'I was wearing that ridiculous *saree*!'

'But you were still beautiful,' he said softly. 'Then I had to go back to the UK. I decided that the time wasn't right then.

259

I hope it is, now. Will you have dinner with me some time?'

'I'd like that,' I said, too distracted to think things through. Looking up at his handsome face, I felt an unfamiliar fluttering in the pit of my stomach. Was I flirting? After all this time?

'It's a date, then,' he said, gently, closing his other hand over mine.

Something about our body language must have given us away because Maya came barrelling up. '*Punchi* is mine,' the little girl screamed, pushing her way between Bhatiya and me. 'Don't you touch her!' she yelled, kicking Bhatiya with considerable force in the shin.

CHAPTER 30

The Duck Pond

'Take a load off,' Rohan said as he held out a glass of wine. Maya had had a tantrum just before bed and consequently I was wiping yoghurt off the kitchen benches. 'Don't worry about it now,' he said, when I hesitated for a moment. 'The cleaners are coming in tomorrow morning anyway.'

I ripped the rubber gloves off my hands, tossed them in the sink and gratefully accepted a glass of Merlot. I followed Rohan out onto the balcony overlooking the Yarra and curled up on the rattan outdoor couch, as he lit the chimenia already stacked with wood to ward off the bite of frost in the breeze of the crisp autumn evening.

'I gather feeding the ducks down by river this afternoon didn't go well?' Rohan asked as he flung his long, lean body onto the adjoining couch. At forty and with grey now feathering his temples, he'd transformed from hip to debonair gradually and seamlessly. And losing Amani had permanently wiped the streak of smugness from his character.

'It went reasonably well to begin with,' I replied. 'She fights so hard against liking him. One minute she is all over him like a rash and the next minute, she turns into a little brat.'

'Tell me what happened. I thought Bhatiya had bought his way quite effectively into Maya's materialistic heart the other day. I didn't know there was a Barbie dream mansion as well as a Barbie BMW!' Rohan said, referring to the stack of gifts that Bhatiya had bestowed on Maya in a bid to get her to like him.

'Bhatiya picked me up first from work and we picked her up together from pre-school.'

Bhatiya and I had been steadily dating each other for the last six weeks. He was intelligent, well-spoken, drop-dead gorgeous and without any obvious character flaws that I could see. He was the perfect candidate for a relationship and I wanted to believe that something between us could work.

'Hey, princess,' Bhatiya called out as the swarm of pre-schoolers ran out of the classroom in search of their loved ones. My little girl was easily identifiable, even in the sea of fairy floss-coloured clothing, by her halo of curly hair.

'Hi, Uncle Bhatiya!'

I stopped to say hello to a few of the other mothers gathering up their offspring, watching out of the corner of my eye as Maya and Bhatiya walked slowly towards his car. Somehow, Maya had convinced him to carry her miniscule school bag and was leading the charge while Bhatiya followed a step or so behind, like a loyal vassal. She was brought to an abrupt halt when she didn't see the familiar Volvo I drove.

Bhatiya pointed to the large BMW four-wheel drive parked a few cars away; Maya gave a whoop of delight as she scrambled towards it. It never fails to amaze me how even children as little as Maya can be so completely brand conscious. Bigger is always better.

'*Punchi, Punchi*! Look!' Maya squealed from the back seat as Bhatiya switched on the in-built DVD player. I groaned inwardly as the familiar panpipe music of the Waybuloos blared through the crystal clear surround sound system. Did we really need to have a DVD on for the few minutes it took to drive from the pre-school into Warrandyte?

'You really don't need to spoil her like this.'

'I love to,' Bhatiya said, angling a quick glance back at Maya who was now engrossed in her show. He gave me an indulgent smile. 'You don't let me spoil you, so at least let me spoil her.'

Bhatiya was referring to my refusal to accept his invitation to join him and his colleagues at an all expenses paid spa retreat last weekend. Somehow, I didn't feel comfortable at the lightning speed with which he wanted to move things along. Maybe I just wanted to get to know him better first.

'We're here!' Bhatiya called out as he pulled into the parking lot behind the tennis courts near the river. It was a lovely day; the autumn sun glistened through the heavy canopy of gum trees lining the nearby river and there was a hint of smoke in the air from the wood-fired bakery. In the distance, I could hear cyclists ringing their bells as they rode up and down the winding path next the river.

Only Maya didn't even bother looking up. She was now too engrossed in her show to care where she was. I knew she'd crack it if Bhatiya switched off the in-car entertainment system. So I held up a conspiratorial hand at a perplexed-looking Bhatiya who was wondering why Maya was now completely uninterested in playing.

I opened the passenger side door closest to the river, letting the sound of running water, quacking ducks and the squeals of excited children waft into the vehicle for a couple of minutes. Then I motioned to Bhatiya to reduce the volume a couple of notches.

'Maya, look! A duck and ducklings,' I said, pointing to the duck and its brood which had congregated not far from the car. They were being fed by an excited gaggle of kids; though judging by the size of the birds, they needed more exercise and a lot less food.

Still no response.

I waited a few minutes more before I tried enticing her again.

'Maya, I think I just saw a little puppy. A Labrador!' I said in faux-excited voice. Maya spotted the tone and knew at once that I was lying. She didn't bother to raise her eyes from the DVD screen.

'Shall I go up to the bakery and start ordering our coffees?' Bhatiya asked, beginning to get bored and exasperated with Maya's inexplicable delaying tactics. 'What would you like?'

'Look Maya! Some 'roos have come down for a drink,' I exclaimed, pointing to a mob of kangaroos that had appeared at the edge of the river.

But Maya remained entranced by the Waybuloos, her little rosebud mouth hanging open.

I flung my hands up in the air, giving up. I turned around to Bhatiya. 'Can you get me a soy flat white? And one of those fruit flans? I don't think *mademoiselle* here will have anything.'

One of these days I was going to have to explain to Bhatiya that effective parenting was all about preventing trouble where possible, rather than scraping up the ensuing mess. About leaving the eggs inside the fridge, rather than unscrambling the omelette.

Bhatiya gave a frustrated grunt and turned to get the coffee, when a piping voice called out from the leather-lined interior of the BMW.

'*Punchi*, tell Uncle Bhatiya that I want a muffin. Joe from the bakery keeps one for me.'

I help up a delaying hand to stop Bhatiya from rushing back to the car to get the little miss's order.

'You know Joe only keeps them until 2.30 pm and it's nearly past that. You need to tell Uncle Bhatiya quick.'

'I can't. I'm watching the Waybuloos.'

'Well, Uncle Bhatiya can't hear you.'

'Well, you tell him then!'

'I don't want to shout across the carpark. That's rude!'

'Please?'

'No. I think I see Emily's little girl going into the bakery. Doesn't she love muffins too?' I asked craftily.

'Let me out!'

'Say please.'

'Let me out! Let me out!' the little girl screamed as if I had imprisoned her in the car.

'Say please!'

'Okay, *please.*

I ducked into the car and unbuckled her and helped her down. Her haste to get to her muffin had her outstripping the long-legged Bhatiya in the race up the hill. Not that Bhatiya was exactly hurrying. He seemed to be doubled over, laughing.

'The two of you ...' he gasped between chortles, '... are amazing. She knows exactly how to push your buttons. And you push hers like a pro!'

'Like any mother and daughter,' I responded with an arched eyebrow.

We spent the rest of the afternoon down by the river feeding the ducks and getting to know each other. Well ... actually, it was more a case of Maya whittling Bhatiya's ego down to the size of a pea.

'*Punchi*, can we go down and feed the ducks?'

'Sure, honey,' I said kissing her curly hair as Bhatiya and I drained our coffee cups and stood up.

Maya led the way down the little embankment to the river, where she promptly turned to Bhatiya, gave him an assessing look as he reached into the bag of stale bread, and said, '*Thathi* walks faster than you.'

When Bhatiya threw a few bits of bread into the river to entice more water birds, Maya's only comment was, '*Thathi* can throw bread further than you. And he can get more ducks to come.'

Things didn't improve from there. When Bhatiya, Maya and I walked a little way up the track to look at some of the riverside stalls, Maya kept up a stream of comparative comments.

'*Thathi* smells really nice. Uncle Bhatiya, you don't smell as nice,' the little girl said, wrinkling her nose when Bhatiya picked her up momentarily to walk over a puddle of water.

'She's starting to like me,' Bhatiya commented laconically at Maya retreating back as soon as he set her down.

Things went further downhill once we got into the car to return home; the stream of disparaging comments turned into a raging torrent. The high tech diversions in the car no longer held any interest.

'*Thathi* sings better than you,' Maya commented when Bhatiya hummed a couple of bars of the Wiggles' 'Rock-A-Bye Your Bear'. And *Thathi* is nicer than you, more handsome than you and smarter than you!' Maya yelled as we pulled into the driveway. The temper tantrum had ignited after Bhatiya had momentarily held my hand in between gear changes.

I snapped.

'Maya, Bhatiya and I will not take you out again until you are nicer to him. Your manners today have been awful. Now, go to your room!'

'My *Thathi* is better than him,' she yelled from the upstairs window when she spied Bhatiya kissing me goodbye.

Rohan was laughing uncontrollably by the time I finished my story. 'You should not let her wind you up so much.'

'Easy for you to say. You weren't on the receiving end of a SWOT analysis of your boyfriend.'

'So, is he your boyfriend?'

'Don't change the subject. How are we going to deal with Maya? I mean, she *hates* him.'

'I wouldn't be so sure,' Rohan said, refilling my glass.

'Why?' I asked, genuinely perplexed. If Maya had been a teenager, I'm sure I'd have found a voodoo doll with Bhatiya's countenance stuck through with needles.

'Well, all she could talk to me about this afternoon was him.'

'Really?'

'Yes, really. I had to endure a very similar afternoon!'

'What? Did she tell you all about how awful Bhatiya was?'

'No, she told me how much *better* than me Bhatiya was,' Rohan responded with a smirk.

'Excuse me?'

'Apparently my Volvo no longer cuts the mustard; I must get a BMW like Bhatiya. *Thathi* drives a silly car, apparently. Bhatiya apparently has a nicer smile and a better watch than me – I have been told to buy a Breitling, by the way. She said he always buys her muffins, and he was very nice to the ducks, and did I notice how tall he was ...'

To say I was gobsmacked would have been a gross understatement. 'The way she speaks to him, you'd think he'd murdered her favourite soft toy.'

'Nuh, uh, she adores him ... or at least she gave me a very good impression she did. She loves his clothes (not boring like *Thathi's*) and most of all, she loves his accent. She says she wants to go and live in England and learn to speak like him. I must confess I was feeling a little jealous of him by the time you came home.'

'You don't think she's trying to ... you know ...' I said, gesticulating furiously to the two of us, as the outlandish thought struck me. I wondered, as some wine sloshed out of my glass, if the two glasses of wine I'd already consumed had gone slightly to my head. Both Rohan and I jumped in with the napkins to mop up the spill on the floor and banged heads together in the process.

'Nah …' Rohan denied, rubbing his sore temple. We were still both crouched together in the tight corner between the two rattan couches. We were so close that I could smell the wine on his breath mingled with the mint tea he habitually drank after dinner. 'I mean she knows you and I are like …'

'Yeah … we're like …' I said, dismissively waving my hand, though my heart did skip a beat when I saw the firelight reflected in his deep brown eyes. I mean, I have known Rohan since forever, but he was always Amani's man.

'Don't worry. I'll set Missy straight on that tomorrow morning. But getting back to you and Bhatiya, why don't you and he just stop pretending and call yourselves a couple?'

'He wants to,' I mumbled into my wine. But Rohan heard my muffled words.

'So, what's stopping you?'

'He always orders roast lamb or spaghetti.'

'Huh?'

'He has the most boring palate known to mankind. I can't believe he's Sri Lankan! We've only been dating each other for six weeks and I know what he'll order when he goes to a restaurant. What'll I do after thirty years?' Rohan looked at me as if I were insane.

'Oh, for the love of God, Shani! So what if the man likes roast lamb? Have you considered that? It's not a hanging offence and you know it. I think I'm hearing a little bit of a bullshit excuse here. What's the real reason you are holding back?'

'Maya.'

'That's bullshit too!'

'Why is it bullshit?' Maya's feelings were really important to me.

'It's bullshit because you know Maya should not rule your life. You are an adult – an independent woman of thirty-five – and Maya will just have to live with what you and Bhatiya decide to do,' Rohan replied, crisply. Clearly, the wine had affected him too, and he wasn't pulling any punches. 'Lord knows, you've been amazing these last three years, Shani, and I have thanked you many times for everything you've done for Maya ... and for me. I seriously doubt we would have survived without you. My mother would have taken Maya back to Sri Lanka and I would probably be sleeping on a park bench somewhere. But it wouldn't be right to hold you back any longer. It is time you moved on with your life.'

'Do you want me to move out?'

'No!' Rohan said, in a rush. 'You are a non-negotiable part of our family and you must stay as long as you want. All I am saying is that we need to work out how Bhatiya will fit into this family. Maybe we could look at some sort of arrangement where you and Bhatiya have a place of your own next to us, or something like that,' Rohan said, throwing his hands up in the air. 'You know there will be a way to work it all out. So, what's really holding you back?'

'Bhatiya'll want to get married,' I said in a small voice, leaning back against the couch. From my vantage point, I could see the landscape in oils Rohan had painted for me last year for my birthday, hanging over the fire place. It was of my favourite view from our deck onto the river. He said that way we could enjoy the Yarra no matter what time of year it was.

'And your problem with marriage is?'

'I never thought of myself as the marrying kind. I hate big weddings and the like.'

'I don't know why you're so hung up about weddings. Marriage has nothing to do with weddings, in the end. A wedding is one day. Marriage is about two people building a life together.'

'But do you need a piece of paper to do it? If you're committed, you're committed. You don't need to apply to the state to prove how serious you are.'

'I agree with you. But it may be important to him.'

'And he'll want kids.'

The penny dropped for Rohan.

'Just because Amani had post-natal depression does not mean that you will too,' Rohan said in a gentle voice. 'Tehara didn't.'

'That's because we all pitched in and made sure she was well looked after,' I replied.

'What makes you think we wouldn't do the same for you?'

'Because we really tried with Amani and she still ... What if that happens to me?

'We need to be able to say it, Shani. No, "what ifs". We need to *say* what really happened,' Rohan said softly. 'Amani committed suicide.'

The Coroner's Report had called it accidental death by overdose of anti-depressants. But the fact that Amani had expressed enough breast milk to last Maya fourteen days and had the bottles labelled carefully in the fridge spoke of a hidden agenda. Amani had been organised to the very end.

'Shani, Amani would never have wanted to leave Maya if she had been in her right mind. Depression is a disease – it kills just as effectively as cancer or heart disease.

'And I am sick of hiding. Sick of the averted gazes and the whispers! Yes, my wife committed suicide. She had PND and I didn't know how to help her. I never knew it could *kill* her,' Rohan said, emphatically. 'I am not ashamed of Amani or what happened. I am no more ashamed of the fact that she died from depression than if she died in a car crash. It was not her fault. And – this is much harder to say – it was not mine, either.

'You know what Amani used to say about you? She used to say that you'd find any excuse not to love someone completely, because you were afraid that you would not be able to do it forever,' Rohan continued relentlessly. 'But Shani, you are the most loving person I know. *You care*. You care about everybody and what you've done for us is nothing short of amazing,' he finished softly, now crouched on the floor in front of me. 'Take a chance on Bhatiya, give him a go,' he urged softly, wiping away the tears on my face with his thumbs.

I nodded wordlessly. He was right. And Bhatiya was a good man. He was kind, generous and smart. I should seize the opportunity with both hands.

'So, Shani? Do we brave the gossips?'

I lifted my shoulders and looked at him in confusion.

'Let's go to the Peiris wedding. Let's put our glad rags on and party with Bhatiya. Let's go to a good old, hoe down Sri Lankan wedding. It's time we lived!'

'Amani would have liked that.'

'She was the life of a party,' Rohan said with a sad smile, remembering.

CHAPTER 31

Family Day!

In an attempt to broker peace between Bhatiya and Maya, Rohan and I decided to invite Bhatiya for one of our family day outings – so that we could impress on our young princess that we were in charge of the situation and not her.

Our excursion down to the Mornington Peninsula started off brilliantly. It was a warm autumn day and we'd decided to head up to the gardens at Heron's Wood before going down to the beach.

Maya had only whinged minimally at the change in car seating when we'd all piled in Rohan's car. 'But *Punchi* always sits in the front next to my *thathi*.'

'That may be case, Maya, but Bhatiya has longer legs than me and I am sure he does not want to ride in the back seat all crowded up.'

'But why? Your place is next to *Thathi*!'

'No Maya, my place is anywhere I want it to be. I care about Bhathiya and I want him to be comfortable,' I replied patiently.

Bhatiya smiled widely when I said I cared about him.

'But why do you care about him?'

'Because he is a lovely guy.'

'My *thathi* is a lovely guy,' Maya replied with maddening logic while shooting Bhatiya a greasy look.

'But I thought I belonged to you, Maya?' Rohan asked. 'And you don't like sharing me with anyone.'

'But sharing you with *Punchi* is not sharing at all ... it's like sharing ...'

And we spent the next hour of the drive talking about things we didn't mind sharing. I rolled my eyes with resignation when Bhatiya shot me a look of boredom halfway into the conversation. At least he'd never had to deal with the constant discussion of poo we'd had when we'd been toilet training Maya!

We'd walked around the gardens at Heron's Wood, enjoying the beautiful ornamental vegetable plots as Maya chased fairies among the various different trees.

'Look,' she cried, pointing to an invisible playmate up a lemon scented gum, 'a gumnut baby! *Punchi*, I am going to play catch with her.'

'Amazing imaginations kids have,' Bhatiya commented, draping an arm casually around my shoulders. I gently disentangled myself from his hold, shooting him an apologetic look. I still wasn't quite sure what I thought of us yet. And I didn't want Maya to get upset if something didn't work out. And what if Maya really liked Bhatiya and then he decided he didn't like us ... and ... and ... and ... yeah, I know I am thinking too much about it.

'And some have more imagination than others.'

'I guess it is important to keep encouraging her imagination. Speaking of which, did she like the My Little Pony collection I bought for her last week? I didn't see it out this morning.'

Oh my god, Bhatiya had fallen for the old marketing tag – hook, line and sinker! 'Actually Bhatiya, kids play really well with few or no actual toys. For years Maya'd play with the boxes the toys came in – so I put some of the toys you bought for her away …'

'Why? She loved them! And she really likes me each time she starts to play with the stuff I get her …'

'Well, that's exactly the point. I want the two of you to start liking each other without the bribes. You can't keep buying her things everyday.'

'Oh yes we can!' Bhatiya contradicted, using his trademark faux American accent to emulate the US President.

'Actually, no Bhatiya, we can't. Rohan and I like to set limits on how many things we give her or she'll grow up without knowing any boundaries. She's already at risk of being completely and utterly spoiled anyway,' I emphasised as Rohan picked his little girl up and swung her up in the air, eliciting high pitched squeals of delight.

'But it's all educational,' Bhatiya sooked, trying to look cute.

I have to say this – sooking grown men can be cute. But sooking as a pull factor diminishes exponentially as soon as a woman has a real child to care for. And since I did, I gave him a withering look that made him grow up in a microsecond.

'Explain to me how My Little Pony with twenty-five different attachments to comb her fluorescent hair is in anyway educational.'

'It teaches her to care for pets?'

Maya chose that moment to turn into a pony herself and came galloping towards us. I fielded her adroitly and sent her back to Rohan.

'How do you keep up with her?' Bhatiya asked.

'It's really not that hard. What we read to her pretty much drives her imagination – so Rohan and I seed it with things which are nurturing and positive.'

'Isn't all kids' literature nurturing and positive?'

'Not all – and some things she's just too young for. I point blank refuse to buy any of the Bratz doll crap and I'll not let her go near any of that Diva pop porn stuff.'

'It's all a bit of harmless fun, correct? You're not one of those harpies who want to ban porn and make little girls just wear long frilly dresses, are you?'

'You're kidding me right? Harpies?

'Yes, harpies. Some of these femi-nazis can be such killjoys!'

'Hey, what are you guys arguing about?' Rohan asked with a gentle smile. He must have spotted some tension in my shoulders.

'I was just telling Shani she ought to lighten up. There's nothing really wrong with little girls' Playboy T-shirts or the like. It's all a bit of fun.'

'Actually, I agree with Shani on this. We keep Maya away from a lot of the shopping malls and the sexualised toys. The sexualisation of little girls is a real concern.'

Over a beautiful lunch of roast organic vegetables and poached fish, all washed down with several glasses of Sav Blanc, we chatted about how we'd decided to parent Maya. We explained to Bhatiya that we were determined to raise her with a defined set of values and principles that centred on character ethics, rather than personality traits. We wanted her to grow up to be a happy and confident woman.

'I guess I have a lot to learn about this parenting gig,' Bhatiya said with a deepening frown.

'We've had years to think about it though,' Rohan replied with a tight, annoyed smile.

I groaned internally. Yes, I would need to impress on Bhatiya that Rohan is and always would be Maya's father. This whole blended but not blended family thing was getting complicated.

'It's a pity this place is so far away from Melbourne, it'd make a great tourist spot,' Bhatiya commented as the waitress brought us our coffees.

'I disagree,' I replied, turning my face to the afternoon sun. 'I just love it here and would hate for it to be overrun by truck loads of tourists who don't much care for it.'

'Wasn't Phillip Island god awful?' Rohan recalled. 'Shani and I took Maya to see the penguins last Christmas and we could hardly see the beach over the heads of the tourists.'

'I remember when the Penguin Parade at Phillip Island meant that you drove up after lunch from Melbourne and hid in the sand dunes until the little fellas came in!'

'You are just being nostalgic. You're pining for the good old days that will never come back,' Bhatiya challenged.

'I may be nostalgic but I do believe in responsible development.'

'But the way you speak, one would be forgiven for thinking you are anti-development.'

'I am not anti-development. I am just for sensible development. But I thought you were all about sensible development – Mr I-Work-In-Renewable-Energy.'

'I am, absolutely. I think it is the new way forward and I want to be there as the global economy changes.'

'So you agree that any development needs to take into account the impacts it will have on the surrounding environment? And if the environmental impact is too negative, alternatives need to be sought?'

'Not really ... just because something will have short term impacts does not mean it needs to be abandoned if the long term outcomes are favourable to the community.'

'Excuse me?' I asked. Had I read Bhatiya completely wrong?

'Come on Rohan, help me out here,' Bhatiya replied, turning to Rohan for assistance. 'You used to be a developer. Didn't you design some resorts up in Queensland and some in South Australia? You understand the need for development.'

'I did – in Cape Tribulation and on Kangaroo Island. But they were all eco-resorts. We made sure that we kept them manageable and did not encourage too many visitors. They really turn a profit by appealing to visitors who can spend ...'

'See Shani, you need money to visit Rohan's resorts! That's not exactly equitable, is it?'

'... we also built sufficient budget accommodation so that people with little means but the want to visit could,' Rohan added quietly.

That was one of the many things I really admired about Rohan. He was practical. He did sensible things without grand-standing.

'I am bored,' Maya chimed in, having become completely frustrated with the conversation. She'd been exquisitely well behaved over lunch, playing with the car puzzle I brought along for the trip.

'Okay, Miss Bored, let's go to the beach then!' Rohan suggested. As Bhatiya and Maya raced down the hill to the beach, Rohan pulled me aside. 'Shani, give the guy a break. He is trying, and trying very hard. You'll have years to mould him into what you want,' he advised. 'His heart is in the right place, but like the best of us, he has a bit of foot in mouth. It took Amani years to beat me in to good form.'

The beach was perfect too. The sun was high in the after-noon sky and the cool seabreeze made it just perfect for a little girl to race up and down the beach chasing seagulls.

Bhatiya and I strolled along the water's edge, chatting about nothing in particular, till we got to a clump of rocks further along the beach.

'I am sorry,' I apologised. 'Ever since I lost my house I am a bit sensitive about profits-over-safety developers.'

'I am sorry too. And I am also sorry about the crack I made about you being a harpie.'

'Don't worry about it. Not everybody will share my views. Actually, I have evidence provided by the Australian Electoral Commission that nearly half the population of Australia thinks quite differently to me. It's just that as a parent you have to be so aware of everything you do and say. Bhatiya, I need to know that you're potentially up for that kind of thing.'

'Of course I am up for it. Why do you think I have been trying so hard?'

As we stopped for a moment, Bhatiya spied Maya running in and out of the shallows with her bucket.

'Should she be doing that?' he asked.

'Yeah, she'll be fine.'

'You Australians, you are so nonchalant.'

'See, that's a word we would never use. Nonchalant!' I giggled.

As Bhatiya dipped to kiss me I pulled away – not only because I didn't want Maya to think that there was more going on than there was, but also because I heard a piercing cry that could only mean one thing: Maya had tumbled into the water.

As I spun around to make sure she was okay, a look of intense rage flashed across Bhatiya's face. But then he raced across the beach, outstripping Rohan who had to navigate over the sand dunes, to fish the little girl out of the water.

'My hero!' Maya cried, clinging on to Bhatiya for dear life. Not that she'd been in any danger at all. The swell had barely come up to her ankle.

Bhatiya carried Maya to the car and the concern he displayed as he towelled the little girl was palpable. Once he made sure she was dry, he sang her a song to calm her down and told her silly jokes until she finally smiled.

And it was in there, in the carpark on the Dromana foreshore, with seagulls fighting over stale chips in the background and the acrid smell of charcoal chicken wafting through the seabreeze, that I fell in love with Bhatiya Fernando.

CHAPTER 32

How Many Sambols is Too Many Sambols?

The process of becoming an established couple is a curious beast. It's relatively easy when you're young. You pash some boy a couple of times at a school dance and half the people in the eastern suburbs know you have a boyfriend. Sometimes, even your own parents know before you do. Things, however, get a bit tricky if you pash a boy who is Sri Lankan. You can bet your bottom dollar that, once she gets wind of that stolen kiss, your future mother-in-law will have made an appointment at the David Jones Wedding Registry by the end of the evening. Which is one of the many reasons why I have steered clear of Sri Lankans as prospective boyfriends for a good many years.

This, naturally, put me at great disadvantage when it came to Bhatiya. I had forgotten the protocol. First there needed to be the acknowledgement between Bhatiya and me that there might be a little more going on than just a casual acquaintance. I took the fact that the man happily groped me at every given chance, and put up with the abuse Maya flung his way with amazing grace, as a good sign. He also seemed to like my company. Proof, surely, could be seen in the way he laughed at my stupid accountant jokes.

And he'd used to utter the ominous words 'I'd like us to be a couple' regularly. But in my foolish desire to get to know him before I committed myself openly, I had evaded the question. So now that I knew how I felt about him and was ready to commit to him, I didn't know how he felt about me anymore.

Ever since our outing down the Mornington Peninsula, Bhatiya had been strangely reticent. Disconcertingly distracted and uninterested.

What if he'd changed his mind? What if he'd only seen me as a short-term fling while he was in Melbourne? What if he was no longer really interested in me? What if he was trying to find a graceful exit? What if he actually did not like Maya? Disaster loomed before me and panic erupted.

So, I did what I always did in times of panic. I called a summit. With Tehara and Una, of course.

And a tub of Nuts About Chocolate. And a couple of bottles of wine. Old habits die hard.

I wound up drinking most of the wine myself as Una was pregnant and Tehara reminded me that James liked to bounce on her chest at 6 am every day no matter how hungover she was.

I won't go into the details of our rather fabulous girls' night, but suffice to say, we came up with a plan. It involved the Collette Dinnigan blue floral strapless dress I had bought last season for a fundraiser at work. And it also involved the Dandenongs.

Now let me explain the Dandenongs. Melbourne's mountains of luuurve.

The Dandenongs are an arc of blue-green mountain ranges that border Melbourne to the east like a royal sentinel. The place has all the ingredients for romance, in spades. Long, windy, misty roads laced on either side with sooty great ghost gums and moss-laden tree ferns. Hundreds of vein-like lanes that lead off to secretive little B & Bs with names like 'The Mill on the Floss' or 'The Lavender Heaven'. Townships that dot the tourist road with gorgeous little gift shops and quaint old English-style pubs.

And what was the cherry on top of this rich dark chocolate mousse of romance? The scenic lookout at the highest point. It not only provides a spectacular vista of Melbourne thirty kilometres away, but also a well-wooded carpark that affords young couples opportunities rarely available in parental lounge rooms. I'd be a rich woman if I had a dollar for every person who lost their virginity in the back seat of a car in those misty hills. I'd never have to work again, come to think of it.

So, about three weeks after our excursion to the Mornington Peninsula, I invited Bhatiya out to the Dandenongs. I suggested that we drive up to watch the sunset, then dine at one of the delectable restaurants on our way back. The Dandenongs could induce even the severest of sceptics into romance and hopefully it would renew Bhatiya's declared intention for us to become a couple.

I gave Una and Tehara a quiet mental salute when Bhatiya picked me up that evening. He looked a little grumpy as he pulled up, but his eyes widened in appreciation as I dashed out the front door, with my evening bag under my arm and matching blue cardigan draped loosely around my shoulders. I knew the strapless dress showed off my curves to good effect. Bhatiya didn't skip a beat before saying, admiringly:

'You are looking very beautiful tonight, Shani.'

'Why thank you,' I replied, with a wink.

'Is it a special occasion?'

'No … I just thought I'd spice things up a little.'

'Oh spice away, honey, spice away. I am Sri Lankan, after all,' he grinned.

Oh, this was going to be so easy, I thought gleefully.

But Bhatiya's mood kept changing as we drove up the hill. One minute he'd smile and the next he'd look grumpy enough to throttle a chook. And he seemed more distracted than I'd anticipated. I wasn't even sure his mind was completely on me.

Finally, I decided to tackle it head on. 'Are you okay?'

He sighed and looked seriously at me. My heart sank a little. Was this about to be the great break-up speech? 'I am so glad you asked. I really wanted to talk to you about this.'

I could literally feel my heart falter. Was it hot in this car or something more worrying?

'I've had it on my mind for the last couple of weeks.'

Yup, it was coming. I braced myself for it. It would not be the first time a guy had broken up with me, although usually it was the other way round. But I was a big girl, I could handle it.

'It's my sister and her family. I don't know what do about them.'

Urgh!

Bhatiya had five sisters. And no brothers. I had initially thought that this would make him a mama's boy, but no. He was completely independent. He'd even made me dinner at his apartment in the Docklands a couple of times.

'Which one?' I asked, settling back into my seat.

'The second one.'

'Shanthi, you mean?'

'No, Laksmi.'

'Oh, I though Laksmi was the youngest.'

'No, that's Vasana.' I know he's explained them to me like a million times, but their names and the sequence they come in just do not stick in my mind. I hoped it wasn't a Freudian sign of trouble to come.

'It's Shanthi, me, Laksmi, Karuna, Jaya, Vasana,' he repeated patiently. I blushed. I remember the sequence of the Bennett sisters from *Pride and Prejudice* (Jane, Elizabeth, Mary, Kitty and Lydia) but I can't remember the names of the women who could potentially be my sisters-in-law. Maybe I deserved to be dumped.

'So, what's going on with Shanthi?'

'Laksmi … ,' Bhatiya continued, pausing to emphasise the name, '… wants to go back to school and study.'

'And she can't, because …?'

'She has two children.'

'Isn't that Karuna?'

'No, you're thinking of Jaya. She has two children, too.'

'But I thought they were, like, eight and ten years old.'

'No, the eight- and ten-year-old kids belong to Shanthi, and she has a thirteen-year-old too. Laksmi's children are twelve and fourteen. But her mother-in-law does not approve.'

And it went on and on and on and on. Like a bad soap opera. But *this* soap opera would never have even made it to TV. Nobody would have been able to sit still long enough to watch it!

By the time we'd finished dinner I had a brain buzz. Every time I'd come up with a possible solution, Bhatiya would say in frustration, 'I said that to her and she said …'

I was feeling too defeated by the time we walked out to the carpark to return home to carry on with my now-thwarted seduction strategy. In spite of dinner at the Observatory Restaurant, with its show-stopping views over the valley to the bay I had convinced myself nothing was going to happen that night.

But something magic happened in that gentle sloping walk down to the carpark that evening.

A gust of wind.

It blew off the cardigan I had draped around my shoulders, giving Bhatiya a good look at the slender shoulders and plump breasts beneath. And as I bent over to pick my cardigan off the asphalt, another gust flipped up my voluminous skirt, giving Bhatiya an eyeful of thighs, stockings and garters. God bless Collette.

Any further conversation we might have had about his sisters became purely academic.

We hurriedly parked his spacious 4WD in the corner under a large, shadowy ghost gum and somewhere between my exploration of his unexpectedly buff pecs – and other regions – we sealed the deal. In comfort, too. I can confirm a BMW is spacious enough for that.

You'd think, after going that far, the rest would flow smoothly. But no. And that was because I was a complete dunce at Lankan couple protocol.

My first inkling that I had seriously miscalculated the situation came the next morning when I got a rather frosty phone call from my mother.

'Shani,' my mother opened, icicles dripping from her carefully controlled voice.

'*Ammi*?' I said groggily, eyeing the bedside clock which told me that it was only just past 7 am. Not even Maya was up. I certainly could have done with a bit more sleep, having not met the business side of my sheets and doona until well after midnight.

'Is there something you want to tell me?'

This early in the morning? 'No.'

'Are you sure?'

'I was going to talk to you about something when you and *Thathi* came over for dinner tonight.'

'So everybody in the world knows and I'll only be told in the evening! Am I so worthless in your life?' my mother squealed, anger making her voice go straight from calm to screech, skipping 'mild annoyance' on the way.

'Hold on, *Ammi*. What are you talking about?'

'That boy!'

'What boy?'

'That Bhatiya boy you met at Gayani's. I got a text this morning from Mrs Peiris to check my Facebook account and guess what I saw.'

I was shocked. Since when did my mum get on Facebook?

'So, why haven't you asked me to be your Facebook friend?' I asked, hoping to sidestep the whole issue.

'Because I am your mother, not your friend!' she snapped. 'Besides, I don't want you to know what I am doing.'

'*Ammi*, if you were my friend then you would have seen my relationship status,' I said, hoping no one would check and find out I hadn't updated my relationship status yet.

'Oh,' my mother responded, momentarily stumped. But she got her second wind. 'So, Facebook gets to know before me? That's probably why half the Sri Lankan community have been writing on my wall, congratulating me on the upcoming marriage of my daughter.' I had to hold the telephone away from my ear to save my eardrums.

'Don't get your panties in a knot ...'

'Don't you tell me what to do with my *yata andung*.'

'I was planning on telling you this evening,' I semi-yelled back, trying not to wake up Maya.

'And when are we going to meet this boy properly?'

'Tonight. He's coming over for dinner so you and *Thathi* can meet him formally.'

'Oh ... okay.'

'Yes, I'll see you tonight,' I said, hanging up and sinking back under the covers, hoping to be left in peace. Only my phone beeped again. It was a text message from Bhatiya.

Told my sister about us last night. Everybody's very happy.

I had identified the source of the leak!

Things got no better as the day progressed. Mostly because my phone didn't stop ringing.

Just as I was getting ready to go to yoga, my mother rang me back again.

'So, what are you making for dinner tonight?'

'String hoppers, chicken curry, *paripu*, *pol* sambol, *katta* sambol ...'

'Too many sambols.'

'But Rohan likes *katta* sambol.'

'You're not cooking for Rohan. You're cooking for Bhatiya now. I'll bring my ripe lemons for the *pol* sambol. Nothing like fresh lemon juice to give it some zing ...'

'Okay. Okay,' I said, trying to cut her off. I was running late and I hated missing the *Suriya Namaskar*. And I had to go to Gayani's to finish working those bridesmaids' *sarees*.

'And don't forget to make some fresh vegetables – and I don't mean potato curry ...'

'*Ammi*. I have to go ...'

'And don't over-salt the chicken curry ... you have to watch out for these boys and their hardening arteries.'

'*What?*'

'Mrs Jayakody's son was only thirty-two when he had a heart attack.'

'Okay, okay!'

Just as I pulled into the parking lot at yoga, my phone rang again. I picked it up, fully expecting it to be my mum again.

'*Ammi,* why don't ...'

'It's not your *Ammi*, though I feel like a mother to you, Shani,' Mrs Peiris said in a saccharine voice that set my teeth on edge. 'I just rang to tell you how happy I am that your problems are finally at an end,' she gushed. 'Your mother must be so happy. All her children finally married ...'

'Aunty ... aunty ...'

'And to think that you met at my Gayani's house. I said to Gayani that that house was lucky,' she said, triumphantly.

'Aunty, I don't even know if Bhatiya and I are getting married yet.'

'Oh, you will. He's such a good Sri Lankan boy. He'll take you. Don't worry about it. You just need to have babies as soon as possible. You aren't getting any younger.'

Arrggh! I was finally able to shake her off when I entered the lift at the yoga studio and my phone lost reception.

Tehara rang just as I was leaving the studio. 'I gather the Collette Dinnigan worked then?'

'Like a treat. But how did you know?'

'My mother-in-law rang this morning. Apparently, one of your sisters-in-law-to-be is good friends with my in-law's sister in London.'

'Excuse me?' Who is friends with whom?

'Don't worry, I don't get it either. But your sister-in-law-to-be has put in a request for a file on you.'

'Oh, no!'

'Yup, she wants to know what kind of girl her little brother is going to marry. Past lovers. Ex-fiancés. All that kind of thing. The hot question, of course, is whether you are still a virgin …'

'I'd forgotten about all this shite.'

'Luckily, it was my in-laws she asked and they think the world of you, so you got a good rap. You do know though that they'll be cross checking – so you want to word your mum up to spread the good word on you.'

'Roger that!'

'I'll see you at Gayani's.'

I was halfway to Gayani's when my mum called again.

'What now, *Ammi*?'

'I just wanted to tell you that Gehani and Una will be coming to dinner.' And she hung up before I could respond.

I was really enjoying my time at Gayani's, working on the *sarees* with Una and Tehara. It was lovely to work on a serious project together again. Though Gayani could never fill Amani's shoes, it somehow felt acceptable – as if having a fourth person in the circle was central to our group dynamic.

But today I didn't get to glue down a single bead or sequin. The stream of phone calls was endless, the questions relentless. Some called to confirm the news.

'Is this Shani Devapura?' one woman asked, belligerently.

'Yes.'

'Is it true you are with Bhatiya Fernando?'

'Yes.'

Then she hung up. No explanation. No nothing. How rude. And she'd called from a silent number so I couldn't give her a serve in reply.

Others called to congratulate.

'Oh, Shani! I am so happy to hear your news.'

'Hi,' I returned weakly, desperately trying to place the voice.

'So, tell me *everything*. Where did you meet him? Is the wedding date set?'

'I met him at Gayani Peiris's and we don't know if we're getting married yet.'

'Your late father would be so happy that you're finally getting married,' the caller added, tearfully.

'Umm …' I said, completely confused. I was pretty damn sure my dad was still alive unless mum forgot to tell me something. Not that I wouldn't put it past her.

'Isn't this Shani Gooneratne? From Burwood in Sydney?'

'No, it's Shani Devapura from Warrandyte in Melbourne.'

'Well, I didn't want to pay for an interstate call. Especially not to a mobile phone!'

'Here's a simple solution. Don't call!' I responded, cutting off the line.

And then there were those who called to console. This puzzled me.

'*Anay*, Shani,' Mrs Jayakody said, 'your mother must be so happy. All your problems are solved now. Your mother must feel like a huge weight has been lifted off her shoulders ...'

'Hmm ...'

'And you must be relieved too. A beautiful girl like you must have been wondering when the right man would come along. You must be so happy that your problems are now over.' Again, the tone of triumph, completely unsolicited.

Oh really? I hadn't even known I had problems in the first place.

'Now you'll have a husband of your own, you can start your own life. Find a house, have children, balancing everything with a career ... although, I remember my daughter found it really difficult. Why, she nearly had a nervous breakdown when she had her third child and had to go back to work ...'

I was beginning to wonder what I'd let myself in for. Marriage was sounding like a whole lot of trouble.

I was ready to kill the next person who called me. As luck would have it, it was my mum. She rang as I was bolting out of the curry takeaway with my arms laden with the string hoppers and boxes of curry. Okay, so I cheat.

'I am bringing dessert,' I heard her say.

Only the fact that I dropped my iPhone while juggling the containers of curry saved her from the serve she so richly deserved.

By the time my parents arrived that evening, I had well and truly had a gutful.

'So where is he?' my mother trilled enthusiastically as she rushed through the front door, my dad quietly following at her heels. She was dressed in a bright floral top and pale grey slacks with a gorgeous pair of chandelier earrings.

I picked up the edge of the deep red Persian rug in the hallway and looked under. 'He's not here,' I responded theatrically. I then picked up the vase on the hallway table. 'He's not there either.'

'Why are you being so rude to me, Shani?'

'Hi *Thathi*,' I welcomed my dad softly, before turning to follow my mum into the kitchen. 'Because you never stop pushing!'

'I'm your mother. It's my job to push,' she grunted back, as she hefted a couple of heavy shopping bags onto the kitchen counter.

My mother never does things by halves, including dessert. Five different varieties! She'd made *wattilapam* (Sri Lankan crème brulee made with coconut milk and palm sugar treacle), Sri Lankan fruit salad (freshly chopped tropical fruit ruined with sweetened condensed milk) and Marie biscuit pudding (trifle of chocolate mousse with alternating layers of Marie biscuits dunked in sweetened milk and brandy), *petit fours*, and an enormous pavlova. Good lord, if dinner wasn't going to clog the boys' arteries, dessert surely would!

'So, when is he coming?' she asked with bated breath as she cuddled Maya. Maya loved my parents and the feeling was mutual.

'Soon, he's on his way,' I said as I popped a few samosas in the oven.

'Did you buy those from the Curry Hut? They don't use fresh ingredients there, you know.'

'No, I got them from Coles.'

Rohan came in and greeted my parents, giving my mum a great big hug.

'Uncle, I hope you are here to watch the game,' Rohan asked.

'Yes *putha*,' my father responded, gleefully eyeing Rohan's massive flat screen in the TV room.

'Mahinda, we're here to meet Bhatiya. So don't spend the whole evening just watching the cricket,' my mum scolded. I saw Rohan and my dad share a quick wink. Rohan'd take care of Dad.

But things got really busy from that point as Una and Gehani arrived. Followed quickly by Bhatiya. I met him at the door.

'Are you ready?'

'I think so,' he replied with a worried little smile. 'I am so sorry I spilled the beans earlier. My sister rang while I was driving home and it came out in conversation.'

'That's okay.'

'I thought you had two brothers,' Bhatiya queried as soon I finished introducing him to Gehani. Maya had mercifully saved Dad by demanding that he model for her Barbie Hair Salon before the match started.

'*Anay*, yes,' my mother butted in, bumping me aside with her ample hips and linking her arm through Bhatiya's, pulling him towards the couch. 'My other son – Gamini – he's an aeronautical engineer and he lives in Sydney now. He has two children and another on the way. Gehani and Una got married last year and they have a *putha* on the way. I only have Shani left. So, tell me about yourself!'

Una, Gehani, Rohan and I moved into the kitchen, ostensibly to sort dinner, but keeping a watchful eye on the proceedings from a distance.

Bhatiya started his standard spiel, grinning when he saw me roll my eyes.

'And you got your initial degree from Oxford?' my mum asked, with a huge smile. Her social collateral was going to skyrocket if she had an Oxford graduate for a son-in-law. 'Now tell me, do you have any brothers or sisters?'

'Five sisters.

'Too many sisters,' Rohan commented conspiratorially, as he opened a bottle of wine.

'What? No brothers?' my mother asked worriedly. She was calculating the dowries Bhatiya would be required to pay for five unmarried sisters.

'No, Aunty, no brothers. But all my sisters are married,' Bhatiya cut through quickly, understanding my mother's angst. He was rewarded by another sunny smile.

'What a good boy you are! It is a good, traditional boy who waits for his sisters to get married before getting married himself. And where is your *thathi* from?'

'Kandy.'

'And your *ammi*?'

'Also from Kandy.'

'Ahh … a good hill country family. We are of course from Colombo, although my brother married a girl from Kurunagalle.'

'Is Kurunagalle anywhere near Kandy?' Gehani asked Rohan while my mother continued with her interrogation.

'Yeah, somewhere on the Colombo to Kandy road.'

'Excellent, we must have some social collateral then,' Gehani replied, tongue in cheek.

Twenty minutes into the 'conversation' Bhatiya looked around at us, a little wide eyed. My mother had by now moved on to his sister's in-laws and their family circles. We gave him the thumbs up, which seemed to steady him a little. Courageously, he re-entered the fray.

'I am amazed she hasn't asked him for his underwear size yet,' Una commented.

'I'm sure that'll come,' I returned cynically.

Once my mother had established that our family circles were reasonably compatible and that any children Bhatiya and I were likely to reproduce would not come out with two heads, she moved on to the really serious business.

'So, *putha*, shall I ring your *ammi* for your horoscope?'

'I have it here,' Bhatiya responded, pulling out a delicate piece of papyrus with his astrological chart etched on it. He carefully took the fragile piece of paper and checked it over for a few moments.

'I am amazed she hasn't ripped it out of his hands,' my brother commented, noting the fact that my mother's hands were now tightly clenched on her lap.

'Thank you,' my mother said, gleefully, when Bhatiya finally handed over his horoscope. She quickly grabbed her reading glasses from her handbag.

'I didn't know *Ammi* could read horoscopes.'

'She can't really, but I gave her a rundown of the basics before we came.'

'*Puthay,* it says here you will be rich,' my mother commented, pointing to a particular configuration of stars. 'It also says that you need to start before you are thirty-eight to have healthy children.'

'Can you really tell that kind of thing from a horoscope?'

By now I felt Bhatiya had suffered enough, and I needed to put the conversation to an end. I was about to cut my mum off when she turned her steely gaze on Bhatiya once more. 'How old are you now, *putha*?'

'Thirty-eight.'

'Well, you had better get on with it then!' my mother commanded sternly.

'*Ammi!*' I remonstrated, aghast.

'At least she hasn't demanded you copulate in front of her like a pair of performing seals,' my brother commented a little too loudly.

'Gehani!' we all yelled at him. I was completely mortified by my family.

CHAPTER 33

Threading

Where the hell were Maya, Rohan and Bhatiya? I had been waiting for them for fifteen minutes outside the reception room. If they didn't get their act together in the next couple of minutes, Maya was going to miss her part in the wedding procession.

I looked down frustratedly at my iPhone. Surely Rohan could at least have returned my call. Why oh why had I let the little girl out my sight! I stamped my foot in frustration and crinkled my forehead. Which only made my eyebrows sting, reminding me why I had let Maya go off with Rohan and Bhatiya in the first place. Damn it!

But I need to back track a little to earlier in the proceedings. Perhaps to the point where Maya conned Jayani, the bride, into making her a flower girl? Neither Rohan nor I were able to find out how Maya did it, but somehow she convinced

Jayani that she should be made the seventh little flower girl, thus breaking the perfect symmetry of the wedding party. Not that either Rohan or I had a problem with that. We thought Maya looked cute as a button in her rose pink *lama saree*. But such beauty had come at a price. The little girl had been impossible to live with over the past week.

When Mrs Peiris brought over Maya's outfit for her to try on, she insisted on wearing it for the full afternoon. This was initially a blessing as Maya usually has ants in her pants and is rarely able to sit still for two consecutive minutes. The fear of the sequins and beading falling off her pretty clothes had her seated like a statuette on the couch. A pose that, sadly, only lasted for about half an hour.

Once she convinced herself the sequins and beading were not of weak disposition and were not going fall off with the passing breeze, she spent another hour looking at herself in the mirror. This in itself was innocuous enough but it led to her practising her walk up the aisle in front of the mirror. To ensure the experience was authentic, she not only denuded the late blooming rose bush at the front of the house to get rose petals to walk on, but she also insisted on playing the god awful song that Jayani had chosen as a bridal march, 'Said I Loved You But I Lied', by Michael Bolton. Repeatedly.

Blessedly, we had spaghetti bolognese for dinner that night and it was an easy enough task to convince her that her outfit would not survive unscathed from ribbons of pasta drenched in red meat sauce. However, we had *hoppers* for dinner the following night and Maya was sure she could manage dinner without spilling curry on her outfit. I was not. But after we argued for about thirty minutes, I gave up and let her get on with it. Then the inevitable came to pass; she spilt chicken curry on the skirt of her *lama saree* and thus began my rather unwanted relationship with the local dry cleaners.

After the third trip to the dry cleaners, I hid the outfit in Bhatiya's 4WD. It seemed to me to be the only place the little girl would not look for her rose pink fantasy creation.

Which brings me back to why Maya was currently missing.

'Maya, honey ... could you get away from the balcony?' I had asked as Mrs Fernando pinned the last of the hot rollers in my already straightened hair. 'Honey, *now*!' I said in a sterner voice. 'Shani, you are going to have to sit still if you want me to thread your eyebrows,' Mrs Fernando puffed sternly. I grimaced. I'd had to sacrifice my waxing appointment for one of the repeat trips to the dry cleaners.

'Maya!' I yelled, leaping across the room and pushing the tea cup out of the way before the dregs of tea landed on Maya's skirt.

Ruefully, I pulled my iPhone out of my handbag and called Rohan. He and Bhatiya had been down at a Sport Lounge several floors below our room at Crown. You guessed it, they were watching the cricket. It is such a tragedy that wedding season corresponds with the Indian Premier League. I can't remember the last time I saw a Sri Lankan male actually paying attention at a wedding. They all walk around like secret service men, with ear buds in the ear, listening to the cricket on their iPods.

'Is she driving you nuts?'

'Yes, come and get her!'

I opened the door of the hotel room a crack and pushed Maya out to Rohan.

'Should I take her to hang out with the other flower girls?' Rohan had asked through the door.

'No. We are keeping all the flower girls apart. They fight.'

'What do you suggest we do?'

'Take her for a quiet walk down by the river. That'll calm her down. Just make sure she is at the bottom of the stairs in about thirty minutes.'

'She's like a daughter to you, *nay*?' Mrs Fernando commented as she pulled out an innocent-looking spool of cotton. I sat down, arched my neck back and closed my eyes as she started twisting individual eyebrow hairs off at the skin by running a corded length of cotton across my face. The depilatory action comes from the knots of cotton picking up the hairs and slicing them off. Yes. It hurts. A lot.

Halfway through the threading process, Rohan called.

'Maya says that you said that she could have a snack before the wedding. Is that correct?'

'Nope. She's having you on. I made her have a snack before I dressed her. She can only have tiny sips of water. Ouch!' I gritted as Mrs Fernando moved on to the skin between my eyebrows.

'Cheers.'

Mrs Fernando had moved onto the next eyebrow when the phone rang again.

'Shani, I am so sorry about this, but Maya really, really needs to pee and I can't find any family restrooms. Can we come back up to the room?'

'Sure,' I gasped, hanging up as Mrs Fernando finally threaded off the sensitive hair at the end of the eyebrow.

One of the good things about losing one's house was that I could really re-invent my wardrobe. I was no longer held back by fashion faux pas from adolescence or shoes from a bygone era. And since I was returning to the Sri Lankan scene, I wanted to do it with a splash.

But I could not face going back to Clow Street in Dandenong. Memories of washing Amani's vomit off Tehara's car tyres were still fresh in my mind. And somehow, I didn't feel like mustering Una and Tehara for a group shopping expedition either. So, I'd gone *saree* shopping with my mum. She was so happy at being asked you'd be forgiven for thinking I'd donated her an internal organ.

Only I'd never realised quite the extent to which her demanding nature translated into the art of *saree* shopping. We visited at least fifteen different '*saree* boutiques' hosted in various sheds, garages and rumpus rooms across Melbourne. And we found it in the last and least likely. I called it my Sri Lankan curry takeaway. It was the most beautiful vintage silk *saree* that I had ever seen, even if I did have to hang it out to air for ten days to get rid of the stench of *thunapaha*.

The *saree* was the palest of pale grey silk. The fabric was so fine that it was almost gossamer while retaining the suppleness of silk. I felt as if I was cloaked in a fine sheen of diamond-faceted water. The hem was beaded with vintage Swarovski crystals in a cursive flower motif. The most spectacular part of the *saree* was the crystal beaded *pallu*. The cursive flower motif was transformed from the border into an amazing paisley montage that was highlighted by crystal beads of every hue. The *saree* glittered and shimmered from every angle. Combined with the suppleness of the fabric, the beading made the *saree* a poem in fluidity.

And damned hard to drape.

It had taken Mrs Fernando a good thirty minutes and three separate attempts to drape this *saree* on me. The first time, the uneven weight of the beading had meant that my under-skirt could be seen in a couple of places around the hem. I had thought we were done and was about to leave the room.

'*Aiiyoh!*' Mrs Fernando had screamed.

'Excuse me?'

'Your *yatasaya* is showing,' the woman squealed, furiously waving her hands, coming towards me like a bullet. I took a hasty step back, but my escape had been blocked by the closed door.

'So?'

'*Cheekaya*, only *kara* girls show their underskirts. You'll have the boys taking bets on who gets you to … you know?'

Mrs Fernando said in a hushed, urgent voice, mimicking the actions of lifting one's skirt.

To placate her, the *saree* was unpinned and re-draped. The second time the *saree* gaped quite openly in the front. Even I didn't need to be told that I'd cause a stir walking out like that.

Third time was a charm, as they say, except that halfway through, I looked up and noticed the time. Rohan had said they'd be up fifteen minutes ago. Yes, Maya was toilet trained, but three-year-olds have notoriously weak bladders. Especially if they are excited. I sent Rohan a text message and hurried Mrs Fernando along as much as I could.

'You are not supposed to run wearing *saree*!' Mrs Fernando called out as I hightailed it to the elevators. 'Ladies in *saree* walk demurely!'

I resisted the urge to flick her a birdie and I rushed to the meeting spot at the top of the stairs that Rohan and I had prear-ranged. I surveyed the crowds below from my high perch and my heart gave a tiny frightened lurch when I didn't see my girl, Rohan or Bhatiya. I pulled out my phone again to put in a call. The Crown complex was a big place. Maya could get lost very easily.

I was so busy punching in Rohan's number again that I didn't hear a familiar voice calling.

'Hey, *Akki*, we're down here!' Gehani called up, rounding a corner, firmly gripping a bouncing Maya by the arm.

I was so relieved to see Maya, her gown intact, that my descent down the wide spiral was executed with more haste than elegance.

'What took you so long?' I asked Rohan, crossly.

Both he and a very wrung-out looking Bhatiya were bringing up the rear. I didn't have the time to listen to their excuses; I quickly dropped down to my haunches to inspect Maya. She looked fine, though a little sheepish. Her outfit didn't look worse for wear and her roses were still in her hair.

'We lost her,' Rohan admitted quietly.

'Oh my goodness! *Baba*, are you alright?'

'She was only lost for ten minutes,' Bhatiya defended hotly. Wrong move.

Rohan knew better, and wisely kept his mouth shut, his eyes firmly glued to a spot on the carpet not far from my jewelled high-heels.

'Honey, do you still want to be in the wedding procession?' I asked the little girl. She nodded wordlessly.

We made it just in time, slotting Maya into the procession as the bridesmaids made their way past the doors. No one was any the wiser. The bride was still a fair way along and the flower girls pushed and shoved their way up the aisle behind a motley crew of older ladies singing a Lankan love song. *Phew!*

Tehara had saved us a spot up front close to the bridal podium because I was still supposed to go around and pin the bridesmaids *sarees* as well.

'What took you guys so long?'

'Rohan and Bhatiya lost Maya,' I muttered between clenched teeth.

'We didn't exactly "lose" her,' Bhatiya defended, hotly.

'Then what exactly happened?

'Maya did a runner into the Disney shop when Rohan and I stopped to get cricket scores.'

I do believe honesty is the best policy. But there are times when lies are possibly a safer option, and this would have been one of them. They lost Maya while watching the *cricket*?!

'That's not exactly true,' Rohan quickly contradicted. 'I was looking after Maya while Bhatiya was looking for the rest rooms when the Playhouse Disney show came on the big screen. We looked away for an instant, we thought she was watching the show. She just disappeared.'

'So, how did you find her?'

'Actually, I found her,' Gehani said, raising his hand.

'We came across Rohan and Bhatiya absolutely frantic, looking for security when we were coming from the carpark,' Una interjected. 'So we started looking for her.'

'And where did you find her?'

'Near the popcorn machine.'

'Which is just around the corner from the Disney shop!' Both Bhatiya and Rohan looked as if they wanted the earth to open up and swallow them.

'We panicked.'

'Silly boys,' I said, shaking my head in disbelief, but thought it wiser not to give them a bollocking right there. I turned my attention to the bridal party. Jayani was coming with her seven flower girls and six bridesmaids. Maya gave a tired little wave when she spotted us in the crowd.

'*Anay*, those bridesmaids' *sarees* are sooo plain,' one woman next to us commented audibly. 'Vinitha Jayasekara's bridesmaids' *sarees* were just beautiful!'

'*Chick vitharak*, those bridemaids' *sarees* are like *cheethe* you buy from Spotlight. The Peiris's should have better spent the money on the bridesmaids' *sarees* and not have another wedding here at Crown!' another complained, the envy plain in her voice.

At long last, Jayani came into view. Bhatiya stepped in closer, jostled by the crowd straining to get a glimpse of the bride. He took it as a chance to get close and put his arm around me. 'You look beautiful tonight,' he quietly whispered in my ear.

Finally the business side of the wedding finally started. Vows were exchanged. The bride and groom had their pinky fingers tied together and their palms were filled with grains of rice for a bountiful marriage. This was my cue to go and pin the bridesmaids's *sarees*.

'Be back in a tick,' I said, pecking Bhatiya quickly on the lips.

As I disentangled myself from his grasp, I glanced round to give Una and Gehani a grateful smile for finding Maya. Only I noticed Rohan standing a little way behind us. He was looking at me as if he'd been clubbed over the head with a cricket bat. I couldn't help catching his eye and giving him a saucy little smile.

The pinning of the bridesmaids' *sarees* was a simple job. While the crowd was distracted watching the newly married couple light the traditional oil lamp – a humungous brass monstrosity topped by pair of necking swans – I ducked around the bridesmaids who were now standing in an arc behind the happy couple facing the wedding guests. I took the top edge of the elaborately beaded *pallus* that Una, Tehara, Gayani and I had spent weeks beading and gently pinned them to their waists, fanning the fabric out into an elegant drape.

'*Anay lasanai*!' a little old lady enthused when the bridesmaids filed out behind the bride and groom.

'Those have to be the prettiest bridesmaid's *sarees* this season.'

'They must cost a fortune. Beaded *sarees* are so expensive.'

'Where did Jayani get those *sarees* from?' I heard Vinitha Jayaskera ask hotly.

Una, Tehara and I high-fived each other. Mission accomplished.

'Where's Maya?' I asked Rohan, as we scanned the retreating crowd. Our little girl was difficult to spot in the sea of brightly dressed, jewelled wedding guests rushing to their seats before the bridal dance started.

'There she is!' Bhatiya said, pointing to a tiny forlorn-looking figure hiding next to a large pot plant by the curtains.

'Hey, honey,' I said holding out my arms. Maya tossed her bouquet away and toddled up. 'Are you okay?'

'Yes, *Punchi*.'

'Did you have fun?'

'No. I don't feel well.' There was an ominous rumbling from her little tummy. 'My belly is empty.'

'Let's see if we can get you a dinner roll or something,' I said as the DJ started the pre-dinner music and the dancers were getting into place for the dance extravaganza.

'Give her to me, I'll get her something to eat,' Rohan said, holding out his arms. 'You two go off and dance.'

Maya clung like a limpet. She was getting a little weepy. She needed a little ginger ale, a bit of bread and sleep. 'Honey, I'll be back in two minutes,' I promised as I tried to disentangle her. But she kept clinging.

'The best bits of the song are going to start in a few seconds. And we need to get a good spot on the dance floor so we can be seen,' Bhatiya urged hurriedly.

I slowly started disengaging Maya's sticky fingers from around my neck. Her grip was surprisingly strong. Rohan put his arm around Maya's waist to pull her off, but she countered this by wrapping her sturdy legs around my hips.

'Maya, please? I just want a quick dance. I love you.'

'I wove you, too, *Punchi*,' she said with a little hiccupping sob and released her arms and legs and fell into Rohan's waiting arms.

Bhatiya immediately grabbed my hand and we ran onto the dance floor. As luck would have it, we got pole position next to the bridal couple. And I fell back into my groove. I had forgotten how much I loved to dance! The rhythm, the music and being able to truly let go and allow the beat to drive my body. The first song was great and I had an admiring little crowd gathered around me by the finish. I cast my eye over to Rohan and Maya – they were sitting quietly together, with Maya chomping away at a bread roll.

Before you knew it, I had been on the dance floor for a good twenty minutes. And loving it! Tehara and I were having a Bollywood dance-off with the four girls who had been leading the bridal dance. Tehara and I would do a particular dance move and then the other four would scramble to copy us. And they were failing. Dismally. Such amateurs.

But all good things needed to come to an end. Muthu was losing the battle to contain James and looking desperately over to Tehara and his parents for help.

'Having fun?' Bhatiya asked, dancing away furiously.

'Yeah,' I said with a bright smile. 'Where are Maya and Rohan?'

'I dunno. They were there a minute ago,' he said.

I was a little worried, so I dragged Bhatiya off the dance floor to go in search. We looked around the entire reception room, stopping to chat to people along the way. I was pleasantly surprised at how much I enjoyed being introduced to people as Bhatiya's girlfriend. By the time we'd made it back to our table, another good fifteen minutes had passed, and I was really getting worried.

'Oh, where *are* they?'

'They're probably fine. Come dance with me?' Bhatiya asked, holding his hand out. They were now playing some Lionel Ritchie mood music. 'This is more my style and I want to hold you close.'

'Just give me a sec,' I responded, reaching for my iPhone and putting a call in to Rohan. In all likelihood, Maya had conned him into taking her back to the Disney store. However, Rohan picked up straightaway and I knew immediately that something was wrong.

'What's going on?'

'She's sick, Shani. She's been chucking up for the last half hour.'

'I'm coming up!'

'No, no. I have this in hand. It'll be alright,' Rohan protested, though he was cut off by more sounds of vomiting in the background.

'Rohan, I'm coming up!'

'He has a point, you know,' Bhatiya said quietly, holding firmly onto my hand. 'Let him manage.'

'What do you mean, he has a point?'

Perhaps I said it a little loudly, because a few heads turned our way, so Bhatiya and I shuffled to a little alcove near the exit.

'I mean, let Rohan handle the situation.'

'But she is my girl.'

'No, she isn't. She is not your daughter. She's his. Let Rohan handle it.'

'No!' I said hotly. 'I have been looking after her since she was four months old. She needs me and I always go to her when she needs me.'

'What happens if we are away? God help us, what if we're on our honeymoon? Will you leave me to go and be with her?'

'Don't ask stupid questions!'

'No, Shani,' he said, grabbing me by my arm. 'This is not a life or death situation. Let Rohan handle it.'

'I just want to make sure she's okay,' I pleaded. Something in my eyes caused him to let me go immediately. He took a step back, shaking his head.

'You know, I thought I could do this. I thought I could …' he shrugged, spreading his hands wide, as if to encompass the situation we were in, '… make this work. But I don't think I can. I mean, I always feel like I come second best.'

'Bhatiya, get a hold of yourself! I am not *leaving* you for good, I am just going up to see if Maya is okay and I will be straight back down. Don't make a mountain out of a molehill!'

'No, actually, I really can't do this. I can't take on the responsibility for Maya,' he said in a low voice.

'Nobody is asking you to!' I snapped.

'By being with you, I feel that I do. I was so frightened when we lost her today I didn't know what to do.'

'Dufus! I'm not blaming you for that. Her own father lost her too. We parents do stupid things like this all the time,' I said, understanding dawning. I remembered vividly how I had panicked the first time I had cocked up with Maya. I had accidentally locked her in the house and it had taken ten minutes for Rohan to come and rescue us. I had had a total meltdown until Rohan me reminded of the dozens of mistakes he had already made. 'And she's still here!'

'Shani, listen to me. I am not Maya's parent. It'd be different if I had raised her from an infant like you have. But I can't do this. And I don't want to lose you either.'

'What do you want me to do?'

There was a tiny pause, and then: 'This is not the way I imagined doing this,' he said stiffly, pulling a Tiffany's jewellery box out of the inside pocket of his immaculately tailored jacket. 'Marry me? Marry me and be with me.'

'You mean, choose you over Maya?' I desperately tried not to be distracted by the Rock of Gibraltar-sized solitaire diamond ring nestled in the velvet confines of the dark blue box.

'Let Rohan and Maya move on with their life. Let's start our own life together.'

'But Maya is part of my life. I've been part of her world her entire life. I can't give that up.'

'But I don't think *I* can be a part of her life forever.'

I felt as if I had been slapped. Time stood still, the moment shattered by the ringing of my phone. I saw immediately that it was Rohan and picked up. 'Shani, she's screaming for you.'

'I am on my way,' I said and turned to Bhatiya. 'Can we talk about it in half an hour?'

'No Shani, I think I know how it'll pan out.'

Another call came through. It was Rohan again. 'Shani, I'm going to call the ambulance! She's chucking up bile.'

'Just wait for me. I'll come back and we'll talk,' I said to Bhatiya as I hoicked my *saree* up to my knees and sprinted to the lifts.

'You are not her mother!' he called out.

'Yes I am!' I yelled back, telling him the truth I had known in my heart from the moment I had been able to settle Maya into a comfortable nap at her mother's funeral three years ago.

CHAPTER 34

Can a Girl Have Some Privacy To Cry? Or Do You Really Want To See Me Snot Myself?

My mother always said that the reason I did so well at school was not because I was a genius (thanks, Mum!) or even because I was of average intelligence, but because I could shut everything else out and focus on one thing. So while other girls whinged and whined about boyfriends or weight gain or celebrity marriages during Year 12, I could – and did – shut everything out and just focus on my exams.

When Rohan called to say that Maya was chucking up her guts and my boyfriend quasi-dumped me, I was able to shut the latter out to focus on the former. And it was just as well. Maya really needed me this time. It was something akin to a barf fest that greeted me when I got up to the hotel room.

'Rohan, tell me what happened?' I asked urgently. He was holding Maya's limp head over the toilet bowl. Her vomit-splattered clothes made a trail from the door to the bathroom.

'She said she was feeling sick about ten minutes after you left, so I brought her up here. She almost started chucking up in the lift, but I was able to get her in to the room before the worst started.' Rohan's tailored jacket had been tossed into a heap in one corner of the bathroom and his tie, which was liberally sprayed with vomit, was sitting in the bath.

'When did she stop vomiting?'

'About two minutes ago.'

At which point, Maya proved Rohan wrong by heaving her little stomach again.

It took me all of ten seconds to unpin Mrs Fernando's carefully draped *saree* and get down on the floor in my underskirt and blouse to help Maya. I took over the job of holding her head over the toilet bowl as a seemingly unending volume of bile-coloured gag exited her mouth. Rohan was halfway through the job of stripping off his soiled trousers when his phone rang. It was Tehara.

Rohan picked it up and put it on speaker phone.

'I just saw Shani run out of the reception and Bhatiya storm off. What's going on?'

'Maya is really sick,' I called out. Maya punctuated my statement by being violently sick again. 'I can't believe she's got anything left to throw up!'

'Muthu and I are on our way up.'

'Did you give her anything out of the usual to eat?' I asked.

'No. I only gave her a couple of sips of water.'

'*Punchi*,' Maya cried weakly. 'My tummy hurts so much.'

'I know, my baby, I know,' I crooned, holding her close. And she was violently sick again. 'Rohan, could you get a hot, damp face washer?'

'Do you think we need to take her to the hospital?'

'Let's just wait to hear what Tehara and Muthu have to say,' I said worriedly, as I took the face washer and mopped Maya's wan face. As she doubled over, crying in pain, I felt her abdominal muscles clench and spasm as wave upon wave of agony gripped her.

I started to panic too. I could not lose Maya. I'd sooner follow Maya into the grave than let anything happen to her. The endless moment that followed as both Rohan and I desperately tried to calm the little girl was shattered by the knock at the door.

'When did she start vomiting?' Tehara quizzed brusquely, gently picking up the child and laying her flat on several thick towels on the tiled floor. 'Muthu's gone to get the medical bag from the car,' she explained when I looked over her shoulder for her husband.

'About forty-five minutes ago.'

'What has she had to eat today?'

I gave Tehara a quick rundown – just the normal everyday stuff. Just as I finished my list, Maya piped up with a tiny voice. 'I was so hungry, *Punchi*, I ate a spring roll.' Where on earth did you find a spring roll?'

'In a bag near the lolly machine.'

'Near the Disney store?'

She nodded, as images of salmonella poisoning flashed before my eyes. Not to mention a host of other bugs.

When Muthu arrived with the medical bag, they picked Maya up and lay her on the bed. 'Food poisoning,' Tehara explained to Muthu.

'Maxalon?'

'Yes. She'll be fine.'

Tehara pulled a small hypodermic needle out and quickly pulled a dose without letting Maya see. Meanwhile, I gently held Maya as Muthu used an alcohol swab to disinfect a tiny area on Maya's bum.

'I don't want a needle. I don't want a needle!' Maya screamed as soon as her mind put two and two together. But Tehara was too quick; she'd already given Maya her shot. Within five minutes, Maya had fallen asleep. I could feel the spasms in her stomach ease off.

'We'll wake her up in about half an hour and see if she can hold down some lemonade or ginger ale,' Tehara said softly, as she sank into the couch next to Muthu. I was on the bed next to Maya.

'Do you think we'll need to take her to hospital?'

'Let's see how she pulls up in the next hour or so. She'll probably have a sore belly for a couple of days and then she'll be right as rain. Kids are resilient …'

'Where's James?' Rohan asked as he walked back into the room, pulling on a tight-fitting T-shirt and chinos.

'With my parents,' Muthu replied. 'They've taken him to their place for the night – supposedly to give Tehara and me a break. But they let him sleep in their bed and eat whatever he wants, so we'll need to spend the rest of the week de-programming him.'

'So, what happened with Bhatiya? I saw him storm off,' Tehara asked, looking me straight in the eye.

'He asked me to marry him.'

'Oh, congratulations!' Muthu started, but Tehara cut him off mid-sentence.

'He wasn't exactly behaving like a newly engaged man. You didn't refuse him, did you? I thought you loved him.'

'I do love him … but …'

'But *what*?'

'I told him to hold the thought while I sorted out Maya.'

'You really are the queen of romance, aren't you?' Tehara commented, rolling her eyes. 'So, what are you waiting for? She'll be fine, now.'

'I am not sure he'll be waiting for me,' I replied, starting to feel the pain of a breaking heart heading my way.

'Well, there's only one way to find out, isn't there?' Rohan said, leaning against the door jamb to the bathroom with a curious expression on his face. 'Go get him, girl!'

I stood up in my underskirt and *saree* blouse and looked askance at him as if to say, 'Like this? Surely, you've got to be joking!'

'Here, let me help,' Tehara said, bounding off the couch.

Blessedly, Maya had not christened the supple silk with her bilious regurgitations. So, between us Tehara and I were able to re-drape the *saree*. Well, almost; it didn't gape at the front though my underskirt did show through in a few spots.

Halfway through the draping process, we'd woken Maya up and given her a couple of sips of lemonade. She held that down well and by the end of the *sareē* draping, she had demanded a bread roll. I almost ran into the room service waiter as I bolted out the door. I turned around and said, 'Rohan, let me know how she's going.'

'Yeah, sure,' he replied, tonelessly.

I texted Bhatiya from the lift, asking him to meet me at the wedding. I knew it would still be going full pelt when I got back downstairs. People were dancing, eating and generally having a whale of time. This made it difficult to find him through the throng. Every second person was drunk and wanting to pull me onto the dance floor.

By the third circuit of the reception hall, I was ready to throw in the towel and call it a day. I was dragging my sorry jewelled high heels out the doors of the reception room and getting myself ready for death-by-minibar when I was ambushed by Gayani.

'Shani,' she called from across the lobby.

'Have you seen Bhatiya?'

'Yeah, you just missed him. He told me to give this to you …' Gayani said, handing me an envelope with the Crown Casino crest embossed on the top right-hand corner.

I didn't want to read the letter anywhere near the wedding. If I needed to break down, I wanted to do it in somewhere reasonably private. So I caught the lift up to Breezes restaurant and convinced the maitre'd to let me sit at the bar.

I took a deep breath and slit open the envelope.

Dear Shani,

I have spent the last few hours thinking seriously about us. And I don't think I can do it. I thought I could handle being a step-dad to Maya, but I can't. In some part of my mind I will resent the time she takes from me, and eventually our own children. I can't love her like a dad. I thought I could. And I don't want to tear you apart by making you choose. I know that Maya needs you more than I need you. She needs your steadying influence and your love. I need you too. But I can't be what she needs me to be.

Shani, I'd like to thank you for the best two months of my life. I have loved every moment I have spent with you. It's breaking my heart to end this. But I'd rather do it this way than have you hate me because I can't love Maya as you do. So please, Shani, let's make this easy on ourselves and end it now. Tonight. Let's not try to contact each other. I do not want to see the disappointment in your eyes.

May the Triple Gem bless and keep you. I will only ever want the very best for you.

Yours,

Bhatiya Fernando.

'So, this is what it feels like to have a broken heart,' I said softly to myself, as tears clouded my eyes and splashed down on the letter, blotting the ink of Bhatiya's words. I felt the deep sobs shake me. I shoved my fist in my mouth to stifle the sound.

'You will survive. You're a survivor,' Una quietly said from my elbow, handing me a hanky. I turned around abruptly.

Behind her were Gehani, Rohan, Tehara and Muthu.

'How did you guys find me?' I hiccoughed through my sobs.

'Gayani saw you go towards the lifts and texted me.'

'And I figured you'd end up at the bar. It's so lovely up here,' Tehara added, pointing to the outdoor balcony dining area.

'Let's get a table,' Rohan said.

But Muthu, in his usual unobtrusive manner, had already organised a quiet table in the corner of the balcony away from the rest of the diners. And a bottle of Ben Nevis single malt whisky. No wonder Tehara loved him.

'Is it over?' Una asked.

I nodded and handed her the letter, taking a large gulp of fiery whisky that Muthu had poured for me. My friends, being my friends, rallied around me in their usual way.

'What a tosser!' Una said with heat as she got to the end.

Tehara got the letter next.

'Who's looking after Maya?' I asked.

'*Ammi* and *Thathi*,' Gehani replied.

'I never really liked him. I thought he was fairly light on,' Muthu added as Tehara made a sound of disgust at the end of the first paragraph.

'I didn't like him either,' Gehani added. 'He talked right through the cricket game and not only that, I just thought he was weird. He was just too perfect, you know …'

'I thought he was bit of wanker, too. He went around big noting himself as an environmental saviour, but he had a four-wheel drive.'

'And if he were serious about being an enviro-warrior, why the hell was he commuting from the Docklands to the Yarra Valley each day? That just didn't make any sense. How much petrol did he run through?' Tehara added.

None of them wanted the sodden missive, so I folded it and put it away in my handbag, eyeing them all sceptically.

'If you guys didn't like him, why didn't you say anything?'

'Because it seemed like you finally found someone you liked and we didn't want to jinx things,' Una said, with feeling.

'We thought that you were in love and we were willing to do anything to see you happy.'

'Oh you guys! I'd much rather have known.'

We spent the next couple of hours bitching about Bhatiya, comparing him to a host of ex-boyfriends and ex-girlfriends. Jacob Thuan, my psycho ex got a good outing, as did Una's previous crush on Hugh Jackman. But after a while, the group started to dwindle. Una and Gehani were the first to call it a night, Tehara and Muthu following not long after. Which left me alone with Rohan.

'Shani, you know he was a fool to let you go,' Rohan said softly. He had been strangely silent during our bitch session.

'Yeah, I am such a prize, I am,' I replied sarcastically, blowing my nose loudly on Una's hanky. Then something occurred to me. 'Oh, God, what am I going to say to my mum?' I started to cry in earnest again.

Rohan put his arms around me. 'Don't worry too much about Aunty Jayanthi. She told me just before we came down to find you that she'd had Bhatiya's horoscope faxed to an astrologer in Lanka. You'll be pleased to know that your horoscopes didn't match nearly as well as she'd hoped, after all.'

'But I thought our horoscopes tallied perfectly.'

'No, no! Remember, it was Gehani's horoscope that tallied perfectly with Bhatiya's. If only they were gay!'

I giggled at this.

'Besides, your father'll be really happy. He kept giving Bhatiya the evil eye right through the game when Bhatiya was talking. He told me never to invite him to watch a game again.'

I giggled some more. I must have had way too much of that single malt. I looked at the bottle on the table. It was empty.

So I blame what happened next on the alcohol and the sweet warm breeze that was wafting over the Yarra that night, 'cause before I knew it, Rohan's lips were kissing away the salty tears on my face and tasting the whisky on my lips. And we were at it, pashing on that outdoor couch like a couple of hormone-driven teenagers 'cause it took us more than several moments to realise that someone was shouting at us.

'You slut! You complete and utter whore!' Bhatiya raged. 'I knew you were fucking him behind my back.'

'You shut the fuck up,' Rohan raged back, standing up abruptly. 'Nothing has ever happened between us.'

'So what's happening now? Were you feeling her *saree* blouse to check for structural integrity?' Bhatiya yelled, pointing to Rohan's hand.

'You dumped me! What the hell are you doing back here?' I asked.

'Because I was wrong. Gayani texted me to say that she'd seen you cry … she came up to find you and saw your friends consoling you. I couldn't bear for you to be hurt. So I came to see if you'd take me back.'

'Bhatiya …' I said softly. I was completely confused. 'We … nothing … I mean …'

'No. My sister was right. There has been talk that something's being going on between the two of you. Maybe for years. Maybe that's why your wife committed suicide,' Bhatiya spat out venomously. Rohan flinched as if someone had punchd him clean in the solar plexus. 'I certainly do not want to have anything to do with a dirty whore like you,' he spat.

At which point Rohan moved faster than I had ever seen him to grab Bhatiya by the lapels of his jacket and shove him against a wall.

'Don't you dare,' Rohan said menacingly, nose to nose with Bhatiya. Both men were about the same height, but against Rohan's stocky build Bhatiya seemed almost adolescent.

'Okay … Okay …' Bhatiya said, holding up his hands in surrender.

Rohan let Bhatiya go. I looked imploringly at him, and held my hand out to him. I could only see the heartbreak in his eyes. Surely we could work this out. He looked at my outstretched hand and then at me. He gave me a dirty look and then turned on his heel to walk off.

CHAPTER 35

Conundrums

One of the best things about having a good friend who is a psychiatrist is that you don't need an appointment to figure out if you are going certifiably insane. And I certainly felt as if my grip on sanity was slipping two days out from Maya's fourth birthday, when I arranged to meet Tehara at the Prahran market. The plan was to get her to write me a script for anti-psychotic medication while picking out fruit and vegetables.

'Shani, you look like shit,' Tehara said as she met me at the market, threading her arm through mine.

'Thanks,' I replied in a wobbly voice, feeling a little emotional.

'Has the fallout from the break-up been that bad? How's your mum coping?'

'*Ammi* is fine. She's been distracted since Kieran was born and has barely paid me any attention.' Una and Gehani's baby had arrived two days after Jayani's wedding.

'Yeah, I gathered that. Una said that she's never been as well fed in her life and that it was a joy to wake up every morning and find all the laundry done, floors swept and the house dusted. How does your mother do it?'

'Gehani gave her the key to the house with the strict instructions that she could do it as long as she made no noise if the baby was asleep.'

'What about the gossips in the community? Have they been bad?' Tehara asked as we sat down at a café and ordered a couple of lattes.

'No, not really. Bhatiya has been really good about things, telling everybody that it was not my fault that we broke up. He even called Mrs Peiris and made up an excuse about an ex-girlfriend back in the UK. He's a really decent guy, you know,' I said, swallowing a sob.

'If you love him, Shani, have you tried patching things up with him?'

You see, I hadn't told my friends about my little indiscretion with Rohan. One of my best friend's husband! What kind of person does such a thing? It didn't matter that Amani wasn't here anymore, I still felt like a skank.

Meanwhile, I had to answer Tehara's question.

'I don't think that's on the cards,' I said softly, raising my devastated eyes to look my friend straight in the face.

'Honey, I've seen couples pull through worse. Gambling, adultery, bigamy ... you name it, I've seen it. Do you want me to set up a couple's counselling session with a colleague of mine?'

And that undid me. I looked down at our intertwined hands on the table and between sobs blurted out everything. I told her how I'd kissed Rohan. I told her how we'd gone up to our separate rooms in stony silence, mutually appalled at what we'd unleashed. And that alcohol had not brought the amnesia I craved the next day.

I expected her to remove her hand from mine in disgust. I expected her to rail and yell at me and tell me that I'd ruined our close circle of friendship. I needed her to call me a slut. I needed her to hate me as much I hated myself. But when I was finally able to look up at her, she was smiling. There was no judgement. No hate.

'What's wrong with you?' I blurted in desperation. 'Why don't you hate me?'

'Shani, Shani.' she said urgently, holding on to my hands, smiling gently.

'What?'

'Amani died four years ago. You and Rohan did nothing wrong. You're both adults.'

'I betrayed my best friend!'

'No you didn't. You can't betray someone who is dead,' she said firmly.

'But I betrayed her memory …' I cut across her, hotly. Tehara held a hand up to silence me.

'When Amani died, you stood up and you looked after Rohan and Maya. You did what few people could do or would want to do.'

'That does not give me any rights to her husband.'

'He *was* her husband. He's now a healthy, attractive man. You are a beautiful, kind, intelligent woman. Things happen,' Tehara said, before looking me straight in the eye and asking the most important question. 'What's happened since?'

'Nothing. The only way to keep going is to pretend nothing happened. And he's doing the same. We just avoid each other. He's asked me to have a wine a few times out on the deck, but I've just said I had a headache or something …'

'Basically, you've put your head in the sand,' Tehara finished wryly. I nodded. 'So what's the plan?' she asked.

'The plan is that we'll both forget what's happened and we'll continue as before, of course.'

'You know that's not possible. You *know* that!'

'Sure it is,' I said, stubbornly.

Tehara knew when to quit a line of questioning and move on to the next. 'But how do you feel about him?'

'Like I have always done. He's like a brother to me, much like Amani was the sister I never had,' I replied flippantly. A little too flippantly, perhaps.

I knew I was lying, hoping that Tehara didn't hear through the fib. I had to admit that I noticed Rohan now like I had never done before. I literally had to restrain myself from jumping the man every morning when he made breakfast for Maya and me, wearing only his sleeping shorts and dressing gown. Mannerisms that were previously familiar had taken on a new sweetness – and sexiness. My hands ached to bury themselves in his thick dark hair and draw his mouth down to mine. I wanted his eyes to light up just for me. I wanted him to love me as much as I loved him.

Falling in love with Bhatiya had been an analytical process; I had measured his positive personality traits and negative, and decided the good outweighed the bad. I had decided to fall in love with Bhatiya, knowing we had all the ingredients for a good relationship.

But falling in love with Rohan didn't require thinking. It was the absence of thinking that was my undoing. Falling in love with Rohan had been as simple as breathing and as natural as walking, or watching him sketch at his architect's easel every evening, with his glasses perched on the edge of his nose ...

Get a grip on yourself, I told myself firmly, pulling back to the here and now. You're here to ask Tehara for help.

'So, what now?' Tehara asked, eyeing me suspiciously.

'Well, the thing is, I have a little problem. Ever since that night, I've been dreaming of Amani. I think I am going insane.'

'It's quite normal to dream of someone, especially if they are close to a situation you are trying to sort out.'

'I am afraid to go to sleep. Every time I close my eyes, I dream of her.'

'Tell me what's happening between you and her in your dreams,' Tehara said smoothly, switching to analyst mode.

'In my dream last night, she was wearing that Lisa Ho dress she wore to the Desperate and Dateless Ball when we were at uni ...'

'The cream one with the off-the-shoulder diamante beading?'

'Yes, and she was wearing those fabulous heels she got down in Adelaide when we went there for grape grazing the summer before ...'

'The cream peep toes with the sweetheart buckle at the back?'

'Yup. Anyway, she's angry with me for choosing to drink the merlot ...'

'Where were you?' Tehara asked, looking completely bemused.

'At some swanky party. She kept telling me to drink the pinot noir.'

'And why didn't you?'

'Since when did I ever do what Amani told me to do? We ended up having a massive fight and I left the party in a huff.'

'Good point. What else have you been dreaming about?'

'The other night I dreamt that we were at the races. The Melbourne Cup ...'

'Had you scored any invites to a marquee?'

'Yup, we were at the Emirates marquee and Amani was wearing those Miu Miu platform sandals ...'

'Those nude sandals? She looked absolutely fabulous in those ...'

'And she had a fabulous vintage frock on too. But we started fighting again. She insisted that I back the horse she picked. She would not let me pick my own horse. In the end, Jennifer Hawkins and Megan Gale made us settle our differences by mud-wrestling. Right there in the Emirates marquee!'

'Were Hawko and Megan involved, 'cause Muthu'll want a blow-by-blow account of that,' Tehara giggled.

'Can you be serious?'

'Who won?'

'She did, of course! Remember all the time she spent on the rowing machines? Well, she has really strong pecs even in the afterlife. She got me in a really strong head hold and changed my bet with her other hand ...'

Tehara was rocking with laughter by now.

'Not funny,' I replied with a sheepish smile. 'I never used to have such crazy dreams.'

'At least you get to see Amani! What I'd give to spend another few minutes, or even a few seconds with her.' We sat quietly for a long moment.

'Come on, hon, let's get shopping. Remember, green beans need to be cut on an angle,' Tehara added, imitating Aunty Chandra's bossy voice.

'What about my drugs? I haven't slept in weeks! Can't you give me some drugs? Zoloft, Valium, anything?'

'No, love. I won't give you drugs. That's not how I work. But I can refer you to a psychologist who can help you sort yourself out.'

'But the drugs will work faster. And I won't go insane.'

'You're not going insane. Why don't you try some valerian for a few days until you can get an appointment with the psychologist?' she said as she marched me to the vegetable section of the market.

***

The second year after Amani's death, Rohan and I had decided that we'd stop commemorating her death anniversary. It seemed so macabre. So we started a tradition of celebrating Maya's birthday with a *Dhanay* to acknowledge the wonderful woman who'd given her life instead. Of course, we also have a kids' party with cake, ice-cream, balloons and clowns later in the day, but we always have the *Dhanay* first.

So on the morning of Maya's fourth birthday, I started cooking at the crack of dawn. No, I wasn't cooking fifty different dishes – just enough for the handful of family and friends who were coming. I focused on Amani's favourite dishes – red lentil curry with hot fried onions, calamari stuffed with broken rice and cooked in a tomato sauce, peppery Spanish mackerel cooked in a claypot, and fresh green beans lightly steamed with a splash of lemongrass-infused coconut cream. As you see, I have learned to cook. And as I inhaled the blend of aromas, I knew that Amani was with me once again.

'Tell me when you're ready for me to start up the wood fire for the fish,' Rohan said quietly, startling the wits out of me as I stood by the sink chopping the vegetables.

'No, it's all good.' I said brightly, trying desperately to avoid looking at his broad chest peeping through the folds of his dressing gown. 'I stacked the fire last night, I just have to light it and it'll be ready to go.'

He busied himself getting the tea going. 'Just the way you like it, Shani, white and sugary,' he said with a smile.

'Thanks, Rohan,' I said, ignoring the outstretched mug. 'But I've already had mine.' I could see his wounded expression in his reflection in the stainless steel microwave.

'Is there anything you want me to do?'

'No, I've got everything under control!'

'Okay, I'll go and do some work in the study for a while then,' he said hesitantly, before walking away.

The crew started trickling in at about 10 am. Gehani and

Una were first with little Kieran in his carrycot. Tehara and Muthu followed with James; as did Gayani, Sarath and Mrs Peiris. A hush of expectant silence fell as my parents' car pulled up. We all lined up, single file, along the hallway to the lounge room where the *Dhanay* ceremony was to be held.

My father jumped out of his car and held aloft a large orange umbrella to provide a canopy of shade for the Buddhist nuns who were officiating.

First out of the car was *Bikuni* Patachara, previously known as Aunty Chandra, Amani's mother and Maya's grandmother. She walked slowly, meditatively and gracefully up the path to the house. Her bowed, shaved head gleamed in the morning sunlight.

Maya rushed out to greet her grandmother, prostrating herself dramatically on the front lawn before giving her an exuberant hug. I held my breath for a moment as I noticed, for the millionth time, the resemblance between the two. Identical bone structures – high cheek bones, wide eyes and delicately arched brows.

Every year *Bikuni* Patachara made the journey from Rangoon in Burma where she'd been ordained as a nun six months after Amani's death, to Melbourne to celebrate her grand-daughter's birthday. And somewhere along the way, I'd finally been able to stop blaming Aunty Chandra for her part in Amani's death.

So it was with a genuine smile that I was able to greet her at the door. No one was perfect. I understood that now.

Once the three nuns were seated on the thick cushions on the floor draped with a white sheets, the ceremony started in earnest. Rohan, Maya and I sat in the front row, our hands clasped together in prayer.

Namo tassa, bhagavato, arahato samma sambuddhasa.

Homage to Him, the Exalted One, the Worthy One, the Supremely Enlightened One.

Buddham saranam gacchami.

I go to the Buddha as my refuge.

While the prayers were said, I was able to find respite from the accusing voice in my head but it unfortunately returned as soon we started serving the nuns with their alms. Rohan and I supported Maya as she carried the heavy plate of rice from nun to nun, serving spoonfuls of the delicately steamed grains into their begging bowls. I was even able to maintain a cheerful facade while we had our lunch in the kitchen, making sure everyone had second serves of the deliciously smoky fish, spooning out large servings of dessert – fruit trifle with mangoes and peaches.

But I knew I could not run away from myself as we sat down in front of the nuns for the final blessing and sermon. It was guilt that caused tears to course down my face as we prayed for Amani, pouring water from a simple tea pot into a cup and saucer to overflowing to symbolise our love for her.

> *As river, when full must flow*
> *and reach and fill the distant main*
> *So indeed what is given here will*
> *reach and bless the spirits there.*
> *As water poured on mountain top must*
> *soon descend and fill the plain*
> *So indeed what is given here will reach*
> *and bless the spirits there.*

Then *Bikuni* Patachara raised her fan to deliver her sermon. Her voice was calm and steady.

'I am not going to speak of charity. I know all of you well enough to know that you have hearts purer than gold. I am not going to speak of my late daughter; that would be dwelling on a past that cannot be changed. But I am going to speak today of happiness because I finally understand that that was the

Buddha's true message: That we need to live in happiness, in the present moment, without dwelling in the past or worrying about the future.

'To this end I will speak of courage because it takes courage to cast off the past and the future to live in the present. And there are few women in the Buddhist canon who exemplify courage than Mahaprajapathi Gothami, the Buddha's step-mother, his mother's own younger sister, the first Buddhist nun ...'

And I knew she was speaking directly to me. How she knew my secret I didn't know, but she did.

'She relinquished the care of her own children, Nanda and Sundara Nanda, to the care of nurses so that she herself could care for the young Prince Siddharta. She supported the young Prince's widowed father. She led her family in accepting the Enlightened One when he returned to Kapilavastu and challenged the Buddha to starting a lineage of nuns ...'

I felt Tehara take hold of my hand and Una put her arm around my shoulder.

'The life of a lay Buddhist,' *Bikuni* Patachara continued, 'is as blessed and important as those who follow a monastic life. For it is they who support the *Sangha*. As you lead your lives, live them with the love, courage and compassion that Mahaprajapathi Gothami did.'

I didn't know what to say.

And then I didn't have to say anything, as the house was invaded by a horde of pre-schoolers all dressed as fairy princesses. Thus began an endless, breathless round of serving chips, settling toy disputes and ensuring all the children were entertained, fed and watered.

After the last party favour had been distributed and the final child, hyped up on red cordial and lollies, had been despatched with a weary parent, I was finally able to walk onto the deck for a few minutes of peace, to gather my thoughts. My dad was stretched out on one of the outdoor couches, listening to the cricket.

'Shani,' *Thathi* said, pulling his headphones off. 'I've been hoping that I'd get a chance to speak with you. Sit, *puthay*, sit,' he said, swinging around to make some space for me on the couch.

'*Puthay*,' he started, looking really uncomfortable, 'Rohan is a good man. He's not like that Bhatiya ... or Jacob Thuan, And yes, I know that Shamil Udabage is gay, never mind what your mother says,' he fumbled along.

'Mahinda!' we heard my mum call from inside the house. 'Where are you? Are you watching the cricket?'

'Look, I'd better go. There's another five overs left in the game,' my father explained, furtively looking through the French doors to make sure Mum was still inside. 'My Shamini, just know that it's in your hands to make this work for you. Do what your heart tells you to do,' he said tenderly, as he bolted out into the garden to hide and listen to his game in peace.

CHAPTER 36

Decisions

I was standing in front of the fireplace, looking at the landscape Rohan had painted for me last year for my birthday, when I felt his presence behind me. I knew I could not run. We would have to talk. Whatever happened, I wished it would be quick, even if it could never be painless.

'I never painted anything for Amani. In the ten years we were together, I didn't paint her one thing. I did the mural for Maya in her room and painted lots for myself, but not for Amani.'

'Why?'

'She could never make up her mind what she wanted. And, to be honest, I was afraid.'

'Of what?' I was surprised. Rohan had always struck me as confident, almost smug.

'That I would not live up to her expectations. Don't get me wrong, I loved Amani – she was complex, intelligent …'

'And beautiful.'

'She was more than beautiful, Shani ...'

'I know, Rohan.' I turned around, my heart breaking. How could I ever hope to compete with Amani – alive or dead.

'No, you don't know, Shani. Amani was a very complicated woman. Her demons weren't just inflicted on her by her mother. She was always ...' Rohan said, shrugging in bewilderment '... fragile.'

Strange, Rohan and I had talked so much about Amani in the months ... years ... since her death, but we'd never talked about their marriage.

'Why are you telling me this now?'

'Because I need you to believe me when I tell you I need you.'

'Rohan ...' He held up a finger.

'Shhh! Let me speak. I loved Amani for all the reasons a young man loves a woman. She was everything I ever dreamt I'd want in a woman. But that was what I wanted *then*. I know what I need now. And I need you. Not just because you're great with Maya and certainly not just because you are the sweetest person I've ever met. But because I can't see my life without you. I. Need. You.'

And that was it. There were no romantic declarations of undying love, eternal devotion or promises that had little hope of being kept for life. I had come to learn that after the first fierce burst of love, emotions are lowered to a simmer.

I also knew there was no certainty of marriage with Rohan, either. But there was the acknowledgement of need, of the common necessity for companionship, partnership and abiding contentment. And that was more profound to me than libraries devoted to flowery protestations of romantic love.

The tiny distance between us suddenly seemed like a vast ocean. The choice before me was clear – I could either hang onto Amani and the past, turning her into an obstacle that, in life, she would never have wished to be; or I could step across the void and face the uncertainty of letting go.

* * *

In the pre-dawn moments of the next morning, I dreamt of Amani again. She was wearing a gorgeous lace ensemble that looked suspiciously like something out of Vera Wang's Winter 2010 catalogue with a pair of Alexander McQueen boots.

Damn it, the girl had fantastic taste in fashion, even in the afterlife.

For the first time in a long time, she and I weren't arguing. We walked in silence for a while; she smiled, kissed me and walked off into the distance. I knew I could not follow her. Not yet anyway.

And then I awoke to a pleasant ache between my legs and a beloved weight on my chest. Maya was deeply asleep, cuddled between Rohan and me.

GLOSSARY

Aiiyo lamayo Oh dear child.

Aiiyoh Oh my god.

Aiyubowan Good day.

Akki / Akka Older sister.

Ammi or Amma Mummy or mother.

Anay Oh.

Anay balandako Oh please look here.

Archie Grandmother.

Bhangra Style of music originating from the Punjab in India which fuses traditional melodies with western styled music. Awesome music to dance to when you are completely drunk as it requires wild gesticulation and no coordination.

Bhuja mix Spicy mix of nuts, peas and fried noodles made of chickpea flour.

Bikuni Nun.

Bindi Not to be confused with the daughter of Steve Irwin, but it is a coloured dot placed between your eyes on your forehead. Traditionally, this dot is placed over the third eye to stimulate spiritual awakening but is now more of a fashion statement.

Buddham saranam gacchami I go to the Buddha as my refuge.

Chee chee chee Yuk yuk yuk.

Cheekaya Yuk.

Cheekaya Disgusting.

Cheethe Cheep cloth.

Chick vitharak How ugly is that!

Devas Gods.

Dhanay Donation.

Dhobi Washerwoman.

Divaina A Singhalese-language newspaper.

Dukka Sorrow.

Dupatta Scarf worn for modesty.

Gagra Choli The traditional garment of the women of Rajasthan that is now worn through out the sub-continent. It consists of a tight blouse and pleated skirt which leaves the entire midriff bare.

Guliyak A clump of raisings or water that has been charmed by a witch doctor to bring about a certain outcome.

Hoppers Bowl-shaped crisp pancakes made of rice flour and coconut milk.

Kabhi Khusi Kabhie Gham A block buster Hindi Movie that was released in 2001 staring Amitabh Bachchan, Jaya Bachchan, Shahrukh Khan, Kajol, Hrithik Roshan, Kareena Kapoor and Rani Mukerji.

Kara Sly, devious, crafty.

Katta Sambol A spicy condiment made of chilli flakes, onions and crushed dry-fish.

Kaun Deep fried oil cakes made of rice flour and Palm treacle.

Kokis Deep fried crisp biscuits make of coconut milk and rice flour.

Kumari Princess.

Lama saree The traditional garment for a Sri Lankan little girl consisting of a blouse cut up to the bust line and a skirt with a frill around the waist.

Lasanai Beautiful.

Loku-amma A maternal aunt is also addressed as mother but a distinction is made based on whether the aunt is older or younger than your own biological mother. Loku (meaning big) refers to maternal aunts older than your own mother.

Machang Mate – this term is used exclusively amongst younger people and between friends. One would never call an older person *machang*. Unless you had death wish of course.

Magul Wedding.

Mahataya Sir.

Mahive A song from Hindi movie *Kal Ho Na Ho*.

Mangala Yoga The specific time in your life that you are most likely to get married.

Modi Stupid girl.

Mung Kaun Cakes made of roasted mung bean flour and treacle which is then dipped in a batter of rice flour and deep fried.

Namaste Clasping hands together in prayer and bowing as a sign of respect; symbol of a truce or promising not to do any harm.

Namo tassa, bhagavato, arahato samma sambuddhasa Honour to the Blessed One, the Exalted One, the fully Enlightened One.

Nay A negative confirmation of facts.

Nekath Auspicious time.

Nona Madame.

Pallu The fall section of a saree that is heavily embellished and is worn over the shoulder.

Paripu Pink lentil curry that is made flavoured with turmeric, curry leaves and cinnamon. It is staple of the Sri Lankan diet, but to say one has eaten a good 'paripu' is to say that one has been had or been deceived.

Patiyo Young one.

Pau Poor thing.

Pisu Crazy.

Pittu A roll of steamed crumbly bread mix made of coconut flour, grated coconut and coconut water. Frequently made for either breakfast or dinner.

Pol kiri hodi Coconut milk curry made of tomatoes, coconut milk flavoured with turmeric, curry leaves and chilli flakes.

Pol sambol A condiment made of grated coconut flavoured with green chillies, onions, lemon and Maldive fish.

Ponrondang In Vedic astrology, your chart consists of more than just the astrological signs placed in the various twelve houses of the zodiac. You also have *porondang* which are totems of animals, plants, trees and the gods. So when two horoscopes are matched for marriage, these totems are matched as much as the squaring of astrological signs to understand the compatibility of the couple.

Poruwa A decorated podium on which the bridal couple stand on to get married on.

Punchi-ammas A maternal aunt is also addressed as mother but a distinction is made based on whether the aunt is older or younger than your own biological mother. Punchi (meaning little) refers to maternal aunts younger than your own mother.

Puthay or Putha Son.

Rahu Apala Mars returns.

Rupavahini Sri Lanka's national television broadcaster.

Sambol A spicy condiment. Sambols by their very nature are eaten sparingly as they are used to add either tartness or heat to a meal.

Sangha The tradition of monks and nuns who are the caretakers of Buddhist philosophy.

Saree A garment made of an uncut cloth which is tucked around the waist, pleated and then flung over one's shoulder.

Seeni sambol A condiment made of caramelised onions, sugar and cloves.

Shawa Shawa One of the chart topping songs featured in the movie *Kabhi Khusi Kabhie Gham*.

Suriya Namaskar The salutation to the sun. The first position in most Hatha Yoga practises.

Swarminwahansa The respectful title given to a monk.

Thathi Dad.

Tho-il karaya A Sri Lankan witch doctor.

Thunapaha Sri Lankan curry powder made of coriander, fennel, cumin, pepper and curry leaves.

Tikka A pendant on a chain that is pinned into your hair so that pendant lies on your forehead.

Wattilapam Sri Lankan crème brulee made with coconut milk, eggs and flavoured with cardamom, nutmeg and cinnamon.

Wokuma Maya has a lisp and can't quite pronounce 'L', so Loku becomes 'Woku' and she has contracted 'Amma' to 'ma'. So she means to say 'Loku-amma' or mum's older sister aunt.

Yata andung Underwear.

Yatasaya Underskirt.

Su Dharmapala is a writer and blogger.

She was born in Singapore and grew up between Singapore and Sri Lanka before immigrating to Australia in 1989. She completed her Bachelor of Arts (majoring in French and German) and Bachelor of Science at Monash University in 1997.

After graduating from University, Su worked in technology for some of Australia's Fortune 500 companies.

Su took a two year break from her professional career after her son was born and it was during this time her love for writing was re-ignited. And when she is not writing or mothering, she is a political junkie with a passion for food. There is nothing Su enjoys more than cooking large feasts for friends and family and debating the political issues of the day over a glass (or bottle) of chardonnay.

She lives in the leafy eastern suburbs of Melbourne and is currently working on her second novel.